HENRY G. INGRAM

A U T H O R

"WHAT?!"

– NATHAN TUCKER,
THE HUMAN SENT FROM EARTH

THEN DIMITRI MOVED NEXT. HE POINTED AT ME AND SHOUTED THAT SAVAGE, COLD-BLOODED WORD.

"MURDERER!"

– DIMITRI VOLKOV,
THE OTHER CRASH SURVIVOR

As the guard pointed her to the jaws of death, the girl took care not to let slip any cry of distress.

She did not move or speak, but her quivering eyes voiced that she understood full well her imminent fate. Using his spear, the guard nudged her toward the dangling noose, and she stepped across the wood hesitantly.

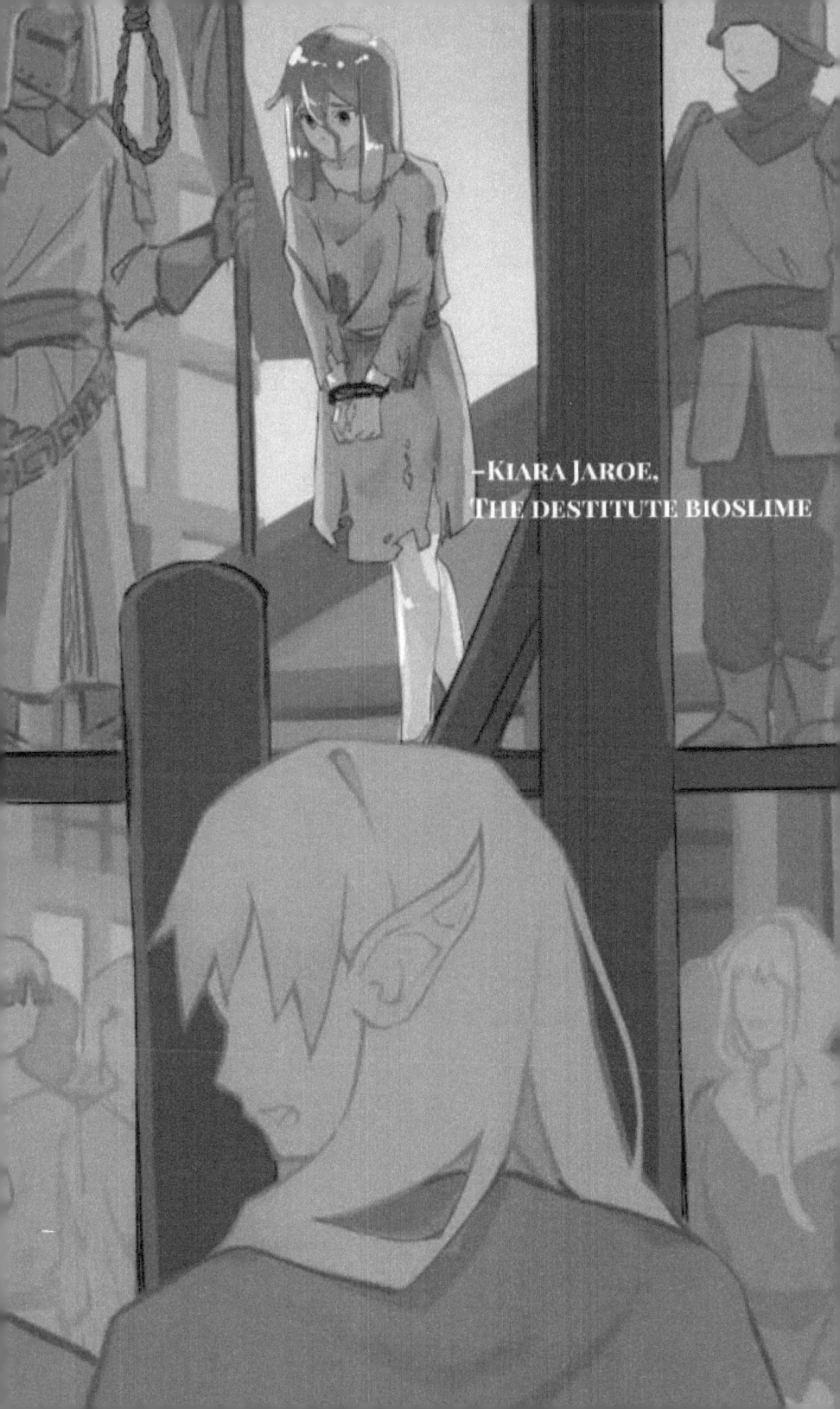

—Kiara Jaroe,
The destitute bioslime

"THIS HAS TO BE THE AETHER SEAL."

"IT MUST BE."

ALIEN STRIKE

STRIKE

THE NEW FRONTIER

A Novel by

HENRY G. INGRAM

Paperback ISBN: 979-8-9911422-0-5
eBook ISBN: 979-8-9911422-1-2

CONTENTS

PROLOGUE

Though the spacecraft had a crew, there were no astronauts. Instead the crew comprised four amateur youngsters. That's the last thing you'd expect of the most important space mission ever, but Mr. Gonzalez, NASA's administrator and our overseer, had a nasty old habit of working in mysterious and shady ways.

Being among the four crew members, I had the pleasure of meeting the other three upon boarding.

"So, what's everyone's story?" I asked through the rather coarse radio in our bright orange spacesuits. We were busy strapping into our seats in the narrow cockpit, which was a vibrant cage of state-of-the-art tech that wildly surpassed what I thought was possible. There were countless glowing buttons and glaring screens and blinking lights larded about the room, which were all far beyond my understanding, and the fancy patterns and designs that adorned the ship inside and out echoed the freshest flavors of modern style.

We sat huddled elbow to elbow, facing the front window overlooking the spaceport, two on my left and one on my right. The guy seated at my right answered:

"I'll go first. My name is Dimitri Volkov. I'm from a Russian town called Vorkuta, which lies north of the Arctic Circle where it's freezing all year. I've independently been studying aerospace engineering, which somehow caught the American government's eye. At first I was skeptical when the agents from NASA approached me, but I took the bait pretty quickly."

Dimitri spoke in a thick accent. He fared the eyes of a hunter and a sharp jaw, and his posture was drawn tight. He was the tallest in the group by a healthy margin. There was a fair amount of muscle on his body, but there wasn't too much; rather his figure was sculpted just right. His voice was potent and exuded a bold confidence as if he were positive that our job would go swimmingly. He was probably the oldest of us.

All four of us were young adults, certainly an odd age range for a space mission. We weren't trained as astronauts either, but the ship was entirely automated and, to our astonishment, could supposedly carry us to our destination with the press of a few buttons. No one ever suspected such advancements in space travel would come speeding over the horizon so soon.

"The bait? Was it the money that made you decide to do this?" asked the guy seated at the far left, who had a distinctly British accent.

Dimitri stalled before saying, "Well, yeah. My town's financial standing is rapidly deteriorating. We don't eat well, and the weather doesn't help much. I'm here because I want to support my home." Another pause. "I look forward to starting a new life," he finished, a hopeful smile playing across his face. I wondered what he meant by *starting a new life*.

"I'm Hinata. Hinata Sasaki," said the only girl in the crew, who sat at my left hand. "I'm from Japan."

Beneath her big and bulky spacesuit she sported a slender frame, and any privilege of boasting about height eluded her. There was an air of modesty in her voice, yet she presented herself with some subtle note of vigor and let slip just a bit of authority too. *That* was a sweet balance any fellow of good taste could respect.

"My dad works for JAXA," she said. "When he got his hands on the intel concerning this secret mission, especially that NASA wanted young adults for it, he pestered them till they let me in."

"So you're not here by choice?" I asked. "Your dad's making you do this?"

"Oh, no, I definitely want to be here. My mom is in the hospital with leukemia, but we don't have the money to help her. I'm doing this to pay for her treatment. She's..." Hinata fell silent, possibly to choke back tears, but I couldn't tell through her helmet. "...Running out of time, so this is my last resort."

"I'm sorry," I said, then for some encouragement, "You'll save her soon...once this is all over."

Hinata gave a wan, childlike nod. Dimitri sighed. Then the third person, the one with the British accent, spoke.

"My name's Dutch Aldrich. I'm from England. I'm the winner of last year's International Olympiad on Astronomy and Astrophysics. The agents from NASA visited me the other day and told me everything—said they could use someone like me. And since I'm an astronomy whiz by nature, I accepted their offer in a heartbeat."

"What about the reward?" asked Hinata. "Aren't you interested in the money?"

"Ah, sure, the money's great. I won't deny that. But I really just want to explore the universe. I've spent my whole life pining to see more of what's *out there*, and I feel blessed to have this opportunity. Sometimes it feels too good to be true."

As an Englishman, his English flowed smoothly. Actually, Hinata and Dimitri were strikingly fluent for nonnatives, but their accents were so sharp that it sounded like they'd learned English no more than a few days ago. I figured it was the work of the *injections*.

I gazed out the window as Dutch told his story. The windowpane was planted beyond the giant control panel, and it provided a breathtaking view of the Johnson Space Center from an awesome height. A broad beam of morning sunlight filtered in and brushed against our glass helmets.

"That reward..." said a tentative Hinata. "...It's one million dollars divided among us, right?"

No one said anything for several seconds. Then Dutch's voice was the first to break through.

"No." With a slow and shaky voice, as if disturbed by such a huge number, he said, "One million dollars...*each*."

Such was an opportunity that echoed every ripe dream: that someday a chance to strike gold would appear out of nowhere.

And so it was that we were a team of pilgrims wrapped in the throes of a gold rush. We four were just a lone group of pawns doing our part in the struggle for the good of tomorrow. Each of us bore the same duty, called here by the supposedly inerrant word of our most hallowed leaders.

There was a big catch to our deal. Our mission today was simply the first step in a much grander plan—a plan that could sway the fate of all creation. It was a plan to halt the destruction of the universe. Our failure could usher in the demise of all existence, and no amount of money could pay for that. The stakes were high and the pressure was on; if we failed, a million dollars would be meaningless because everyone—all life as we knew it—may soon lay dead.

Today, our one small step for man would be one giant leap for mankind. It seemed there was no way of telling what to expect of our futures—neither for ourselves nor the human race. What would become of us and where we would find ourselves were things only the passage of time would reveal. We could only hope that the road ahead wouldn't skin us alive with its jagged stones.

After a fleeting moment of silence, the group looked over at me.

"So...?" Dimitri prompted me to speak. "What about you?"

What about me?

"Well..."

CHAPTER I

THE SIREN AND THE SAILOR

It all started with my Uncle Rod, who was the most remarkably unremarkable fellow you'd ever meet. He worked at a smoke shop, owned the rustiest and oldest car ever to roam the roads, and was chronically single at the ripe age of forty-three despite his best efforts. Still, he was my dear uncle and the only family I had—but I'll get to that shortly. I found it perfectly appropriate to blame his singleness for wedging me into a secret space operation. "And how might *that* have happened?" you might ask in disbelief at the wild prospect.

Well, I suppose everything *really* started with my father, Mr. Stuart Tucker. Let's go back a little further to where it all began.

My father served as an astronaut. He was no ordinary astronaut. No, Mr. Tucker was among the first people to walk on Mars...

...Or he should have been.

When he set out for the task, NASA oversaw him and his crew. My age could still be counted on two hands when he was dispatched to the red planet, but even as a child, I knew how important the mission was. Setting foot on Mars was a huge deal, and the general populace knew it too. In fact, the mission gained a sensational wave of momentum, drawing the support of many people from across the United States, and in some instances, across the world. But everyone knew the voyage to Mars was a marathon, not a sprint, and the wave of hype naturally flattened and died not long after the blastoff. Weeks later, the spacecraft mysteriously vanished in the darkness of outer space. Gone. Disappeared for good. What had gone wrong, no one could say, but NASA pronounced the crew dead soon after the tragedy.

And with that my old man's body was never recovered.

My name is Nathan Tucker. At this point I'm eighteen years old and a senior in high school. It was an ordinary quiet Sunday, and I'd gone to the library to do some studying that afternoon.

There were two others joining me named Nora and Mason. Being stuck in the drudgery of our last year in high school, we all felt the menace of college entrance exams looming over us. We lacked confidence in our testing abilities, so we agreed to band together and tear into our studies as a team. Along with being my primary study partners, we also relished each other as close friends.

However, today my focus was scrambled. I was in some mystical trance at the moment. My partners were busy arguing over a math problem while I zoned out there in my seat. My gaze zeroed in on the television across the room. Often it showed its typical gloomy news networks, but what I saw was much more peculiar. Presently my vision blurred and I only perceived a flickering black and white static. Then as I completely tuned out Nora's stern voice, I saw a bleary figure of a girl. I had never seen a girl like her. She had a blue tint and didn't even appear human. But she wore a beautiful sundress and stood in a flowery field with the gleam of the rising sun behind her, and although her figure was merely molded together by pixels on a screen, I felt a strange connection to her that seemed to exist beyond the bounds of time. My mouth hung open as I stared at the projection. As she reached out her hand affectionately as if inviting me to take it, she flickered away and the pixels merged into what appeared to be a mythological creature, but *nightmarish* was probably a better word. It was a strange amalgamation of body parts. It had an enormous eye in the center and six wings studded with smaller eyes.

A voice that sounded like my own preached down:

The rule of Our Lady shall eclipse you;
Her holy love will reach you.
Her grace shall triumph o'er the heavens
and of your bondage breach you.

Then came a feminine voice that fell smooth like a drop of honey, crooning my name. *"Time to wake up, Nathan. Wake up."*

The words made me snap back to reality at once. "Wake up, Nathan! Hellooo, Nathan?" said Nora sharply. "Earth to Nathan! What's gotten into you?"

"Uh...what...?" I sputtered in a hazed confusion. I brought my hand to my chin, intending to stroke my beard, only to stop short remembering I had no facial hair. When I looked at the television again, it had relapsed into showing the news as usual.

"You weren't even paying attention, were you? At this rate, there's no hope for you two!"

"Oh, uh...sorry. Where were we again?"

My question elicited a sigh from Nora, but she patiently pointed out what we were working on and started explaining the concepts I had missed until I eventually caught back up.

Nora was passionate about her studies and always kept our workflow on track. She was a tomboy with big emerald eyes, and locks of rich sunlit gold that rolled just below her shoulders and tickled her upper back. Outside of studying, she was an outdoorsy girl who never passed up a chance to unleash her spontaneous and cheerful self. That was something we two men did *not* share in common with her; our social habits lay much more low-key.

Minute after minute ticked by. Our study session had been going well until Nora suddenly asked an odd question I never thought I'd hear again.

"You know, Nathan, I've been curious about this lately. Ever since your dad died out in space, have you heard anything from NASA? I mean, do you know if they're thinking of sending more people to Mars?"

"Um...why are you asking?" I'd moved on from all of this. Why was she bringing it up now?

"It's just been on my mind recently."

NASA had broadcasted nothing but radio silence in recent years, and there had been little talk of retrying their shot at Mars. I had actually assumed they'd abandoned their aspirations for the planet entirely.

"No idea," I answered. "I haven't heard from those nerds in years."

My father was long gone, so I had lost the perks of having a relative who worked for NASA. Any insider info I could have nabbed from my old man had evaporated into thin air thanks to his disappearance and death, which left me in the dark just like every ordinary citizen. Ever since *that day*, NASA's secrets had been pried out of my reach.

"Maybe they're hiding something from us, but I don't know," I added, granted that their recent silence had left me very suspicious.

Right after I spoke, Mason dropped his opinion.

"You think maybe they're developing a secret weapon of mass destruction? Like a nuke big enough to destroy a planet?"

Typical Mason response. Nora and I looked at him.

"And *what* would they use that for?" I asked defiantly.

"I mean, I was just having some crazy thoughts about this the other day. People think aliens will invade us someday, right? But what if we invaded *them* instead? How easy would it be to dominate them by just threatening them with weapons that are totally *cracked* with power? If we do that—boom!—we can make an entire race of aliens fall to their knees and conquer their home world!"

I traded an incredulous glance with Nora and drifted my head back toward him slowly. What kind of absurd power fantasy was going through his head?

Mason was a big oaf. A gym rat by nature, he was tall and meaty;

all muscle and no brains. Nora and I shared a fancy that he took anabolic steroids, but he was too adroit in the art of changing the subject whenever we confronted him about it. His academic life wasn't particularly high in priorities. Nora was the opposite. Stark against Mason, she was the brains of the group (even I found her overperformance on every homework and exam annoying).

Still, for an oaf, he gave an interesting case, though I wasn't sure if his logic would hold up.

"I mean...yeah, but..." stammered Nora, hoping to refute his ridiculous vision. Eventually, some counterargument flashed before her, and she formed the words. "We haven't even found life apart from Earth. Besides, if we could invent such a weapon of mass destruction, wouldn't the aliens do the same? They're probably more advanced than us. They would've beaten us to it."

"You really think so?" Mason leaned back in his chair in a relaxed motion. "What if the aliens are still living in their own stone age? Maybe they're stuck in their corner of the universe chasing their food and sleeping in caves."

"But think of how old the cosmos is compared to humanity. This universe is billions of years old, and we've only been around for three hundred thousand. Chances are they've had way more time to develop than us."

"Mm...what do you think, Nathan?"

"Whatever..." I said as their drivel ended and pointed at Mason's worksheet. "...Hey, Meatbrains, you did that problem wrong."

Mason, whom I nicknamed Meatbrains, betrayed a look of alarm at my sudden rebuttal and scrubbed his work away with his eraser.

"We should probably get back to work," said Nora, realizing our focus had veered off its path.

Nora had been my friend since the earliest days of our childhood. When I first moved to this small town after my father passed on, *she* was the loud and troublesome tomboy down the road who welcomed me with wide-open arms (new neighbors were instant new friends in her innocent eyes). For a scared and confused little child like myself, my first sense of belonging in my new home sprouted through her. Every day, that hyperactive girl invited me over to play, and presto, we grew attached quicker than two strips of tape. Even as the years rolled by and we matured beyond those daily playtimes, we were dearly close, and we stuck together ever since. I was grateful for her. She probably didn't know it, but looking back on it, I certainly would've been a vastly different person if not for her random acts of kindness.

Fast forward several years, we met Mason. We didn't have much in common in the beginning, but he was a charming hulk of a man who always managed to brighten our day, so as we talked more, he eventually assimilated into our group.

And this was our little triad of friends. Our bonds had carried us through the rough toils of high school, and we hoped things could stay that way beyond our youth.

After studying ended, Mason went his own way as he wanted to hit the gym, leaving Nora and me to walk home together. I lived on the same street as her, so I saw her off at her house. However, just as she was heading inside, she stopped and twisted round for one last thing.

"Also, Nathan, come over tonight. I want to show you something."

"Huh? What is it?"

"What, you want me to spoil it for you?" she giggled playfully. "Nice try. You'll know soon enough. Also, make sure you come after dark."

She was already closing the door as she finished speaking, and I didn't have time to respond before she vanished inside. Well, it looked like I had plans for the evening. Knowing that, I shuffled down to my own place and headed inside.

Uncle Rod had taken me in after I had nowhere else to go. It was just us two in this run-down place. It was a frowsy little house we inhabited, kept with low maintenance and minimal polish. The knobbed side of the front door sagged, and its corner scraped across the hardwood floor. All the deep-set windowpanes were murky with stains and dust. Our furniture had scratches and tears and splotches of discoloration that had all surfaced over the years. Last year, pale streaks of paint had started to peel off the walls. We lacked the money to fix any of these issues, and they festered with age.

As my uncle was hard at work and wouldn't be here until later, I was left to my own business for the afternoon. His car pulled into the driveway as the sun started setting that evening, but to my surprise, two people—not one—exited the vehicle. As expected, out hopped Uncle Rod from the driver's seat holding a pair of grocery bags, but the one who emerged from the passenger side was an unfamiliar face.

Looking through the window, my amazement kindled when I saw the drop-dead gorgeous woman at his side. She sported perfectly kept hair which was smooth, long, and blonde, and it suited her delicate face, with a slightly younger look than Uncle Rod. Below her head was a tight blue dress that was casually dashing; it boasted her curves and had a short-cut hem that showed off her tall legs. Just who was this lady?

Like a hungry cat who'd spotted a mouse, I eagerly rushed outside to greet them. "Hey, Uncle Rod! Who's this chick?" I asked breezily, trying to seem cool.

"*This* is Florence," he said, stepping onto the porch. "My new señorita."

"Hey. Nathan Tucker," I said as Florence scanned me up and down and smiled.

"Oh, so you're Nathan!" She spoke unhurriedly as she gazed into my eyes. She extended her hand and I shook it. Based on looks alone, she seemed capable of making most guys drool, and her voice only added to her beauty. I never figured out how Uncle Rod could sweep such perfect women off their feet. The likes of Florence seemed way out of his league.

The moment I heard her sweet voice, I was immediately flustered, and my face blossomed bright red like an overripe cherry.

"Uh, yep, hi, nice to meet you," I awkwardly stuttered.

"It's nice to meet you too." A look of satisfaction played about her confident smile. "Now, why don't we get inside before the sun burns us up?"

We headed inside, where it was much cooler. I lived on the outskirts of the Woodlands of Texas, north of Houston, where the southern heat straggled late into the afternoon. Uncle Rod's new partner immediately set down her purse in the living room and plopped onto the scruffy old sofa, unshy to make herself comfortable.

Typically, when Uncle Rod got home, one of us would make dinner or we would order in. Looking at his groceries, I presumed the former.

"Why did you go to the store?" I asked. "I thought we were finishing those leftovers from last night..."

As soon as I spoke, Rod pulled me into another room where Florence couldn't hear. Keeping his voice low, he said, "Listen, man, do you really think a chick would appreciate leftovers? Get a grip! No wonder you're still single! Ladies love a man who can whip up a good meal—a meal that'll make her feel special."

With a sigh I asked, "So what's on the menu?"

"You just leave it to me," he said with a wink. Then he gravitated back to Florence.

I sighed at his mulishness and let him take the reins.

Dinner turned out to be some incredible filet mignons that *had* to be beyond his budget. He baked them in the oven before searing them in a pan and basting them with butter. On the side were mashed potatoes, richly enhanced with heavy cream and more but-ter, and it was all garnished with a fresh chimichurri sauce. Also, a bottle of red wine to wash everything down. Uncle Rod obviously had run the extra mile to impress Florence. Just how much did this cost anyway?

"Thank you for making this!" she exclaimed gratefully.

Luckily for Uncle Rod, his new date appreciated the food, so it looked like he would walk away from the table victorious.

As we started eating, I asked, "How did you two meet, anyway?"

The smiling pair, whose seats were practically nuzzled right up against each other, exchanged glances, and the lady spoke. "Well, I just moved here from downtown Houston the other day, and I had to check out the nearest smoke shop. That was where Rod was working, and since then, ah, *everything* fell into place from there."

"Hah! Must have been the almighty universe that led you to me!" Uncle Rod spoke in a flirtatious tone and put his arm around her. Florence let out a silly giggle at his comment.

For the rest of the meal, I stayed relatively quiet. They seemed perfectly happy together without me dabbling in their business. As I didn't particularly want to be labeled a third wheel, I was the first to excuse myself.

"Thanks for dinner," I said as I stood up and tossed my plate, sil-verware, and wine glass (Uncle Rod let me drink) into the dish-washer. "Well, um...I'll leave you two to it." I nodded awkwardly and took my leave.

Despite Uncle Rod being over twice my age, he didn't display a typical guardian's energy. We were more like roommates—perhaps brothers—and I had noticed that my day-to-day lifestyle had al-tered drastically since I moved in. That was one pleasant advantage of living with my uncle. He was less authoritative; he was unlike the type to demand that I be home before dark or get on top of me about grades, and I enjoyed the degree of freedom I gained from living with him.

The sun had fully set by the time I finished eating, which meant I had somewhere to be. I got ready to leave and hollered at Uncle Rod that I was heading to a friend's house before walking out the door and making for Nora's place. Oddly enough, she immediately opened up when I knocked on the front door.

"Thanks for coming," she said smiling. "Come on in...it's a really clear night for this."

Knowing not what she meant, but curious nonetheless, I followed her inside. She led me out to her backyard with an eager grin.

"Oh, Meatbrains! You're here too!" I remarked upon seeing Mason waiting out there. He sat in an Adirondack chair on the back porch alone. He acknowledged me and we exchanged small talk for a few moments before getting back on track. "So, Nora," I got straight to the point. "What was it you wanted us to see?"

"Over here." She led us deeper into the backyard where a particular instrument was set up.

"Your telescope? What about it?"

We bought her this telescope for her birthday over the summer. Astrophysics was her passion and aspired field of study, which was why Mason and I decided to pitch in some savings to gift her this fancy gadget. In fact, she'd let us use it before, and it truly was magical. It could zoom so deep into the nighttime heavens that even planets like Jupiter and Saturn were visible at times.

"I spotted something that I wanted to show you," she answered while situating the telescope's position and adjusting its knobs, a process I didn't much understand. She made it look easy. After fiddling with it for several minutes, she peered through the telescope and said, "Okay, it's ready. You can look now."

I looked at Mason to see if he wanted to go first, but he merely motioned for me to go ahead. Stepping up to the telescope, I bent down and took a look.

"I don't get it...it's just a group of stars," I muttered, confused. "I don't think it's zoomed in enough." It seemed like the telescope wasn't focused on anything in particular. All I could see was a typical night sky. Was I missing something?

"Do you see how some stars are more oval-shaped? Almost like they're being stretched out?"

"Yeah...?" I said in response to Nora's instructions.

"If you imagine lines connecting all of those stars, it should make a circle."

After I connected the dots in my head, the result checked out. Peculiar indeed.

"Huh...you're right." The oblong stars were arrayed in a perfect circle. They even seemed to be curved along the circle's perimeter. Although it was a strange sight, I didn't understand where this was leading. "What does it mean?"

"I'm not sure," she replied. "But it wasn't there last week, so the view of the stars must be distorted somehow. The light from the stars is being warped by something. I just don't know what." Her words were getting a bit too sciency and were hard to keep up with. "Normally, these kinds of distortions are a sign of a black hole."

"You found a black hole?!" I stiffened and gawked at Nora.

"No, dummy. I thought so at first, but that can't be the case because there are also stars *inside* the circle. If it was a black hole, the center would be pitch-black. It must be something else."

Then what in the universe was this curious thing?

"Well...you have any ideas?"

She looked away as if to say she had no clue, and then Mason chimed in.

"Maybe it's some undiscovered phenomenon. Time's up, Nathan. Let me see." He put his eye against the telescope after I stepped aside. "Whoa, that's neat. I wonder if NASA knows about this."

"Maybe. Thanks again for coming," she said with a honeyed tone. "I'll try and look into it on my own. Just need to do some more research."

"Keep us posted," I said. I hadn't the slightest smattering of astronomy, but I was interested in my friend's discovery.

The early autumn sun always beat down cruelly in Texas, but at night, the heat ebbed and poured away as if being nudged elsewhere by the wind, dissipating into a pleasant coolness that felt especially good this evening. Spending nights like these with friends was what made a person relax, and it reinforced some threads of meaning in a world where meaning was rare. These thoughts brought a smile to my face, and I looked at Nora, who seemed satisfied after showing someone her discovery, and I couldn't help musing upon her reaction when she first unwrapped the telescope we'd given her. The way her eyes lit up with that lustrous delight was a sight I'd never forget.

We all exchanged goodbyes and I headed home to settle down for the night. As I moseyed down the hall, I spotted Florence trail Uncle Rod into his room. Letting out an exasperated sigh, I went to the bathroom to wash my face. I examined myself in the mirror. I was somewhat lanky, standing slightly taller than most men, my slim physique passing as mediocre or less. My hair was naturally messy, full, and chocolate-colored. I had hazel eyes.

After drying my face off, I headed to my room and climbed into my empty bed. I could hear tender, faint voices from Uncle Rod's room, mingled with chirped songs of crickets outside. Fortunately, I wasn't bothered by noises at night, so I fell asleep without interruptions.

One thing I couldn't sleep through, however, was bright lights, which woke me after only an hour. It was a sudden glare that filtered through my window and, my eyes being accustomed to the darkness, nearly blinded me. I got up to check the source of my room's illumination, which turned out to be a jet-black van parked outside the house with its high beams on. Supposing it was none of my concern, I closed the blinds and went back to bed.

But after several minutes, the luminosity strengthened. It shone burningly even through the blinds and simply couldn't be ignored.

Stupid car, go away! I raged in my mind.

I made for the window with powerful stomps, furious that the van was infringing on my sleep. But as I peered out the window, I noticed that another van had appeared, just as fancy as the first one. My gut twisted. Why were there two now? Why in front of *this* house?

That was when I heard Uncle Rod scream.

CHAPTER II

A FOOTPRINT OF STUART TUCKER

I jumped madly at the sudden noise. The shout was out of clear shock, imbued with genuine pain. There was no time to think; I had to take action and was on my feet right away.

Adrenaline coursing through my veins, I burst through my bedroom door and bolted through the dark house to my uncle's room. I was covered by no more than my pajamas, but the situation was too dire to care. I should've known Florence couldn't be trusted. Uncle Rod had so effortlessly picked her up and brought her home; no rational person would fall for something like that. As I cursed myself for not knowing any better, I kicked open the door to his room but was greeted by a shadowy female figure standing in the doorway, pointing a gun-shaped figure at me. Uncle Rod was on the ground, motionless.

Was he...dead?

When the silhouette pulled the trigger, I was the next to scream. My legs quickly gave out, and I dropped to the ground as if every muscle had shut down. My whole body tingled like it was on fire, and everything tensed up as an intense wave of pain crashed over me. My muscles were locked up as if caught in a snare, and all I could do was suffer until the electrifying agony went away.

My attacker, who I knew to be Florence, stood over me and watched as I writhed on the ground in pain. "I'd suggest you hold still if you don't want to get tased again."

Although my body stopped aching after a few lasting seconds, I shied away from making any sudden movements. The notion of taking another shot from that awful gadget was terrifying.

"*Pant...pant...*Urgh..."

I heard men shouting along with the sound of the front door bursting open, after which several hardbodied units rushed over and pinned me down. When I realized who these people were by their black suits, it occurred to me that these people were among those my father worked with, and a spell of confusion blended with anger flared from deep within my memory.

"The CIA? What?" I muttered puzzled jabberings as I watched a familiar older man approach me.

"Apologies for being a bit loud." He knelt in front of me with his signature materialistic smile. The image of this man was welded on the frame of my entire childhood. He was the man behind NASA's ambitions of landing on Mars, and his hands soaked up a great deal of my father's blood.

"Dominic Gonzalez...administrator of NASA," I managed to grunt.

He didn't do his work for the spurring of human progress or the expansion of American prosperity. He was in it for money, and money alone. He grinned maliciously. Anyone could spot the wide chasm between his amusement and my revulsion. "Nice work," he said to Florence.

My head spun like a whirlwind. I couldn't believe it...that dirty Florence was an operative for the CIA! She put on the nice-lady act and backstabbed us!

"Why are you doing this?!" I bawled. More specifically, I wanted to know why NASA and the CIA were working together.

"We're leaving." Mr. Gonzalez ignored my question and started his way outside with his brief command, and the men holding me down hoisted me up and escorted me outside.

The two vans parked outside waited with their doors open. I must have looked like a criminal being lugged away by the law.

Thankfully, everyone was asleep and didn't know what was happening.

All except for one.

Several houses down, my eyes met Nora's, whose rock-solid gape showed absolute dismay. There she was, standing on her front porch in her pajamas. She must have been awake into the night, and upon hearing the raid's commotion and seeing the cars parked before her childhood friend's house, she was naturally inclined to investigate. She was always a fearless child who never flinched at horror movies or got frightened by scary nighttime noises, hence she could investigate anomalies such as the booms and shouts coming from my house. *That* quality stuck with her to this moment, when she rushed outside to check out the sounds. She surely thought the same thing as me: *What's going on?*

The men shoved me into the back of the second van and drove off, bringing up the rear of the first one. Nora watched us disappear around the corner. Mr. Gonzalez sat in the front van. Florence sat in the passenger's seat of the rear van, and alongside me were two men, and there was also a driver. Both vehicles hummed along the dark, empty roads, and the car was dead quiet until my consternation tapered off. Anger set in, giving me the courage to speak.

"Hey," I leaned forward to gain Florence's attention, but her motionless head stared ahead as if she didn't hear me. "Hey...what's your problem?" My eyes remained fixed on her frozen head. She imparted no response. "I know you can hear me."

The men beside me watched my attempts to make verbal contact but took no measure to stop me. Her body and mouth were static, and I wondered if she had gone deaf. But I wouldn't give up so easily: I wanted answers.

"Listen, you invaded my uncle's house and attacked him. You at least owe me an explanation."

"..." Florence adjusted her posture and looked out the window to her side.

"What about that steak? That was an expensive cut. He bought it just for you."

Florence finally reeled her head around and spoke. Her grimace was beyond irate.

"I've never been much of a steak gal," she hissed. "You should reconsider running your mouth so much. Do you think I *want* to be here? Do I look *happy* doing this?" Her head floated back to a neutral position following her embittered response. Her gaze was downcast and gloomy as she faced forward, as though a flood of intense guilt had inflamed her conscience. "...You don't even know who I am."

"What do you mean? Who are you?"

"Be honest. Do you *really* think your dad's spaceship magically disappeared in outer space?"

"I...I don't know. NASA just said they lost contact with him and his crew. They never elaborated much further."

"Of course you think that. Of course you blindly listened to the powers that be, when they told you the spaceship randomly vanished. That's the problem with you people—you'll believe *anything* they say. You think they'd never lie to you? You think they *don't* look down on you all like a herd of sheep? Think again, sunshine."

My confusion swelled with every word she spoke. I wanted these cryptic messages to stop—I wanted to know what she meant—but although I struggled desperately to make sense of what she was suggesting, I couldn't bring myself to ask. All the other men in the car sat silently with their muscles tensed, stiff like stone, and I could only describe the spectral air radiating throughout the tiny space as an aura of the damned. The driver breathed out a sigh that sounded like a ghost's somber moans.

After silently continuing down the road for many awkward minutes, the route brought us to a gray but illumined office building. The fluorescent lights were eerie at this time of night. Every adjacent building was lightless, which only magnified the morbid uncanniness of how this lone structure stood out. The driver switched off the car, and the two men beside me dragged me out. Mr. Gonzalez and his men waited for us at the building's entrance, and as the agents escorted me over, I kept my eyes glued to the ground. My bare feet were scrunched against the rough concrete since I was given no time to put on shoes.

"Welcome, gentlemen...and lady," he said, aiming the last part at the tired Florence behind us.

She responded dryly and opted to light a cigarette. Mr. Gonzalez gave a pained smile at her apathy and turned to the other men.

"Stay out here, all of you. I'll handle the rest."

The men acknowledged his command and released their grasp, but although I was free to move, I didn't dare to try and fight or run. The mere thought of getting tased again made me wince in pain.

"Florence, you're coming with us—and drop the smoke, too."

"Yeah, yeah, whatever," she said in a mildly disaffected tone. She puffed a smoke ring into the air before tossing the cigarette on the ground and stomping out the embers.

Inside, many people walked around in suits, some working on computers, some sorting documents, and others engaging in meetings. There was constant tapping of keyboards and clicking of machines. The place looked like a white-collar company but, erratically, operated in the middle of the night. What happened to the traditional nine-to-five? Since there were no signs or labels on the building's face, there was no telling who owned the establishment, but I had a pretty shrewd idea.

A secret CIA building, entered the words into my mind. Our group filed into a room that looked like an abandoned office. There was a table with various old tools splayed across it, a worn-out hospital bed with a thin, tattered mattress, and a set of grimy chairs. A deep incessant thrum came from a fan in the corner. The dank, bleak space was unsettling.

"Sit down," said Mr. Gonzalez.

I took a seat, as did Mr. Gonzalez, but Florence impassively sat atop the edge of the table with her legs crossed. Before anyone spoke, I had a question that had been grating my mind for a while.

"Why'd you do it?" was the first thing I asked. "Why'd you raid my uncle's house?"

"Federal agents have reported that their most recent interactions with you, Nathan, have been met with hostility and insolence," he explained. "You've been labeled as, quote, 'a nasty, aggressive troublemaker of a child,' unquote. I was just taking extra precautions. I was given authority to make you submit by any means necessary."

Since my father's death, I had spoken to men working for the government a couple of times, but those interactions never struck me as particularly special. I'd thought of them as average run-ins that occasionally happened to everyone, and I most certainly didn't think they made note of my conduct. I couldn't have denied my unkindness toward them since I had moved in with my uncle, but how could they blame me? It was their incompetence that took away my father!

"So what? Why *wouldn't* I behave that way?"

He grinned and leaned forward. "Well, yes, I have an inkling as to why you do. You see, the CIA knows a lot more about you than you think. For weeks now, we've been keeping an eye on you. We've been in the shadows preparing for this for some time now. If you don't believe me, ask my boys outside."

"You've been spying on me?!" I sprang from my chair, contending with his smug pride. "How could you—?!"

My sentence trailed off when Mr. Gonzalez's hand strayed to his belt where a taser was affixed. Perhaps another one of his so-called extra precautions. Without any sudden movements, I glared daggers at him and slumped back in my seat.

Mr. Gonzalez wasted no time in getting started.

"Now, I assume you remember what happened to your old man?"

"Yeah, I remember. You sent him off to space so he could die in vain. Then my mom ran out of money and went missing. I never saw her again. You're the one behind it all...isn't that right, Mr. Gonzalez?"

He chuckled at my choice of words.

"Yes, that's right," he said. "Actually, I've looked into the situation about your mother. Get this—this is funny! After she abandoned *you*, she traveled all the way up to D.C. and totally cracked! She put on the red light for all kinds of people! There were lots of crazy adventures, I tell you." He held back laughter as he talked excitedly and leafed through the pages of his memory. "If I recall correctly, she did it with a few congressmen, a communist party leader, the president's eldest son, also, um, an FBI agent, a presidential cabinet member...let's see...a Klan member, a mafia boss—"

"Stop!" I cried, unable to take it anymore, but he kept going.

"—some famous rappers, the president of a multibillion-dollar corporation, uh, several neo-Nazis, some crazy cult leader, and, oh yeah!—even a big-name televangelist, I think. Now that last one just baffles me. Well, she must have been a real freak. Oh, and she recently died! She overdosed on drugs! Ha-ha-ha!" He cracked up and slapped his knee.

I closed my eyes and dropped my head as my heart sank deep below my stomach. How did she fall into shambles so easily?

"Why are you telling me this?" I asked with a shaking voice.

"Because I know you *love* arguing. I'm just showing you that my men and I know leagues more than you do. That way, you'll realize there's no point in arguing with everything I'm about to tell you." He moved the subject back to focus. "Anyway, for the first several years, we really *did* think Stuart's space crew was dead. We left it at that. But a few weeks ago...something changed." He stalled for two seconds. "It'll take some explaining. Tell him, Florence."

"*Sigh*...fine." Her tone was notably flat, and she avoided looking me in the eyes. "I guess I can't dodge this any longer. The truth is: I was on the spacecraft with your father."

My head whipped upward. "You were with him?! That's impossible! They're all dead! If you were on that spacecraft, how are you still alive?!"

Just then, a new possibility flashed in my mind. If Florence was alive, what did that mean for my old man? Could I see him again?

"Just listen to me. We were en route to Mars. Everyone was so excited to become the first people to set foot on it—thought we'd put Armstrong to shame. One day, we woke up in the middle of nowhere—I don't know—somewhere far outside the solar system. Ground control was uncontactable because it was out of range. We had no idea where we were or what to do. Then...we found it: an exoplanet. It looked like Earth from up high, with water and green land but distributed differently so that we knew it was a different planet. So, seeing as we had no better option, we touched down and found out the world was called Kadaan...at least, that's what the inhabitants called it."

Inhabitants. The word jumped at me. "Like...like aliens?" I asked.

"Exactly that. But once the Kadaanites found us, it all went to hell. We couldn't defend ourselves because we didn't have weapons, so we had no choice but to capitulate. They took us in and treated us like rats; they tortured us, ran experiments on us, and stripped us of all the dignity we had left. To this day I can still hear the screams of my crewmates. We lost hope of returning home. At first, there were five of us. After three months, it was just me. But I was determined not to die in that godforsaken place. The longer I stayed there, the more I found out what the Kadaanites were planning. The Kadaanites have their eyes set on this other planet called Anbizia."

Florence paused, and then said slowly, deep and ominous like a phantom, "Their goal...is to conquer and exterminate every Anbizian!"

My gaze tipped to the floor, and a thin gust of breath quietly escaped me. So much had unfolded tonight, and it was beginning to wear on my mind. Florence also gazed down after her explanation ended, a certain emptiness graying her eyes.

"So there's two alien planets. And one of them wants the other dead," I repeated in disbelief, making a sour face.

"Yes. I still don't know why the Kadaanites are so bloodthirsty, but I immediately didn't like the sound of it. Eventually, I escaped Kadaan and reached Anbizia, and the folks there were sure as hell friendlier than those other jerks."

"Wait, wait, slow down," I interrupted. "How did you get to Anbizia?"

"You ever heard of Einstein-Rosen theory?" Mr. Gonzalez tried to step in for her. "They're like...uh...portals...."

"Wormholes," she said. "Bridges between two points in spacetime. The Kadaanites can create wormholes that lead to another point in space. I don't know how. But they're not made in *outer* space like you'd expect—they're made on the ground. And they're small too, like doors that can be walked through. I fled to Anbizia by sneaking through one of their wormholes. The Kadaanites usually send troops through wormholes to attack Anbizia, and I took the opportunity to escape by slipping through the gates.

"After I learned to communicate with the Anbizians that saved me, which involved many months of learning their language, they told me their planet was in peril. They wanted humanity to help them, and they agreed to help me get back to Earth if I promised to send humans to prevent their extermination." A shadow passed over her eyes, tinted with gloom and rue.

"I don't get it," I said. "How can we win a war against a civilization that can create wormholes? Doesn't that give them a massive advantage?"

"Ah!" said Florence with a sigh. "That's a little complicated. For so long, we humans assumed aliens were more advanced than us. We always imagined them as little green men who fly around in UFOs and shoot plasma guns and abduct kids. But *these* aliens are nothing like that. The truth is that we're technologically superior to both planets. It's best said that they're practically living in their own version of the Middle Ages. And *that* raises a huge problem that needs solving: if we're technologically superior, why can the Kadaanites create wormholes when *we* can't?"

Only when she finished speaking did I realize my mouth had been completely ajar. With two blinks I closed it as I tried to digest the new information. None of it seemed right. To think that a less advanced race had the power to manipulate spacetime was too ridiculous.

The Middle Ages were a time composed of little more than princes and paupers, swords and stones, castles and cathedrals— they didn't have any flair for space exploration. If those aliens were so medieval, how could they produce such a miracle like wormholes? It simply didn't add up!

"The wormholes are the only level of high ground they have over us. That's where you come in," said Mr. Gonzalez. "One-third, Nathan...the Kadaanites have already claimed the lives of one-third of Anbizians. Right now, the war is hopeless for them. My boys ran hundreds of simulations...the results are all the same. It's a losing fight."

"One-third...and the Kadaanites want to eradicate all *three*-thirds of the Anbizians," I said. There was no option to fold and submit. It was either fight to the bitter end or face death. Although it was a losing battle, Anbizia could only let it rage on and on. "But why do you want me to know this?"

Mr. Gonzalez continued, "If we can figure out how those wormholes work, we can use them against the Kadaanites and wipe those rats out. Let me get straight to the point. NASA is going to send you to Anbizia as part of a research team to uncover the science of the wormholes."

My breath hitched at the declaration. This was insane. My eyes were wide but quickly narrowed. "No."

I trusted in my first instinct. Getting shipped off to a war-torn alien planet? No thank you. I had a life on Earth that I didn't fancy leaving behind, especially for some conflict that didn't affect me.

Moments earlier I had been so invested in Florence's tale, hoping it would lead to some positive tidings about my father. But there was no rising from the grave.

"You play a vital role in all of this," said Mr. Gonzalez. "This is very important—more than you could possibly imagine. The war has already earned the title of the Great Alien War among the Anbizians. That alone should tell you how massive it is, but even still, its scale will only get larger as time goes on. Understanding the truth about the wormholes is our first step in defeating the Kadaanites."

"I said no. Find someone else. I have better things to do than get involved in a war that's not my problem." I was agitated by Mr. Gonzalez's insanity. He knew full well I had every right not to be interested. I slouched deep in my chair, folding my arms across my chest like a sulky child.

His proposal sounded like an adventure, for sure. However, I couldn't accept it. I had my priorities—I was still in school and needed to focus on getting into a decent college. I couldn't waste time dealing with alien barbarians.

But even though I denied Mr. Gonzalez, he knew better than to throw in the towel so soon.

"We aren't looking for someone else. NASA wants *you* specifically because you're the only son of any of Florence's crewmates. None of the others had any kids. Besides, our estimates say it'll only take around two weeks, and when you return, we'll reward you handsomely."

Two weeks? I was expecting the journey to take months or years, but I could handle two weeks without taking a massive blow to my schoolwork.

"What kind of reward are we talking about?" I asked earnestly.

"One million dollars."

I nearly toppled off my chair. It took me some time to conceptualize that number. But when I did—a million dollars! I wasn't sure if Uncle Rod had made that much in his entire life!

Yet at the sudden thought of my uncle, my gut caved toward my stomach, and the memory of his rotting corpse on his carpet decked me like a bullet. While the money was indeed compelling, I couldn't overlook the atrocities that had unfolded at my home, so I couldn't very well do Mr. Gonzalez's bidding. After all, I never favored the man and wasn't keen on kneeling before him.

"I'm sorry..." I hissed icily at Florence. "...You killed my uncle. How do I know I can trust you?"

Mr. Gonzalez kept a neutral expression, unfazed, but as he began to respond, Florence opened her mouth to speak as well.

First, Mr. Gonzalez, "I was advised to detain you by any means—"

Then Florence, "Wait, what are you saying? I didn't kill him. I knocked him out."

"Oh..." was my short reply. I was relieved. It had been hard to tell in the acute darkness, so I'd simply assumed the worst.

"So what's it gonna be, Nathan?" asked Mr. Gonzalez. "We need your help in defeating the Kadaanites. If that fails, they'll destroy Anbizia and come for *us* next."

"Why does it matter if they come for us?" I countered. "*They* don't have guns. Wouldn't it be easy to mow them down as soon as they arrive?"

"Yes, but there comes a huge risk with that. Even if that *did* happen, that would regrettably mean the destruction of Anbizia and lots of gross bloodshed on our side. But the cardinal risk comes down to this: if the Kadaanites can create wormholes, our chief fear is that they could create a weapon even worse—something we could never counter. It..." There was a deep pause as if his heart wouldn't allow him to say it. "...It could even destroy the universe."

This statement hung in the air for a while. The room felt more silent than ever. Now it was becoming clear just how urgent the deal was.

Mr. Gonzalez knew far more about this subject than I did. Of course, that meant that every argument I pitted against him, he had a response. I couldn't fight off his orders forever.

" If there's even the slimmest chance that the universe faces total annihilation, it has to be dealt with at once," he said. "This sphere we call the cosmos is infinite and ethereal, but that infinity is at stake now. The fate of all things may be resting in our hands. So, will you do your duty to your country—or rather, the universe?"

I stared ahead blankly and thought to myself for a moment. A million dollars was more than an adequate boost for poor Uncle Rod and me. It could be the pillar of my future if I spent it judiciously. And a mere two weeks would be well worth it. I could see the material gain projected in my vision and simply wanted to reach out and grasp it. Two short weeks for a million dollars...I would be rich in the blink of an eye. It was a simple adventure that could set me up for my entire future. A funny image of me bathing in green paper bills came up in my mind, its comicality drawing out a faint smile.

There was another concern. Time had made my memory of my father's face blurry. "What happened to my dad?" I asked Florence.

She hesitated before saying, "I don't know. One day, while we were in Kadaan's custody, he just disappeared. But I never saw his body. For all I know...he could be alive."

This was likely my only chance to find him.

"I'm in. When am I leaving?"

"You'll set out tomorrow," said Mr. Gonzalez. "We still have some work to do beforehand. Firstly, the Anbizians don't speak our language. Of course, you won't be able to get around in that world without being able to talk to anyone, but we don't have time to teach you a new language by traditional means."

He was insinuating something unorthodox, but I had no guesses.

"Brain modifications," continued Mr. Gonzalez. "Our scientists developed a new experimental method, where we can essentially inject information into the human brain. By loading injections with Anbizian vocabulary and grammar, we can basically upload a new language to your head."

I shifted in my seat uncomfortably as a nervous feeling crept its way into me. The possibility of syncing information to another brain was unheard of, and being one of the first subjects for this experiment roused queasy feelings.

"...Is this where it's happening?" I asked, my voice trembling slightly.

"Yes. We'll get started immediately. Don't worry about the needles. You'll be unconscious throughout the whole operation."

"Sure," I said, but I would have liked to say, *It's not the needles but more that I'm being a lab rat!*

"Good, then let's get going. Florence, go tell the operators that we're ready. Nathan, lie down on that bed."

Florence nodded and left the room while he indicated the rusty hospital bed. I found it rather uncomfortable. The place was lit very dimly compared to the rest of the building. A single bulb was suspended from the ceiling in the exact center.

While I waited for the scientists or doctors or whoever was due to perform the operation, I wondered if I'd experience any side effects. As several men in lab coats filed into the room, Mr. Gonzalez stuck a needle attached to a tube into my arm.

"General anesthesia—it'll put you to sleep for about half an hour." Then he said ominously, "Sweet dreams."

I said nothing, and my muscles quickly gave in to relaxation. I started feeling drowsy, and more and more people poured inside as I lost consciousness...

Several moments passed.

At first I perceived nothing.

Occasionally there was a sharp pain in my ear...

...And I could hear movement accompanied by hazy voices. Eventually they became clearer.

"Uh...sir?" A man spoke. "You should come and take a look at this."

"What is it?" The second man who spoke sounded familiar. Mr. Gonzalez, I think.

"It's the patient, sir," the first voice replied. "His brain is giving beta waves. He's still out cold, but his head is active. Should we pause the operation in case he wakes up?"

"No. This is exactly what I wanted."

There was the sound of footsteps treading closer.

"All right, Nathan, I hope you can hear me because this is important. *Arithas*. Remember that name. *Arithas* deserves death. If you get the chance, you do what needs to be done. Don't forget that."

Arithas? Who's Arithas? It probably doesn't matter.

Another wave of intense pain washed over my ear, and I couldn't help but black out once again.

When I woke up, the room was empty save for Mr. Gonzalez, who was staring at a strip of paper.

"How'd it go?" I asked curiously.

I certainly didn't *feel* bilingual. All the thoughts playing in my mind were in English. My head ached with that name *Arithas* burning in my skull.

"It was a success." He handed me the scrap. "Give this a try."

My eyes fell upon glyphs I had never seen before, scratched across the paper with fine, sharp pen-strokes, yet they were somehow legible:[1]

ᒍᗅᎩᎵᘻ ᒪᗆᎵ Ꮀᖵᗅ̇ᐱ ᐸᗅᒍᒪᗆᎵ ᐸᒥᐪ ᒐᖵᐱᐱ Ꮅᗅᒥᛡ

"I can read it. 'Abandon all hope ye who enter here.' What's that supposed to mean?"

"Nothing." He shot me his most reassuring smile. "Just...an old saying."

"Ah," I said, scratching behind my ear.

"We'll have you set off tomorrow," he said. "You can go home now." He led me to the building's near-empty parking lot and, unlike last time, entered the same van as me.

The entire way back, he blathered on about everything that was to follow. His men would pick me up in the morning and drive me to the spaceport, where a rocket would be waiting to take me to Anbizia. When I asked how an ordinary spaceship would reach an exoplanet so quickly, he explained that there was a giant wormhole orbiting Earth. No one knew where it came from or why it appeared, but to NASA's knowledge, it had been there for several weeks and was a direct gateway to Anbizia. This was proven because Florence testified using that wormhole to return to Earth. And yet, not even she could say much more about it. It just...materialized. Out of nowhere, it seemed. It made hardly a lick of sense, but there was no time to dig into that mystery, for the wormhole only had a few weeks of life left before its inevitable collapse. We could only use the anomaly to our best advantage.

Hence, I would reach Anbizia through a wormhole. It was already out there, circling Earth, waiting to take me to the distant

---

[1] Romanized, this reads, *Nazmú hem bjålt vaxhém voi rikt máng.*

planet where my task lay before me.

Also joining me in my journey would be a company of three. We were to work together to solve the mystery of the wormholes, and although Mr. Gonzalez didn't divulge their identities, it was good knowing I wouldn't have to brave the task alone.

He also explained that the spaceship was almost entirely automated. What typically took months upon months of training now took a brief conversation and the punching of a few buttons.

Which would leave us with a perfectly straight shot to Anbizia.

He talked about many other things, but I eventually tuned out his prattling. That man droned on way too much, and my head hurt, and a sore drowsiness weighed on me as the anesthesia was still waning.

The only other thing he mentioned was an armory on the spacecraft with firearms and explosives in case of an attack by the Kadaanites. It seemed like an unrealistic scenario because we wouldn't be on Anbizia that long, so I didn't think much of it. I had no plans to get caught in the bloodshed during my short visit to the planet.

When the van reached my uncle's house, Mr. Gonzalez unlocked the doors and said, "Get some rest." Then looking at me glumly, "You have a big day tomorrow."

"Okay," I said, disgruntled, aware that his concern was totally superficial.

I bundled into the dark house, omitting any glances over my shoulder, and hurried into Uncle Rod's room. When I got a good look at my uncle, it turned out Florence was right. He was not dead, just unconscious.

"Uncle Rod. Wake up," I said as I knelt on the ground by him, at which his obnoxious snores blared on. I tried to shake him awake. "Come on, you dope! Wake up!" Then I gave his face a hard smack.

With a squawk he jolted awake. "N-Nathan? W-what happened? Where's Florence?"

"You're an idiot! She tricked you! She totally played you!"

His expression was brimming with perplexity, and I groaned and paced about the floor. The whole situation was his fault. If he weren't so arousable, so readily tempted, Florence wouldn't have gulled us in the first place.

"W-wait, what?!" he drooled. "Where is she now?!"

"She's gone! You gotta stop falling for every woman you meet!"

He blinked a few times in confusion as if he couldn't imagine such a thing, and I had to control myself from falling into greater furor. He had to be more selective with his heart. Right now, he was the type of fish to bite every hook in the sea.

Uncle Rod opened his mouth to speak, but it sealed shut as if the words got caught in his throat. A silent moment crept by, and he changed the subject and murmured, "...How long was I out?"

"I'd say an hour. Maybe two," I answered in a silkier tone. "It turns out Florence was secretly working with NASA, and while she had you napping, I was getting lectured by NASA's administrator. You remember Dominic Gonzalez? You know, the guy that never shuts up?"

"Oh, you mean NASA's administrator? What did *he* tell you?"

My wonder of whether he'd believe my tale drew a wry smirk. And so, sitting on Uncle Rod's bedside, I told him everything, and at the end of my story, I added, "Ah! They probably didn't want me to tell anyone about all that. Oh, well, not my problem."

Uncle Rod maintained a neutral expression the whole way through, and I could tell he took me dead seriously. This was no conversation of jokes or games. He heeded every word in understanding.

"So...you're leaving?" he asked.

"For a few weeks, yes."

Silence seized us for a solemn moment.

"...Are you mad?" I asked nervously.

Very slowly, he adopted a smile and shook his head.

"No, Nathan. Actually, I think this'll be pretty good for you."

I cocked my head, and I couldn't tell if Uncle Rod had finally gone crazy. "What do you mean by that? Do you mean the reward?"

"Oh no, I'm not talking about the money. I mean this is your chance to become a man—to become your best self. You'll be more of a man than I ever was. Look at me. I work at a smoke shop, drive a crummy car, and have barely a penny to make ends meet. Hell, I can't even keep a chick from backstabbin' me. I ain't the man you wanna be. You gotta follow your own path. Make your own name. That's what being a man is all about, and it's something I've been missing all my life."

"Oh, Uncle Rod," I said on the verge of tears but beaming nonetheless. With a dart I flung myself forward and wrapped him in my arms. "You're right, Uncle Rod! I swear I'll come back a better man!"

"That's the spirit!" He clapped my back hard, and I laughed, not minding the pain it aroused. "Hey, you'll kill it out there!"

We split our sides until it started to hurt. At length I remembered how late it was and opted to go to bed, for I really did need some shut-eye. I didn't want to be sluggish for my big day.

While I fell asleep in my bed, I was thankful to Uncle Rod for helping raise my spirits. Although I was eager about the proffered million dollars, I was feeling anxious and a bit downhearted about traveling so far away. Uncle Rod's humble abode never felt a more desirable home than it did now, and I dreaded leaving it behind so suddenly. I didn't even have time to savor this last night in my bed. On top of that, I'd been worried my uncle would be disappointed, so his mellow reaction had eased my mind. I wanted to ensure no one would fret over my sudden departure, and I wanted them to understand that my trip would not last forever. A mere two weeks would fly by quickly. What's more, if I could make extra short work of my task, I would be able to return sooner. It technically depended on how fast I could uncover the science of the Kadaanite wormholes. Two weeks was simply an estimate.

The good news was that I wouldn't be alone in the task because I would be joined by three partners whom I still had yet to meet. I wondered what kind of people they would be.

Upon the next daybreak, a similar black van was parked outside waiting for me. I threw on a blank shirt and a pair of dark blue jeans, and just as I was about to head out, I suddenly froze at my bedroom door, remembering my smartphone. It was beside my bed. My task at hand pulled me toward the exit, but my phone stared me down enticingly as if begging me not to leave it behind. Though I hesitated for several moments, I soon gave in to my burning instinct and took it with me. Saying one final goodbye to Uncle Rod who was still in bed, I left the house and hurried outside.

I expected Mr. Gonzalez or one of his men to be waiting at the door. Oh, how wrong I was! The girl who greeted me just beyond the front door was someone I hardly expected, though I shouldn't have been surprised.

Nora.

We exchanged silent stares for several lasting moments—actually, on my end it was a dumb gawk. The dark look on her face was some unsettling union of fury and terror that stung my eyes greatly. She should have been well on her way to school by now. What was she doing here?

"...You mind telling me what's going on?" she eventually asked.

"N-Nora? I...uh..."

I rummaged through a jungle of mental havoc for a response, but she promptly strutted up to meet my face and spoke.

"Nathan, I saw what happened last night. You don't have to keep secrets from me. You know if anything's wrong, you can tell me."

There she was, my childhood best friend; but I couldn't find the words to answer her. This brought my heart to my mouth. Our eyes locked, and I could see the layer of emotion glimmering in her pupils. They looked as though one wrong word on my end could fill them with tears.

"I have...to go somewhere. I'll be gone for a couple of weeks, probably."

"Where are you going?"

Nora had always been this way. It was always out of genuine concern, but she tended to get on top of people about their new feats. And judging by how we'd always been close-knit since childhood, I frankly wouldn't be surprised if she trailed me all the way to Anbizia.

"Somewhere far away."

"But where?" The fire in her voice said that she wouldn't let me keep any secrets.

I gently drew her into an embrace as a desperate means to calm her down. It was hurtful seeing her act so worried. Ultimately, my departure from Earth wasn't fussworthy because I would return in due time. I wouldn't be away unbearably long. It did no good to overreact; there was no point dwelling on this thing.

"You don't know it, but it's a place called Anbizia," I said. "It has something to do with my father."

My childhood friend slowly pulled back and tried to make sense of my words. Her eyes quivered and darted all over, deep in thought, and when they met mine again, she managed with a sigh to squeeze out a weak, "Okay..."

With a mouth slightly agape, eyes wide and weary, she delicately held onto my sleeve with her small fingers. She didn't have the strength to ask how my father was involved in this.

I wouldn't have had the strength to answer.

"...You'll be back soon, won't you?" she finally asked.

"I will. I promise."

We hugged each other one final time. The way she held me was the same way one holds a family member about to get sent off to war.

And when I get back, I'll be rich, murmured my mind.

Surely Nora had enough evidence to piece my words together. She was a smart girl—she could draw the right conclusion. This adventure was related to my father, and with that she could unravel that I was heading to no terrestrial land. Still, neither one of us was willing to say it aloud.

Heaving a deep breath, I said, "I have to go now."

"Be safe," she said softly. Then she whispered, "Go find your dad."

Unable to bear looking at Nora any longer, I lowered my gaze and slowly pushed her arm off my sleeve. I trudged toward the awaiting car. There was only a driver inside. He looked at me with ill humor as he must have witnessed the whole exchange. "How touching," said his expression sarcastically.

Against my expectation, Mr. Gonzalez was not present. This was fine by me, however. It was actually pleasant knowing that he wouldn't spend the whole ride chirring in my ear.

The car sped off without delay and headed southbound to Houston. Our destination was the Johnson Space Center. NASA had constructed a spaceport there many years ago as part of a program that involved a spree of establishing launch sites across the country, and since the Johnson Space Center was snugly planted there in the city, it was a perfect spot for a new rocket pad. My father blasted off there amidst its early days of operation, and it was where I was to do the same.

I was also due to meet my three new crewmates there. NASA was sending so few people on the mission to keep a low profile. This entire operation on top of the so-called Great Alien War was kept secret from the public, and to my knowledge went unbeknownst even to the president of the United States. According to Mr. Gonzalez, the strategy banked on utilizing as few resources as possible to avoid alerting any sentries. Sending droves of non-astronauts to space would raise suspicions.

Which of course meant the government had not granted authorization to execute this mission.

Mr. Gonzalez had also told me about my exact target for landing on Anbizia. I was to touch down in a country called Neiklof, a kingdom relatively unsullied by Kadaanite barbarism. NASA had already contacted their officials and alerted them of our coming; the king expected us. He avidly supported cooperating with the human race, and I would soon have the honor of meeting him. Like Earth, a broad variety of Anbizian tongues stretched across all the planet's nations. The language implanted in me was called Falian, Neiklof's official language.

As the morning sun steadily inched its way skyward, we presently arrived at the Johnson Space Center. I caught a glimpse of the aluminum-clad rocket towering over the spaceport, the upward orange face smiling warmly down on its white hull. The sight was spectacular and stirred in me a subtle flurry of excitement. Envisioning the cutting-edge technology dressing its interior, and eager to see more of the scientific wonder, I stepped out of the car, and the driver walked me to the launch site.

And that led me to meeting Dimitri, Hinata, and Dutch.

This has been the prelude to my involvement in the Great Alien War. In the last two chapters is my detailed account of the events that led me to the day I left Earth, but my crew, upon asking, only heard the shortest version I could string together. Just the key fundamentals I told them, if you will, not much deeper than *their* respective stories.

At the time I didn't know I was saying goodbye to everything I knew. Had I known what my near future had in store for me, I never would have agreed to this mission. One million dollars wasn't worth the taste of hell looming ahead in my life.

CHAPTER III

A GRENADE IN OUTER SPACE

M y new peers and I sat side by side in the airtight cockpit. The machinery laid out before us, with its various neon glows and flashes, emitted a prismatic half-light that diffused the air like a wispy mist. Through my half-tinted helmet and the room's wide polished windowpane, I gazed out fixedly at the Johnson Space Center. Swept out before us was a fantastic view of the spaceport; other buildings were sprinkled across the rest of the campus. A cylindrical metal tower was erected on the site's eastern tail similar to the control tower of an airport. Its shadow, guided by the young sun, loomed over to our ship like an outstretched arm.

There was one oddly striking thing about this mission. Granted the United States was this operation's sole organizer, my crew was international. One would expect NASA to be limited to the boundaries of its homeland, but it wasn't. My best guess was that Mr. Gonzalez and his cronies were riding on the CIA's intelligence.

The pumpkin-colored suits encasing our bodies were dreadfully unwieldy. They were tight enough to induce aching throughout the body, and I could feel my own mobility repressed with every twitch and squirm. Our helmets were equipped with headsets connected to a private radio channel. American flags were stitched on our left shoulders. There were pouches on my suit's Nomex husk, so I stuffed my phone in one of them.

"Hope you're all ready to say goodbye to Earth." Mr. Gonzalez's voice buzzed in our headsets from ground control. "I'll see you again once you have the proper...intel. Remember, we're promising each of you a million dollars for this. You'd better not disappoint."

"Don't worry, comrades," chimed Dimitri over the radio. "We'll get through this together, and then we'll live on easy street."

"Let's get it over with," I said. In truth, although I was excited about the cash, the upcoming job itself filled me with a nameless dread. We were about to touch down on a planet no human (except Florence) had ever visited, all spurred by the goal of probing a phenomenon that could spark a brand new era of space travel.

Since the dawn of time, all humanity had lodged comfortably in its corner of the cosmos, living blissfully in ignorance of the affairs of the rest of existence. But today was the dawn of a new age, and *we* were the pioneers. Gone were the days of our solitude, and the hand of human progress now guided us beyond the soil of Earth.

The next hour was spent touring the various controls of the ship. Mr. Gonzalez expounded instructions on how to get the ship off the ground. The automated mechanics had us expecting easy travels—all we had to do was launch, steer, and land.

After much waiting, we ignited the rocket's thrusters, and the engine roared to life as the rear erupted with flames. Outside I saw dense fumes of smoke blossoming into the sky as if the launchpad had become a steam room.

"Here we go..." Dutch muttered under his breath.

The ship lifted off. The room quaked as we took to the skies. Gravity bore down on us as if fighting our ascent, and soon came the feeling of my weight tripling or even quadrupling, as if a huge man sat on me trying to squash me. From my view, the terrain below grew ever smaller until the ship's nose speared through the clouds, and eventually there was a sight of raw magnificence: the regal face of planet Earth. Everything about her stuck out—her rugged green land, her murky blue ocean, her frothy white clouds, all blended together in a painting of the place we called home.

"Easy now..." said someone from the ground control team. The hull tilted as the thrusters brawled against gravity with all their might. "You'll be out of the planet's atmosphere in five!"

"There you go! You got it!" Mr. Gonzalez hooted and hollered. The radio was hard to hear over the screeching rocket, but I could make out the words faintly. "...Aaaaand that's it! Welcome to world's largest observatory, folks!"

After crossing the atmosphere, the unduly encumbered feeling eased off until I nearly felt weightless under my harness. We'd finally escaped gravity's domain. My gaze rose from the shrinking planet and met something of similar splendor. In what could be painted as a beautiful mural, an array of stars and space dust came together in a medley of the most exotic night sky I had ever seen. The majestic view could be taken in from every direction, and it was so much more vibrant than the empty, light-polluted sky one saw on the ground. On Earth, the city lights drowned out the stars, leaving the heavens only as a blank slate, or a dark canvas. But out here, not a single torch could meddle with nature's true image of nighttime.

"It's beautiful," said Hinata, stun shining clear in her voice. A lonely satellite outside the window floated by, catching her attention.

"I've always dreamed of catching a real view of space," added Dutch. "I wish I could take a picture."

I thought about whipping out my phone to do just that, but, "Let's stay focused," came Mr. Gonzalez's voice. "Go find that wormhole. Keep your eyes open." His voice had a subtle sense of urgency. He had a habit of wanting to make quick use of the people he worked with.

So began the next phase of our journey to Anbizia. The wormhole was orbiting the planet somewhere. How or why it appeared was not for us to ask. Our job was simply to track it down and use it.

*   *   *

We steered the ship west, moving against the Earth's natural rotation, which would make it easier to intercept the wormhole as it drifted toward us. Because Anbizia was so far from Earth, traveling there through traditional means would be stupid. The planet lay hundreds of light-years away from our solar system, hence a journey there would take centuries, even at light speed. No one could cope with such a waste of time. This meant that our only option was to take a shortcut. I knew not how wormholes worked in the slightest, but I imagined it as a portal. It could essentially compress a thousand-year voyage into a trip of a few minutes.

As we slowly traced around the planet, we took in the majesty of the fair Milky Way. In every direction you looked, there was something of stunning richness to enjoy, be it the elegant Earth, the dazzling sun, or those delicate stars. What a shame it was that most everyone would be grounded for life, never to see this vast universe's true ethereal grandeur.

"Look!" cried Hinata. "The wormhole! I see it!"

"Whoa..." murmured Dutch.

The wormhole looked like a marvel well beyond the limits of human imagination. Nearly forgetting to catch my breath, I found myself staring in awe at a giant ball of distorted spacetime. Pale rings of light warped around the structure's edge as if being orbited by the sun's gold. Though its edge was deformed, its center maintained a regular shapeliness. Such a sight was a portentous symbol of the universe's enigmatic beauty.

However, it bore a certain familiarity, one with gnawing eeriness. I couldn't shake the feeling that I'd seen something of this sort before. Looking closely, I noticed that behind the figure's edges, there was a distinct deformity in the stars...like the distortion of spacetime had stretched out their image.

"Gasp!" I drew in my breath when I made the connection. *So this is what Nora found!* I thought.

There was no mistaking it. This was exactly what I had seen in the telescope the previous evening. It reminded me of a black hole, but rather than a terrible mass of shadow waiting to devour us, there lay a wall studded with more stars and space on the far end.

The ship accelerated into the gaping rift, and as we entered the wormhole's bosom, the distorted space expanded in our view and ensnared our ship like an animal's jaw. The beautiful rings of light pranced by, and I watched the wormhole itself extend and warp in an inexplicable fashion, space dust flowing like a river and the wormhole's borders churning as if we'd entered the belly of some eldritch horror.

"This is where we part ways," said Mr. Gonzalez. "The wormhole disfigures radio waves, so it'll eventually cut off our contact with you. Remember, the *real* enemy is—*bzzt!*" He went static.

"Looks like the cat got his tongue," Dimitri commented. "But I don't get it. Why can't radio waves travel through wormholes like we can?"

The question came as we sailed deeper into the wormhole. It was hard to even pay attention to him while watching the changes in space around us.

"Wormholes distort light." It was Dutch who spoke. "Radio waves are a form of light. That means the wormhole distorts radio waves. I think it affects the frequency, so we can't receive transmissions on this channel anymore. That's why ground control is static now. The radio only works between *us* because of the safety of the spacecraft."

"I see," said Dimitri. "You've certainly done your homework."

"Mm, well, you learn a lot when you're tasked with winning the International Olympiad on Astronomy and Astrophysics," replied Dutch proudly.

The ship started to shake with sounds of metallic creaking. It sounded like it might collapse in on itself at any moment.

"Hey, uh...?" Hinata called out amid the rumbling. "Are you sure this thing works?"

"Only one way to find out," I answered. As nervous as I was, we were beyond the point of no return. There was no escaping the craw of the wormhole once inside. All we could do was let it decide where to take us.

As we whizzed through the tunnel of formless spacetime, I wondered how long it would last. I could see its tail opening, but it was impossible to properly gauge its distance given all the contorted light and dust. Every passing thing came as endless and disordered rapids. These spectacular spectacles were impossible to take my eyes off, and the others were undoubtedly as mesmerized as I was. We all watched as the wormhole's shams played out. Eventually the quaking subsided, and space expanded outward until the cosmos returned to its ordinary form. All the illusions had ended in the blink of an eye.

We had arrived.

Since the wormhole wouldn't last forever as this new discovery of man lacked stability, we would have to leave within a few weeks regardless of our mission's success. If the structure collapsed and disappeared, we'd be stuck here.

"Hey, check it out!" Dutch hollered. "I can see the planet from here."

"Wow, you're right!" crowed Hinata. "It's even prettier than Earth!"

Out in front of our spacecraft, I could see it too. Floating there in solitude, was a blue and green planet inviting our approach. It was like a sister to Earth, the only significant difference being the distribution of land and perhaps a slightly more vibrant sheen to its colors.

"Amazing," I whispered before turning toward Dimitri. "Isn't this..." I trailed off mid-sentence when I looked at Dimitri's seat beside me.

Empty! Dimitri was gone! I glanced around but found that he was nowhere in the cockpit, nor had he left behind a trace.

"Uh...guys? Where's Dimitri?"

I had been so captivated by the wormhole that I didn't even notice his sudden disappearance.

"I thought he was sitting next to you," Hinata said when she, too, noticed his absence.

"He *was*. He just...vanished."

At the very least, he could have announced where he was going first. We needed all hands on deck to land on Anbizia, which would spawn problems if he didn't return soon.

"Dimitri, where'd you go?" I asked through the radio. "Come in, Dimitri. Talk to me. Dimitri?"

No response.

Where had he gone? Had he fallen victim to motion sickness and made for the waste to hurl? If that was the case, it was definitely worth checking on him.

I decided to take it upon myself to find him. "I'll go look for him." I unstrapped myself from my seat and stood.

But as I made for the cockpit's exit, I stopped when I heard a loud but distant *crash*, followed by a *bang*. I listened closely. The others glanced around in confusion. My head canted sideways as the strange noises continued to sound out, low and ominous like a huge drum.

Boom...boom...BOOM!

"Whoa—!" I cried out as the last boom, a far-off explosion, caused the entire ship to shake violently. The vibration threw off my balance, and I caught myself on the nearest wall. The lights flashed red, alarms blared, and the place rumbled like an earthquake. More low explosions screamed throughout the ship. "What's happening?" I cried over the sirens.

Then a robotic voice from the ship's system started preaching at us.

"Warning! The engine has sustained significant damage! Threat level: ten! Abandon ship immediately!"

"You've gotta be kidding me!" said Dutch exasperatedly at the sudden announcement.

Hinata and Dutch quickly released their fastenings and bounced up.

"Let's go!" yelled Hinata. "There should be a lifestation with escape pods on the lower deck! If we hurry, we can make it!"

We ran. Spending no time dawdling in the cockpit, we scrambled our way to the lifestation. It didn't help that we were at the spacecraft's nose, which was farthest from the lower deck. The ship was about to go under, so we would have to hightail down to escape in time.

My heart raced like a torpedo. I didn't understand how this happened. Was this our fault? What could we have done to cause this meltdown? We were untrained astronauts, so we never had a chance to digest everything about the spacecraft's technology. Had there been some careless slip-up? Then again, the wormhole was an unrefined phenomenon, unchecked for errors. Perhaps something about it strained the ship, causing a loss of stability. Maybe Dimitri slipped away because he noticed something wrong and felt compelled to investigate. I hoped he was all right.

It blew my mind that NASA never tested the wormhole. I couldn't believe Mr. Gonzalez and his cronies would be so careless, but I didn't have time to dwell on that.

More ear-piercing explosions fired throughout the ship as we bundled through the ship's chambers and corridors. Flames spat through cracked metal walls, and steam fizzled out of damaged pipes like a hot kettle.

"Warning! Hull integrity is at fifty percent!"

"No time to lose! Hurry!" came a cry, maybe me or maybe someone else—too much a kaleidoscopic blur to tell.

We ran as fast as our bulky spacesuits would allow, if you could call it running, and although they were heavily restrictive, they did not stop us. We couldn't afford to lag behind lest we go up in flames with the doomed ship.

There was still no sign of Dimitri. Nor was there time to worry about him. All we could do was pray for his safety and hopefully catch him before reaching the lifestation.

"Warning! Engine damage has reached critical condition! Abandon ship immediately!"

With each announcement from the system, the new information weighed on me heavier and heavier. Our window to escape narrowed every second, and my hopes for safety were being dashed.

We entered a tight metal corridor. It was so narrow that we each had to go one at a time. I went in first. The explosions had gotten worse, much louder and clearer than what was heard in the cockpit, and I was getting increasingly on edge out of fear that a blast would occur right below my feet. A silent moment passed, and *crash!* my ears flared up with intense ringing. In the heat of the moment, my balance betrayed me, and I fell forward, though I could not tell whether it was of my own accord. Part of me thought I had dived, but another part of me thought I'd been shoved. As a portion of the ceiling crashed down in an avalanche where I previously stood, it dawned on me that an explosion had occurred directly overhead. However, the others were behind the point of impact, and with that we were separated. Hinata and Dutch were stranded on one side of the fallen debris, and I was on the adjacent. I staggered to my feet and peered through a tiny gap in the pile of scraps.

"Is everyone all right?" I shouted over the sounds of explosions.

They stood frozen and nearly shell-shocked, facing back at me. Fortunately, the falling metal had not crushed either of them.

"We're fine!" answered Dutch. "What about you?!"

"I'm all right!" I said. "Let's hurry and move this junk!"

They signaled agreement, and we started by grasping a big metal bar that topped off the rubble blocking our path. One look was all I needed to tell how heavy it was.

"Warning! Hull integrity is at twenty-five percent!"

"On three!" Dutch yelled as we prepared to lift the metal mass. "One, two...three!"

"Hngh!"

Failed. The bar was too stubborn to move a hair. Not even all our strength combined could lift that debris.

"What's this thing made of?!" I groaned in frustration. "Let's try again! This thing has got to move somehow!"

We grabbed it again and tried, tried with every reserve of strength to spark some movement.

"Aaaghh!"

It simply wouldn't budge. The bar of metal was attached to some part of the wall, keeping it immovable. Our time was dwindling. If we couldn't get this rubble out of the way, we'd be consumed.

"Again!" I urged furiously.

"Warning! Hull integrity is at fifteen percent!"

If we were here when the hull integrity reached zero, that would be our end.

Despite my insistence, the two stood still, looking on soberly with little hope left in their expressions. Even so, I grasped the debris and tried to move it myself. But the strength of us three combined was not enough to yield results, so of course I alone couldn't make any difference. My efforts were so futile that I looked like an idiot for even trying.

"Nathan." Hinata's quiet, sedate voice ran through my radio.

"Come on! Please! We can move this!" I begged.

"No, Nathan, we can't!" she said with more zing. "Just go on ahead! We'll be fine!"

"I'm not leaving you all behind!" I protested.

"There's no time! If we stay here, we'll all die! Just go! We'll find another way around! The lifestation should be just ahead!"

How did hell break loose so quickly? What happened to the simple and straightforward mission ahead of us? We'd gotten swept up in a windstorm of misfortune so soon, and it only raged on. Just how much worse could my luck get?

I didn't believe Hinata one bit. Nothing back the way we came would save them.

"Just wait! I can get you out of there!" Weirdly I said this, but I didn't know how to save them, and there was no time to mull it over.

"Warning! Hull integrity is at ten percent!"

"We're wasting too much time!" cried Dutch. "If we want to go, we have to go now!"

"Wait, don't!" I urged them to stop.

But despite my best efforts, they turned and ran, and I watched their swift recession helplessly. Just as Hinata was about to round the corner, she whipped her head over her shoulder for a final, fleeting look.

"Good luck, Nathan! I'll see you on Anbizia!"

She turned tail and disappeared into the crumbling spaceship along with Dutch. All the same I yearned to mend this horrific turn of events, but I knew it was too late—I couldn't fix a problem out of reach. I pivoted and ran with frustrated stomps, shaken by my own uselessness, trying to clear my mind of my failure until I came upon the lower deck's entrance. A small sigh of relief slipped out, and I almost spun a hopeful smile at the incoming safety. But as I closed the distance of the final stretch, someone came into view, already prepping one of the escape pods.

"Dimitri?!" I called out in shock.

He spun toward me with unmatched speed. His expression swelled with surprise at my arrival, but once his mind registered the situation's urgency, his alarm assuaged, and he replied, "Nathan! Hurry, my comrade! We're nearly out of time!"

I didn't think twice about following his order. With the strides of a bull, without slowing down, my body crashed into the escape pod. Dimitri immediately slid the door shut and initiated its launch. Neither Dutch nor Hinata was in sight, and there was no time to wait for them. Their only chance at survival was to take their own boat. I desperately hoped they would make it in time.

"Warning! Hull integrity is at five percent!"

A broken cry came from me, "Let's get out of here!"

"Da! We are leaving now!" said Dimitri.

With the press of a final button, the ship spat our lifeboat out into the dark space. I leaned over Dimitri's shoulder to assist him with the controls.

"Pull right!" I told him. "Head straight for Anbizia!"

We veered the pod in the direction of the planet, and as we blew toward its earthly face, I turned my attention back to the destructing spacecraft. I waited several anxious spells for another escape pod to shoot out the side of the hull, hoping to dear heaven that they'd make it. But there came nothing, nothing at all. Hinata and Dutch only had seconds before the ship would be reduced to dust and echoes, and I didn't want them to be part of that. I watched out the window through each crushing moment as the ship's body hawked up little fireballs from within, which blasted outward before dissolving into the nothingness of space. Then came the final explosion. At last the body caved in on itself, folding into one enormous fireball that soared over our tiny cabin with the magnitude and devilry of a nova. It was a glaring blast, yet specter silent, for sound could not travel through the vacuum of space.

"No no no!" I bawled in earnest while banging on the window.

For several moments, I stared at the searing remains of the ship, hoping for another escape pod to come gliding in our direction, but no one came. Leaning on foolish hopefulness, I wished their pod might emerge from the blast like in those children's stories, where everyone thinks the hero is dead but then he valiantly rises out of the flames victorious.

But this was reality. The real world was no place for such miracles.

"They...they didn't make it..." I lamented when the horrible truth was clear, voice quavering and eyes racked with tears.

"Nathan! We have other problems!"

When Dimitri clenched my shoulder and pulled me round, I saw that we were caught in the planet's well of gravity. Our speed accelerated while flames broke out on the escape pod's nose, and the sky gradually changed from black to blue upon falling into the atmosphere.

"Parachute, parachute! Deploy the parachute!" he shouted.

He punched a button on the control panel, and I gazed out the back window. A flap opened up and released a parachute that could slow our descent. It surfed through the sky behind us attached to cords. But there was a problem. The escape pod was still speeding up; the parachute wasn't opening. It flailed around uselessly in the air, and only when I checked the cords did I realize what was wrong.

"It's tangled!" I wailed.

We were speeding at full throttle to the ground, the parachute being the only possible remedy for our rapid descent. I could do nothing but watch in hope that the cords would miraculously untangle themselves. And though it tried, the snarled parachute couldn't capture our fall until finally, its strings lost their grip, and it went sailing away with the wind.

"Not good! We must have been going too fast!" I slumped in one of the seats and slung the straps over my shoulders and across my chest. "We're in for a rough landing!"

Our lifeboat swept through the clouds, and, beneath them, revealed nothing but a massive range of snowy mountains.

"Brace yourself!" said a panicking Dimitri as he buckled up in a seat.

"Hold on tight!"

Before we reached the ground, I noticed he'd torn off the American flag on his suit's shoulder at some point.

With a nosedive the escape pod crashed into the white fluffy landscape with unbridled force. It was so unbearable that I couldn't stay conscious.

"..."

It was cold.

"...Gah! *Gasp...pant!* Ugh..."

The severe bite of the frost jolted me awake, gasping for fresh air.

I scanned my surroundings to assess the situation. It was dark out, the roaring wind echoed through my ear, and the dragging snowfall scintillated in the moonlight producing an elegant glow. My body stung sharply in many places, the taste of my own blood dancing on my tongue. My helmet was shattered, its glass shards spread about the crashed escape pod which was dressed with dents. Patches of snow and blood plastered the floor.

Mewling in pain, I tried to get up, but my body was met with resistance. I struggled harder, and— "Augh!"

A scalding twinge flared in my left breast, and I felt a warm runnel of liquid trickling down my midsection. A prudent surmise told me this:

Something had pierced my chest.

Any sudden movements would surely broaden the wound. Although my torso was pinned down, I could move my arms freely, so, without moving anything else, I moved my hand to my buckle and released the straps holding me down. Being unable to see in this inky capsule, I couldn't tell what had wounded me, but it must have been wedged inside the spacesuit. I resolved to remove each piece of the suit slowly and gingerly, starting with the helmet. I moved with care at a snail's pace to avoid provoking any injuries I had sustained. As soon as the helmet came off, the frozen air pricked my head brutally like a stiff robe of tiny nails. I could feel my cheeks redden instantly under the chill.

Still wheezing and choking with agony, I chucked the helmet to the ground and peeled off my silicone-coated rubber gloves. The spacesuit had depressurized at some point in my unconsciousness, so I could slip out of it more easily, but I needed to hurry before my hands froze too solid to bend or wiggle. With haste I reached over my shoulder until my fingers found the little zipper and un-zipped it.

After I shimmied out of the suit, I moved my legs around to make sure they weren't broken...and they weren't, thank heavens. Relief washed over me, and it would've been satisfying had my conscience not been lost in everything else going wrong. Now, having shed my suit in full, my skin quickly broke out in goosebumps as it lacked protection from the frost, and my teeth chattered turbulently de-spite my efforts to stay them. My undersuit scarcely warmed me up at all. The chill put me in a horrible tremor and sapped what little energy to move I had left. The scotches and bruises blemish-ing my body didn't help.

When I looked down at my chest where I'd been wounded, my undersuit was painted red with blood. The spandex didn't absorb my blood, leaving the crimson fluids to ooze down to the ground. I tried touching my chest where it stung.

"Agh!" The pain flourished immediately at the contact, an in-tense rise in heat. Out of curiosity I took a look at my suit to see what had cut me. "W-what the...?"

What I saw only made the situation seem even more like a night-mare. There was the hilt of a knife sticking out of the suit's pierced fibers. Fear seemed to slither up my whole being, enwrapping me like a serpent. The only possibility was that someone had gone out of their way to try and stab me while I was out, though I could hardly conjure a guess as to who or why. The knife hadn't carved deep enough, thankfully, for the Ortho-Fabric was thick enough to halt the blade. Still, I couldn't imagine who would do such a thing. It was a small utility knife, so, figuring it could prove useful later, I folded it and stuck it in my undersuit's pocket.

Then I reached inside a certain pocket on the spacesuit, searching for my phone. But it was gone. I was sure I checked the right pocket, but it was empty. So where was it?

I was too cold to think about my phone. I halted out of the escape pod, shuddering tumultuously. Looking around the mountains, which were bleached white with glowing snow, I spotted zero signs of Dimitri. Neither he nor his spacesuit was in the pod, and there were not even the faintest tracks of footprints in the heavy powder. He must have left quite some time ago if enough snow had fallen to cover up his tracks, but how could he just up and abandon me?

"Dimitri?!" I called out weakly, my voice rattling in broken ripples. "...Dimitri?!"

But the only response was the howling wind. It sang a ghoulish song of everlasting loneliness. It was then that I realized I was all alone out here. My one partner was long gone; I was the only sign of life for miles. My panting quickened, my legs quivered with more fervor, and a weariness I could describe as deathly came over my already harrowed heart. I was falling into a deep panic, and as much as I wanted to let out a scream of terror, my windpipe was too frozen to produce such loud noises.

Dwelling here was useless—that was for certain. If I wanted to get out of this icy storm and find warmth, I needed to move. When I tried to walk, my legs barely had the strength to support my own weight.

I forced myself to slog through the fluff. Sticky snowflakes touched down on my face, swirling in the wind, piling up and benumbing me. There was no way I could endure this for long. Across the mountain range, I saw not even a speckle of light...and where there was no light, there was no warmth. Still, I exerted all my willpower to press on, and after many lazy trudges, I came across a bright orange mound jutting out of the snow. I stooped and brushed off the sheet of accumulated ice.

The whiteness revealed a spacesuit. It could only have been Dimitri's. He must have wrested it off shortly after venturing into the glowing silver wasteland, and I wondered just how long and how far he'd gone.

What if he...?

I winced at the horrid thought. Things were bad enough as they were, and I had already lost two of my partners. I could not stand to lose another. I warned myself scoldingly not to think of the possibility.

Still, what would I do now that the spacecraft was history? Was I stuck on this planet?

"Ah! It's so cold! I can't..." I murmured as a strong clap of wind came and sent me into a ruthless wave of shivers. Snow was thick in my hair, and my legs sank into a pool of fluff up to my knees. White glistering ropes eddied in whirlwinds around the summits of mountains under the black, angry clouds.

I needed to tune out the river of thoughts flowing through my head and focus on the matter at hand. Leaving behind his spacesuit, I kept wading the powder, trying with all sincerity to follow Dimitri's path, but the fresh drifts of snow had covered his tracks.

Deep down I knew this blizzard would be the death of me despite my search for safety. Mere minutes passed before my body gave out to the demanding cold. I collapsed face-first, blood staining the snow in dull red streaks. My last reserves of strength had been shuffled off, and now my muscles were little more than a hollow, empty void.

My vision slowly faded out, and I wondered if anyone would find my body in all the snowy mass. Before all went black, there was the sight of shadowy humanlike figures, and then, nothing.

CHAPTER IV

ANCIENT ECHOES OF THE DEVIL

The only thing that woke me was the balanced stream of my breath. All was silent and placid, making way for a gentle awakening. I didn't bother to open my eyes in the thick bliss of comfort.

All the horrible memories piled up in my mind as I adjusted to the quietness. The explosion, the crash, the snow—it had all been so violent, so brutal. I'd been convinced I was done for. The thought of enduring such a terrible episode made me twitch slightly under my covers.

What a crazy dream, I thought.

But the nightmare was over, and now I enjoyed the state of serenity, melting in my bed's warm embrace. My breaths were not shallow nor uneven, rather I took in the smell of the autumn air in deep drafts. I smiled in the sheets. Knowing I could continue my quiet life without hurdles, I started thinking about what would come next. I figured I would wake up, go to school, see my friends, head home, study, and relax. What a wonderfully simple life. I adored the lovely notion.

Better yet, there would be no aliens, no spaceships, and no snow. Oh, what a relief! Even though I knew it had been a dream, the horrors in my memory felt so uncannily real.

Better get up soon—

My thought was cut off as soon as I opened my eyes. My awakening wasn't greeted by the room I knew. I was in bed, but I wasn't in *my* bed.

No, I wasn't even in my house.

"Uh...where am I...?" I groggily asked nobody in particular.

I sat up and looked around the room through drowsy, slanted eyes. The bed had a narrow frame with a straw mattress and pillow, both criminally lacking in fluffiness. The lineny blanket was light and slim. In three directions there were gray stone-brick walls; in the fourth there were iron bars. Water droplets plunked down from the ceiling in long intervals. The place reeked of rot and waste like a sewer.

This place was not palatable as a bedroom in the slightest. It made me feel like a peasant—an animal.

"...!"

The new notion struck me like a charged bolt. I had a sudden shift in what I believed to be true, realizing at that moment that my recent memories had never in fact been a mere dream. I flung the thin sheet off, rolled up my shirt, and peered at my chest.

It was still there.

A massive stab wound. My chest was caked with excess blood that had dried into a burgundy crust, which sealed the slit from further bleeding. But what was left was a tremendous scar running across my left breast. The splitting crack was like a deep gully chiseled into my flesh. Nothing—neither medicine nor time—would ever fully heal it.

So the nightmare had been real after all.

Taking a long breath I unconsciously put my hand on my chin, my thumb just brushing over the upper lip. If it wasn't a dream, did that mean I was on Anbizia? And if so, why would the aliens lock me up in a dungeon?

As my thoughts raced around in every direction, I stood up from the crude bed and made for the metal bars. Outside my enclosed box were rows of empty cells on both sides of a long corridor. A stairwell spiraled up at the end of the hall, which was probably the only way out of this dank, corroded place.

Also I found myself wearing a distasteful, rough-hewn outfit. It was a deep brown shirt and a pair of olive pants, which combined looked nothing short of ugly and felt grainy on my skin. I also had on a pair of hide shoes, their black skin scuffed and faded.

Just then, as I was looking sourly at my unsavory fashion, the sound of footsteps came from the stairwell and slowly picked up in volume. A shadow bent down the spiral and expanded as it inched closer. Someone was coming. But the person that slipped into view was no human. Although he bore a humanoid, bipedal shape, his skin was milk-white, as was his hair, though the ends of his tresses faded to blue. His ears curled upward with a sharp tip. All in all, his bearing didn't deviate too much from a standard human appearance, but I knew undeniably that he *wasn't* human.

Which could only mean he was one of the aliens.

When he noticed me standing at the edge of my cell, a smirk beamed between his cheeks before he spoke.

"Well, well. The human finally awakens." The alien, who was dressed in a soldier's hauberk, stood on the other side of the bars. "It's not your lucky day. Bah, who am I kidding? Do you even understand me? You probably don't."

"What makes you say that?" I said in a somewhat mocking tone.

Surprise blanketed his expression. If NASA hadn't injected a new language into my brains, we wouldn't have understood one another's speech. He didn't speak English, but it certainly didn't come as gibberish. I comprehended him without difficulty and could reply with flawless fluency. I'd been told that the Falian language was the dominant Neiklofian tongue, so if that was the language this soldier spoke, then this place must have been...

"Hmph. Welcome to Neiklof. It's a real shame we can't give you a warm welcome, but you brought this on yourself. It's nobody's fault but yours that you've ended up in this pickle."

"Why am I locked up in here? Is this how you aliens treat your visitors?"

He shot me a belittling glare. "Don't play dumb—you know why you're here. You're sorely wrong if you think you can get away with what you did."

"I don't understand."

"Also, *you're* the alien, not me. Who are you to set your feet on *our* planet and call *us* aliens? Learn some manners and know your place. *You're* the one with foreign blood."

"Um...sorry," I squeaked sheepishly.

I didn't mind conceding that I was alien to the Anbizians since I had come knocking on *their* front door, but that was the least of my concerns. Never mind that—what about the things he said before? He berated me like a criminal, yet I had no idea where I went wrong. Everything he said only stoked my confusion.

"It really is pathetic," he went on. He swiveled, leaned back on my cell's bars with crossed arms, and reeled his head around to keep eye contact. "You had a master plan—thought you were a little genius—but it failed! Now it's biting you right back! You should've thought it through better!"

"Hold on...I think...I don't know what you're talking about." At this point my shirt was sodden with sweat, brewing what seemed like a swamp on my chest and back, and nausea grew in me.

He ignored my confused pleas and prattled on condescendingly. He raised his voice with feverish excitement and started making fun of me. "I mean, come on, how stupid *are* you? Why didn't you plan ahead? From the moment you touched down on this planet, your scheme was already going wrong. You landed in the middle of a snowstorm in the Saulos Mountains, and when you came to, you up and abandoned your only shelter, you idiot! Great idea! Walk out into the middle of a blizzard with no protection from the cold—how could that possibly go wrong?! You did have *one* small stroke of luck, though. The Astra Mercenaries found your collapsed body sprawled out in the snow. If those merciful dolts hadn't taken you all the way here, your corpse would still be collecting ice. You'd be too frozen solid to decompose. If you ask me, they should've left you there! Ha-ha-ha!"

It wasn't easy thinking of a response when half of this guy's words only raised more questions. My mind reeled, and my ghastly stare seemed to phase through him; my thoughts raced too wildly to spin up something to say. I decided to keep quiet and wait for his amusement to run dry.

After a series of one-sided giggles, he said, "Just give me some time to spread the word that you're awake. Soon you'll finally pay for your crimes."

I gulped. The guard headed toward the stairs. He didn't waste time giving me another glance.

"Wait...I don't understand..." I tried to speak, but he ignored me. "What's going on?!"

He ascended into the stairwell and disappeared as quickly as he'd appeared.

What was that? I was irritatedly tromping back to my bed and lying down as my imagination ran amok. I could hardly relax as I lay there. My legs fluttered bouncily against the mattress out of nervousness, and my breaths lacked evenness. An eerie feeling buzzed in my mind as I pondered the conversation, trying to fit the pieces together. What crimes had I committed? Maybe they simply hadn't realized who I was. They probably thought I was some random human who illegally crossed into Neiklofian territory; there must have been some species of border laws here. It seemed reasonable to arrest me because they didn't expect me to come crashing down on the planet in such a theatrical fashion, and they also didn't foresee that I'd be the only human.

The only human.

The words throbbed in my head, and the memory of the others came flooding back. Hinata and Dutch had bitten the dust, no doubt about it, but what about Dimitri? I hadn't witnessed his fate firsthand, so there was still a chance that he survived. If the Neiklofians found me and rescued me from those frost-coated alps, they could have crossed paths with him, too. There was still a dim ray of hope for him. But at the same time, locating a man in such a massive mountain range was akin to finding a pond in a desert. It may have been right to consider my safety a miracle.

But if Dimitri hadn't made it, did that mean I was the only human left here? And with the ship in ashes, was I stranded?

I shook my head violently as if shaking the soul-crushing notion out of my head. I still hadn't figured out why that soldier had called me a criminal. *Think, Nathan!* said my inner thoughts. They knew we humans were inbound, but they expected four of us, not one. It was likely that they mistook me for someone else. If they wanted to convict me of coming here illegal, I could simply tell them what happened. Surely they would understand.

It was all just a big accident surrounded by a horde of misinformation. That *had* to be the case. A simple explanation would definitely clear things up.

I waited for at least an hour, holed up in the tiny prison. It could have been longer. My sense of time felt muddled.

"Get up." The soldier returned and unlocked the cell door. He grabbed a fistful of my hair and yanked me off the bed before I could react. "We're going to the Stiadev Welyn. It's time to face the consequences of your actions."

"Ah...not so rough," I murmured as he dragged me out of the dungeon.

On the way to the Stiadev Welyn, more soldiers outside the prison appeared by my side to escort me, seemingly hell-bent on keeping me in line. They hemmed me in on all sides and trained their halberds at my neck threateningly, meaning any attempt to run or fight would get me sliced up.

The vast city outside the dungeon didn't have much of a modern look; the buildings were made of stone and wood, and the cobbled streets were traversed only by pedestrians and carriages. Being the only human, I must have drawn the attention of every passerby, but I kept my head hunched low, my gaze downcast. The pointed weapons stalked me with their foreboding tips, which kept me from admiring this new world.

And this brought me to this enormous arena.

The Stiadev Welyn's shape was attuned to an ellipse rather than a perfect circle and had exquisite architecture of gray limestone that really painted a stellar picture of an ancient world. The building was roofless, letting the sun toss its fair rays down onto the floor in bright bursts. The walls were erected thirty fathoms or more into the sky, with seating sloping up the whole circumference like a stadium. The many stacked tiers of seats were jam-packed with Anbizians. Their clothes, being very classy, bore a very medieval style. Such fancy getups only befitted the wealthy; this was no place for an ordinary boor. There was a wide, open ring in the middle, a vast expanse of gray stone, which gave a swell view for the eyes of the audience.

The royal soldiers towed me out to the center and threw me to the ground with deliberate force, leaving me on the cold stone floor like a wretch. More guards stood at the ring's walls, ready to intervene at a moment's notice.

When I had first entered through the gaping tunnel in the back, the crowd had been baying with a restless, oppressive sense of fury, making a low-droning din but as soon as I made my entrance, the chatter tumbled over and hushed abroad, and the once booming atmosphere fell ominously still. Everyone in the audience watched me fixedly through grave expressions. All their attention was undivided; no catastrophe could occur that would knock their focus out of balance. No one produced a whit of sound, not even a whispered conversation with their neighbor. Only silence. An unearthly feeling crept up the back of my neck like a spider. I felt sick, my throat was parched, and I could sense bits of sweat emerge on my skin in crystalline pearls.

The spectators had the same alien features, with pale skin and ivory-white hair, but the tips of their hairs differed in a rainbow of colors. Blue, yellow, black, green, red, etc.—a diverse spectrum, which was probably a genetic thing.

Up in the crowd directly ahead, opposite the entrance tunnel, a very eminent onlooker caught my eye and, with his presence alone, demanded my fullest attention. He was an older Anbizian man sitting in a fancy private box that looked like some royal pedestal. His carmine robes and golden crown embellished with jewels pegged him as nothing short of a king. Standing at each side of his lofty perch were hulking cataphracts who must have boasted ranks among the highest of knights.

And there was one more person on a platform near that monarch, his eyes burning red with anger.

"*Gasp*—Dimitri?!" I sputtered uneasily. "H-hey, what's going on—?!"

Wham! Another soldier's halberd blindsided me haft-first and broke my words with a cruel blow. Had my mind not been bouncing off the walls with questions, I would have gotten hold of myself to keep my balance.

But I didn't, and as I took a sidelong tumble and slammed into the hard stone, the soldier barked, "You speak only when spoken to, you filthy trash!"

Before I could even begin to catch my breath, two other soldiers lifted me by the shirt and set me back on my knees. I felt like a helpless sheep cast into a pit of slobbering wolves, their fangs hacking and slashing without pity.

Why was this happening? Why were these aliens treating me this way?

"Now that you're here, let us begin," said the king, his tone gray and warmthless, but composed suitably for his royalty.

Then Dimitri moved next. He pointed at me and shouted that savage, cold-blooded word.

"Murderer!"

As if the sky had suddenly collapsed and come down on me, my eyes widened at the revolting accusation.

"What?!" was my only response.

Murderer? Me?

The king grew furious at my mystification. His voice boomed, "You dare feign ignorance before me?! Why, to think that this human would commit such a grave offense and try to play us for fools!" He put his palm to his forehead impatiently, his skin pulsing with rage.

The spectators looked on in fear and bitter disgust. Each look I returned met me with the same eyes of disbelief that a low-life like me even existed. All the same I hadn't a ghost of a notion how I offended them.

"What are you talking about?!" I shot back, flummoxed. "I don't even know what I've done!"

But my words only sparked greater fury in Dimitri's outburst.

"Is that how little our fellowship meant to you?! You have the nerve to throw away the others' lives only to deny it?! You swine!"

He hurled the accusation at me the way a god would hurl a strike of lightning, and the bolt smote down with a splitting crack. He was pinning the disaster on me for no reason! Why was I getting credit for the deaths of the others? What good would it do playing the blame game?

"H-hold on, this has to be a mistake! I didn't kill them! The ship malfunctioned and self-destructed! They didn't make it out in time! That's why they—!"

"Silence!" the king roared, echoing across the arena. "Do you know who I am? I am His Majesty King Frieval Neiklof III! You *will* tell the truth, otherwise I'll take your head!"

Judging by his last name, which was the same as his country, he must have been born into a royal family. I could picture him spending his entire upbringing in luxury, looking down on all the peasants below him. I suspected it was maybe within his very nature to walk over commoners like me.

"You thought you could hide your schemes?" Dimitri stepped forward in King Frieval's elevated bay. "I witnessed everything with my own eyes. You sabotaged the ship—rigged it to explode! I saw you doing it when you thought no one was watching! If I hadn't acted so quickly, I too would've succumbed to the blast! My most grievous regret is not being able to save my dear friends, Hinata and Dutch, let alone warn them!"

"You're kidding!" I said.

I never sabotaged anything! At first, I thought Dimitri misunderstood the situation, but now he was preaching blatant lies, and he knew it! I couldn't think of a reason why he'd accuse me of murdering the others. Why the calumny? And why were the aliens so quick to believe Dimitri and not me?

"Y-you don't even have any proof of that!" I argued. "You all can't just take his word!"

"Oh yeah?" One of the knights standing behind the king sprang into the argument. "If you didn't blow up the ship, then explain these explosives found tucked into your spacesuit!" He produced two M67 fragmentation grenades and flaunted them aloft for the eyes of all.

A roar breathed out of the throats of the spectators at the sight. It was a potent gasp, followed by a low-vibrating surge of chatter. I could hear their repulsed voices:

"Who would do such a thing?"

"What a scumbag."

"Are all humans like this?"

A knot in my stomach tightened as the audience shared whispered murmurs. I was dripping with cool sweat. They only saw a cold-blooded killer—a monster—and I couldn't think of any way to sway them otherwise.

"Reportedly, there was also a knife in your pocket when you were found!" the knight added. "There's no doubt about it! You must have been behind it all!"

The astounded growls and hisses among the audience built up in a crescendo like a wave, cresting with fierce indignation. How, how did things end up this way? They assumed I was guilty without a second thought.

The grenades he produced were preposterous. I had never once seen those things, not on the spaceship nor in the mountains. Every new falsity made me dizzier. Dimitri and I were supposed to be a team. We had already lost the others—we couldn't afford to lose anyone else. So why did he rat me out for something I didn't do? I mulled over these questions on the ground, but before any answer turned up, something else hooked my attention—something that shed light on all of my present troubles.

There was Dimitri standing beside King Frieval's throne, no one watching him but me. And suddenly his face didn't express the same anger as his previous attacks and gestures. It was the exact opposite:

Dimitri was smiling.

It was a twisted smile, not of some colorful jubilation or comic hilarity but of pure rampant wickedness. Within his vile beam lurked a subtle tinge of satisfaction as well, as if some risky ploy of his had finally paid off. Everyone's attention was too fastened on me to notice him, and I only caught a small glimpse, but that sole expression revealed everything.

The truth flashed upon me like a revelation. Dimitri had set me up from the start. *He* sabotaged the ship and destroyed it. Hinata and Dutch died at *his* hands, not mine. That must have explained his disappearance while we were in the wormhole. We were mesmerized by the unfurling magic at the time, giving him the perfect opportunity to slip away and fire his grenades in some critical area.

Upon analyzing the situation more carefully, I figured he expected me to croak alongside the others, but I survived, so his backup plan was to pin it all on me. Mr. Gonzalez had mentioned something about the ship having an armory. That must have been where he accessed the grenades.

Why would he pull such perfidy? Why murder his comrades and destroy his only ride back home?

I remembered him mentioning the plundering penury of his hometown, Vorkuta, and his desire to help. One might think NASA's reward of one million dollars was adequate to procure financial freedom, but for Dimitri it may not have been so simple. A million dollars was a lot, but it wasn't *that* much. Saving his town would require a much greater abundance; a mere million wasn't enough.

Vorkuta's economy must have been maimed by ineluctable circumstances. Things like the freezing climate, isolation, and low production were what kept his community pinned down. There was no cure to the starvation and bankruptcy that ravaged his home. He was a slave to an interminable cycle of poverty that no wealth within reason could solve. So, what better way was there to loose the bonds of such slavery than to run away? By settling down here, those fetters of his home would dissolve, and he could start over in a new land. After all, his modern brain would be unleashed in a medieval society, doubtless a recipe for success.

However, we, his teammates, were the biggest obstacle in fulfilling his vision. There was a reason why he had to eliminate us. Suppose we had all cooperated and pushed through the mission. It would follow that, through the junglelike toils of our task, we'd develop an affinity for each other. If Dimitri then confessed his desire not to return to Earth, he would surely face resistance. The truth, though I wished I could deny it, was that we wouldn't readily leave him behind, regardless of how much he wanted to stay. We would contend and argue about it and maybe even resort to force. So by wiping us clean from the slate, we wouldn't be able to stop him from staying here forever. There would be no one to try and convince him to come home.

The way his motives intertwined with his actions was terrifying. He just wanted to abandon everything and start a new life! And so far, his plan was working, and he knew it!

He must have been responsible for the knife jammed into my spacesuit in the escape pod. The blade's tip had carved the surface of my chest and left a huge scar. That must have been Dimitri's second attempt at killing me. When that didn't work, my suit being too protective with its firm and thick fibers, he squirreled away the grenades in my pockets to frame me. That way the evidence piled up.

I glared at him as he concealed his smile with his hand before anyone else noticed. Even in spite of his failure to take me down, his amusement soared like a rocket. He may have been discovering that this new arrangement was better than his initial plan: he enjoyed watching me suffer.

"It's settled," King Frieval said in a disappointed vein. "The human used explosives to kill his own companions. I'd hoped that as an advanced race, you humans would be above this depravity, but it seems your advancements have not yet prodded your people beyond sin. Wickedness abounds in your civilization. I'd been advised that not all humans were trustworthy, but I didn't think the rogue would strike so soon. I thought we could sniff you out in time."

Idiot! The rat is right there with you! I screamed in my mind, my jaw tightening.

The king had it all mixed up. He thought I was a nefarious imposter on a hunt for blood, but that was a description far more suitable for Dimitri.

What a sick country this was. King Frieval was Dimitri's puppet, dancing under his strings of sadism without even realizing it. These realizations fired up a spasm of wrath in my soul. Anger had been circulating throughout the Stiadev Welyn, but none of them could surpass the rancorous steam filling my system. This place was awful, and the people were hideous. I wanted to make them burn and rot. It sickened me how everyone had let Dimitri manipulate them. They weren't thinking for themselves; they were like a herd of sheep, blindly following the herdsman to the slaughter. The entire royal body was kneeling before him as though *he* were the king instead.

"You're a devil!" fumed Dimitri.

"Go to hell!" I shot back.

King Frieval ignored our mutual slander and shouted, "Enough! It's time for you to see your punishment! Your execution is at hand!"

"Execution?! No—that's absurd!"

This couldn't be happening. He was trying to slice my head off with a pair of spinning blades turning in the wrong direction. I wasn't ready to die—not for something I didn't do!

"Mr. Volkov, I'll let you do the honors!"

Two guards poised their halberds around me to prevent me from resisting. I was going to die by Dimitri's hand, just like the others. I couldn't accept it. I couldn't!

"Dimitri! You bastard!" I erupted into mayhem. As the soldiers tried to stop me, I grabbed onto the stalks of their weapons and struggled against them, my feet planted stiffly. More guards darted over to join the fight. High wails and gasps came from the observing nobles. In the midst of the tumult, a thicket of more spears and halberds appeared in my vision, all unanimously trained on my head. We were frozen in a flock of reciprocal struggle; the soldiers and I pushed against each other as opposing forces with the two halberds being mediums in between. However, I knew that if I tried to make a move, the others would immediately cut in and neutralize me.

As I gripped the shafts with all my might, the next image that blinked into my mind was not repulsive but delicious. I could see the future laid out before these aliens, paved by the horrible truth that my mission commissioned by NASA was a failure. Half of our crew was dead, our ship had burned to mere embers, and a losing war loomed over the whole ordeal. We'd come here to investigate the wormholes engineered by Kadaan, but now, that field of research had flown far out of reach. Our mission was supposed to be the first step in saving Anbizia—or the universe—from Armageddon. And yet, it was becoming robustly clear that the first step wouldn't be taken today. The Anbizians would be crushed under the poundings of genocide, and it was all thanks to Dimitri, and Dimitri alone.

A small nip of my mind thought maybe the king knew the truth. Maybe he and Dimitri were conspiring with each other to frame me. After all, he never took a single chance to hear my side of the case. They both wanted to screw me over. What kind of rigged justice system would do that? This entire royalty was rotten to its core. The king, his soldiers, the nobles...they all made me sick. For a moment I lost memory of why Mr. Gonzalez sympathized with them. Why was I expected to help this accursed planet? Why cooperate with a race full of unbridled hatred?

My lips curled upward as I mused upon the insanity. I even started to laugh. My dryness of throat was audible in my cackles. As I was unable to stifle my feral gaiety, I must have finally gone mad in the moment. No sane person would laugh in the face of everyone else's deathly glares. These last moments of mine would be spent as a psychopath.

"Ha-ha-ha-ha! Ah-ha-ha-ha-ha! Go ahead!" I screamed with hysterical laughter. "Go ahead and kill me and let that good-for-nothing moron lead you to hell!" The soldiers tried to push me out of our locked struggle, but the shafts of their weapons were too long to apply any practical amount of strength. I kept a firm grip on the

halberds. "Do it! Kill me, and go prancing back to your royal or-
gies!"

My ribald advice drew an emphatic, repugnant gasp from the audience, followed by a strain of silence. I knew well that these people
held status more dearly than all else. To let slip so much as a snicker
at my language was to stoop to my debased level—a level of status
even lower than a dead person. I didn't care that I was further sul-
lying my dignity. I was about to die anyway.

"W...What...I don't..." gibbered a confounded Dimitri, incapa-
ble of forming a sentence. He groped for a comeback but found
nothing, and it was hilarious. "Y-you piece of—!"

"Enough squabbling!" bellowed the king, who was among the
few who hadn't stiffened in shock, instead maintaining a cool, perfectly regal composure. "It's time to expel you from Anbizian soil!"

Everyone recollected themselves for the forthcoming execution.

A knight walked up to Dimitri, stooped to one knee, and presented a bow and arrow. It was crafted by the finest bowyery a pair
of human eyes had seen, its grip inlaid with gold. Dimitri accepted
it.

He took a dogged step forward, nocked the arrow, and drew back
the bowstring. He held his hand steady.

"Take the shot, sir! Don't worry about hitting us if you miss!"
yelled one of the soldiers struggling against me.

"We have armor! We can take it!" added another.

"Monster," I muttered under my breath while staring him down,
my expression scorched with lividity.

All eyes watched in anticipation as he took aim. Things were
looking depressingly black. I was about to die, and these alien no-
blemen and women planned to celebrate it.

My burning gaze slithered up the shaft of his arrow, beyond the
fletching, into his slate eyes. Our eyes locked onto one another as if
a taut chain bound together our stares. The bilateral staring drew

out for several seconds. All I saw in him was sleek relaxation, immense pleasure, because *he* had won, and I had lost, and he knew it.

But while I thought destiny had come to sweep me away, I did not take any arrows that day. His bowstring twitched slightly, and then, to a stupor of amazement in every spectator, he pulled forward the bowstring and plucked the arrow off.

Everyone's jaws dropped open in puzzlement at whatever he was playing at. I couldn't tell what his deal was either. What were these new games? Did a change of heart suddenly arise from an influx of mercy? Or was he trying to fool me for one last laugh?

He chucked the bow and arrow from the tiered seating down to the bottom level that held my lowly person. It clattered in the ring of stone with a sonorous racket that echoed across the arena. Then he pumped his fist over his head and exclaimed in a bold, gallant tone.

"There has been enough bloodshed! It is my cherished belief that hatred is solved by love, not more hatred! We must come together and strive for peace, not violence! You all say, 'Put him to death!' But I say: let him go!"

The audience silently took some time to absorb Dimitri's speech, and then, everyone erupted into laudatory cheers. Even the king couldn't suppress his respect for such rectitude. Only I didn't applaud. Instead, I released the pair of spears and collapsed on my knees, mortified.

"Your wisdom is truly something to behold, fair Dimitri!" remarked King Frieval. "You and your friends were the victim of his wrongdoing. I see no reason to punish him beyond your discernment. But I must ask: would this be the wish of the fallen?"

"Certainly," said Dimitri. "We humans are not vengeful creatures. They would not want their deaths to steal more blood." More lies masked by eloquence.

The aliens adored him. He'd manipulated them so perfectly, so unfairly, securing his image as their flawless guardian angel. It was like he had precisely calculated each word necessary to win the Anbizians over. He had twisted the truth in such an exact way that there was no questioning him. From there it was just a matter of revving up the multitudes by sounding heroic, and they would be hooked.

But heroism was a far cry from his true colors. He mentioned peace and love, but who was he to speak with such allure? He only wanted to control people. He wanted the world to think of him as a public benefactor—a savior. There was no corruption tainting his public image, no deception. It was all robed in a veil of purity and benevolence. The people would believe everything he said, and they would applaud every one of his actions.

And anyone daring enough to expose the lies would be silenced, if not merely brushed off as a crazy conspiracy theorist.

Moreover, Dimitri willed all of this. He wanted to wedge himself into a position of power for his personal gain, and those gains would sprout from manipulating naive people and defaming his enemies.

There was nothing I could do to bring the truth to light. I was powerless. In everyone's eyes, I was a villain who wanted to watch the world burn. History would favor Dimitri as a hero, and I would be the infamous devil whom he had triumphantly defeated. The fact that he'd chosen to spare the bad guy was a monument to his heroism.

I couldn't take it anymore. I couldn't watch him thrive on the foundation of his dishonesty. It was an offense that made me want to shatter the world into a million pieces.

"Be grateful for Dimitri's pity on you, human," said the king. "He may be letting you go, but make no mistake: you won't go forward without penalty. The public already knows about your heinous crime. You'll start your life in this world with an irreparable reputation. You'll walk our lands as a monster, a devil; you'll find no joy, no friendship, no meaning. While *our* hands may not do away with you, the people ought to tear you apart instead."

"So be it," I said, putting every morsel of spite into my tone. "You can dump Dimitri's trash on me all you want, but it won't matter. I'll leave this dirty planet as soon as possible so that I won't have to deal with you losers any longer. Just keep your circus out of my way."

If there was nothing at my disposal to change their minds about me, then I wanted out of here. I stood and brushed the dirt off my knees, but as I started for the arena's exit, Dimitri seized my attention.

"Hey Nathan!" He spoke in English so that no one could understand him. Reluctantly enough, I looked back. "I believe this is yours!" He reached into his pocket and produced my phone, which hitherto had slipped my mind. He launched it across the arena, and I subsequently caught it and put it in my pocket without any movement of my lips. My rage was too thick for words. "One more thing..." He produced a utility knife. It was the same knife he'd tried to stab me with in the snowy mountains. He must have taken it when the soldiers found the grenades. "...A parting gift!" He folded the knife and tossed it to me, and I caught it. "Don't die out there, dear comrade."

Dimitri...he was mocking me. After putting on an act to trick everyone, he had the audacity to mock me? And to think he would display such spinelessness by doing so in English. He knew what a disease he was. He knew it full well, which was why he wanted only me to understand his present words.

He had already dealt enough damage. No amount of hurt could affect me now. I wouldn't show him any more weakness.

"Don't worry about me," I responded, likewise in English. "I won't die. Not until I crush your empire of lies. I've lost everything because of you...but now I have nothing to lose."

Dimitri grinned.

"Godspeed, Nathan. Godspeed."

This was all a game to him. I gave him a venomous glare before heading for the exit.

As the aliens had no knowledge of our tongue, they only spectated in confusion at what they heard as gibbered chants. The king was confused too, but he seemed to shrug it away. I left the arena without another word.

A dreadful feeling stirred up in me as I took my first steps into the unknown world of Anbizia. I was about to enter a grueling, unforgiving society that was already pitted against me. My life was going to be hideous and brutish, and happiness would slip to the domain of mere fantasy. All the while, Dimitri would live perched on the bosom of society's praise.

Earlier, I had wondered how much worse my luck could get. The world had answered my question.

The Stiadev Welyn grew smaller behind me, and I heard the king's voice ringing behind me: "Let it be known that Dimitri Volkov, our brother, may be counted among all the people of Anbizia!"

I ground my teeth as the people exploded in thunderous cheers.

CHAPTER V

WOE TO THE TRUTH-SEEKER

Just like that, I had lost everything before having gained anything. The wind had swept up all my trust and respect, carrying it away. Worse, the bent ways of the man behind my falling were shrouded in the fog of deception.

To make matters worse, my troubles were set in cold stone. I was stranded on this planet, and all alone too. I had fallen into an abysmal trench with no way of clambering out. It seemed unlikely that I would see home again. Thinking about it only weighed more on my heart, but it was impossible to steer my mind elsewhere.

I stormed away from the Stiadev Welyn and headed into the city. I advanced against a strong headwind, and the sun beat down on my neck, piercing the poor fabric of my clothes. When I reached the inner city, the streets were vibrant with alien people. The moment I entered their view, silence washed upon them as I became the focus of all those inhuman eyes. Murderer or not, a terrestrial being on an extraterrestrial planet would inevitably draw attention, but with the black frame around my head, their stares were more smarting than ever. I knew not how long I'd been unconscious following my wintry peril in the Saulos Mountains. Surely the news of my treachery had already spread far and wide.

The commoners, who were more dressed down than those nobles in the arena, retreated to the avenue's shoulders to keep a safe distance. I must have parted the crowds the way Moses sundered the sea. I kept my head down as I ran the gauntlet of those foreign and stabbing eyes, past all the shops, taverns, and houses. "Mommy, what's that funny thingy walking in the road? It looks weird!" said a little boy among the herd, but his mother gave no answer. The woman shielded her son's eyes to obstruct his view. I was in a spotlight of scorn. Everything was humiliating.

My troubles seemed inescapable. Even still, there were more important matters at hand. For one I had to find shelter before dark. The air was bringing down a slight chill and would only worsen come dusk. Since this planet wielded a medieval spirit, an inn was probably my best bet at finding warmth for the night.

That was, assuming anybody would take me.

If that wasn't problematic enough, inns required money. At some point in my walk of shame, I heaved a great sigh while reflecting on my besmirched reputation and empty wallet.

I knew I ought to do something worthwhile, but I couldn't depart from the plagues in my mind. I needed some time in a place removed from the mean leers of aliens. So, striding swiftly I hastened for the city walls, hoping to cut myself loose from the crowds. Beyond the walls lay a vast steppe. Greenery rolled gently, and dirt roads spanned in all directions. It was a massive open swath of land that gave a person more than enough room to run free. The roads extended into the unknown backwoods past the grassy sweep, and I could see the domes of mountains peeking over the horizon.

A line of people stretched roughly a furlong outside the city gate through which I exited, waiting to be granted entry by the two soldiers standing guard. Many sat atop carriages, but some were on foot. The carriages were pulled by odd reptilians (I later found out they were called traxids) such as no pair of human eyes had ever seen. They had the stature of Jurassic bipeds, their hind legs bulging with muscle in contrast with their short, wiry arms. Their bodies were clad in large white or gray scales, scales much fatter than those of earthly reptiles, and their backs were saddled with hard tortoise-like shells. Their snouts and heads had heavy and colorful plumage.

As I dragged my feet through the dirt, I hung my miserable head low while skirting the string of extraterrestrial men and beasts. Toward the end of the line, I looked up and found myself face to face with one of those traxids. It gazed at me with its ophidian eyes, probing my foreign, human form. It reached out a webbed claw, as if preparing to grapple me, and I swiftly stepped back out of caution.

"Don't be scared, now," said the driver of the animal's carriage. "She's an outgoing one—gets real curious when meeting new people."

I relaxed in the alien thing's presence but didn't go any closer. I had just begun to resume my walk when the driver grabbed my attention again.

"Hey, I heard about what you did. Don't worry, I won't give you any more trouble than you're dealing with. I just want to know: where are you headed?"

I glanced between the enclosed city and the naked field. To tell the truth, I didn't know where I was going. I just wanted solitude from the glares of strangers.

"Just...anywhere away from here." I gazed down the train of people and carriages. There appeared to be a kind of inspection process for the people to undergo. I couldn't imagine that the line was ordinarily so severe, so I figured there must have been some special event or circumstance exacerbating it. Most everyone among the chain looked miserable too, as if having just emerged from a catastrophic occurrence. "What's with the long line?"

"Refugees," he said with a predatory smile. "This is a big city, so it gets a lot of people who've been displaced by the war. I think these people are mostly from Norscha up north, which fell not too long ago. I'm a merchant, you see, and selling goods to desperate folk like these here makes for easy money!"

Beside the driver sat his lady companion. It was unclear at the time what their relationship was. She looked straight ahead with little interest in our man-to-man conversation. She wore a brown mantle with a hood that suspended a shadow over her eyes, which made it hard to discern any features beyond the base layers of her face. When she noticed me looking at her beneath the sunlight, she acknowledged me with a silent smile and kept enjoying the good weather.

"If you come back, come and find me," said the merchant, whose scalp was wrapped in a kerchief. "I have some things that might benefit you."

An offer? He had to be lying. Why would anyone be friendly to me? I was a murderer, and he knew it. He was probably fishing me in so he could strangle me privately. In spite of his blatant trap, I didn't have the spirit to call him out or argue, so, for politeness's sake I mumbled, "Sure...whatever," before being on my way. My mood still abject, I haphazardly wandered away from the city.

There were plenty of reasons to steer clear of that man. The king had warned me that the people would encounter me with extreme hostility. In other words, trust no one.

I got lost in the anguish clouding my mind. After a while I regained my misplaced consciousness, and I found myself standing before a lake adjoining the city. No one was to be seen. Finally, I was alone.

I went in the shade of a lone tree atop a bluff overlooking the water. Beyond the deep blue plunge was a view of the city, and I had my first view of the elevated castle and its stone spires cresting in the long blue sky.

Suddenly an animal concealed in the tall spikes of grass spotted me and maundered closer. I stared at it, and it stared back. It had fluffy vermilion fur and great round eyes. The whiskers were of an otter, shooting from a nose that was much too small for the largeness of its eyes. A hefty pair of roundels sat on its head like a mouse's ears. Its figure looked frail and bony like a malnourished squirrel. It was an ugly little critter.

The animal (which was called a kreplim as I would eventually learn) curiously inched closer to investigate the strange species it had discovered. This was certainly its first time seeing a human. I wanted to snap at it and scare it off, but it acted a moment sooner.

"—!" The piping treble it suddenly produced could not be mimicked by human tongues. At best it was describable as a strident shrill, which, while not so cuttingly loud, was obscenely irksome as I'd strictly come this way for some peace and quiet. The thing's eyes shifted to an angry bright red, and it pounced at me, latching onto my leg with its large front bucktooth. I nearly screamed in pain, but I held my tongue upon realizing there was no pain actually worth my screams. Its teeth were far too blunt to penetrate my flesh, no matter how hard it clenched its jaws, so it hung there pathetically as it gnawed at my skin. Its chops must have been built for soft fruits and the like. I stood in exasperation, ripped it off my leg, and held it up by the fatty skin on its neck. The creature kicked and flailed about in the air, focusing on me with its bloodthirsty eyes.

The roils came rushing back. "Buzz off," I spat, throwing the kreplim on the ground. The impact evoked a cry of pain, and the thing scuttled away into the lush grassland bleating hurt whimpers.

Alone at last, I slouched against the tree's bole and closed my eyes. But although I could see nothing with my eyes closed, the faces of all those people of retrospective horror were still plain in sight. Their images burned in my mind—Dimitri, King Frieval, those soldiers, even Hinata and Dutch—they were all there.

My face scrunched up from a growing sense of malaise as I wrestled with my bogeys. Eventually, I opened my eyes and pulled my phone from my pocket. I turned it on, but still, there was no signal. This was a foreign planet: of course there would be no cellular service here. The battery was low too.

Shipwrecked and with no way home, I would have no choice but to adapt to this new planet.

And that meant leaving behind my past life.

Unleashing a caterwaul of bloodred rage, I hurled my phone into the lake, and the water billowed up in a great splash before the bubbles consumed my device forever. With the last remnant of my old life gone, I sighed stressfully, watching the rippling rings from the splash shudder and die out.

When I was finished absorbing all the reality of my black future, I rose to head back, when suddenly an irregularity in the landscape took my attention by storm. What I saw hadn't been present when I first came to this precipice—it had appeared at some point. I knew not how or when it got there, for it arrived in stealth unbeknownst to me, brooded upon by the element of surprise, and my skin crawled realizing the thing could have been there for many a moment amidst my ignorance. Even more unsettling was the sheer enigma and abnormality of the sight, which was almost paranormal in nature.

Someone was standing on the other side of the tree.

He was leaning against the trunk. His stare was dead set on me like a laser. His face was veiled with a wooden mask. His clothes seemed noble but suited for combat, befitting a high-ranking military officer, and a huge black jacket hugged him like a trench coat. There was plenty of room for the imagination save for his raven hair, which cascaded down his shoulders, and his maroon eyes, visible through the mask's eyeholes. He bore little resemblance to the aliens I'd seen so far, but he wasn't human either, despite his similar bipedal shape. We both stared at each other for a few moments until he murmured slowly, deeply.

"You...you're a human."

"What do you want?" I asked.

"Your name," said the masked man. "Tell me your name."

Most everyone back in the city should have known my name already. Did this man not recognize me? Figuring it would be just one more person, I decided there was no harm in answering.

"Nathan Tucker."

"Good..." he said, and in his voice I could hear the smile growing behind his mask.

"Who are you?"

At my question, the masked man straightened his posture and drew closer. There was a certain menace about him. While a sheet of cloud had rolled in over the whole skyward dome during my time alone, leaving the Anbizian land gray and umbral, there was a gleam in the man's eyes that was of someone who didn't flinch at the world's horrors.

"I am nobody," he said. "...Nobody here, at least. You can call me Tebaldus." We were standing face to face by the time he gave his name. "You don't want to be here, do you? You hate this planet. You want to go back to Earth. You see, I can help you get home."

"H-how would you—" I started stammering, but before I could finish, Tebaldus drew a dagger, threw his arm around me, and reeled me in from behind before I could steel myself. He perched the blade on my throat, ready to slit it at a moment's notice.

"Or I could kill you now and free myself from the ghosts that haunt my nights!" His hot breath flowed down the back of my neck.

If I moved even a little, his knife would skate clean across my neck. What was he talking about? How would killing me free him?

"I've got nothing left to lose anyway," I managed to squeeze out.

"Don't say that. You'll make my prey less satisfying."

Being his prey, I had no hope of squirming free from his arms. My only option was to stay quiet and let him decide my fate. At this point I hardly cared about life or death. I had already lost everything, so what more was there to lose?

But a bead of mercy must have arisen in him, for he withdrew the blade and put it away. "Ah, I shouldn't do this. Not yet," he said. "Death is mercy. Killing you now would be a waste." He released his hold; the hawk decided against devouring the rabbit.

"Then what do you want with me?!" I demanded while retreating several paces away and adopting a defensive stance.

"I just want you to see the truth. Then you'll know why..." He bridled his tongue. His way with words was painfully cryptic. It seemed like everything he said was a riddle with no solution.

"What *is* the truth?"

"Be patient, Nathan. You'll learn one day." His glare bit me, and flashingly there was a spark in his eyes, appearing to blaze with hatred. "The day you see the truth is the day you see my vengeance."

With those words, Tebaldus strolled away. But he didn't head for the city. He headed the opposite direction, off to the wildwood beyond the grass expanse. I watched him go, grimacing under a mountain of fear. What his words meant, I knew not a flicker. Neither did I know why he was here, where he came from, who he was, or why he hid behind that mask. I wondered whether or not the truth he mentioned would set me free. One thing I knew for certain, however, was that we would surely meet again.

My return to the city was met with that line of refugees outside the gates, which was still vigorous in length. I blundered up to the tail, having little memory of who or what I was, and the line inched forward, slow and steady. One by one, the two guards inspected each wagon and pedestrian before allowing passage. Perhaps the process was a measure to catch illegal smugglers or sniff out spies. Tight security was only logical in a state of war after all. The problem was that the inefficiency made everyone else's head throb.

Unsurprisingly, every preceding person was in the clear. The probable lack of alarming incidents these guards handled must have goaded them to slog through their jobs with little effort and enthusiasm. Their minimal interest had them moving like sloths, which held up the line. If one wanted to smuggle something, a plan wrought with shrewd acumen—add a sprinkle of luck—could easily turn success. But their apathy was suddenly squelched when it was my turn. Although I was obviously empty-handed, the guards tensed like rheumatics and stood erect when they saw me. Now they behaved as though they had the most critical jobs in the kingdom.

They began the process with knotted scowls, and they examined me far more thoroughly than anyone else. Only I had to let them pat me down and scour my pockets.

"Your shoes," said one of the guards just as I thought it ended. "Kick 'em off."

"This is ridiculous! You never made anyone else do any of this!" I carped.

My complaints hardly fazed him. The guard stared at me with detached, motionless eyes, with lips somewhere between a smile and a frown. There was something lifeless about his vacant look, as if he were focusing through me and into a vast abyss of nothingness.

"I'm just following orders, sir."

After giving him a cold, hard glare, I complied. *So be it*, I thought. If they were selective about who received heavier law enforcement, it fell upon me to prove them as hypocrite fools. Disgust, disgust, disgust settled in my mouth, knowing they would choose their rigor based on who they liked and disliked.

Of course they found nothing, which left them sorely disappointed. They probably had their hopes up to get some long-awaited entertainment by inventing an excuse to arrest me. I eyed them smugly as they let me through, to which they glowered back in contempt. As my public image wasn't exactly a portrait of virtue, I knew I'd have to get used to discrimination from the law and the people alike.

"By the way," said the guard who'd snooped in my shoes. "There's a place here that's suited for your kind. You'll find it if you head down that way." He pointed to the right of the main avenue.

This advice was certainly not intended to be helpful; it was an insult. Without acknowledging him, I trod the road of his suggestion.

Looking down the city streets, I couldn't deny the liveliness of the castle town. Even under the cloudy sky, the city was constantly astir with heaves of activity. I'd been too absorbed in my thoughts to notice the thriving movement during my first walk through these streets. But this bright climate was a poor fit for my gray situation. There was somewhere more proper—a more somber place—a graveyard of gloom which suited me perfectly according to the guard.

It was a district for people just like me: people with no money, dignity, or future. It was a cold ring of poverty, the vale of the economically inviable, the most degenerated part of town. Its denizens would be wise to oust any dreams of success. I eventually found it to be called the lower district.

While I walked toward the city's supreme hellhole, the buildings turned more and more cadaverous, and the air itself seemed to fall into depression. The bustling place's color seeped out of the environment like a canvas painting left sitting in water by mistake. Buildings were more dilapidated and uninspired in architecture, roads and alleyways grew thinner, and the volume of cracks and potholes in the cobblestone increased. The entire district seemed to molder with little possibility of salvage.

There was an observable shift in the people too, their clothes becoming more frayed and fusty. Not only that, but this area's people were variegated with different physical quirks compared to the aliens I'd seen beforehand. There were many people with features of animals such as horns, claws, or even tails. Some features were bestial but strange and foreign to the human imagination. An immediate dawning struck me—a realization that, to my stupefaction, hadn't so much as tapped my mind: these differing alien beast-men were of the same element as the various races of Earth's men. Something peculiar about these fellows tugged my attention. Why were all of these unusual strangers clustered up in this place? I hardly saw such breeds in the other districts of the city. Why did they dwell in such a squalid place? Could it have been that these more exotic specimens were stamped down in the lower brackets of society? Perhaps there were the folks you could view as ordinary, who enjoyed superior living standards over a rancid place like this, as opposed to those who were more offbeat or undesirable, cast aside like dogs to receive the scraps from the social ladder's higher rungs. What a pitiful way to organize a city.

Another difference among these people was how they looked at me. Unlike the nobler classes of townsfolk, their expressions didn't betray the same fear or hatred in my presence. Rather, they looked disappointed that I had misplayed my cards so poorly that I ended up here.

Near the district's center was a central square from where the neighborhood branched out. The decrepit buildings were chiefly low-end shops and alehouses, clearly the worst, cheapest businesses available. They only appealed to people who couldn't afford anything better.

I was thinking about where to go first when I heard a familiar voice. "Hey, kid! Over here!"

My head reeled toward the voice, only to see the merchant on the carriage who had beckoned me earlier. His wagon was nuzzled into an alley, and he had set up a stall with goods to sell. His woman was still with him, too. They both waved affably, so I took the bait and approached with cautious, dubious steps.

"So, you came back after all!" He flashed a smile, pleased to see me. "I figured I'd find you here."

"What do you want with me?" My suspicion shone clear in my

tone, which he quickly caught onto, so he tried to alleviate my worries.

"I'm dying to ask..." he said. "...Why'd you *do it*?"

It took some time to think up the right response. Everyone was adamant about disbelieving me, so there was no point in trying to plead innocence. If I had to shoulder the blame for the crimes, the next resort was to gloss my actions as justified.

"I did it...because humans are evil. I hate them. They make me sick. I didn't want their filthy hands to poison this great planet, so I slaughtered them like the animals they are."

"But *you're* a human, no?"

"That's my biggest regret every day."

The man's eyes twinkled with benevolence, which I found smitingly curious. He laughed. "That's what I like to hear! Well said! You're not wrong for killing those humans. For all I care, you can kill as many of your kind as you want. Just keep them off our planet!"

I looked at him tentatively before responding. "You don't view me as scum?"

"How could I? You think I want more nasty humans coming here to desecrate our land? Not to be rude, but Anbizia doesn't belong to your kind, which is why I wanted to thank you for at least reducing the number of humans landing on our soil. I'd say you're...one of the good ones."

Ah, so that was how it was. He only appreciated my alleged transgressions because he believed humans were inferior. He simply assumed niceness in spite of my humanity because my supposed crimes aligned with his values. So long as he didn't impose his hatred directly on me, I didn't care how he regarded us Earthlings. I could withstand his beliefs if we could cooperate, for I felt similar disdain: I didn't harmonize with his people either.

"The name's Goldwin," he said, moving the conversation forward. "Gad Goldwin. This is my wife, Elowen."

"Pleased to meet you," said the cloaked woman.

"Listen, I like you, kid," said Goldwin. "You sacrificed your reputation to keep a few humans away from us. As someone in the business field, I respect your guts. That's why I wanted to give you a little something." Goldwin produced a small drawstring sack and dropped it onto the table. Its contents jiggled with metallic clinks. It was money. "This bag has thirty Merth Silver coins. That should be enough to get you started here."

"..."

Not knowing how much a Merth Silver coin was worth, I reached for the bag of coins tentatively. But obnoxiously he snagged it back at the last second.

"Not so fast, boy. I need something in return."

I scoffed. "Fine. Shoot."

"I'd like you as a regular client."

"Why?" I asked. "Why do all of this if you don't like humans?"

"Because assets are assets. And correct me if I'm wrong, but..." he leaned in close as he spoke. "...I'm assuming you aren't fond of Anbizians given how everyone's been treating you. I can see it in your eyes: you hate everyone here. I get that being stuck on another planet full of trash people isn't a pleasant feeling. You and I may be separate by DNA, but we really aren't so different in our ways of thinking. That's why I think we'd do well to trade luggage from time to time."

He spoke like a typical merchant. I didn't want to surrender my wallet to a greedy businessman. And yet, I needed his proffered money, and I couldn't afford to turn down a potential positive partnership. Such opportunities would be seldom henceforward.

"You can count on it," I said, and Goldwin forked over the coin purse.

But before I could leave, he said, "Wait a sec. I have something else for you. I was selling clothes in my last town, and I have some left over. Elowen went and put together a nice outfit for you."

He asked his wife if it was ready, and she answered, "Yes. Just a moment, please." And she disappeared in the carriage's bonnet, rummaged around for two moments, and emerged with a set of clothes. She handed them over so I could take in their style. "I know you stick out like a sore thumb as a human, so I made sure the outfit's colors will help you blend in," she said.

The outfit had a sable pair of leathery boots and a belt. There was a collared undershirt—also black but more faded—and a tan sweater vest complemented by dark gray pants. To top it off, it sported a supple brown utility jacket that looked useful for work and travel. Everything was fairly clean except for a few travel stains here and there. The clothes were of decent quality, had conforming and harmonious colors, and were an obvious upgrade over my current attire.

I knew my current appearance sank below that of peasantry. I was wearing these rags when I first woke up in Neiklof, and while I wasn't entirely sure who dressed me, I surmised it was likely the mercenaries who found me.

"You won't get very far with the tatters you have now, so I want you to have these," said Goldwin. "Normally, I would charge you a fair amount, but you can have it for free. Consider it a first-time customer deal."

"Oh..." It took great power to cough up the next word, which was caught in my throat by my surprise. "...Thanks." I fully understood that kindness would not commonly be tossed in my direction. That was why I couldn't help feeling skeptical at the merchant's generosity.

"To be honest," he said as he indicated my current wear to leave one final thought. "If that's how you humans dress, then may the gods help us all."

As I walked away, I didn't respond or laugh, not because his joke was poor taste, but because I had nothing to laugh about, let alone smile.

CHAPTER VI

BIOSLIMES AND OTHER FUNNY CRITTERS

A string of days drifted by. I escaped the melancholy only in my sleep. The atmosphere was dull, gray, and sluggish. There had been little movement on my part since *that day*. I stayed in the poorest inn I could find. Its stench had notes of rancid grains and moldy cheeses. The odor was probably from the inn's chef's constant waltz to brew his foul meals, which were only worth eating in deep spells of hunger. The prostitutes who peddled their bodies at these types of inns didn't help either.

The new jacket hugged me warmly and kept the nightly chill at bay. I abandoned my old clothes in a random back alley, figuring I'd never see them again.

Still, my situation could have been worse. Many refugees from other war-torn regions were forced to sleep in places like the nearby stables or even outside the city (which was called Cordea) when they couldn't afford inns, but looking at my rapidly dwindling silvers from Goldwin, I feared I was soon to join them.

Over the days spent at the inn, I had learned more about Anbizia and the Great Alien War. Allow me to share my gatherings. I expect you have many questions by now, and this information may answer some of them.

Most importantly, the wormholes were Kadaan's crucial advantage, which was why Anbizia was itching and sweating to secure Earth's support, because if it didn't, the fight was already over.

As Earth was far more advanced than both warring planets, we humans had the power to turn the tide completely. Even so, mankind was stumped by this celestial phenomenon of the wormholes. No one knew how such an innovation was achievable, especially for a less advanced Kadaan, *especially* when it was beyond terrestrial technology. So the chief issue was that the Kadaanites could readily deploy their troops on Anbizia, but the Anbizians couldn't retaliate. They couldn't invade Kadaan—only defend.

Though it seemed like this war's outcome could be swayed by the hands of mankind, the fight was urgent because there was that dangling fear that the Kadaanites could create a weapon even more powerful than the wormholes. Then the tide wouldn't be so easily turned.

Despite Anbizia's jeopardy, her strongest nations had not formed an alliance of any sort. You'd be right to anticipate everyone banding together in a supranational coalition to avert their annihilation, but the planet's more powerful nations were adamant about navigating the sea of blood alone. The Kingdom of Neiklof was among the planet's strongest nations, so it naturally had a higher degree of security. The nearest Kadaanite-occupied territories were far north, but the enemy's advance was quietly impending, constantly clawing forth, battle by battle, inch by inch. The enemy line creaked along the land as each Anbizian line of defense broke, and the alien invaders prowled the soil looking for quarry.

I sighed as I thought about the alien invasion.

Although the wormholes were the mystery I had originally set out to solve, I needed to shift focus. My spaceship, my only way home, was reduced to ash. My new top priority was to forget the research and find a way off this planet. I had nothing to do with this war anyway. But until I could devise an escape from this prison, I'd have to make a living here somehow.

And what were the chances that I'd never return home? It seemed plausible since the Anbizians lacked space travel. Perhaps

I'd die here without ever viewing Earth's noble face again. Adapting to this new planet would be grueling, and I would give anything for an alternative.

But what other choice did I have?

And how would I make do in this otherworldly land? Staying at the inn had cost me just over half a Merth Silver coin per night, and the food and drink hadn't affected my budget much, either. I could live on these thirty pieces for a while, but they wouldn't last forever.

I painfully reviewed these items in my head as I sat at the inn's bar, sipping what few drops of diluted fruit juice remained in my cup, and headed outside. The morning sun had scaled just a pebble into the sky, glimpsing over the city walls and blaring its vivid rays onto the streets from the cloudless plane of blue. Looking around the immediate area, I was nearly thunderstruck by the lower district's rare barrenness. Usually the streets in this precinct were overflowing with people, but that hustle and bustle was absent today, and it was a rather quiet morning. The lower district was already the most desolate part of Cordea—now its dreary temper redoubled by its emptiness. It wasn't a problem by any means. Actually, it meant I could walk without dealing with people pushing and shoving.

I took a brisk walk past the few pedestrians at hand until I came to the old well. My face needed washing. I drew up some water and scrubbed. My scrubbing was eccentric in a manner you might call vigorous or even violent, and I probably teetered on grinding rashes into my cheeks. When I finished, I leaned on the well's wall and breathed deeply, staring down the cavity into the black abyss. I figured the midnight silence of the hole was the most peaceful part of the city, terrifying and lonely as it was. Driblets of water slipped from my face and dove into their cold, dark place of belonging. I took a long, drawn-out breath. The empty staring lasted several moments, after which I dried myself off with my sleeve and took to the lower district's main square.

You may still be wondering about the different kinds of Anbizians. Here, I discovered that Neiklof's most common and dominant people were called falia (the singular form is falius, mind you). Those closely resembling the falia but with physiological aberrations (such as animal parts) were called demifalia. Most of the lower district was full of demifalia. There was additional intelligent life on Anbizia called nonfalia, existing outside the first two categories, but such breeds were scarce in these parts.

Interestingly, I heard booming voices as I drew closer to the square. When I turned the corner, it was packed with people. It looked like the purlieu had been sucked into the area as they congregated around the middle as if something had stolen their attention. However, I couldn't see what allured their interest. The morass of demifalia blocked my view. I shoved my way through the flock until at last I could see the target of all those eyes. It was enclosed there in the circle of spectators: gallows, erected tall, complete with a noose for hanging and topped with soldiers on duty. Standing among the soldiers was a girl. She looked about my age— maybe a year or two younger. She was the first nonfalius I ever saw, and the sight of her, as distinguished from the commoners, had a rather sublime touch.

The girl's body was cerulean like the sea and translucent, and though she had a humanoid figure, her texture wasn't like typical flesh. Shimmering under the sun, her body was a watery-looking substance that constituted her entire being, including her hair and eyes which were also blue. This was why she stuck out like a sore thumb.

Currently I had little knowledge of her race, but I will use this moment to share what I eventually learned. While demifalia and nonfalia had trouble finding belonging in Neiklof, this girl had it worse than most. She belonged to a species known as bioslimes (commonly shortened to slimes), one of the rarest and most unique races on the planet. Their differences from the falia flamed more brilliantly than anyone else; even humans were more similar to falia than these slime people. This race was doomed to live subject to scorn and disgust. Casting them under the umbrella of nonfalia was inappropriate in the eyes of many. To some, slimes were much closer to animals or even monsters, but ultimately their existence as intelligent beings narrowly salvaged their status. Granted the humanoid forms of the Anbizians, you should expect them also to have humanoid minds and thus humanoid desires, and one of man's preeminent cravings is power above all else. And the only way to gain power in Anbizia was to stamp your neighbors into the dirt and enforce their lowness of status. The falia had simply beaten the other races to that punch. Of course, the thirst for power was unquenchable by nature, so this social divide only yawned with greater width as society aged.

The slime's clothes represented the very soul of the lower district, with tears and dirt strewn across the brown threadbare rags. She kept her chin tucked into her neck with a downcast gaze, misery writ all about her face.

It looked like the soldiers were here to present some very bloody morning entertainment, and the slime girl atop the gallows was the star of the show.

"Good morning, good people of Cordea!" announced a soldier, clearly the executioner. His hauberk had a crest that looked like an axe cutting a tree. "Today we come together as Ystaria's beloved children to witness the deliverance of justice! This slime here has committed a horrible crime! She's been caught in the act of stealing clothes! We all know how offensive it is to infringe on another person's nice attire, and for a nonfalius, it's punishable by death! This is our chance to quell this injustice and rid our great city of such unfairness, and as servants of Our Lady Ystaria, it is our duty to send the depraved to Her!"

What kind of savage would execute someone for stealing alone?

And to speak of justice? The hypocrisy cowed me. Listening closely, I sensed a subtle hint of apathy in his manner of speaking. There was a façade of enthusiasm, but he wasn't speaking from his own heart. He seemed to recite a script in his head, and his perfunctory speech operated like a machine.

The girl looked as though the man's preaching fell on deaf ears. She had probably heard his words but was too absorbed in her own thoughts to listen. There were too many things churning around in her head to surrender attention. On the outside, she was only a shell, a mere entity—the real her had withdrawn fully to the interior. Her only existence was adrift in the formless and lightless world of her mind. If I had to guess, she was probably contemplating how her missteps had led her here.

"Now, before we continue, does anyone object to this execution?" asked the executioner. "We have quite a low price for her life today. You can purchase her life for only twenty Merth Silvers!"

Neiklof used a system that allowed one to bail another out of execution. If you had a friend about to be put to death, you could pay a hefty fee to break that person's chains, though it was often wholly unaffordable. Executioners were inclined to set prices in such a way to far exceed the crowd's price range. But this offer for Twenty Merth Silvers—almost half a Golden Sol—was indeed cheap. Bioslimes were so widely regarded as lesser that the executioner didn't need to set a high price—no one would sacrifice a portion of their wallet for her anyway. The reduced price came from a combination of the world's scant pity for slimes and the already shallow pockets of the lower district's regulars.

The executioner surveyed the audience in search of a hand raised above the canopy of heads, but no one was throwing in their lot. Each pair of arms hung low at their sides, denying the girl any shred of sympathy. Unfortunately for the girl, no one felt it was worth throwing away twenty Merth Silvers for someone like her. Neither did I. I did have enough money to afford saving her, but the purchase would set me back, and I didn't see what was in it for me.

"Well, slime, it's time for your departure. All souls return to Ystaria's hands. May She hold you gently."

As the guard pointed her to the jaws of death, the girl took care not to let slip any cry of distress.

She did not move or speak, but her quivering eyes voiced that she understood full well her imminent fate. Using his spear, the guard nudged her toward the dangling noose, and she stepped across the wood hesitantly.

When she put her head through the noose, another soldier confronted the executioner and murmured something.

The executioner nodded, cleared his throat, and said, "Ah! Pardon my forgetfulness, kind citizens, but I intended to present the stolen clothes!"

Another guard stepped forward with the clothes and held them up. Everyone beheld the outfit with little interest. No one seemed to care for the ratty clothes...no one except me. The moment they came into view, I suddenly wanted to shout, but my mind blanked.

It was my old outfit—those rags I'd worn on my first day here!

How could she have stolen those clothes when I abandoned them in an alley? It was understandable that she would snatch them for herself out of desperation if she was penurious, but that wasn't theft. Besides, those clothes were way too big for her frail, starved frame—why would she risk arrest to steal them?

So did she...it couldn't be...

...Did she get falsely accused too?

"These clothes are what wrote her fate!" The executioner exclaimed as another guard tightened the noose. "Let the original owner of these clothes—who we regrettably couldn't locate—witness justice!"

"Yeah, yeah!" shouted a spectator. "Just get on with it already!"

Justice? These people had no right to speak of justice. Their vision of the law was twisted, yet they thought the truth favored them. But no, they had long been under truth's curse.

As the executioner prepared to seal the slime's destiny, her oceany eyes met mine for the briefest moment, and she quickly looked down. But that infinitesimal glimpse told me everything I needed to know. Her eyes traveled into me with waves of innocence. Not only that, but behind that thick layer of misery, a burning desire to redeem herself through any means necessary crackled in her eyes. From then on, I knew she was guilty of nothing. There was potential in her, and I could see a glimmer of resolve in her expression, like the stars spitting sunbursts of hope. If only there was something to spark the flames of her future, those flames could shimmer brilliantly throughout the land.

I understood now.

She didn't want to die. Not like this.

"Before justice is served, would you like to share your last words?" the executioner asked. A silent beat passed, and the hopeless girl shook her head.

A torrent of anger blasted up my spine when he mentioned justice again. My scowl must have been bent in a way that looked inhuman. I couldn't watch it any longer. I reached into my coin purse and jangled the pieces out of nervous playfulness. I was partially responsible for the girl's position—I'd abandoned those clothes in the wrong place—so I felt obligated to rectify the situation. To stand still and do nothing about the injustice I caused...how could I call myself any better than that sorry executioner?

I can handle the price, I thought. The cost of her life was substantial but not unbearable. *I can handle the price*, I repeated to myself.

Right when the executioner placed his hand on the lever to open the floor and suspend the rope, my voice rang out.

"Those clothes are mine!"

The entire audience, plus the soldiers, looked in my direction, dumbfounded. Everyone was unanimously in disbelief at the words that ground the execution's dramatic flow to a screeching halt. Even the girl, who had been staring downcast at the wooden planks of the gallows, lifted her gaze for me.

"Stop the execution!" I demanded.

"N-nice try..." stammered a very befuddled executioner, doubtlessly recognizing me. "...Silly stories won't save her."

"Then I'll buy her life!" I declared.

I held my coin purse aloft, plowed through the assembly, and soared up the stairs two steps at a time. The soldiers showed clear irritation at the sudden turn of events. When I handed the executioner twenty silver coins, our eyes met with a shared silence. I knew his glare questioned why I would save someone whose name I didn't know. His unwinking alien pupils, his twitchless and emotionless mouth, his inarticulate wryness asked the question: "You murdered your fellow humans, and yet you show pity to the likes of a slime?" All the watchers saw the exchange, and they must have been thinking likewise. My hypocrisy was an absurdity.

After loosening the girl's noose and unbinding her hands, the guard shoved her toward me with a level of force far beyond warrant, and she barely caught herself from stumbling. The crowd, disappointed after being robbed of their morning excitement, dispersed and returned to their business.

I descended the stairs, and the girl followed, looking down, her posture tense, her face still displaying that hopeless emptiness. "You didn't have to do that," she said in almost a whisper at the base of the gallows.

Yes, I could have let her die, but I couldn't stand to watch another unjust death. I turned around and looked at her. I didn't care much for her comment, so I didn't say anything in response, but it was a look deep in thought. I wondered whether or not she was a worthwhile purchase.

This alien was now bound to me by the chains of debt. As long as her debt persisted, she was under my control; her fate rested in my hands. A feeling of power came with knowing I could do with her whatever I liked. It was an emotion molded by the human longing for control—a foul, terrible longing arisen from a black heart. A purehearted man would scold himself for holding an emotion such as this, and yet, to me the feeling was deeply satisfying.

As she kept her head hanging low, I spoke at length.

"Your name...let's hear it."

"..."

"Speak up!"

"Kiara."

She answered in a reluctant murmur. Her fear was the leash by which I controlled her. That was what I wanted. For my convenience, fear meant obedience, which meant she wouldn't dare defy a single order. Right now, the law allowed me to do unto her as I pleased. My plan was simple: if she followed my orders, she would be fine. If she didn't—or if she proved to be useless—then she would suffer consequences.

"Kiara it is, then. Let's go," I said, walking away from the gallows. She had an awfully human-sounding name.

I led her through the once again busy streets. Now that I had an extra pair of hands, things would be twice as easy assuming she was competent. I could use her as momentum to take care of business. Making ends meet was my current priority. I wanted to work, but no one wanted to employ me. There was, however, one line of employment I found that would take me, but first I needed to make preparations.

All of a sudden, the realization crossed me that the soldiers never returned my old clothes. Although I didn't particularly need them, I wished Kiara were wearing them instead of her current excuse for an outfit. Right now I was witnessing the most pathetic style in the universe. It was embarrassing to be seen with such an unsophisti-cated dresser.

So I made my way to a person who could fix that.

"Hey there, kid!" Goldwin smiled and greeted me when I ap-proached his wagon in his usual alley. I had tried to give him my name before, but he seemed insistent on calling me *kid*. "Who's the girl?"

"I bought her out of a public execution. She's going to work for me."

"Uh...wha...?" He gawked at me for a few moments, startled by my outlandish declaration. It really was considered a foolish prac-tice to place trust in worthless creatures like slimes. Eventually, Goldwin's shock fell away and he came back to his senses. "Geez, you paid all that money for a slime? Investing really isn't your strength, is it? Maybe you can trade her for someone better, but you'll need some sharp bargaining skills to score a good deal."

His resentment toward demifalia and nonfalia was a point of commonality between him and his fellow falia. In fact, Goldwin seemed to hate everything that lacked pure falius blood. A fair question would be, "Well, then why is he in the least falius-dense part of town?" Perhaps he thought it was easier to prey on custom-ers who weren't falia. "Conquering an animal is easier than con-quering a person," he might say. But perhaps he was here for rea-sons beyond the understanding of my foreign nitwit brain. He may have cherished many ethical, practical, and philosophical values that would never cross the human mind, and even if humanity were to learn of them, there was a very real possibility that we simply wouldn't be able to wrap our heads around such other-worldly logic.

"Are you interested in getting involved in the slave trade?" he asked. "It's a very profitable trade, and I have a friend of mine who can show you the ropes if you—"

"That's not necessary," I cut off his proposal. "I'm just looking to buy some things for her."

Did he expect me to sell Kiara into slavery? This was my first time hearing about Anbizia's slave trade, the thought of which sent chills up my spine. My image of this merchant had long since devolved to that of a greedy pig who would put material gain over anything else, regardless of whether it made people suffer. That willingness to hurt others for personal gain was beyond my power to respect, regardless of whatever beliefs shaped his behaviors. But he had dealt me many favors, and as long as I kept reaping the benefits of our relationship, I saw no reason to fear him.

"Pick whatever you want," said Goldwin, indicating his table of goods for sale. He did a lot of trading in this city, and his daily inventory often changed. Today he sold clothes, but on other days he had provisions or tools. "I'll keep the prices low for you."

My disapproval of his selective price adjustments was a source of sour unamusement, but I didn't find it worth the trouble to interfere. I could only afford to stand on business, not ethics. I didn't need the additional headache of objecting to his twisted practices. What mattered was that his way of business availed me, and that was my only concern.

"Give me something she can wear for work. Make it fit for combat, too." The work I wanted to do would require some fighting capabilities. Additionally, I had too many enemies—too many people wanting to hurt me—to be unprepared for strife. I needed this girl to help me survive. If she couldn't hold her own line of defense, she would surely buckle when faced with whatever bullets should come our way. "Oh, and make sure it doesn't look stupid on her. You can tell she's not much of a fashion whiz."

Kiara shrank away in embarrassment at my last comment.

"Hmm...let me see here..." Goldwin dug through the vast collection of clothes. He picked out a few outfits and placed them in front of me. "These should be the best choices for work and combat."

"Which set is cheaper?"

"That would be this one." He pointed to the outfit on the far left. "This was tailored in the faraway lands of Scheff. You can have it for six silvers. A good deal, don't you think?"

To my surprise it was a very fine outfit. It had a pair of brown lace-up boots reaching up to the knee. There was a short skirt that was white down the middle and ultramarine on the sides, which paired well with its indigo fur-lined hem. Long sleeves spanned the whole length of the arm, and it was all topped by a small black coat. Being intended for work and combat, the attire came with a brown pair of gloves and a hide breastplate, and a belt was included to keep the skirt from flying out.

Goldwin spoke. "If you want, I can remove the gloves and breastplate to reduce the cost to five, but you said you were looking for good work clothes..."

"Keep them in," I said, reaching into my bag to produce six Merth Silvers, which was a pleasantly modest price for its quality. Still, I was running my coin purse dry. "These clothes better be worthwhile. This is almost the last of my money."

"Ha-ha! I'm sure they'll do you wonders!"

So much money I had blown through in a single morning. I'd only scraped together a few extra pieces since receiving Goldwin's aid of thirty Merth Silvers. I didn't have the financial freedom for the big spending I'd pulled this morning. Now I was utterly broke, save for a few coppers and maybe two silvers hiding at the bottom of my coin purse.

"Go and put this on." I gave the clothes to Kiara and pointed her toward the wagon bed, which with its tall bonnet would hide her from onlookers. "...Don't just stare at it! Go on!"

Terror seized her like a demon. She recoiled at my raised voice and scurried for the wagon in earnest. I waited in silence as the minutes passed. While she changed, I couldn't help but notice a foreign emblem on the carriage's timbered sides. It was some crest that had the look of something from a science-fiction film, and while its freakishly modernistic design—consisting of a bird amid a spirally shape surrounded by stars—was queer beyond doubt, I didn't feel compelled to ask the merchant about the heraldry.

Rustle, rustle.

"Hurry it up in there!" I barked. Moments later she appeared from the wagon in the new garments.

"Oh-ho! A perfect fit!" The remark came from the merchant, but it sounded less like a compliment and more like he was boasting about his intuition to fit her in the perfect gear.

Her old tatters were gone in favor of the refit, partially dissolving her pathetic style, but the misery polluting her face had yet to fade. It seemed her forlorn demeanor wouldn't be curbed so easily, and I still felt a bit awkward being seen with such a mopey oddball. Still, the clothes suited her, and the navy-blue color contrasted well with her body's lighter shade of azure.

Looking at her face, I only saw indifference. Perhaps her despondent mood stole her energy to show emotions, or maybe she was unenthused about working. It may have been that today's events shocked her to the point of death somewhere within her soul. Whatever the case, she was little more than a slave, and the happiness of slaves didn't matter. The consideration of feelings was a privilege not reserved for one like her. A slave's value hinged only on competence. If her depression reached the point of crippling her ability to work, I would have to decide a new fate for her.

Kiara hopped down from the wagon and plodded closer. Although her hands quavered slightly with her head tilted down, her body language seemed to ask how it looked.

"It'll do," I said. "Let's get going."

With my hollowed-out wallet, I frowned at the idea of spending money at an inn. There was always the option of settling for the streets or stables, but the horror stories about those experiences repulsed me.

After a moment of poring over my options, an idea struck me. If I needed Kiara to be capable of work and combat, then I needed to toughen her up. Why did she deserve the luxury of a snug bed in a warm inn? Why make her hands softer when they needed callusing? Sleeping in Dirul Field was more favorable. After all, many impoverished refugees preferred to sleep outside the city over the grime-clad streets, so the plan wasn't out of the ordinary. While it made for itchy and stiff bedding out there, you could keep warm and stave off bugs by taking the trouble to start a fire. Better yet, there was no noise or odor of the inner city.

So I set my sights on a new crash pad beyond the walls of Cordea. Kiara followed me toward the gates, and after navigating through the sea of people and the web of buildings, we trekked across the grassy low-undulating field. The dry clods of earth crunched beneath our boots as it had been more than a moment since the last bout of rainfall, which portended a very prickly sleeping arrangement. I headed toward the edge of Dirul Field, near the brink of the unpeopled backwoods, and picked the smoothest patch of grass I could find.

"This should be a good spot for tonight," I said. Those who camped outside the city usually stayed hunkered down by the walls, so it was nice and quiet in this outback. "Start gathering firewood in the forest. If I call your name, come over immediately."

"Yes sir," she said quietly.

We plunged into the neighboring forest together. A bright sun smiled down through the crowns of trees; the wood was thin and modest in shade, but the air was cool and in some sense lightweight. Blades of grass and weed stabbed up and licked my pant legs as I went about my way.

We broke apart for our separate tasks, and while Kiara went to collect ingredients for a fire, I began the search for dinner. I wasn't much of a hunter, and I couldn't face off with a large animal, but there was a sure food source I had in mind. It came as sound advice for travelers that, when camping in the wild, it's best to start preparing for the night earlier than assumed necessary. That would leave time to resolve any unforeseen issues. After combing through the trees and brush, I came upon a glade where I found it: a kreplim—that puny squirrel-like critter I'd encountered by Lake Dirul. It quickly noticed me, and we were hence frozen, staring each other down with malicious eyes of mutual bloodlust. We anticipated who would attack first. The brainless creature eventually made up its mind and pounced, baring its teeth. Of course, its teeth were still too feeble to drill into my skin, so the attack hardly dealt any pain. I called Kiara's name, and she appeared in the glade moments later.

"—!"

With a gasp she succumbed to a tremor and dropped the bundle of sticks cradled in her arms. The animal was still nibbling at my leg. But I was unmoved, and I produced my only utility knife—yes, *that* utility knife—and handed it to her. Then I firmly squeezed a handle of fatty tissue on its back, wrested the creature off my leg, and held it up for her. It bayed and squalled helplessly, swinging its limbs around in hope of hitting or grappling or squirming free, or really taking any desperate measure to earn deliverance from this subdued position.

"Kill it," I ordered.

"Huh?!"

Her eyes bulged at the struggling kreplim. She dithered and backed away, so I repeated myself.

"Use the knife. Stab it until it stops moving."

"But I—"

"Come on!" I boomed, my indignant outburst making her jump.

Was Kiara too soft to kill this stupid animal? I wouldn't accept such uselessness. I could have killed it myself, but this was my opportunity to learn whether she had the grit to spill another's blood.

This was her only chance to demonstrate her capability of following orders. There would be no second chance, and I would not ask
again. What little freedom she had was this dilemma: slay the animal, or pay the price of disobedience. The choice was in her hands.
Fearing her case was hopeless, I started sorting through potential
punishments in my head.

As she swallowed the truth of what needed to be done, her expression saddened out of sorrow for the kreplim. Following several
moments of hesitation, the bloody energy finally overtook her. She
made her move, but there was reluctance in her forward charge,
and I could tell she wasn't harnessing all her power. Nevertheless,
a shrill squeal chimed across the forest, and the knife punctured the
animal's belly. Blood sprayed onto our hands from the piercing.
The creature piped and howled in agony, but the blade hadn't dug
deep enough, for it thrashed even more violently.

"It's still moving. Do it again," I said as Kiara pulled out the
blade. A river of blood trickled from the puncture. But the girl
stood rooted, her heart in her mouth, unable to inflict another
draft of pain. "You're only prolonging its suffering by stalling! If
it's pity you're feeling, finish it off and set it free! Lay it to rest!"

Her expression teemed with contrition at my command. Perhaps
she was right in thinking that this beast deserved a better fate. But
she couldn't afford to lack the gall to kill things undeserving of
death. In this world, you'd be stupid to waste time weighing
whether or not the object of your blade is a just kill, for that would
quickly result in your demise. The only way to survive was to de-
sensitize yourself to the feeling of bloodstained hands, to tune out
that voice of virtue, to fight and earn your right to live. That was
why any sympathy within her needed to be dashed.

Whatever feelings shook her soul, she took a moment to suppress
them and charged once again. "Yahhh!" she shouted, and with
much more *oomph* into this thrust, the trickling of blood turned
into gushing. Only a few seconds passed before the animal stopped

moving, and my hands got dyed red with blood.

Looking at her, I saw Kiara's face pale with remorse. She hated what she'd done. Not that I cared a feather.

"Good job," I said, though my gruff tone persisted. "Did you find some firewood?"

She nodded and gathered up the dropped pile of wood. It looked like she had garnered enough for a fire, and now that we'd secured dinner, I figured we were at sufficient capacity to head back to the site.

"Right. Let's go back," I said.

We started heading out of the swell of trees, but a sudden gale of excitement from Kiara brought me to a halt.

"Oh! Those are—!"

She stumbled over her words and hushed. For a very ephemeral moment, she perked up like an eager pup before realizing her error of speaking freely, and at once she shied away. She seemed to berate herself for making such a grave mistake.

"What is it?" I asked, curious at what warranted the eruption granted her yellow temperament. My eyes followed Kiara's gaze through a dense patch of undergrowth, which led to some colorful plants next to a small pond. "Flowers?"

"N-no sir. Those are rare herbs."

"What about them?"

There were two distinct genera I could see. One was a nettle with black leaves springing from a very dark green stem, and the other had rose red leaves and a barbed chartreuse stem.

"They're valuable, I think," she said. "You might be able to sell them."

The petals were curiously colored, and I was intrigued about what made them valuable. I drew closer to the place of interest and reached for one of the black herbs.

"W-wait! Don't!"

Despite Kiara's admonishment, my mind registered the words a moment too late, and I placed my bare fingers on the dark petals. Big mistake. "Ow!" came a startled cry. A stream of heat transferred to my hand as though I'd touched a screaming hot stove. Fiery pain bloomed causing me to spring back. I flapped my hand around to wave off the searing flare-up.

"That...that herb's leaves are known for having intense burning properties," Kiara explained nervously, afraid I would take out my flub on her.

"You don't say," I replied as I started plucking the herbs from the earth, handling them by the stems, wary of letting the black leaves touch my skin. "Let's take these with us so we can sell them."

We got on our knees and picked as many as we could safely fit in our arms. The red herbs were harmless to the touch. We also used the pond to rinse the kreplim's blood from our hands. With our arms filled with the herbs, firewood, and our slaughtered game, we made our way out of the wooded land.

After taking to the meadows and assembling the firewood, I made a stack of dead grass as tinder and hitched a tepee of sticks over it for kindling. Suddenly amidst my dread of running the trouble of igniting a flame, an idea seemed to grab my shoulder.

"Hey," I snagged Kiara's attention. "Do you think I can use the black herb to start a fire?"

She shrugged. I decided I might as well try. It seemed like a worthy experiment since the petals had so-called burning properties. Perhaps they could act as a natural fire starter. I took a black herb by the stem and placed it on the tinder. Within seconds the dead grass shriveled and turned black under the heat, and it glowed scarlet with candlelight. Gradually the flames budded until eventually maturing into a beautiful, hearty campfire. Kiara watched in awe as the magic unfolded before her eyes, but she timidly snapped her mouth shut upon realizing it was agape.

Night was soon to fall. As the fire dazzled peacefully in the wide open Dirul Field, it looked as a sort of beacon in the broad sphere of darkness. Its appetite had grown to require larger fuel, and it chawed away at the heftier chunks of wood. Travelers were always happy to fall asleep to the gentle crackles of flame, laying in the grass and admiring the star-speckled night sky. Such was the kind of view that reminded you just how tiny you are in the scale of the universe. It made you feel lost, knowing you were nothing but a speck of life floating on a rock somewhere in this illimitable macrocosm called space.

As I hadn't eaten anything since morning, I was famished. I figured the gap since Kiara's last meal was even longer, which furthered my conviction that it was dinnertime. I skinned and disemboweled the kreplim, drained its remaining blood, split it in half, and prepared the meat for roasting. My servant tried to look away from the lurid scene, but I forced her to observe so that she could learn these skills. Next, I skewered both halves on sticks and poised them above the fire. The flames tickled the meat's lower end, roasting it. An occasional drop of juice fell onto the burning wood and sizzled a sweet hiss.

Eventually the white meat turned golden brown. I was a somewhat novice cook and wasn't sure what doneness was required for kreplim meat. Was it safe or unsafe at rarer temperatures? I decided overcooking was more prudent than undercooking, even if it meant the texture would match tire rubber.

As I held the skewer over the burning wood, I noticed Kiara's queer behavior. She sat across the fire, but with great distance— too much distance for its heat to reach her. A chill had brewed upon dusk, so her avoidance of the fire's warmth was unwonted. Was it that slimes had a special tolerance for low temperatures? Was the warmth not necessary? Or maybe—and this was more likely—she sat thither because she was afraid of me.

What I noticed was that she'd been eyeing the roasting meat for quite some time now. Her round eyes were awake and full of desire, but she immediately averted them when she realized I could see her staring. With her body being almost entirely water, Kiara's cheeks reflected the glow of the fire like a mirror, which was a fascinating sight. Her face appeared flushed orange.

When the meat was cooked to my liking, I removed both skewers from the heat, padded across the little lawn between us, and with a brief, "Here," offered one to Kiara.

She fancied the usual stubbornness. The incredulous girl looked back and forth between me and the meat several times, carefully discerning truth from trick.

"Uhhh..."

"What's wrong?" I snapped, to which she yelped in fear. "You don't want it?"

She frantically took the stick of kreplim meat, imagining what terrible things would befall her if she didn't. I took to my spot again and started eating.

The meat turned out to be as dull as I'd envisioned. The lack of even a grain of salt left the food bland beyond palatability, and as the drippings all rendered into the fire, it was dryer than overcooked chicken. My water flask did little to allay the unpleasantness when washing it down. But my hunger commanded service, so I accepted the meal nonetheless.

"..."

When I looked up from my dinner, I spotted Kiara looking at me, seemingly on the rack. Her skewer was still in hand, food completely untouched.

"What are you waiting for?" I asked. "Aren't you hungry?"

"This is...for me?"

"Why else would I give it to you?"

"But...why are you feeding me?"

"You can't work on an empty stomach. And you looked hungry."

Did this girl seriously think I would let her starve? That was ridiculous. I wasn't some sick tormentor. All I needed was someone to work with me. She wouldn't be useful if I let her energy drain until her death.

Slimes had drastically different biology from everyone else, so I was inclined to question if their weight fluctuated on food intake. There wasn't an ounce of muscle or fat in Kiara's scrawny frame. She was twig thin—she needed to eat more. She must have been poorly fed in the days leading up to her execution. That piteous thing must have been like a stray mutt. A lousy vagrant, cast to the bottom ends of society, forced to live off of others like a parasite, taking the scraps of meals, and sleeping out on the cold curbs.

She seemed to want to say something but relented at last and brought the food to her mouth. Her eyes darted to me several times to confirm safety and finally paid the meat her full attention to take the first bite. After swallowing once, she gave in to the greedy temptations and wolfed it down like a vacuum, hardly taking time to breathe between bites. She treated the bland meat like a grand feast.

I returned to my food. In contrast to what could be seen in Kiara's dining etiquette, I wasn't delighted by the taste. It truly tasted like bland chicken, something only a starving peasant would find tasty. The kreplim I'd hunted was stripped of dignity even after its death, cooked until it knew no flavor or texture but only sustenance.

When Kiara finished her meal, I was only through half of mine. She'd eaten in total blitzkrieg fashion, after which she tossed aside the leftover stick and bone. But although she looked satiated, she still looked unhappy. Her posture was stiff with discomfort. She looked off into the night, squirming like a restless cat.

"Hey, aren't you cold?" I asked, indicating her unreasonable distance from the fire.

"N-no!" Kiara crimsoned and shook her head bashfully. "No sir,

I mean! I'm not!"

My brow furrowed unconsciously. Her defensive tone rang blatant dishonesty.

"Whatever," I said. "If you're gonna sit over there, you'd better not freeze to death."

"Okay..." She looked away.

While I finished the rest of my meal, I noticed that her gaze kept shifting to the fire. There seemed to be two forces in her mind playing tug-of-war. After a while, she gave up and drew closer to the fire with an abashed sigh.

I also noticed the heaviness of Kiara's eyes as they stared into the dancing and humming flames. "You tired?" I asked.

She shook her head without words. Yet another lie.

"Really? Well, I'm getting some rest."

I lay in the grass and dropped my leftover stick in the orange fire. Having chosen this campsite carefully, I found that the ground was rather soft, but it was not comfortable. Darts of grass pricked my back as I lay, and a harsh itch crawled about my skin. Such was the virtue of sleeping in this prairie. Kiara soon plopped down by the fire as well, and we stared at the darkling night sky dotted with thick white stars, like spattered drops of milk. Anbizia had two moons that shone brightly. The larger moon was named Ild, and the smaller moon was named Ald. Oddly enough, Ild was only a dim sickle, whereas Ald was full and glowing above the distant mountaintops. But no matter how brightly the two moons shone, one was objectively bigger, and Ald couldn't mask its smallness forever. Their current sizes were a stubborn illusion caused merely by perspective. One day, sunlight would strike them both at a perfect angle, and all truth would be revealed.

CHAPTER VII

SHOPPING AND SELLING SPREE

*S*nore...snore..."

Kiara, who had previously denied being tired, awoke me with her snores. She looked so relaxed in her sleep. The grass made a fine bed for her.

When I sat up, I decided to let her sleep a bit longer. I was painfully short on sleep, for I had spent the majority of the night keeping watch to make sure she wouldn't try attacking me or fleeing. I simply didn't trust her enough to fall asleep around her. Seeing as the sun was beginning to expose itself, I got up and scattered dirt over the fire's dying embers, but I was careless to keep down the noise, for Kiara stirred soon after. Then, as if possessed by a spirit, she sat up and tipped her head back, puffed out her chest, and stretched her arms laterally.

"Hahhh..." she heaved a huge yawn. Her eyes sagged. She was still half asleep.

However, she quickly remembered who, what, and where she was, and she covered her mouth sheepishly as though trying to hide an embarrassing blunder. Her fear suggested a belief that I'd castigate her for her ditziness, but I only returned an absent stare for a few seconds and returned to my business of clearing the fire.

"Get ready," I said, packing my things including the new herbs. "We're going back to the city."

We were on our way after she tied her bootlaces and tightened her belt.

The city of Cordea was Neiklof's capital city and was the heart and soul of the country. On one side it was the stronghold where the pompous claimed hegemony and where the avaricious savored wealth. The other side was starving. The social divide was, in a sense, brilliant, and while to many such disunity seemed deplorable, I couldn't help but hold it in a particular fascination.

We reached the city and paced through the streets, moving toward the market district, and the morning church bells pealed over the city. It was a regular custom that occurred at the same hour every morning, signaling the official start of the day's business while also reminding the citizens of the ultimate being for whom they toiled. That bell meant all hell would break loose in the streets, for it was the signal to open the marketplace and served as a whistle for people to leave their squalid dwellings and set to work. Right away the streets filled with people, and we got caught up in the droves. Then followed the occurrence of lots of pushing and scuffling; many ribs were jostled by elbows, and many boots were clipped by carts. I did my best to worm through the labyrinthine crowd.

My first concern was getting the herbs off my hands. Avoiding contact with the black leaves was a real throb of the nerves, so the sooner I could rid myself of them, the better. An apothecary was one who could deal with such herbs. In the marketplace there was a medicine booth with the services I needed. Stalls like these operated humbly, acting as a shadow of larger shops that occupied buildings. They usually attracted different types of customers, like people seeking products that were more modest and inexpensive. They were also a fairer option for those looking to sell lesser goods, as the owners of more reputable shops might chase you out for wasting their time if your things were laughably cheap.

"Excuse me!" I seized the attention of a stall owner, who faced the other way, concocting some elixir in a pot, which smelled of cinnamon and sweet ginger.

"Ah, welcome! How can—" the young falius man's words trailed off as he turned around and realized who had approached him. A few seconds passed. The thoughts skipping through his head must have teetered on the lines of, *Should I turn this person away?* At length he probably decided that a customer was still a customer and a profit was still a profit, and finished his greeting. "How can I help you?"

Owners of these small shops couldn't afford to deny service to a precious customer. Even if public opinion considered it honorable to snub a guest who was particularly rejected by society, those slack morals were easily tossed out the window when the opportunity for profit arose.

I emptied my pack of herbs onto the counter. "How much will these sell for?"

He examined the herbs before sorting them by type with nimble and swift hands, likewise avoiding contact with the piping black petals. The lad evidently knew what he was working with.

"Well, sir, these black herbs are utterly worthless."

I swallowed the urge to slam my fist on the table and asked, "Are you serious?" I gave Kiara a sidelong glare, who stood tense and nervous. *She* had declared the herbs valuable, only to turn out mistaken. No doubt her lapse in judgment was a cause for sour consequences. I communicated my thoughts to her with my needle eyes, to which she shrank in fear.

"Yes sir. They're called ravenblazes, and they hardly fetch a penny. This world is at war. Materials are valuable when they benefit the armed forces; if they aren't useful in that way, their prices tumble. An herb that's simply hot to the touch won't help anyone on the front lines. It won't boost the abilities of our soldiers or serve as a viable weapon. It's just not something anyone needs. Now, if you're wondering about the red herbs, which are called lifeweeds, you'll be glad to know you can score a fair deal with them. Lifeweeds have very potent healing properties, so they're useful for soldiers who get roughed up on the battlefield, especially those who take a blade or an arrow."

A sigh escaped my mouth as I weighed my next options. My potential to make money with these herbs had been crunched. I wondered if the value of concoctions outweighed their raw ingredients.

"Would it be more profitable to brew the ravenblazes into a solution before selling them? Would they go up in value that way?"

"No, that would be worse. Ravenblazes just aren't good for much. Nothing you can concoct out of them would fetch a decent price. And if you compounded the medicine on your own, you'd have to buy the necessary tools for doing so, which I have little doubt would put you in a deficit. Sorry, kid."

Well, at least the stall owner seemed honest about these hurdles. It seemed that the gains of compounding medicine only went to the professionals—not amateurs like us who were looking for a quick one-time profit. Accusations of sorcery were common among apothecaries as the line between apothecary and alchemy was somewhat blurred. This conflation made some sense because apothecaries excelled at making their practice look shady with all the queer substances they dealt with. The thought of getting framed in that way triggered a certain anguish in me, and my hands quivered restlessly at my sides.

Those ravenblazes were a thorn in my side. I wondered if I ought to sell them anyway—perhaps I'd gain at least a few Neiklof Copper pennies. It may have been my best option, seeing as my wallet was a barren wasteland.

As I mulled it over, Kiara gave her thoughts.

"If the lifeweeds are valuable, you could buy them and we could pay you to brew something with the ravenblazes. Then we'll take whatever you make with the ravenblazes for ourselves."

I was surprised to hear her speak this much. Her idea seemed clever.

The apothecary counted the leaves and performed some mental calculations. "Yes, that seems like your best option. Accounting for the fee to make the concoctions, you'll turn, um, ten Merth Silver coins. Is that a deal?" he asked, directing the question at me.

I glanced at the ravenblazes. No doubt they would fill my pack with goods, but it seemed their low value boded poorly for their utility. But alas, there existed no better outcome, and all I could do was make the most of what I was offered.

"It's a deal," I said, though I was not the least bit enthused. "You'd better make something useful."

"I'll do what I can," he said, rolling his eyes, taking the herbs, and sparing me ten silvers. "I'll have your things ready by this afternoon."

After expressing my approval, I left the shop with Kiara and hustled along to our next place. The outcome wasn't satisfying, but it could have been worse. At least I didn't walk out of there empty-handed. My servant's quick thinking had served as an asset. If not for her bright idea, I would've suffered a loss.

Back in the chaotic streets, my next destination of interest was a weapon shop. The bitter truth was that I needed something to defend myself, be it against wild animals, malicious assailants, or, in the darkest of scenarios, Kadaanites. My feeble utility knife couldn't stand head-to-head with a swordsman vying to kill me, and sharing the tiny blade with Kiara only exacerbated the hopelessness of it all.

When entering the first promising weapon shop I happened upon, I was met with the threatening gaze of the shop owner, which seemed to demand that I either buy something or get out. He was a slender, older man who looked as though he wanted to be elsewhere. The walls were arrayed with brands, pikes, and axes of various sizes and metals. Plated armors were displayed on stands about the floor. There were bows and quivers of ammo in one corner and bulky shields in another; altogether the shop was well-equipped to fit new warriors.

"I need a cheap pair of swords," I said, approaching him.

With a smirk he said, "You can have these for two silvers each."

He picked up a bucket near him and set it atop the table with a crisp *thunk*. "I'm sure they'll suit you perfectly."

Doubtless he knew who I was, judging by his snide mockery. I couldn't keep my expression from shriveling in disgust at his uncouth humor. The bucket was filled with short, dull wooden swords. They were toy swords for children. He was making fun of me.

The man chortled with amusement as he watched my reaction. My face was numb, my gaze icy and unmoving, existing as a disparity from his mirth. "So you're a comedian, are you?" I asked. Not in the mood for this ridicule, I tried to suppress my frustration and leaned over the table. "Listen, I'm only going to ask this once. I'm looking for swords, not twigs."

While the shopkeeper and I got swallowed up in our exchange, Kiara quietly snaked around the counter and took the big book on top, but I paid her no mind, and the shopkeeper didn't notice. She leafed through the pages.

"What's wrong with these swords? They're sturdy and they pack a mighty fine punch. They'll give you and your fellow kids hours and hours of fun!"

I pulled away, tired of the stupidity. "Who am I kidding? Everything you sell is probably dull and rusty anyway. Forget it. I'll let everyone know your whole shop is a scam."

Dismay affected the shopkeeper as I started toward the door. His attitude transformed at large when his regular clientele was at stake. His surprise waned, and he seized my shoulder.

"Just a moment, please!" he urged, and I looked back. "I was only jesting, sir! Lighten up! I didn't mean nothing! My cheapest swords are those iron ones over there. They're eight Merth Silvers each."

He pointed at a set of swords dangling from the wall. They weren't notably sharp or long, but they seemed apt to cut and pierce things and were likely sufficient for self-defense. I took two and handed one to Kiara, and although I could barely afford it, I reached for my coin purse and produced the silver coins. But Kiara stopped me from paying. She glared disapprovingly at the shopkeeper before setting the weapon down and returning with all focus to the book, through which she pored rapidly. Then, stopping at a specific page, she made a few jumping glances between the swords and the book. As I was about to ask what she was reading, the shopkeeper realized trouble was unfolding and went on high alert.

"Hey, what are you doing with that?!" He asked. Evidently the book was for his eyes only. He tried to take it from her, but she pulled it away and turned her back to him.

"You're wrong, mister. This sword is worth six Merth Silvers." She spoke to the shopkeeper with bold sharpness, her eyes fastened to the page.

At that moment, I knew what book she held. It was a ledger.

"Are you trying to rip us off?" I asked with a nasty look.

"Well, uh..." A sweat broke out on his forehead. A fright clearly sneaked about him, and that did not help him think up a response. My stare continued to penetrate him. "Th-the price of weapons recently went up, s-so I—"

"Not true," Kiara interrupted, bewitched by the fresh ink written on the page. "Earlier this morning, someone bought this same class of swords for six silvers." She closed the book with a *thud* that seemed to permeate the room. Then she stared at the shopkeeper blankly. "Have prices really gone up so quickly?"

"Are you selectively adjusting prices on people?" I asked with considerable bile. "How does a crook like you turn a profit?"

Standing in this pig's presence made me sick, but I couldn't very well walk away. This man deserved to be taught a lesson, and now that I held a sword, I was thoroughly equipped to do some teaching. I drew closer to him aggressively, sword in hand but hanging it low at my side. At the same time, the shopkeeper grew tremulous and sweaty. His posture stiffened, his breathing grew irregular, and he backed into a shelf behind him, rattling it.

"S-sir, please calm down. I'm trying my best to run a business here."

"Yeah, and *you're* its biggest liability." My veins started to swell with indignation. A cyclone was blowing in, and it would cause wreckage beyond repair upon striking. Out of the corner of my eye, I noticed Kiara becoming afraid as she watched our exchange, but I didn't care. A kind of chastisement was in order for this man. "You should think more carefully about who you pump up prices on!"

Intending to rock him with fright but not harm, I was about to thrust my sword before his face, but at the last second he relented. "A-all right! You win! Please, sir, just don't cause any trouble!"

Luckily for him, the shopkeeper narrowly deflected the storm. His desperate bid to fan it off into the horizon worked, and the surrounding air's pressure slowly relaxed. Our eyes were glued to one another as if trying to burn each other with our vision, and as my rage defused, I calmly slid across the counter twelve silver coins—six per sword. He cursed himself under his breath as he took the payment, indicating the door with his silent expression. I'd damaged his ego plenty enough, and he couldn't take this torment anymore. He wanted nothing more than for me to leave.

Seeing no reason to dawdle any longer, I left without delay. As I made for the door, Kiara, frozen in astonishment at the show of drama, failed to realize her mouth was hanging wide open, but came to her senses with haste upon seeing me at the exit. She didn't forget her new sword on the way out. We affixed our blades to our belts. I had to give Kiara credit for being a detective and uncovering the actual prices of the weapons. Had she not been there, I would have fallen into a troublesome scam. In recognition of her perceptive move, I turned and spoke.

"You saved me some money back there. Good job."

She had spoken to the shopkeeper with a confidence I had yet to witness till now, but it certainly proved useful. Perhaps the girl's gloom was more of a privation of vivacity, as if her spirit had departed from her and left her to wilt. Now that spirit seemingly wanted to flirt with her again so that her true colors could return. She was like a sponge being rehydrated.

A wary look fell upon her face, and she seemed astounded at receiving praise. She probably thought it was a trap. With her eyes still on me, she deflated and said, "Um...yes sir."

I started through the streets, but after a few steps, I stopped to consider where to go next. My halt was abrupt, and Kiara bumped into me from behind with a froggy croak. She looked every bit contrite as a result. But I was busy thinking, and she watched as I meditated on my next choice.

Noticing a sun that shone directly overhead, I started to ask, "Are you..." I cut myself short. I had planned to ask if she was hungry, but her unwavering secrecy of her needs the previous night had probably siphoned to today. I had no grounds to believe she would answer truthfully. "Let's get some food," I said after a moment of dithering, resuming my walk, and Kiara followed.

Soon I came across a tavern with a sign hanging over the entrance which, translated from the Falian words *Traxidná Tjaluik*, read: *The Tricky Traxid*. I went inside and sat down at a table near the back. The lights were dim, and the room was hazy with pipe smoke. A young lady came over, welcomed us, and tried listing the available daily food options, but brusquely I spoke first.

"Two of your cheapest lunches, and two cups of your cheapest ale."

The tavern girl, who was probably a daughter of the alewife, acknowledged me and walked away. Drinking was standard even among kids on Anbizia due to the lack of drinking regulations, so Kiara and I were both free to sip on alcohol as we pleased. Still, the only things I could afford were dirt cheap small ales and diluted wines, neither of which pleased the senses much, and they certainly didn't come close to knocking me over.

Kiara's glances at the dishes of other guests suggested that I was right to assume she was hungry. Her eyes were wolfish, darting between tables when she thought I wouldn't notice, and she breathed with a subtle slurping noise as if holding back drool. A full stomach always prevailed over an empty one, but she still seemed to take me for one who neglected to feed her, and lacked the prowess to request sustenance.

When we received our ale, Kiara immediately gave me a look that eagerly asked, "May I?" I nodded, and she reached for the drink without a moment's delay, which almost made me laugh. She seemed to appreciate the (albeit thin) alcohol as she took the first sip, letting out a blissful sigh. I had a hunch that she was so hungry that she'd be equally happy to eat the malted barley that brewed the ale. Actually, the drink must have been made from some other grain—it was unfounded to assume Anbizia had barley like Earth. Whatever grain it was, it seemed to have a similar taste.

We'll be sleeping outside again, I'm sure, I thought, admitting only a few drops of my drink into my mouth. That wasn't an enjoyable situation, but such tribulations were inevitable for those without plump wallets. I had scored some coin with the apothecary, yet I'd already spent more than the lot of it on the swords. It was so hard not to blow through my earnings immediately. *One more night,* I told myself. Then I would try my hand at that guild I'd caught wind of. It was often poor form to make a living solely by selling items to vendors as I had done with the herbs, and I didn't need to draw attention for flawed etiquette. I was better off leaving everything behind to perform life-risking feats in the name of profit. If anything, that was my only option.

I took another drink—more of a swig than a sip. Of course it was too diluted for sensual gratification. That's what happens when you settle for the cheap stuff. Before long our food arrived, and our concept of manners turned null, and we did not hesitate to dig in.

The dish was a vegetable stew with clear, flat broth and was luke-warm at best. Given how hungry I was, it was easy to trick my tongue into believing it almost tasted good.

"Hey, easy on the ale," I told Kiara, who was drinking more liberally than I liked to see.

Noticing her slipping of temperance, she blushed and put the cup down. The ale was far too washy for inebriation, but the sight of her rolling around in the juice gave me an ill feeling. As my servant, she was disposed only for work, not for leisure or pleasure.

"Um...sorry," she said out of embarrassment.

Kiara ate voraciously, and while perhaps I needed to keep a watchful eye on her drinking, I was actually inclined to encourage gorging so that she could cure her gauntness. When we finished our meal, I left my payment on the table and made for the door. Kiara's ale had totally disappeared since her first sip. Conversely my cup hadn't diminished much at all.

"Ah, what a waste," she muttered to herself. To my dismay she trotted to where I'd sat, picked up the half-empty cup, and downed all of the ale with relish. Her cheeks were tinted rosily at the rush of alcohol, and a satisfied smile took shape as she set it down.

"Geez...let's get going already," I said with a nettled sigh as I waited for her, raising a palm to my forehead. "Come on. Those herbs are probably ready."

This time Kiara moved with a new energy unlike before. The alcohol seemed to animate her, and there was more color in her eyes. After leaving the tavern, we ventured back into the indefatigable streets and got lost in the swarm of people for a while.

When we returned to the apothecary, the medicine order was ready. He vanished into the curtained brewery behind his booth to fetch our goods. While I waited, I took an interest in the products on display. They were nothing like Earth's medicinal products. Assorted on tiered shelves were many small glass bottles and bowls of various compounds, ranging from simple treatments for ailments and injuries to more anomalous admixtures. There were caffeinated stimulants, healing salves, sedative elixirs—ah! even aphrodisiac love potions. These solutions made some claims of roaring boldness. Did Anbizia have more potent herbs and plants than Earth, allowing its people to draw upon more advanced medical building blocks? And if so, was that a result of luck, or some more transcendent power at play? Maybe the advertisings of these products were just exaggerated claims, garbled for the sole purpose of increasing sales.

I casually pondered these drugs until the shop owner returned with an armful of vials. He stood them on the table, and I scrapped my previous thoughts and snapped back to the present. There were two unique clusters of bottles: a red variety and a black variety.

"What are these?" I asked.

"The red one is a potion for light healing called Nefzing's Touch," he said. "I made it from the lifeweeds. You can pour it on wounds to repair them quickly, or you can drink it to muffle the pain and replenish your strength."

Hold on—that wasn't part of the deal.

"Um, I think you're mistaken," I said. "You already paid me ten silvers for the lifeweeds. You were going to keep them for your own purposes."

"I'm well aware. I was going to save this medicine for a general who was meeting me today for a transaction, but I just received word that he got wounded in an attack from highwaymen on his way to Cordea, so he had to rush to a clinic here instead. Now I'm encumbered with overcapacity. Seeing that I have no other use for this product, I'm letting you have it."

"Oh..." I said, taken aback. How dispiriting that even in the darkest times of war, people still fought among themselves.

He took a deep breath and continued. "This black medicine is a fire potion made from the ravenblazes. It's called Hell's Liquor."

"Hell's Liquor?"

"Be careful with it. It's dangerous stuff. It burns anything it touches like lava, and it can make a man burst into flames. You'd best not even smell it. The vials have thick glass, so they won't burn your hands."

"Oh yeah? And what would I use this stuff for?"

For such a scorching hot substance, the intimidating name *Hell's Liquor* ironically chilled my bones. The ravenblazes had burned me at the slightest touch, and this stuff was probably hotter. I had difficulty foreseeing myself using the product. I could use it to start fires, but was it worth taking up so much space in my pouch for that function alone? What's more, it seemed unlikely as a lethal weapon. What was I supposed to do? Wear a bright simper and offer my foes a drink?

He shrugged. "I couldn't say. Ravenblazes aren't good for much other than Hell's Liquor. They can make a nice seasoning when ground, but it's stabbingly spicy. I figured you weren't looking for spices."

He must have known I didn't like his answer because his suddenly unwelcoming look said, "I'm not arguing with you about this."

I expressed little more disappointment than what would do me any good. This Hell's Liquor was a device to achieve certain ends but not the ends that interested me. It was like an inoperable tool or a nonnutritive food. After all, this was just a cheap stall. I shouldn't have expected any stellar services.

After stuffing the vials into my traveling pouch and letting Kiara carry some for herself, I left as soon as I could, my walk in all likelihood betraying my disgruntled mood.

"We're leaving the city again." I still couldn't well afford the inns, plus I wasn't yet confident in Kiara's resilience.

"Okay..." murmured Kiara with a nameless dread.

Sleeping in the field wasn't the least bit comfortable with its scraggly bristles of pasture, but it was better than trying to roll off on the cold hard streets. Until I made more money, a cozy bed would remain a trophy far out of reach. We traveled beyond the city walls and reached the previous night's crash pad. Black clumps of ash bathed in the dirt where the fire had been. The afternoon was fairly young, so I wasn't concerned yet with preparing a new fire. I sat in the grass examining my new concoctions. Kiara took a seat to boot but kept a distance of about ten paces.

The Hell's Liquor would surely shoulder the trouble of starting a fire, just as the ravenblazes had done so the previous night. I regretted that I couldn't make better use of the substance, but there was no avail in tearing out my hair over what was already done. Setting the black fluids aside, I turned my attention toward the red potions. I uncorked the vial, and the liquid effervesced with bubbles and sparkles. Out of curiosity I nicked my thumb with my knife, waited for blood to squint out, and sprinkled a bit of Nefzing's Touch on it. It fizzed and foamed on my skin, and sure enough, the slit sealed within minutes. I was so fascinated that I wanted to do it again, but my frugal side said to save the stuff for more pressing situations.

I put the vials back in my pouch and, seeing as I had nothing better to do, yawned and sprawled on the grass to bask in the sun's golden light. There were few clouds in the sky save for two or three cumuli, and they leisurely rode the wind across the oceany dome of diamond-blue hanging above. From this spot, Cordea was like a little fortress on the massive carpet of land. Dirul Field swept across my entire scope of vision, and you could probably fit two replicas of the city in its distance from the backwoods here, which spoke volumes as Cordea was huge enough already. With the forest to my right, the open prairie to my left, and the emphatic view of the jewellike Cordea and her neighboring Lake Dirul, there came the feeling that nature herself was the dominant authority here. Out in this realm no one fought over lordship, nor did there exist the foisting of synthetic opinions among the masses, nor did anyone try to force others to submit to their material ambitions. All limbs of nature simply joined the dance to make up one harmonious body.

"Come to think of it," I said sitting up, getting Kiara's attention, for a sudden thought had nagged my mind. "I was impressed by your maneuvers back in the city. You proposed a solution to the herb problem after ravenblazes turned out to be worthless, and you also had a sharp eye when finding out the actual price of those swords. How'd you learn such quick thinking?"

Surprise seemed to infect her face in an instant. Clearly she never expected me to show genuine interest in her savvy.

With effort she wiped away the tangled look and summoned the courage to form a response. "...I had a relative who was a dedicated peddling merchant, so I learned a lot about trading and salesmanship. The value of being totally present when negotiating was constantly getting hammered into me."

Kiara still spoke with shyness. I figured I should encourage her to break out of her shell if we were to work together. Although mere threads of debt entwined us, and I certainly had no concern for her feelings about me, a bond was still a bond. Our tie was better fortified, and cooperation would be easier if she wasn't so quiet and anxious.

"'Keen eyes earn a keen fortune.' That was one of the catch-phrases I heard," she said, looking up at the sky as if reminiscing on old memories. "You have to be clairvoyant to single out potential gains in business—be able to look at deals from the right vantage point. I was always honing those skills when I was little, mostly through silly games, but when I was old enough I started taking a stab at the real thing."

"Mm. Well, you'd better be lavish in those skills when we're out making money."

"R-right. Yes sir," she said, flushing and looking away.

Ah, whatever, I thought. Even if that was all the conversation I could wring from her, it was still a start for now. If her province was an astute attention to detail, I wanted her to employ it to the fullest, for it would undoubtedly prove useful in dealing with crooked swindlers. What I *really* wanted was for her skills to help fill my pockets with money.

I returned to absorbing the view, but my lulling enjoyment was interrupted when I heard the shuffling of grass behind me. The sound was of soft pads, which were light, uneven, hinting at unnaturalness. I turned around.

"Please...help me..."

A child approached with a limp: a little girl of no more than ten years old. She was swathed in bandages from head to toe, which were inked with murky red stains of blood. Her clothes were pitiful torn rags which were too big for her petite shape, and her faded irises which left only her pupils visible and the dark bags underneath made her look lifeless like a zombie. Miserably she hobbled toward us.

Kiara rushed over to the kid by instinct, moved to compassion by the urgency of a child at death's door. She caught the collapsing girl.

"Oh my..." said Kiara said with a heavy heart. "What happened?"

Very calmly I stood and drew toward the two.

"Monster..." mewled the girl, stricken with fear. "...Attacked in the forest...ate my parents!"

Her face was battered with trauma as Kiara tended to her. She was on the verge of tears, and the sight of a child on the cusp of death almost made me forget to breathe or blink. I kept silent, but my muscles tensed with pity, my toes curled in their boots, and my head swam. A pressure awoke in my chest which I identified as my heart weeping for the girl.

"That's..." Kiara searched for words of comfort. "...That's horrible. I'm so sorry." She called on me with desperate eyes. "Sir! She needs that potion."

My thoughts matched Kiara's precisely. I opened my traveling pouch and rummaged for the Nefzing's Touch, but as I groped for one of the red bottles, my hand suddenly went paralyzed. I could hear a voiceless whisper from within saying something was wrong. A growing feeling of insecurity grappled me, and my instincts screamed that I was out of place, compelling me to analyze the situation scrupulously.

My chief bother was that these woods were too thin for the liking of specially dangerous animals; something so ferocious would be stupid to settle here. What monster could possibly lurk beneath this forest's sparse eaves?

Furthermore, her bandages were wrapped skillfully so that it was dubious that she'd done the swaddling herself. Besides, how could she dress her wounds while injured? And when did she have time to do so? But if she wasn't the wound-dresser, and her parents were dead, then who was it? Were those bloodstains even real?

I felt my sword's hilt, loosening the blade in its weathered hide scabbard.

Suddenly from afar came the sound of leaves crinkling, but when I looked toward the trees, I saw no movement. The breeze murmured soft and languid like an idling brook, so the noise couldn't have been a gust grazing the thicket. In the undergrowth, though no sentient movement was visible, there were winkling gleams of white in the bushes. I sensed an inarticulate feeling of strange, barbaric eyes staring me down from the shadows. There was some spectral presence nearby with no possibility of mistake. The aura growing thick in the air whispered words of urgent bloodlust, and I could smell the danger wallowing up like black poisonous smoke. An eerie feeling rushed upon me and seemed to seize my nerves, and my heart begged me to take action.

Kiara hadn't noticed any of this, as she was occupied with trying to comfort the ruined girl. While my servant was indeed sharp and observant, that art of hers must have quailed when harassed by strong emotions.

Unsheathing my sword and pointing it at the bridge of the child's nose, I said, "If you're not out of my sight in ten seconds, I'll slice your lying head clean off." My words bit like burly fangs and were deliberately tailored for fear.

Neither of the girls' expressions captured anything less than immediate shock. Both pairs of eyes bulged wide, their breaths caught, and they looked ready to scream in panic.

"Wha...what?" Kiara was at a loss for words, but her thoughts were enunciated on her face: *How, how could you be so heartless?*

I ignored her and stood my ground. "You heard me! Beat it!" At my terrible words the child sat rooted to the ground, her mouth agape and her mind confused with trepidation. "One...two..." I began counting.

But before I reached five, the girl made a flash of movement. She unmasked her true self; she was not an innocent flower. She was a vile serpent.

The following bedlam was too chaotic to describe in full detail. I knew I'd been showing the girl too much mercy—I should've pierced her thick skull sooner. There was frenetic energy abounding in all the next movement, which seemed to explode outward beyond us three, as if all the air's pent-up tension had been discharged like an erupting geyser. Everything was a blurry scene, but what was clear was my wail, "Get back!" as I shoved Kiara back as the child drew a dagger and swiped at her.

You couldn't trust anyone on this planet. No matter your place in the hierarchy, deceit was your greatest tool. If you could master the art of subterfuge, you could stand to gain anything. Here we had nearly become flies caught in the spider's web.

"Get your weapon ready!" I shouted at the aghast Kiara.

The next thing I knew was that I was facing down a swarm of savages who had dashed out from the forest's shadows as soon as the girl's dagger left its sheath. They took her side. Their clothes were frayed and smeared with dirt. They held crude, rugged weapons whose semblance was almost tribal, and they leered with wide haggard eyes—eyes devoid of irises, simply burning white except for the black pepper flakes which were their pupils, and even those were much too small. Those phantasmic eyes perfectly mirrored the eyes of the little girl.

I couldn't gather what those bulbous eyes meant, but I did know the meaning of the attack.

Bandits.

The word appeared in my mind as the barbarians coalesced in a formation.

There was far more to that girl than met the eye. After administering her first strike and failing, she sprang up and took cover behind her company as if in perfect health. Those injuries really *were* fake after all.

This evil luck was the other problem with camping out away from the city: if you were the subject of an attacker, no one would hear you scream. I held my sword at the ready, my breathing irregular and my distress shaking me. Kiara stood beside me, clutching her weapon tremulously, and her legs appeared like threads of straw, struggling to support her weight. If I was afraid, she was utterly petrified.

Many large animals have little remorse for the lives of their prey. Squelching, eviscerating, and dismembering smaller animals is part of a regular day's business, and they don't care what suffering they cause in their favor. Whatever demonic thing had seized these bandits so as to blanch their eyes had reduced them closer to such animals than civilized beings.

In this case, we were the prey, standing like cattle before our predators.

CHAPTER VIII

IT'S IN THE BANDIT'S NECK

G ive us everything you have!" declared one bandit, evidently
their leader. "Money, weapons, jewelry—all of it! That's the
easiest way to get this over with!"

In addition to the child, there were five bandit men in total. The
group was a mixed band of falia and demifalia. The leader's size was
like a bear—an absolute mountain of a man with heaps of meaty
muscle armoring him. Either he was a falius or a demifalius whose
animality manifested in his physique. His left eye bulged and
sagged limp like a loose marble in his eye socket. He had a great
cigar clamped between his unkempt teeth.

I had no intention of yielding to his unrelenting demands. Our
pockets weren't full enough. My weightless wallet would never impress them, nor would my tasteless weapons or clumsy medicines.

Besides, that bandit girl had already aimed for our blood. Why
were these fiends so quick to kill before offering a compromise? It
was unbecoming of ruffians to greet someone with violence and
then try to de-escalate the situation.

I'd already seen their duplicity once with the girl's little stunt. I
would not be fooled again.

"You plan on killing us no matter what, don't you?" I asked icily.

"Heh-heh. I just can't help myself. After that little military convoy got away from us, I've been yearning to blow off some steam."

"—!"

My gut dropped at that. The apothecary had mentioned an attack on a general by highwaymen. I remembered hearing that the
general narrowly escaped with his life. I ground my teeth, desperate

to wake up from this nightmare. The way people still plundered their own kind in a time of war angered me, and now I was getting speared on the tines of this gray reality. Was there no setting aside differences to unite under one cause? To fight the common enemy? Did everyone require such entanglement in their own enterprises that they were blind to their annihilation galloping toward them?

I didn't want to believe that a gang with the capacity to attack military personnel would set its sights on us next. That alone shattered my hopes of survival. Running wasn't an option either. Two of the ruffians carried bows, and if they could challenge members of the military, their sharpshooting must have been pinpoint accurate. Turning tail would leave our backs as free targets.

"Sir," whispered Kiara, her voice still brimming with panic. "I saw what's making their eyes so empty. They're infected with parasites called neckdiggers. Those things are known for burrowing into people's napes and bending their minds. I noticed its tail sticking out of that kid's neck. They awaken all kinds of brute thoughts and desires in their hosts..." And with a gulp she said, "...They even arouse temptations to cannibalize. They don't just want to kill us...they want to eat us!"

So that was why their eyes were so inorganic and dull. They were the etiolated eyes of possessed souls. Those parasitic things—those neckdiggers—were sucking the life and color from the bandits, leaving their faces cold and corpselike.

"They're infected?" I asked. "How did it spread to all of them? Is it contagious?"

"No. They usually only infect one person. I've heard tell of them laying eggs within their hosts and letting their offspring spread throughout the host's community, but I always regarded those stories as myth. I didn't think it was really possible."

The leader of the bandits laughed. "I daresay that blue lady is more observant than she looks! But there ain't no cannibalism here. You're both nonfalia. When we eat you, it'll be just like feasting on any other animal." The leader studied me closely as if contemplating my appearance. "Say, you're one of those humans, aren't you? Ha-ha-ha...what a lucky find you are. This should be interesting."

It was impressive that a ruffian living divorced from society knew of my kind, but it seemed the news of my reputation had not yet reached these people. Their recognition of my race was not a recognition of my identity.

"Oh, boy! I always love trying new foods, boss!" said a bandit, his voice cracking every few words like a psycho. "Let's butcher him quickly and enjoy his meat while it's fresh!"

"I wouldn't mind that at all!" cackled another bandit. "I've never tasted a slime, either. Hey, Wild Eye, I wonder how smoothly I can take off a human's head!"

"Enough talk!" demanded the leader, who was apparently called Wild Eye, which suited him perfectly given his defective left eye. "If anyone cuts his head off, it'll be me! My blades ache for the taste of his blood!"

Wild Eye's words were like the blast of a war horn indicating a battle. He signaled the bandits to attack, and the chaos was unleashed. It began with the archers drawing their bows and firing. I didn't have time to determine whether they aimed for me or Kiara, but I supposed their most sensible strategy was to divide the task and arrange a two-for-two deal. Whatever the case, we each dove aside in earnest, and the hum of a gliding arrow resonated in my ear. Fortunately the only pain I felt was the impact of hitting the ground, and also a sweet touch of relief reached me upon seeing no arrows lodged in Kiara.

With haste we returned to our feet, and the two other henchmen drew their swords and converged on us. The archers loosed another pair of arrows, and then another, and it was only the blessing of luck that allowed me to evade them unharmed. I felt like a pawn, ducking arrows and trying not to get hit.

After the third arrow whistled by, the rain of fire ceased. By now the swordsmen had advanced too close to curb the risk of friendly fire; a single bad shot from the archers' bows could pierce their ally instead of their target. Knowing this, they discarded their bows, wielded their blades (these were serrated daggers, not swords), and followed suit.

The odds were stacked against me like a mountain. It was just Kiara and me, two bullets against five, like sheep facing down a pack of wolves. And since my enemies had an edge of combat experience, that made them all the more formidable. However, if a gang of ruffians could overwhelm me, I didn't stand a chance against the jagged fangs and black claws of this world. I couldn't die here. I had to survive this ordeal for the sake of my own pride and worth.

One of the swordsmen couldn't contain his excitement and lunged forth. The nose of his sword glinted in the sun, glaring into my eyes, but in the nick of time I blocked it with my own sword to avoid getting cut down. Our blades struggled against one another as we desperately pushed for an advantage, kicking in every bit of strength in hope of gaining an edge.

"No!" Kiara screamed. She ran for my attacker to stop him, but a peal of metal striking metal rang before she reached me. So it was that the other swordsman had slashed at her. By some quick reflex she had blocked the vicious attack, but the strain of force traveling through her arms elicited a groan. They pushed against each other's blades, as did I. When my eyes drifted over, I saw her struggling more severely to keep his edge at bay. Against all my wishes I couldn't fly to her aid.

"Hey, pretty lady!" said Kiara's foe. "I'll tell you what: if you give up now, I promise I'll make your death quick and painless!"

Being a woman, she was at a natural disadvantage. I had to help somehow. With a burst of strength, I kicked my attacker and thrust my blade into his gut. The sharp end tore through his clothes and skin and meat and innards. Blood splashed out, his eyes rolled back, and he collapsed, never so much as to twitch again.

Breathing heavily I looked at my crimson-stained hands. The weight of taking someone's life seemed to crush me. Though I knew I'd acted in self-defense, a voice lurking in the dark depths of my mind murmured words of shame. Those grave whispers were interrogative, like a separate ego, like psychological terrors seeking to stomp me into despair, asking if what I'd done was right, if spilling that blood was justified, if that man truly deserved death. I'd never killed someone before...never felt that feeling...the shame...the guilt...no, there was no time to think about that. My servant—no, my companion—was in danger.

I dashed toward Kiara, who was on the brink of buckling under her opponent's strength. I reversed my sword and bashed the bandit's face with the hilt. He staggered back, wobbling on his feet from the pain (it looked like a tooth or two had flown out), and his state of swaying aswoon opened a window for Kiara to cleave his trunk with a slash, tearing away his balance but not killing him. Kiara looked at me in surprise after the bandit keeled over, confounded by my swiftness to aid her.

"You all right?" I asked.

She did not answer. Her confusion mutated into terror, and she pushed me aside, her sword hoisted up in defense. Presently there was a shrill ringing of iron.

"Damn!" cursed one of the archers. Kiara had blocked the swing of his knife, which had been moving in my blind spot.

I should've held my guard up. Had Kiara not been looking out for me, the ambusher would've caught me off guard. There wasn't room to afford such mistakes—not when fighting to survive.

Having been saved by Kiara, I returned the favor by helping her take down the new assailant. I bounded forth and bore down on the bandit, skidding my blade down his arm. He was too absorbed in his clash with Kiara, thus letting me land an easy strike. A giant cleft opened in his flesh with blood flooding out, and he blenched and stumbled in pain. Then she hacked through his chest. As he swooned I ended it with a sidelong stab. He soon lay prostrate in the grass, lifeless, but suddenly the sight of his nape seized me. Hanging like a sharp fleshy tongue from a breach in his skin among his spilled entrails was a pale pink tail, wriggling and jerking as if sharing the man's pain. That must have been his neckdigger. After a moment the tail went flaccid and lolled, for all neckdiggers die when their hosts die.

"Idiots!" said a seething Wild Eye as he watched his comrades fall. He had been hanging back the whole time, standing like a protective wall in front of the little girl, and hearing him yammer about his gang's failure was ironic considering how little action he'd taken himself.

"Hey, you!" he barked at the last remaining bandit. "Your pride is hanging in the balance! Don't even think about losing to a lowly human and a slime!"

The last bandit acknowledged his command and closed in.

"You've outdone yourself, kid," he said to Kiara. He twirled his knife in his hand. His expression was that of a puma trying to lure out its prey. "I'm impressed that a loser slime could hold off against us. But you've had your fun, and it's time for me to send you to Sedhro, where your kind belongs!"

Kiara's eyes blazed with blue flame at the words. With a fierce shout she charged as if she couldn't contain the tempest of fury. I knew what was happening, and it put me ill at ease. The dark soulless grin emerging on the bandit's face made his ruse obvious. He had a trick up his sleeve, and Kiara was diving headlong into the trap! His previous words were nothing but a means of aggravating Kiara—he was tossing out bait! There were salesmen who could con others by choosing their words carefully in order to present their product as a sound purchase. They constructed their speech so delicately and enchantingly so as to win people into doing their bidding. This bandit had purposely pitched insults at Kiara to sell her into a blind rage. And when you lose yourself in temerity, you become reckless.

"Don't rush in!" I wailed.

Ignoring my cry, the inflamed Kiara swung down with all her might, but even with his smaller knife the bandit knocked her sword away with ease. She'd invested so much power into her attack that, upon failing, the inertia kept her on the move, and her balance abandoned her. Amid her disorientation she stumbled to her rear.

"Ha-ha! Got you!" The bandit towered over her, his shadow darkening her like a threatening black cloud. He let fall his sword, and the slime quailed as doom hurtled toward her.

During all this, I leaped into a vehement sprint, supercharged with all alarm and terror by her sudden peril. Before the knife could shear her flesh, her foe's stroke was cut short, for my blade had appeared in its path like a shield. He bellowed a curse as he was sent back tottering, struggling to stay on his feet.

"Get him, Kiara!" I yelled.

"Hyah!" she yelled as she stabbed him in the heart. He toppled backward with a shriek of icy pain, shuddering and choking in his death throes.

"Keep it together!" I said to Kiara.

She nodded in acknowledgement of her loss of control. The machinery of the mind did not run very well under great storms of emotion. It was better to operate in a breezier state, thus arresting brash tendencies. For us it was critical to get ahold of ourselves, for the selling of our wits to our furor could cost us our chances of survival.

At this point the only remaining enemy was Wild Eye. All other brigands lay dead in the grass—one was left alive but injured beyond ability to fight. The bandit leader, furious, stubbed his cigar in the dirt, drew two giant cleavers, and roared at his smitten lackeys.

"Incompetent and defective you are, fools! Blast it all—I'll handle these weaklings myself!"

He marched toward us, slow and threatening. With his colossal build and massive blades, he was far more formidable than the others. Sweat drenched my face, my body shook with weakness and fatigue, and my sword grew heavy in my hands. However, as we tried to steel our daunted hearts to carry the cross of this clash, the little girl, who had been rooted in a cold tremor watching us pick off her comrades, went paler than ever and clung to Wild Eye's thick leg.

"Papa, please don't! They're too strong and scary! What if you get hurt and Mama yells at you again?"

Papa. The word echoed several times in my mind at an earsplitting volume. She...she called him Papa. That child was the bandit leader's daughter! And that meant that when she first staggered up to us as a moribund orphan, her old man had plainly used her as bait. He had exploited his daughter and her innocence for waylaying. What kind of father was he? To make things worse, I'd waved the tip of my sword in her face, inadvertently trumpeting my willingness to snuff her for her father's benefit, for if I distracted myself by killing her, their ambush would have caught me like a snare.

"Let go of me, you brat!" With a kick he slammed her little body into the grass.

"Ungh!" she whimpered like an abused dog.

Meanwhile the one bandit whom we had wounded instead of killed dragged his bleeding body through the grass, gagging for breath, and clutched Wild Eye's leg. "We need to...*cough*...run. They've already killed half of us!"

"Shut up! Why should I take advice from a failure?!" Fumes of steam seemed to blow out of his head as his murder-laden eyes, which looked like knives, shifted with all fixation onto me. "I planned to finish you off fast, but now I think I'll give you the most excruciating death you can imagine! I'll show you what happens when you harm my brothers!"

Without a moment's hesitation, he bulleted across the short span of grass. His speed, which struck a remarkably discordant note granted his size, nearly caught me off guard. My survival instinct took over, and I evaded with a dive, but his blade whisked through the air and grazed my cheek. A long, thin cut split open, and blood oozed out, dribbling down my face and dripping fast from my chin.

Kiara, who hadn't been targeted, attacked from behind, but with a pivot and hardly a change in expression he raised his blade and stopped her weapon dead in its path. The sound of clashing metal surged out like a high-billowing tide.

Wild Eye's strength was already so peerless, and his two cleavers amplified the challenge beyond fighting a single blade. I got up and reignited my fury. Kiara and I closed in on opposite sides of the bandit and let our blades pounce synchronously, but as if predicting our moves, he broke both our blows with his weapons. He used his beefy muscles to knock us back with our feet stuttering.

Although stunned by his sheer amount of force, Kiara's grip on her balance held up barely, and with a gale of anger she swung again. But the bandit had gained an edge over her wobbly figure, and obliquely he swatted his blade at Kiara's with the strength of a thousand men. The cleaver scraped her sword and sent it flying out of her hands, and her weapon clattered several strides away in the grass. *Thwack!* He kicked her in the stomach, and his strike knocked her off her feet.

I gasped. Her situation was suddenly critical: her weapon landed some ways away from her, too far to pick up, rendering her as easy prey. Seeing her in that defenseless position awoke every crying instinct to save her. From her grounded state her eyes quivered and widened in fear like scintillating bulbs, and she looked up to see the enemy standing over her like a dark portentous spire.

As Wild Eye raised his cleaver to inflict the finishing blow, I charged forward, clenching my sword with both hands, and pointed its shiny tip straight at him. He saw me, and clang, both cleavers thwarted my blade's edge. But as he swiped back in retaliation, something kindled within me. A realization glowed like a beacon and told me that if I wanted to win, I had to get creative.

Only I had a single idea: a huge gamble that would mean certain death if unsuccessful. But the battle was already desperate enough. I decided to go all in and bet my life.

Lurching forward as his blades raced toward me, I subverted his expectations. I dove and rolled through the grass. My weapon left my hands of my own unwavering volition, and I took matters into my bare hands. Wild Eye's strokes went wide and smashed into the earth. Before he could recover or utter a word, I swung around his massive frame, sprang onto his back, grasped his broad neck, and choked him.

"Ack! Kh-kh!" He gagged and dropped his cleavers. My hands weren't large enough to constrict his airways completely, but his breathing was cut thin and his ability was bridled. He swiped at me, but his thick arms had too much bulk to reach his back. His attempt to grapple me died as a pathetic failure. "Stupid human! Get off me!" The bandit resorted to thrashing with violent and relentless turbulence, employing every last means to shake me off from him. I drew my utility knife and thrust it into his shoulder. The small blade didn't cut deep at all, only shearing a few inches into the meaty flesh, but the blow sent him into a roaring frenzy. He howled, and his threshing got so intense that my grip on the knife wrung loose while it was still in his shoulder. I tried to reach it, but...

"Not this time!" He pulled the knife out and threw it on the ground.

Had I known better at the time, I would have set my attention on his neckdigger. By simply seizing its protruding tail and yanking it out, its host would've fallen dead, for you cannot live without your neckdigger once infected. Unfortunately this exceeded my knowledge, so I was unaware of the kill opportunity within my reach.

He jerked forward, and finally my grip gave way. I was shaken off.

"Augh!" I yelped as I flopped on my back, my spine taking a heavy blow. My sword was right beside me, so I picked it up and rose to my feet. But before I could stand fully, the bandit's cleavers hurled down out of nowhere. "—!"

Clang!

"Why won't you die?! Why can't I squash you insects?!" The bandit's complaints were out of frustration when I curbed his attack.

But at the moment it seemed very possible that his anger would be short-lived, for our blades contested each other, and I was at a blaring disadvantage. Our weapons ground in the same manner as our teeth amid our exertion. The metal rang with piping shrieks. I was on only one knee, and it drilled deep into the dirt as the bandit's cleavers tried to squash me into the ground with every reserve of his might. His strike was only restrained by my sword, though the conspicuous difference in weapon sizes ruled our duel at my expense, as if I were handicapped, and I resisted his force with every last fiber of my being. It was a battle of raw strength, but my unlucky commingling of weakness, exhaustion, and inferior weaponry made victory unlikely.

"Kiara! What are you doing?!" I cried. "Help!"

She was still on the ground as she watched our tussle, trying to drum up a way to assist me. Her sword lay many yards out. By going out of her way to snatch it up, she'd give Wild Eye enough time to weed out my strength. Worse, the strip of grass here was too thick to find my tiny knife with timeliness. If she couldn't act now, it was over. I couldn't hold off my opponent's blades much longer.

"Don't just sit there!" I pleaded, my voice straining under the immense pressure. "Take a weapon from one of their bodies or get creative in some other way! Just do something! If you don't, he'll kill me and come for you next!"

Kiara glanced at her offset sword and then at me. Did my companion truly lack the fiber to take action? Was her fortitude really so lacking? My memory suddenly crawled back to the time when I first bought her life. I'd made the purchase only a day ago. Was my financial rashness going to be my undoing this quickly? Could my discretion in investing really be so amiss?

"No...no..." Kiara squeaked, her body quaking with fear. Maybe this battle had shell-shocked her. Maybe the cold bloodbath had activated some trauma lurking in the cell of her mind. But if that was enough to blot out her willpower, then she didn't deserve life. She had to thrust out those qualms to survive—there was no other way.

"Come on! I know you're strong enough!"

The air boiled and bubbled around the grating of our blades. A wolfish grin overspread his face as he watched my resistance wane, as if taking pleasure in grinding down his prey. His crooked teeth glared like a dirty lantern and reminded me that if I died here, I'd be dying at the hands of practically an animal. I didn't want to go out that way.

If Kiara couldn't help me in battle, buying her life was a mistake.

My arms had no more energy.

I'd wasted my money on her.

Why was I thinking about money at a time like this? My life was hanging on the tip of my sword, so my wallet should've been the least of my concerns. It was so ridiculous that I would've laughed if I were given the strength.

Kiara stood and squeezed out the words, "I...I can't lose you too...I won't be afraid."

But once she was on her feet, after only a single step, her leg was caught by small hands, and she tripped and fell face down, for Wild Eye's daughter had latched onto her leg like a leech. The recumbent Kiara looked at the little girl in shock, horrified at that childish attempt to thwart her. There was a kind of purity and innocence in the girl's devices—an intrinsic wholesomeness of youth that, when emulsified with her evil intentions, gave her that nightmare look of an imp.

The girl extended a twisted smile, and drawing her dagger she said in a banshee's voice, "You belong to Udre!" and plunged her blade into Kiara's thigh.

Kiara screeched hoarsely, and my defense wavered when the bloodcurdling noise stung my ears. Wild Eye drove back my blade, and I fell on my back. His round belly bounced with laughter, he stood over me, his thick structure took up my entire view, and he raised his cleavers preparing to finish the job.

But at that a fire sparked in Kiara. At present she was finally fed up with all the trepidation that controlled her and seemed to vow to fight for liberation somehow. She was done being a slave to fear. She snarled in anger and remembered her previous words, and reasserted them: "I won't be afraid anymore!"

With a mighty kick from her free leg, Kiara gave Wild Eye's daughter a faceful of her boot. The girl squawked, released the bound leg, and toppled backward. The dagger slipped out of Kiara's flesh.

My vision had grown blurry, but what I could see in the next moment was a weaponless Kiara making a lightning dash in my direction.

Mere moments before my assailant's blades fell, Kiara's fist met his one good eye.

For good measure I placed a firm foot on Wild Eye's chest. I didn't want to run the risk of him harboring a final trump card, so it was safer to pin him down. His eyes were locked on my blade, whose tip was frozen mere inches from his throat. His defeat was sealed, he was crushed into submission, and all he could do was bare his teeth through the shame and humiliation.

"Why haven't you killed me?" he said. "You won! Sedhro is calling me, so send me away!"

After Kiara punched Wild Eye's good eye, which had since turned dark and puffy like a black pastry, we vanquished him and his daughter with ease. Since then I had looted him and his defeated lackeys to fatten my wallet a bit. Kiara restrained the child and placed a hand over her mouth, which had been burbling with pleads for mercy. Desperately she spat muffled noises and watched with big hysterical eyes that begged me to spare Papa. The only reward left to gain was the savory gratification of revenge.

While the temptation to skewer his neck was all too real, I hesitated. Killing in defense was different from killing in execution. He deserved hellfire, no doubt about it, but could I deliver death so eagerly? Would that not lay the burden of guilt into my hands? Would it not reactivate those grave lashing voices I'd heard after my first kill? It was difficult to distinguish the little devil from the little angel on my shoulder. Which one preached blood and which one preached mercy, I could not tell. But a miscarriage of justice would not ease my mind, so I needed to judge conscientiously.

There were no proper authorities to whom I could submit him. They would never believe me—especially me—if I told them a little girl, her father, and his friends tried to murder us. A poor innocent band of travelers were attacked by that malevolent human and his slime companion: that was the lie Wild Eye would spin up, and he'd use his daughter's innocence to anneal his testimony. I felt a flicker of frustration as I thought about the possibility. Everyone would listen to him, but my side of the story wouldn't even touch their ears. The tables would be turned, and I'd once again suffer the consequences of being branded as a criminal.

What had the little girl said before? Something about her mother yelling at her father for being too careless?

I pulled back and lifted my foot.

"What are you doing?" asked a surprised Kiara.

"What's this? You're letting me go?" asked Wild Eye. Although he was free to move, his bewilderment consumed him, and as if trapped in a block of ice, he didn't even twitch. He might have thought I wanted one last laugh by tricking him, but he was wrong. I was dead serious. The preacher of pity in my mind had moved me to stay my hand. And while this was an act of mercy, it was not an omission of punishment: there was a future for him—a harrowing future fraught with anguish and disgrace, for this day's humiliation would haunt his dreams for many nights to come.

"Yeah," I said. "Instead of killing you, I'm gonna let you go home to your wife. You can tell her you took a beating from a human and a slime."

Wild Eye's face contorted until it adopted a sickly hue. I had degraded his manhood before his wife, and now his hypermasculine essence had suddenly wafted away. Even among aliens the male psyche had an innate wiring for certain passions: power and conquest, adventure and purpose. It seemed the two poles of masculine and feminine were firmly rooted poles, always and everywhere in the universe. As a fellow man I could hardly blame his embarrassment, which made victory all the more delicious. I had humbled him and come out on top the way a lion might overthrow his pride's dominant male. He was no longer the fearless warrior he once thought he was.

"Now..." I said, my glare cursing the air itself and turning it cold and acidic. "...Get lost."

The scathed bandit leader sneered as he struggled to his feet and gathered his daughter and surviving minion. In solemn silence the three limped—with the occasional stumble—away into the timber and disappeared. But as I watched them vanish, a faint noise of footsteps fell suddenly on my ear and quickly grew louder. They were like the footsteps of a rapacious, eager animal, and my tingling instincts tripped every alarm in my conscience.

What had gone awry? Had there been another attacker lying in wait? Was the battle still raging against my realization? I turned around in hope of having time to strike back, but it was too late.

There was nothing I could do to stop the attack.

Of course the blow I ended up taking was not a bloody assault but a tight embrace from my companion. For a new fire was kindled in her heart that day—a kind of confidence which transcended all trauma and past calamity that had put her in such rack and ruin. She flung her arms around me in a manner too violent for comfort, and I nearly lost my balance.

"H-hey! Watch it!"

"We won!" Kiara exclaimed, a smile beaming on her face. "If you hadn't believed in me back there, I don't think I'd have been able to do it!"

She buried her face in my jacket the way a pup nuzzled against its master affectionately, and in return I wrapped my arms around her head and looked off into the landscape, letting out a relieved sigh.

"Not at all," I said. "It was you who saved me. I would've died if not for you."

"Ah-ha-ha...no, you're getting it backward."

But I replied, "Oh no, I'm not."

We exchanged the meaningless but goodwilled back-and-forth for a moment and then fell silent. We enjoyed the repose of the battle's aftermath for a moment, the long seconds tasting sweet like the first harvested sugar canes of autumn. The breeze caressed our bodies with gentle strokes. We were sweating, steaming, and trembling from exertion...but we were alive.

At length I piped up and said, "You know what I noticed?"

"Hm?"

"We were the only ones working together. Those ruffians came

at us of their own accord and pitched their attacks with no formation or synergy whatsoever. We fought them off because we
fought as one unit."

"Ah...I guess you're right."

Of course two pairs of hands were stronger than one. But the
bandits didn't act hand in hand. They kept to their own devices
and fought with no affinity weaving between one another, rendering their toil futile. That was why we survived.

"You did great," I said to Kiara, her body still glued to mine. "As
long as we work together, we'll survive."

"Yes," she said. "Throughout all of history, people looked to their
tribe members, their community, in times of trouble. They produced good fruits with the help of their brethren. That's the way it
should be. I'm glad about the solidarity between us two. It's all too
common among people nowadays to try and challenge the world
alone."

She had a magical touch of wisdom to her. I could see the value
in her—an untapped sense of dependability that seemed to hold
out its hand just for me. There in her eyes was a light that couldn't
be extinguished. It was a blinding light of the zeal to be acquainted
with the scarce good left in this world; it was a fire spitting the same
sparks as the ascetics who sacrifice everything for faith, or the soldiers who give their lives for their country; it was a star whose
beams of heat could flow forth like water and fill every water-
course, deep pool and narrow cranny alike. Who could turn down
a beautiful thing like that?

Our futures had been hideous until we met. They were still paved
with fog and dark, but we were both a ray of hope for each other
in that thickness. Together, we could illuminate the way for each
other.

"Also..." said Kiara, releasing her hold.

"Yes?"

"...What's your name?"

Her question was my first realization that I'd never shared my name.

"Oh...it's—" I started, but I was quickly distracted by the notion that I was missing something of hers too. "Pardon me. You have a last name, don't you? What is it?" The irony occurred to me that despite our camaraderie we didn't know each other's full names.

"Oh, um...it's Jaroe," she answered shyly. "My full name is Kiara Jaroe. Sorry...I should have told you sooner."

"It's all right. I'm Nathan. Nathan Tucker."

"Na...Nathan? I've never heard a name like that. It's nice to meet you."

"Likewise."

CHAPTER IX

IN THE HOUSE
OF MERCENARIES

And so, that was how we came to know each other. I was Na-than Tucker, and she was Kiara Jaroe, and whatever bond should develop between us had been kindled.

We migrated to another strand of Dirul Field that night. Kiara had the clever idea that the bandits might return with the intention of harvesting the remains of their fallen allies for food, and if they arrived with a larger group, the battle would repeat itself all over again. And also we had a fancy that some distance ought to be laid between ourselves and the stink of corpses, so it really wasn't worth staying put. In fact, with the money I'd looted from the bandits, I could afford an inn, but our legs shook from exhaustion, and we couldn't stomach the notion of the long walk back to Cordea. We simply settled for the darts and needles of the itchy grass.

Under the orange glow of twilight's early stages I helped Kiara apply a generous dose of Nefzing's Touch to her stabbed leg while treating my own wounds with modest portions. We finished with still a bottle to spare, which we were pleased to save for later. For dinner we hunted down a kreplim again.

Darkness draped the land. A starlit sky arched over all the king-dom's territory. Ild and Ald floated in the black curtain above in a harmonious, almost romantic fashion. Kiara and I sat around the fire, letting it breathe its warmth onto us amid the nightly jab of cold. The Hell's Liquor had proven useful for starting fires, for it could birth flames on firewood instantly.

"Can I ask something?" said Kiara.

"Hm? What?" I gave her my attention.

Her teeth tore off the only fatty end of her food (marbling and fat caps are seldom in kreplim meat), and after swallowing she said, "What's a human? Is that some kind of rare nonfalius?"

At the question I nearly choked on my dinner. It was understandable that my name had eluded her, but had the very concept of me failed to press upon her? Surely she didn't need my name to know who or what I was—to have awareness of the twisted and criminal deeds for which I'd been framed. Ever since the crashing and burning of my reputation, everyone viewed me as a cold-blooded monster. The dismay with which she regarded me during our first meeting had led me to infer her prior knowledge of me, but now she was confessing ignorance. The previous chapter of her life was probably a period of holding local news in little interest; her destitution commanded the sum of her attention. At the time she'd been too busy worrying about herself: her survival, her next meal, her rotting health, to care about the affairs of others.

Kiara cocked her head with a puzzled look as I swallowed the meat that made me gag.

"N-no," I panted with a burning throat. "I'm from another planet called Earth."

Shock seemed to curse her. She froze, mouth open in bewilderment, and it took her some moments to digest my words before she spoke stuttering. "Y-y-you don't mean...you're the advanced alien race that's prophesied to fend off the Kadaanites?!"

"That's right. But..." I looked into the fire, grief encompassing me like a dense shell. Kiara listened closely. "...My only way home was destroyed. I'm stuck here."

With no spaceship, there was no way home. I could hazard a guess that the wormhole which brought me here would collapse soon, which further cemented my fears of never returning home.

It was best not to tell her about my widespread status as a murderer. She was terrified enough in my presence, and while her discomfort behooved me as it helped me control her, I couldn't have it escalate to the point of causing incapacitation. You can only take so much fright before it devitalizes you, leaving you petrified.

"I guess my only option is to survive here until things change," I continued. "Maybe I'll have to fight the Kadaanites. For all I know they'll probably kill me before I find a way home."

"Um, yeah..." There was melancholy in her frowning face. She clearly couldn't think of a proper response, but I didn't expect one. A conversation with a stranded human wasn't an everyday occurrence for one such as herself. Of course words wouldn't side with her now. Besides, it wasn't like I needed someone to comfort me and tell me everything would be all right. There was nothing beneficial about having someone there to ease my worries. No one could shoulder my burdens or take away my pain. Black knives would always stab at my heart. By now, positive emotions had become foreign, my conscience had reduced to a soup of nameless torment, and my very being felt crannied and sketchy. "I'm sorry," squeaked Kiara at length.

"Let's get some sleep," I sighed as I finished my food and began to unwind. "You're tired after today, no?"

She nodded, but she had the eyes of someone without a spirit. I couldn't tell where her somber silence had come from. Maybe my woes had bestirred her emotions, or maybe her appetite for sleep had grown too ravenous. But I was too exhausted to press.

Our conversation eased into small talk as we wound down, but that too languished after a while, and we retired for the night.

When dawn came, the morning chill was spiky on my sore muscles. A spread of billowy clouds blotted out the sun, but the sky wasn't dark enough to herald rainfall. My back was stiff and required stretching.

"I wonder if a blanket would help..." I mumbled in light of the cool weather. When Kiara woke, I asked, "Are you all rested?"

"Yes sir. Is it back to the city for us?"

"Yeah. I'm tired of living here without purpose. It's time we start making money."

And so our morning began with the long trek along a road spanning Dirul Field that brought us to Cordea. When we arrived, we headed for the market district, the largest and most active part of town, and as usual the armies of people fluttered with life like a parade. Shops, stalls, taverns, inns, and trade guilds lined the streets and threaded the mazes of infrastructure. Every element of the marketplace was a gem for trade, always catering to the cycle of money, as if the whole precinct were a profit-turning machine. We came to Abafide Avenue in the center, the main road which stabbed through the market district and ended at Saint Abafide's Cathedral, which was the district's proudest edifice and was situated comfortably right outside the castle district. But our destination was westward, away from the heraldic masonry of the inner city.

The Nirik River ran through Cordea and acted as a canal. Many a barge rode the dimply water, their foamy wakes sending little pulsing ripples to the canal walls. There was constant docking and undocking at various quays in the market district as they hauled their cargo up and down the river for trading. The boatmen's shouts in arguments over who should get the next open dock were always audible near the water, even over the droning and clamoring of the crowds.

Still treading the length of Abafide Avenue, we crossed the largest bridge over the Nirik. Cambists and goldsmiths sat in trains along the road atop the wide crossings, entangled in their exchanges of coins and jewels. The smell of money from faraway lands wafted into my nostrils as I weaved through the bridge's congestion, and the heavy taxes levied on the place made the fragrance

all the more intense. The taxation was of little surprise, for it en-
sured integrity in the traders' commodities. If someone got caught
committing fraud or handing out fake coins, the taxes would increase, making everyone else suffer. Fear of taking the blame for
everyone's taxes raised great tension that circulated throughout the
area. However, I must stress that this was a pressure to avoid getting caught, not to swear off corruption altogether. Everyone here
was a seasoned swindler. Apprentices were often tasked with en-
forcing the furtiveness of their masters' shady practices; and if it
seemed like the business was in the sentries' sights, they'd signal to
their master that the authorities were on alert—usually by doing a
weird dance, singing a made-up song, or staging a trip-up.

Across the bridge lay more marketplace. The building I was looking for had a fine reputation. It was the home of people willing to
risk their lives for money, and for me it was the only vocation with
its doors still open. Now that I had weapons and also the funds for
the registration fees, I was finally ready to enlist.

After combing the streets, we soon stood outside a building that
looked quite a cozy house, with clay shingles sloping up its wings
and a stone chimney spearing high. A signboard swung on the
eaves with brushstrokes of white paint, reading: *The Independent
Mercenary Guild*. A pair of men armed with bloodstained swords
and plated mail passed us and entered, looking like they'd just
fended off death as part of an ordinary day's business.

"I don't suppose their job is much of a snoozer." I watched them
disappear behind the front door as I murmured the obvious.

Looking at the guildhall, I felt like I was staring down the yawning gullet of a fell animal. Some nameless intimidation gripped me,
but we stood firm against our little itch to reconsider, climbed the
wooden stoop, and went inside. Upon venturing through the
door, we were first greeted with a very homey and spacious lobby
suited with cushioned benches and a hearth that burned dimly.
The fireplace would probably be stoked more generously if the

place was more populated, for the building was currently quite empty save for the men who'd just entered and also some mysterious hard-bitten fellows hanging around. The mild and sober climate made sense given the time of day; it was late in the morning. The adjacent room was a drinking hall, with round tables large enough to seat multiple parties, encouraging a rather social atmosphere. I pictured all the guild members congregating here to eat and drink and make merry after a day's hard work, turning the air carnivalesque.

Beyond the lobby was a room with reception booths that had subtle earmarks of old teller windows. The countertops held quires of paper in messy stacks. Behind the bars of the first booth was a lady who appeared to work there, so I approached, saying, "Excuse me. We're looking for work here."

Dismay shadowed her face somewhat, and I could tell she was reluctant to offer me a place in the guild. She was a grizzled woman who had evidently devoted much of her life to this business. It was a reasonable inference that she spent her youthful days as one of the mercenaries here, taking up jobs and trekking off on adventures. She'd probably settled down in the humbler clerk's position once her age started catching up.

"Very well, mister. Allow me to explain how the guild works. This place is fitted for people willing to face danger for profit. The jobs usually fall under categories in which military or traditional mercenary legions don't specialize. Our clients from other parts of Neiklof can relay them to this guild in the form of contracts, which are then hung up on that board behind you." She indicated the wall past my shoulder, where a spread of paper sheets was plastered. "After that, any guild member can accept the contract. Contracts pay differently based on how much the client offers, and the prevailing pattern is that more difficult contracts pay more. This isn't your traditional mercenary company—its members operate as their own units." She slid two papers and a quill across the desk.

They were our documents for joining the guild and had blank fields that needed filling.

Kiara tugged my sleeve with a nervous look. "Mr. Nathan, would you fill out my form if you please? I can read, but I can't write well."

I arched my brow in surprise, but her unhoned literacy shouldn't have been so jarring. The selective obscurantism of Anbizian society hadn't crossed my mind till now: most nonfalius girls must have beneath the privilege of learning to read and write. It was a wonder that Kiara had the facility for reading on its own. That mind of hers really was something else despite the limits imposed by other forces.

So I honored her request and filled out both forms. They served as the documents for registration within the guild and a release of liability.

"And the registration fee, please," said the woman.

"How much?" I asked with a sigh.

"Ten Merth Silvers each."

While I'd predicted a charge like this, I was not the least bit thrilled. The fee was certainly a ploy to wring extra coins from new members—I could see it plainly in the woman's eyes. This was probably in place to balance the losses induced by greenhorns, who naturally lacked the experience to surmount the challenges of this guild. Many likely didn't return from their first contract. I extracted twenty Merth Silvers from my coin purse and handed them over begrudgingly.

"Welcome to the Independent Mercenary Guild," she said in a businesslike voice, and she bowed, and we bowed back, thus placing the final seal.

This guild would be the road either to good fortune or to my demise. The work here only suited people who valued profit over their lives. Our bowing (the customary gesture for sealing deals among Anbizians) raised the feeling of nails being hammered into our futures, bolting them tight, though I had no idea whether that future shone or dimmed.

My first order of business was of course the contract board. My source of income beckoned me. And soon it came to pass that Kiara and I had set off eagerly to fulfill our first contract, and my appetency for money grumbled a little bit quieter than before.

We'd taken the first steps on the path toward a more meaningful outlook. Living without purpose was a sorry way to live, and I was ready to leave that sad old lifestyle in the mud. It was high time I jump toward the morning sun and toil away for my future. If by the sweat of my brow I could make hard work a daily routine, prosperity would be right around the corner. Duty was calling, and Kiara and I would answer it. That way, we'd bolster each other up as partners in this dark world.

An ancient Anbizian proverb went, "Sloth kills more than all the deadliest weapons, but diligence saves the lives of many!" For the next week, that age-old wisdom seemed to be our guiding light. Our days were filled with engagements in simple contracts.

Our first mission was straightforward. We were to track down the lair of a pack of voldeffs, a class of hexapod animals who were canine in appearance with bristly hair. They wanted nothing more than to sink their razor-sharp teeth into anything that moves. They'd been harrying the nearby village of Lanbur and needed extermination. Often upon detecting potential quarry they let their feral, senseless nature take over and attacked without any shrewd plan or sturdy formation. When we found them camping in an alcove in a cliff, the wolfish monsters rushed at us with their thick greedy fangs, practically lining up for us to cut down one by one. With that it was a rather easy quest. We walked out of it with a fair payment and few scratches, although our clothes had smears of blood, the laundering of which was an extra end-of-day chore. Later we came to find that most days would end that way.

We continued in the following days by taking the guild's more basic, modest contracts. I preferred to keep a low profile due to my befouled reputation, in addition to being among the guild's greenhorns. Strangers still stared at me with wary leers, and I didn't need to pull any moves to draw more attention.

The degree of fulfillment I gained from life in the guild gave me a rare feeling of comfort. Previously my days had been so bleak, so gray, but now I was kept busy from those grave torturous lashings of my mind. Even when a rather dangerous quest presented itself, I enjoyed the process of taking control of my life and reaping the fruits of my labor.

Since our joining the guild, we had transitioned to sleeping in an inn. Our wallets had grown in health enough to support proper rooming and bedding, but still I opted for the cheapest room available—that is, the cheapest room with two beds. This choice was somewhat to Kiara's dissent, but by no means did I have the freedom for injudicious splurging, and I figured spoiling ourselves with unreasonably comfy arrangements would prove bad for both of us. Despite that, I couldn't help noticing a general improvement in Kiara's mood as time passed. Her health and hope grew in strength, which was firmly a good thing as long as she didn't succumb to complacency, so I was more or less glad to see her happier.

One early afternoon, while poring over the board of contracts, a particular case caught my eye which usurped my attention. Excitement grew in me as I plucked the paper off the wall and skimmed its terms.

Client: The Church of Ystaria
Description: A holy relic called the Aether Seal near the remote village of Maratel must be recovered and presented to His Holiness, the Supreme Hierarch. This artifact shall bless the faithful with protection from the Kadaanite invasion and ensure Anbizia's victory against them. It is located deep within a cave and gleams a brilliant

blue light that is said to be a wonderful omen.
  Reward: 100 silver coins

"Aether Seal? Weird name..." I muttered, amused. "Hey, look at this one," I said to Kiara, and she leaned round my shoulder to read it. "I think we've struck gold!"

"Agreed. Let's take it."

The contract seemed too good to be true. Guild members typically accepted contracts based on their risk-reward ratio. If a contract offered weak payment and strong chances of injury or death, no one would take it. In this case, the opposite was true. The payment was astoundingly bold while presumably having a modest danger level. It was almost *too* generous. My luck availed me in that I'd found this contract before anyone else did. A deal such as this ought to be highly coveted.

However, my mind boggled at the Church of Ystaria's relaying of a contract to the Independent Mercenary Guild. The appeals of the guild's reception normally came from laymen and lay communities who lacked the resources to tackle their own problems. And in blunt terms, the Church was a massive institution. Most Anbizian nations recognized the Ystarian faith as the one true religion, and the few countries that rejected it were mostly ostracized when it came to international relations. With its lordly prelates and magisterial authority, it went without saying that the Church's apparatus was more than enough for achieving its ends.

But the contract's bizarreness was hardly a cause for fuss. If it pays good money, then it's a good deal. A hundred Merth Silvers was simply too bountiful to deem refusable. When I brought the contract to the reception booth, the woman working there (whose name I'd learned was Miss Chethyr) logged it in the records without thinking twice. Miss Chethyr seemed totally unperturbed by the anomalous client—well, she seemed too disinterested to bother reading it thoroughly.

As I knew I'd need the contract again later, I furled it up and stuffed it into my traveling pouch. It had a blank signature field that was to be filled by the initial client after the job's completion. That was how we would validate our disposition to get paid.

Maratel was a humble farming village situated at the foot of the Menuil Hills of East Neiklof. Before that was a road running through a dale surrounded by Vethwood, the brush of which was a bit thicker than the modest backwoods beyond Dirul Field. Supposedly there was an old man living with his ulffs (a common Anbizian pet) in a house outside Vethwood, guarding the way to the village. It was a few hours' journey by wagon, so I wanted to get moving before the day had grown too old.

We tightened our belts and moved to the exit. But before I reached the door, someone opened it from the other side and stepped in. Immediately the sunlight sprayed into the room, and my eyes adjusted. When I saw the man standing thither, my chest tightened, my heart dropped to my toes, and the hairs on my body shot up like stiff spikes.

"Whoa! Nathan! Fancy running into *you* here!"

The speaker flashed a toothy smile.

"..."

It was *him*.

His malice-ridden grin was the avatar of every tyrant who rained down suffering on the less fortunate. His posture was charmingly straight with shoulders folded back elegantly, but I could see the latent cancer skulking and sliming around beneath his thin layer of virtue.

Our eyes locked, and the duality of our will, our mental terrain, even our very nature, beamed outward with crystal clarity.

There were three falius women with him, wearing sparsely hemmed and low-cut dresses, standing with arched backs, and sewing their distance from him. They appeared to have achieved mastery over flaunting the divinity of all that was fascinating about the female body. For there is a fundamental wonder to behold about the female; her beauty is treasured by man and woman alike. These ladies had tapped into the most sensual, carnal aspect of that desirable corporeal beauty, and yet it was only to my acrid distaste.

They were drawn to him but repelled from each other, as if existing in a perpetual state of infighting, coiled up in some secret mutual enmity.

My emotionless stare strayed over his shoulder to the door. My eyes showed no sign of life, as I bottled up every feeling that was racking me and set my mind solely on getting out of there. It took some effort to control my temper, but I shouldered my anguish, collected myself with a deep breath, and continued to the door.

But he was too stubborn to give up. He shuffled in front of me and blocked my way. "Hey, it's polite to respond."

The corruption all over his face was markedly plain. That unsavory smile reawakened my memory of the way he'd smiled in the Stiadev Welyn. The gravest torment of this terrible encounter was that he was in total control. He'd wedged his way into a much higher spot in the structure of power, and that superior energy did not sleep but constantly reverberated. There was no fighting back, no giving him a piece of my mind; all I could do was return his gaze impassively and wait for him to move.

"You vermin!' exploded one of the women. "Mr. Volkov is speaking to you! You have no right to ignore him!"

I had no thought of paying her any mind. I maintained my cold conduct and remained inimical to the lady's insolent demands.

People in the lobby and drinking hall took notice of the yelling and started glancing our way, wondering what kind of pother was unfolding. I'd never enjoyed large shares of attention, but on Anbizia I loathed drawing the eyes of strangers. If I didn't fly, our antagonism would engender a very messy scene.

Suddenly Dimitri's eye caught onto Kiara. He stepped out of my way, but then he sauntered up to my companion and blocked *her*

instead. She stiffened. He placed a hand over his heart and bowed his head.[2]

"I beg your pardon, but I reckon we haven't gotten acquainted. I'm Dimitri Volkov. Pleasure to meet you."

Kiara, whom our unnatural exchange had left muddled, hesitated before nervously returning the gesture. "Um...h-hi," she stammered. The disgust I accordingly felt made me want to gag and retch.

"Let's get going," I said in irritation, trying to hide my heaviness of heart. I couldn't spill any signs of weakness. If any weakness shone through the cracks, Dimitri would swoop in like a hawk and use it to his advantage.

"Hold on, Nathan. Not all of us are antisocial like you." After shooing me away like a fly, he redirected his full attention to Kiara. "Anyway, what's your name?"

The faces of the ladies accompanying him were sour with jealousy. Their hackles were probably raised not only because Dimitri was dallying with another girl but also because said girl was a non-falius. But he didn't consider the feelings of his companions—he only lived to satisfy himself. And I had a bad feeling that his volition at this very moment originated in a body part other than his brain. He wasn't thinking in his cerebrum—he was thinking below his waist.

"My name is...Kiara." Her face turned beet red, and she averted her gaze and hung her head low. "It's...uh, nice to meet you."

Dimitri leaned toward me, keeping his eyes on Kiara. "She's cute," he purred. "Didn't think you'd get so tasteful. How does it feel having her at your feet, anyway?"

Why, oh why did he have to put it that way? That shameless aspect of his face, putting forth all the sinister and crooked sadism of his twisted mind, seemed to suggest a kind of inhumanity of his

---

[2] This is the customary greeting gesture for Anbizians.

being. No civilized man could act so brazenly. Kiara fidgeted rest-lessly, embarrassed by his indelicate comments.

As he spoke, I noticed a rolled sheet of paper clipped to his belt. I craned my neck to get a closer look at its contents. *No way,* I thought when I saw what it was. With great difficulty I suppressed a gasp. Most of its writing was concealed, being furled like a scroll, but I could tell it was none other than a contract from the guild.

Which meant *he* was a member here.

The next red flag was the contract's bounty. Written in large, bold lettering was the number: three hundred Merth Silver coins! That was equivalent to six Golden Sols, which was no amount of money to joke about. It was among the highest-paying quests in the guild—the kind of challenge only the most gifted mercenaries would dare to tackle. I couldn't fathom how Dimitri had climbed the ladder to stand among those few.

He continued to stir his soup of impertinent words, this time whispering in my ear so that Kiara wouldn't hear. "Well...you know what they say. Sharing is caring, right?"

A pang of rage coursed through me at his words. I saw the ques-tion coming from afar, and I did not appreciate it one bit. He'd already torn so much away from me, yet still his craving to induce me to misery wasn't quenched. I considered it not my personal but moral duty to stop him, but how would I do so?

"So, Kiara," Dimitri said, sauntering over to her. "You're in luck! It just so happens that I have an open spot in my squad..."

Surely Dimitri created that opportunity *ex nihilo*. The limit of the size of his party was obviously contingent on his will, so he could adjust to his liking. He invented the opportunity on the spot by way of convenience—that was the rampancy of his graft.

Kiara shot me an uneasy look. She was entirely indecisive about what to do, so I shook my head with a wide-eyed expression that urged the admonishment *stay away*. Beads of sweat materialized on her face when she awoke to the fact that this other human was no friend.

"...Is that a cheap iron sword?" he asked, noticing the sword in its weather-beaten hide scabbard fastened to her belt. "Oh, come on, now. Such feeble gear is well below a princess like you. Check this out." He drew his sword and presented it haughtily like a child at show-and-tell. It looked like some legendary weapon out of a fairy tale, sporting a golden hilt attached to the shiniest and sharpest steel blade that was only forgeable by smithery's most excellent hands. His name in Falian was engraved in very tasteless but very ornate fashion at the blade's base, and the whole thing appeared a fine token of the ostentation of royalty and nobility. "See this? This is a gift from His Majesty King Frieval himself, specially forged by the kingdom's top blacksmiths. If you join me, I can get you a nice weapon like this and so much more."

There sparked a twinkle in his princely gaze, but the honor on display was completely artificial. Any benevolent action he performed was only self-serving; for in the deep, dark vault of his mind, he did not value good deeds but only saw them as one of many means to satisfy his egoistic passions. He was a leech, and his black heart sought to feed off all existence like a parasite.

My cornered companion cast frazzled looks to and fro between Dimitri and me. I caught a glimpse of his lady attendants leering at her with disapproval. "Don't even think about it, slime," ordered their snotty expressions. I could tell their annoyed grimaces didn't welcome Dimitri's particular interest in Kiara. Those poor girls— they were blind to the truth that their inclusion in his party was merely a manipulation to serve his self-interest.

"I-I'm sorry, but..." Kiara began, to which Dimitri's face quickly twisted into something that looked suitably offended. "...Mr. Nathan bought me this sword himself."

"Huh?" Dimitri's smile disappeared. "But just *look* at that thing! It's got such a bland aesthetic, and it's not even totally sharp. Besides, I can also have the castle tailors make you some fantastic clothes. Much classier than what you're wearing now."

Kiara's resultant expression seemed to suggest that she saw irony in the offer, seeing as Dimitri's companions' clothes covered an irrationally small area of skin. A mischievous smile reached across Kiara's face. The meaning of this took me some time to understand. The very pompous Dimitri had turned into a very agitated Dimitri, but for some reason his emotional stirring only elicited amused feelings from her.

"I can hear you speaking of all these nice things," she said. "Yet you never confronted any adversities to earn them yourself. They were all handed to you. A meal tastes banal when it's served for free, but when you work hard and earn it yourself, it tastes divine. You say you'll get me all these fancy weapons and clothes, but you're not willing to sacrifice anything for them. Meanwhile, Mr. Nathan surrendered his good money for my gear. No matter how gaudy your equipment is, it'll never imitate the value of these gifts I bear now."

Dimitri took the rebuttal as a flaming insult, but her almost singsong eloquence was impressive. Part of me didn't harmonize with her kudos as I hadn't spent *too* much money on her. After joining the guild, I earned back all that money fairly quickly. She seemed to be inflating the numbers to strengthen her point.

"Also, the fruit that looks most succulent on the outside might have a festered core, the same way your equipment *looks* aesthetic while having no practical value. How can I be sure that your sword is the best just because it looks classy? I've used my current gear to work and fight alongside Mr. Nathan with great success, and I'm already in his debt for that alone. So I'm afraid that I can't accept your offer, as tempting as it is."

Dimitri looked at me suspiciously. "Are you using debt to bind her? Is that how you levy control over her? Wait, you're using that as an excuse to overexert this delicate angel, aren't you?!"

A spasm of ire zipped through me. My patience was tapering. I was supremely fed up with his accusations, and unlike our last meeting, our proximity drew narrow enough to allow my fists to serve him a fresh slice of our strife. I felt like a corked bottle filling with anger, which was bound to burst open upon accruing too much pressure. "Let's go," I ordered Kiara, who was at a loss for words upon hearing Dimitri's accusation. "This place is starting to reek with his scent."

"Coming!"

I opted to leave, and she hurriedly caught up to me, squirming out of the corner she'd been backed into. But Dimitri seized my shoulder firmly, and I twirled, suddenly aflame with an infuriated glare. Very disdainfully I lent him my eyes and ears, but I was ready to batter his face into fine jelly.

"I asked you a question." His voice rolled with a low rumble. He'd discarded his smug, serpentine mien and glowered darkly into my eyes. "What else are you doing to her? What happens behind closed doors? You certainly don't have to restrain yourself when you're alone with her...you could overpower her brittle frame with ease." It was then that through his black expression arose a demonic grin. The curvature of his lips was larger and eviler than I'd ever seen him produce. "...You've been *forcing* yourself on her, haven't you?"

Finally it snapped.

"The hell do *you* know?!" I bellowed. My vision went hot, and my body bounded forward in a sort of knee-jerk reaction. I charged and drove my head into Dimitri's trunk.

A shrill set of gasps escaped all of the women (including Kiara) and bounced off the walls. In the eyes of some, accusations of rape exceeded accusations of murder in gravity, but this was of little concern. What mattered was this: if that bastard Dimitri wanted to paint me as an animal, I'd damn well give him something that typifies one.

After tackling the unsuspecting swine, I pinned him down, and we wrestled on the ground. He scrabbled for defense, but his efforts were fruitless. I grabbed him by the shirt with nailing tightness, but although my fist balled hard enough to match the strength of steel, I only got one straight right on his jaw before several pairs of arms slung under my shoulders and around my waist, and I was torn away.

"What do you think you're playing at, you airhead?!" said one of the guild members restraining me.

"Are you *trying* to get kicked out of this guild?!" asked another.

Other castigating shouts went my way amid the erupting tumult. I careened forward in the men's arms trying to get at my target, but their strength was matchless. Kiara grabbed my arms and held them down while lambasting me with a silent dagger-eyed look. At length the ballistic energy drained from my system and I stopped resisting.

Dimitri clasped his cheek where I punched him and massaged it. A stream of blood bubbled over his lip and crept down his chin, and his companions pampered and tendered to him with every lilting grace of the divine feminine.

"Still haven't let go of your barbaric ways?!" he spat. "You really *are* a savage!"

The comment brought me to gasp with rue—a twinge of self-reproach at having failed to think twice about my actions.

"Yeah! You crossed the line, punk!" snarled one of Dimitri's girls.

When the uproar fully abated, a blistering silence swept over the room, and I looked around at the icy glares of the guild members. Their reprimanding eyes penetrated me, which suddenly aroused a terrible but familiar sense of degradation I'd hoped was well behind me. *Oh, no—what have I done?!* I cursed myself mentally. Everyone already perceived me as a vicious killer who lived for bloodlust, and now I'd practically annunciated to these people that such ferocity really *did* fit my nature after all. No matter what I tried, I'd always be a monster.

As soon as my restrainers released their hold, I sprang forward and stormed out the front door. Kiara, who was drummed with shock, quickly gathered herself and trailed me into the sunlight.

As I crossed the doorway, Dimitri spitefully murmured, "See you around." The door clapped shut.

I traversed the streets with long, quick strides. Behind me was the pitter-patter of Kiara's light footsteps. Even when I gained awareness of her struggling to keep up, I didn't slacken my pace. The only thing I wanted in any capacity at that moment was to flee as far from the guild as possible.

Dimitri was the only other human on this planet, and I wanted nothing to do with him!

"...Mr. Nathan."

I filtered out the voice and kept walking. I tromped over the crossing over the Nirik, past all the cambists and goldsmiths, and deeper into the thick tangles of Cordea's architecture. The electric market district was at complete odds with my morose emotional weather.

"Mr. Nathan!"

When Kiara tugged on my sleeve, I stopped and whirled around faster than a flash of light.

"What?"

My despairing mug was probably a distortion of facial features beyond the way any human face ought to move. She gave me a look of genuine worry and hesitated to speak. My swelled-up anguish didn't deflate as I waited for her to spit it out.

Her gaze fell. "...Nothing."

"What...is...it?" I hissed furiously.

"...Did something happen between you and that human?"

Even a blind man could see how my face burned with redness. Emotions. Too many emotions were ablaze in my system. My head probably looked like a bright red balloon about to pop asunder from too much pressure.

"No."

"…?"

"Seriously. Nothing happened."

"…Okay."

She saw right through my lie, but out of prudence she relented.

I couldn't tell her the truth. No one had faith in my side of the story—why assume she would believe me? Why would Kiara be any different from all the rest?

Everyone's opinion was predestined to be pitted against me. No one, not anyone, would believe in me. The best thing I could do was bottle up my pain. If I did that, it might not hurt so bad.

CHAPTER X

THE AETHER SEAL

The carriage wheels stopped turning after a few hours of travel We had just rolled up to the village of Maratel. The sun was sinking below the eaves of Vethwood behind the wide swaths of farmland.

Having paid the driver in advance, I wordlessly hopped out of the wagon with Kiara and headed into the village. Our stomachs grumbled like thunder insufferably, so we quickly found ourselves drawn to the first tavern we could find, which was called *Merrybeard Alehouse*. It was a cozy run-of-the-mill tavern complete with long tables that seated many a drinking man and some smaller tables where older gentlemen sat with their wives. There was a bar where men shared in small talk, and the braver lads even ventured to strike up conversations with the barmaids, all of whom were quite young and very pretty. A hearth blazed brightly with smoke that smelled of fine earth and herbs whisking up the flue. The building was gurgling with sprightly chatter as we sat ourselves at a vacant table.

"Welcome to our little alehouse," said a lassie around Kiara's age, scampering up to our table. She was a demifalius with droopy, doggy ears on her scalp and four spiky fangs in her smile. "Care for any drinks?"

Our temples were numb from the long trip to the village, so we both requested some strong ale.

"Oh, are you travelers?" she asked with remarkable cheeriness. "I haven't seen you round here."

"Uh...yeah. We're from Cordea," I said, failing to mask my incredulous tone. The effusiveness in her mannerisms put me warily on edge. Anbizians had never been this friendly when dealing with me—I was accustomed to being met with sour, shadowy scowls. This unparalleled interaction felt outside the bounds of reality, as if the laws of the universe had taken temporary leave.

"Is that so? As a kid I dreamed of being an adventurer. Then I had a change of plans and dedicated myself to getting our farmers and other strangers bombed instead, but hey! There's plenty of excitement in this vocation too, don't ya think? I'm forecasting a big booze storm tonight!"

"Booze storm? I'm afraid I don't follow you, miss," I said.

"Just you wait and see what I mean, Mister Handsome. Pretty soon, all these men will be staggering out of here completely dazed!" She giggled and hurried away to fetch our drinks.

Her words brought my gaze over to the bar. The men clutched their wooden mugs and drank in a kind of artistic synchrony. Time would tell whether the lassie's forecast would come true, but she seemed to believe it wholeheartedly.

At the name *Mister Handsome*, Kiara glared at the lassie. My companion pierced her with sharp, blue almond eyes and a furrowed brow before she was out of sight.

With little delay our drinks were brought out. The girls here must have been keenly attuned to the flow of the alehouse: their skills in skipping and scuttling around the place to tend to customers were highly refined. The ale sloshed around in the mugs as they clunked onto the table. Before I could so much as blink, Kiara was already slurping into it with relish. I had grown used to her compulsive quirks as the days went by.

"Mmm, they brew a good ale," she crooned.

The lassie left us with our ales and disappeared into the kitchen, but presently a hairy gorbellied man—presumably the tavern master—bobbed out, screaming through his thick beard.

"Look at you lot, sweating it out in the fields all day just to kick back and guzzle *my* booze all night! I take it your mommas didn't teach you any manners?!"

"Ah, shuddup!" replied a regular. "You're always passing up the ale and diving straight for the mead, Mr. Merrybeard! Maybe if you learned some class and fixed your addiction to that stuff, you'd take more enjoyment from your sorry old alehouse!"

"Addiction?! When was the last time you managed to walk out of here on your own two feet? Honestly, what if someone like General Tebaldus attacks us? You'll be too hammered to hold a sword against him!"

"Hah—my ass! Don't tell me you believe in that myth! They say he's a monster that pillages towns, murders children, and ravishes our women! Buncha scaremongering if you ask me!"

"Aye, I may be a scaremonger, but you my good sir are a whore-monger!"

The other men burst out laughing as the pair jabbed at each other for fun. As Maratel thrived on farming, roistering the night away with drinks in hand seemed popular among plowmen who needed to take the edge off after a day of tilling fields and tending crops in the beating sun. The potations served as a good social lubricant for the men to share good times in this place.

All in all, the people of Maratel savored the contentment of daily life in their little village. Every meal and drink was the bedrock of their community, and they valued every endeavor, pleasant or strenuous, as an instrument to grow in friendship. And in their eyes, health was not a matter of clean dieting or rigorous physical training, but of taking delight in relationships with loved ones. For some odd reason which I didn't understand, I admired their quaint ways. I'd long since abandoned the dream of such simple living.

"Hey, you travelers!" said Mr. Merrybeard, his voice still ringing with gusto. "What brings you to good ol' Maratel?"

Just like the lassie waiting our table, the tavern master's tone was unnaturally amiable. This radical twist of my expectations made my heart pick up its tempo, and I wondered if some trickery was at play.

"The Church sent us," I said. "We've been ordered to retrieve a holy relic called the Aether Seal."

"Aether Seal, eh? Oh, you mean that thingamabob in the little cave just north of here? I heard that thing was deemed cursed. What's going on with that situation, anyway?"

"People were disappearing in there, right?" said one of the bar-goers. "They'd walk on inside to pray in the artifact's presence, and then they'd never come back out! It's like the thing swallows them whole! It got so bad that the village chief declared the cave off-limits!"

This was all news to me. The information produced surprise that merged with uneasiness as the consciousness stole over me that this contract's payment may have been justified after all. Supposing this talk of disappearances was true, the generous hundred silvers started to make sense.

"Now why would the Church want a cursed artifact?" asked Mr. Merrybeard.

"Maybe they're fixin' to uncurse it for us!" said another bar-goer before hailing a barmaid to refill his mug.

"They never said it was cursed," I answered. "They think it's a blessing."

"Well, now, that doesn't add up to me," said Mr. Merrybeard. "There ain't no blessing that turns folk into thin air, unless you got death wishes. Bah, who am I to question the Church? All I do is live by Ystaria's will, and that's that!"

Maratel was fairly close to Cordea, so it was jarring to see the facts flip over such a short distance. Still, I wasn't ready to jump to any conclusions yet. After coming all this way to this remote village, I was pining for my reward and wouldn't capitulate easily.

"Anyway, I must admit it ain't common for a pair of nonfalia to travel alone for Church business," continued the tavern master. "That old supreme hierarch must have gone totally senile!"

A pair of nonfalia? For him to say that, why, he must have been unaware that I was a human. Kiara had made the same error, but her threadbare situation made her ignorance sensible because she was poorer than a pauper. In this case, I had difficulty believing that these men weren't more well-read on current affairs.

"Um...well, right, yep...uh..." I stuttered, sipping my ale. I was too shaken up by these revelations to come close to drawing up a coherent response.

His comment rang more friendly than hostile, but it revealed why the villagers interacted with me so cordially. They had no notion of my identity, so their natural inclination was to assume I was a nonfalius rather than let my humanity occur to them. I gained a sweet sense of comfort knowing that I wasn't a savage in Maratel like I was in Cordea. The populace outside the city must have known little of me, the least of which being what I looked like. Information tends to rack up plenty of wear and tear the more it spreads, so perhaps physical descriptions of me were befogged beyond the walls of the city. If that was the case, I didn't want it to change. Doubtless the ignorance of others would stand me in good stead.

"Well," said Mr. Merrybeard. "If you *do* plan on entering that cave, you should ask Chief Enestir first. He's damn adamant about keeping everyone away from there."

He doubled back into the kitchen to check up on the food, realizing he'd spent too long babbling with his patrons. Suddenly a man at the bar, who had probably taken too much ale for his own good, began a song. The men in his vicinity were quick to join in, and within about ten seconds, all the company had picked up the tune. The throng of customers and barmaids and husbands and wives became a jolly shindy of merry trolling. The lyrics told a ludicrous story about a farmboy and a milkmaid falling in love and running away. Here is the song in full, translated from Falian to the best of my ability:

> *The boy of Ild was a farmer boy;*
> *He tilled and plowed all day.*
> *He worked so hard out in the field*
> *that his harrow broke like clay.*
>
> *The girl of Ald was a milkmaid girl;*
> *So young, so pretty, so pure.*
> *Her totchin kicked her square in face,*
> *And gone was her allure.*
>
> *She met him 'neath the willow tree;*
> *Said "Life's gone awfully gray."*
> *He clasped her hand and squeezed it tight;*
> *Said "Come, let's run away."*
>
> *They frisked along the plots and tracts*
> *with hearts restored anew.*
> *They pranced through mire and moor alike;*
> *Their love was bright and true.*
>
> *But back at home, the plagues alit,*
> *And O, what a taste of hell!*
> *The lightning cracked, the ice poured in;*
> *Disease began to swell.*
>
> *The goddess wilted all the crops*
> *and spoiled meat and grain.*
> *I don't know of the village's sin,*
> *But Her wrath came down like rain.*

When the farmboy and the milkmaid returned,
The village leapt with glee.
The ulffs and olks crowed in delight,
For the village hath been freed.

They ennobled the two with diadems;
Said "You're our king and queen!"
For only when the lovers had flown
were the horrid doldrums seen.

All went to bed a merry bunch;
the per'winkle face stirred up.
And so it was, their rags to riches
ere wintry snare warmed up!

At the very last verse, Kiara performed a spit-take with her ale out of laughter, though I was left thoroughly perplexed. I had difficulty keeping up with the tale, for it contained many Falian terms and idioms that I didn't understand.

When Kiara's laughter dried up, she wiped her mouth and said, "Oh, Mr. Nathan, Mr. Nathan! Did you hear that? Those silly villagers only dealt with hardships because it was winter. It never had anything to do with the couple's absence!" She relapsed into her brisk guffaw.

Though neither of us knew a single line of the lyrics, Kiara had spent the song bobbing her head to the rhythm and shimmying in a sort of pantomimic dance. But personally I found the story itself ridiculous despite the tune's catchiness.

The tavern folk erupted into spirited cheers and hoots and laughs at the song's end, but many were quick to shout, "Once more, lads and lasses! Make the travelers join in!"

Before I could back away in protest of their wish, they were al-

ready at it again, this time with cadent clapping; this time with ge-
nial smiles and inviting arms that urged us to sing along. Kiara was
eager and didn't hesitate to try her tongue, and it wasn't long before I was reeled into the carol too. My ability to match the lyrics
was amateurish, so much so that my participation mostly took the
form of gibbered intonations, but they seemed unbothered by this,
for they were simply taking raw delight in the drunken revelry.

Eventually the song ended again, and dinner was served at last.
Our mouths drooled the moment our eyes fell on our plates. Kiara
had that fang-baring look a hungry animal gets when hunting for
prey.

"No way," she prattled, enraptured. "Is that...meat?! Oh, what a
lucky fortune, Mr. Nathan!"

It was a splendid meal: roasted totchin (the closest Anbizian
equivalent to beef, but for me its taste was probably closer to mut-
ton) and a side of smashed zuyus (sweet dark red vegetables that are
starchy like potatoes). The war had compounded the scarcity of
meat so that it was a treat reserved chiefly for nobles. But ultimately, the farmers controlled the food, and in a close-knit community like Maratel, the villagers claimed nourishment before anyone else.

It goes without saying that this meal was nothing like the krep-
lims I'd hunted and cooked in Dirul Field. These dishes were fixed
by a chef whose purpose was ordered not only to sustenance but
to culinary artistry. The dry, rubbery meat I'd roasted over the fire
paled in comparison to this.

After dinner, which was fittingly delicious, we paid and left
quickly. The hairs of the tavern's thatched roof twitched in the
whispering wind, which seemed to reflect our own drowsiness.
The long day had started to weigh on me. There was an inn not too
far. We purchased a room there, and the two beds we found were
like heaven beckoning us. Sleep was never more delightful than
when you gave into the hysterical hankering to pass out.

*   *   *

In the morning I woke bright and early. I was refreshed, and my energy had returned full and plenty. Kiara was still sound asleep, her snores rising and falling with rhythmic unevenness. She was snugly tangled in her bedsheets and looked like a bulky animal in hibernation.

"Hey, you. Rise and shine," I said to which she yawned and rolled to her other side. Clearing my throat, I tried again. "I said wake up!"

She woke and looked at me with dark and droopy eyes. "Mm...what time is it?"

"It's morning time."

"Hm? Five more minutes..." She returned to her slumber, but I wasn't having any of it.

"Look outside," I flung open the wooden shutters. Pale stalks of sunlight gushed through the narrow window. She yelped as the blinding flash smote her eyes, and she buried her face in the bed-sheets for protection. "The sun's up. Was that totchin too much for you last night?"

Kiara deflated into a pout and dragged herself out from the warm bed.

"An old Orashian proverb comes to mind," said Kiara as we left the room and descended the inn's stairway. It was a tight passage with a trebly creak at every step. "It goes, 'A day filled with hard work is a good day.' Do you live by that precept?"

I'd heard similar sayings back on Earth. This seemed like one of those many points of wisdom that are universal—not confined to any one corner of creation but carved in the DNA of the cosmos. This raised a question which I hadn't reckoned with before. No doubt the universe had innate laws of physics that were unbreaka-ble by ordinary hands, but did it likewise have such laws written in the psychology of intelligent beings? There appeared to be more to the rational will than mere survival and reproduction, for the desire for hard work, for power, for pleasure, for fellowship, and perhaps for something greater than ourselves was seemingly thrust upon us at birth and shared among interplanetary life.

But also as intelligent beings, by sheer willpower we could subordinate such desires to other goals, which brought me to my next thought: cleaving to Kiara's proposed mindset was tempting, but the absence of one integral detail made it off-putting. "Not exactly," I said. "It doesn't matter how hard you work if your enemies work harder. You have to gauge toil by relating it to the people you're trying to defeat. Even if you have the high ground at the present, your opposition will overtake you if their will is more steeled. Hard work is an admirable thing, but that alone isn't enough. It's also about being willing to work hard even when you're drowning in pain and doubt, even when you think your failure is sealed, even when every inner voice is shrieking at you to give up. That's what sets apart hard workers from exceptional workers."

My thoughts seemed to bore her, so she changed the subject. "Well, to answer your question, that totchin last night was delicious, thank you very much. I hope we can have more someday soon." Her tone was cross, but I figured it was out of banter instead of genuine resentment.

We appeared in the main lobby where the innkeeper sat alone, and we left after having him point us in the direction of the village hall where the chief worked.

The village was sunlit with golden morning drowsiness. A pleasant warmth suffused the air and draped across the area like a thick blanket. Winged animals that looked of jackdaws fluttered over the roofs of houses, alighting on the bristly thatch between flights. Walking through the heart of the village, I could hear the singing of men in the fields amid their daily cultivation. We found the village hall near the church building. The way the church's shale roof

sloped up with its overlooking bell tower signaled the robust reso-
nance of the Ystarian faith in this region.

I tried to open the town hall door, but it was locked, and no response came when I tried knocking.

"Huh, maybe the chief's not up yet," I said.

"You mean we got up this early for nothing?" Kiara grumbled. I
extended a look of consolation before speaking.

"We'll have to wait. We have time to kill, so I'll get you some..."

...*breakfast*, I was about to say, before a man came strolling up.

"Can I help you?" He asked.

"Ah, have you seen the village chief, sir?"

"That would be me. I'm called Chief Enestir. What can I do for
you?" He was a rather inanimate, sullen-looking falius who was
slightly hoary and on the stouter side, but not like Mr. Merrybeard.

"We're from Cordea. We'd like to discuss some business."

He showed a slightly annoyed face. "I see. Let's talk inside, then."
The chief unlocked the door and held it open.

Beside me, Kiara made a rolling growl, pursing her lips as she
torched me with deathly eyes like an angry child. She was smart
enough to riddle out how I planned to finish my prior offer—I had
raised her hopes by suggesting the luxury of breakfast. Without
speaking, I patted her head before entering the village hall. This
only fanned the flames of her discontent, as the temper on her face
sharpened before she followed me.

The chief led us through the village hall. A brazen fixture of lights
that looked of a small chandelier dangled from the ceiling between
the wooden rafters, with thin candlesticks that were unlit. He
opened the door to his office and settled down into his chair. His
body language was rather closed, and his expression was exasperated as he looked at us. "Let me guess: the king sent you to inform
me of more taxes on my village, is that it?"

Both Kiara's and I failed to form an immediate answer because our mouths suddenly wouldn't operate. Chief Enestir's words startled me, and they triggered a peculiar chain of thoughts in my head. Was pitiful old King Frieval wringing the village dry by way of taxation? And if so, was it because he was desperate for extra funds, or did he have a personal gripe with Maratel?

"Uh, no. We're mercenaries sent by the Church."

Immediately Chief Enestir swapped his hostility for surprise. "Ah! Um...pardon my rudeness," he said, straightening his posture. He took a moment to absorb what I'd told him. "But this is real dubious. The Church hiring mercenaries? I've heard of no such thing!"

"We're looking for the artifact holed up in the nearby cave. The Church wants its hands on it."

"Ah, yes, the Aether Seal. That's baffling." His hand stroked his beard, a quizzical look crossing his face.

"Is something wrong?" I asked.

"This is just so peculiar. The Church gave us the Aether Seal last year as a blessing. Why would they want it back?"

"See for yourself," I said, showing him the contract.

He skimmed it over, puckering his aging eyes to decipher the small glyphs. "Well," he said. "I'll make no claim of authority to defy the Church, but that cave is not safe."

"So I've heard. People have been mysteriously disappearing in there. Can you explain it?"

"It's true. The cave is actually called Senzaw Cave. Many of the villagers had grown fond of the Aether Seal and would spend time in the cave praying around it, but one day, a prayer group went in and never came back out. Then their families went to search the cave for them, and poof! they went missing too! I eventually ordered guards to stand outside the cave to keep others from sneaking in, but as luck would have it, they disappeared as well! Now, no one goes near the place."

"Do you know what's causing the disappearances?"

"No," he said, looking at the wooden floorboards. "Most have adopted the belief that the Aether Seal is cursed...but as you're just now telling me, it seems like the Church doesn't think so." He ended his sentence making trenchant eye-contact that seemed to bind our gazes with unbreakable tautness.

It didn't seem too troublesome to set an exclusion zone around Senzaw Cave, but this begged the question of how far such boundaries needed to be drawn. This alleged curse seemed to suggest that the Aether Seal had a stomach for people—as if it fished people into the shadows only to swallow them up. So if the artifact really was devouring people, how far did its fangs reach?

"Personally, I'm stumped," he said. "The disappearances only began last month. The very *possibility* that the Aether Seal wasn't a genuine holy relic was unheard of till then. For a while there was a rumor that a platoon of Kadaanites is camped out in there, but most of us have scratched that theory as it lacks any live explanation. I'm sure you can guess why we're all a little reluctant to investigate further—we care about our lives—and I most certainly don't feel proud of letting two *kids* walk right in there."

He paused a spell and sighed. "...But I know better than to rebel against the Church's will. If *they* hadn't sent you, I would've forbidden you from entering Senzaw Cave the moment you expressed interest in going there. Now, if you have any leeway to abandon this endeavor, I'd strongly suggest you do. Otherwise, the cave is at the foot of the crag where the Menuil Hills begin. You be careful in there, you hear? I'd hate for the Church to come after me if you don't make it out."

He spoke those last words with stern authority to which I replied, somewhat disingenuously, "Of course, sir."

We left the building and headed east. The village ambiance seemed fairly undisturbed by the situation with the Aether Seal. Life in Maratel didn't revolve around the artifact; people could continue their days as normal should they steer clear of Senzaw Cave, and *that* seemed of little importunity.

"I still don't see why we needed that man's permission," said Kiara as we walked along the ocher road beyond the village's bounds. She was probably a bit snappish because I had stopped myself from offering breakfast. "We could have just gone in there ourselves."

"We can't just amble into the cave illegally. If we got in trouble for that, we could get kicked out of the guild. Then we'd be out of a job. Not to mention we'd have the Church get upset with us too."

"So, what are you going to do about the curse?"

"We're going in. I don't believe in magic curses or sorcery or any of that hocus-pocus. This so-called curse must have a scientific explanation. We have legs *and* swords, so we can fight or run from whatever's inside."

The crag's head slanted toward the village as if leaning to watch over the area, and its stone face was clothed with ivy. The jagged crests of the Menuil Hills were visible in the east and extended into lands uncharted and uncultivated, the sun poised on top like a pale orb. After climbing a slope past the final building and following a trail that wound through a copse, we spotted the cave burrowing into the cliff wall. We paused at the rim of the arcane shadows and stared into the torchless abyss.

"You ready?" I asked. The cave's dungeon darkness crept up my neck like a piping hot hand.

"Yes," she answered. "If it's Ystaria's will, then it's our duty."

I looked at her, taken aback by the sudden profession of faith.

"You're a follower of the Church?"

"Of course," said Kiara, smiling. "And a proud follower at that. I can't say whether or not Ystarism is a fable—I'm no apologist or theologian. But I *can* say this: faith is what manifests when the people of a struggling society come together to offer their hardships to one that transcends themselves. I'm a believer because it gives me hope in finding meaning during wartime. It's Ystaria who keeps me going through thick and thin."

"That's...an interesting reason to have faith. Well, believe what you want for all I care. But I don't suppose your goddess will light the way for us."

"If She worked in such ways, She would've obliterated the Kadaanites a long time ago."

The tunnel drilled deep into the striated wall of stone. Whatever danger lurked within, this was the crypt of the Aether Seal, a cavity that extended into unknown gloom, the site of our mission. We plodded into the darkness till daylight faded from vision. The interminable shadow engulfed us like black claws embracing new prey.

"Can't see a thing," I said as I felt the cave's wall and groped along the passage. There was no pressing sign of danger, but the loss of my ability to see put my heart at unease. I felt vulnerable, as if sinister hands could snatch me away at any moment. Often it was routine to take basic bodily functions for granted, but at times like these, when fear tried to smother you, you remembered what a privilege eyesight really is. By some extra measure of caution, I put my other hand on the hilt of my sword but kept it snug in the scabbard. The walls must have been arrayed with torches or lanterns when people still visited, but since then Senzaw Cave had become a den of midnight.

Blindly we crept deeper into the thick darkness. Every passing second was a snowballing of the air's tension. I could feel my heart pounding against my ribcage at a horrible tempo.

It was quiet.

Click-clack!

"What was that?" I said, leaping nearly to the ceiling at the sudden noise. By every last lick of self-control I contained a shout.

"Oh, whoops!" said Kiara. "I kicked a rock by accident." After a moment or two, she asked, "Hold on, are you afraid of the dark?"

"Of course not! I just...prefer being able to see."

"I'll take your word for it."

Kiara suppressed a laugh as she cooed the words. My nerves were so jangled that she thought it was funny. I breathed a sigh of relief and tried to pull myself together.

Another worry pressed on my mind that the cave might branch off into multiple paths. The inky darkness alone was daunting enough—I couldn't bear the thought of taking a wrong turn and getting lost. If Senzaw Cave happened to be more fittingly deserving of the name *Senzaw Cave System*, losing my way without so much as a matchstick would be a death sentence. The more steps we took, the more I felt like we were lost.

Just when I was about to suggest turning back, Kiara pointed out an irregularity in the blackness.

"Hello?" she whispered. "What's that?"

Up ahead, the tunnel ended, and there was a wispy blue glimmer fixed on what looked like a small monolith. We drew near it, and the glow illuminated the cold shadows. The source of the light was a glass orb that more or less matched my head in size. It was lined with sturdy metal the color of gold and had an arched handle.

"This has to be the Aether Seal," I said, plucking the glowing orb from its pedestal, upon which I found it was cool to the touch and pleasantly light.

"It must be." Kiara studied it closely. "How is this thing supposed to help in the fight against the Kadaanites?"

"Beats me, but that's not our problem. Our job is to get our hands on the Aether Seal and pass it over to the Church, nothing more. *They* can figure out what to do with it."

"Okay. Let's get out of here."

We headed back the way we came, but this time, the Aether Seal lit the way. The capacity to see my surroundings gave me the peace of mind I'd been craving since entering. My legs no longer trem-

bled, my breathing had grown less shallow, and my shoulders relaxed whereas they were previously drawn tight. Confidence grew
in me that we'd make it out unscathed. All that was left was to take
to the daylight and troop out of the belly of the cliff. It seemed the
rumors of some man-devouring curse in here were true to what
they were: rumors, plain and simple.

But suddenly the crunchy sounds of Kiara's footsteps came to a
halt.

There in the faint blue half-light, I turned and asked, "What's
wrong?"

"I have this weird feeling. I don't think we're alone."

I was sure safety was in our grasp already. This must have been a
prank devised by Kiara as revenge for the promise of breakfast I'd
earlier broken. But I didn't find her joke the least bit amusing.

"Oh, very funny. We can get breakfast after this, so come on."

But Kiara's round eyes did not narrow at my offer.

"No, something's not right. We're being watched."

Terror swallowed her, and she quaked as if she'd been thrust into
a cold pool of slush. She tried to be alert, tried to sense the location
of the danger but with little success. In an instant death seemed to
writhe about the walls. My previous symptoms of fear came flooding back. I looked this way and that, my eyes bouncing off the
dusty floor and sodden ceiling alike, but the tunnel was only a void
of dirt and stone. Whatever made Kiara prick her ears was too sly
for my senses.

"What?! Well, who's watching us?!" I asked, trying to regulate
my breathing. But when I looked at my companion, she was staring
back with a puckish smirk.

"Ha! If only you could see the look on your face!"

"You trickster! You just wanted me to promise breakfast!" While
previously I had been holding my breath, I presently sighed in embarrassment.

Kiara laughed to see her prank successful. "Sorry, but I couldn't help myself! Your fear of the dark is just too good not to toy with!"

Over the drip-drop of the intermittent tears falling from the tunnel's roof, I snorted like an angry bull and said, "Can we just leave already?" I didn't notice the slimy sensation coiling around my pant leg.

"All right, all right," she said, laughing still. "Let's—*gasp!* Look out!"

"Huh?"

But the warning came too late.

In the next moment, a sinuous purple tentacle constricted my leg and yanked me over from below. Out of instinct I dropped the Aether Seal. The arm dragged me back toward the roots of the cave, my back grated through the dirt, and the sharp edges of rocks clawing and slashing at my back agonizingly.

Kiara screamed my name as I cried out for help. But death was only seconds away—not enough time for her to catch up. It fell on my shoulders to defend myself against this assailant. I groped for my sword and drew it. Bracing my core muscles with more strength than I thought possible, I curled into a ball to reach my lower half and sliced through the hungry tentacle. The severed limb let go of me, and I watched in disgust as it flopped and wriggled about on the ground before it went limp.

I looked down the gloomy hall of stone and saw it—the terror of Maratel's villagers, the curse of the Aether Seal, the abomination of Senzaw Cave. It was a hideous beast with eight tentacles waving in the dim air like an octopus. Its arms were pointed at us, and it stared us down with a single massive eye. A circular orifice on its underside had layers of bared fangs and dripped globs of drool— this I could only take for its mouth—the most uncomely mouth I'd ever beheld. The swarthy monster growled angrily and watched us with the intent to prey, and I was left rooted to the ground with horror.

"On your feet, Mr. Nathan!" shouted Kiara, rousing me from my shock and drawing her blade.

"So this is what's been picking people off," I said. "It doesn't look keen on letting us leave. We'll have to fight our way out!"

We stood side by side with our swords at the ready, and they gleamed in the dim blue light. The artifact illuminated the cave some fathoms behind us, so we could at least see well enough to fight back. Two tentacles were flung at us. Their movement was predictable, and we slashed off their tips before they slammed into us. The monster's arms seemed to be its only weapons, which led me to my first battle plan:

"Cut off its tentacles!"

But my companion knew better. Before I could rush into battle, a pale-faced Kiara clasped my shoulder and pointed ahead.

"L-look."

My gaze followed her finger's aim, which targeted the creature's residual limbs. The enemy had hardly quailed, seemingly numb to the loss of its arms. To my absolute shock and dismay, they were rapidly regenerating. Where once our blades had bitten off the arms, the stumps regrew like a lizard's tail into the same healthy tentacles as before.

"Just my luck," I muttered, gaping at the demoralizing sight. I failed to notice the thick purple arm hurling down from above.

"Look out!"

Kiara pulled me out of the tentacle's path, and it smashed into the ground, sending dirt plumes and stone shards flying left and right. Blades of airborne rock grazed our bodies and slashed at our skin, and the hall quaked. Warm blood streaked across our faces, drawn out from our fresh cuts.

Expecting the one-eyed thing to pull back for another assault, I readied my sword. A lithe tentacle slithered past us and looped around the artifact resting in the dirt before drawing it back. The orb's royal glow highlighted the beast's body.

"Look! It wants the Aether Seal!" I cried. Our one-eyed foe

hugged the artifact fast like a stingy child resisting a demand to share his toys. "Mine!" said its greedy look.

But protecting the artifact was only a secondary aim for the creature—its leading priority was food. It stalked us with its ravenous eye like a hunter.

"Our swords are no use!" declared Kiara. "Let's run before we become a meal!"

Sage advice. I wondered if this beast was no ordinary animal. In this cold tomb of nightmares, where we two-legged beings weren't at the crown of the food chain, the notion of supreme beings bore down on me more than ever. While previously I had dismissed beliefs in transcendent bodies as folly, I now felt as if I were facing a being sent by the heavens. Supernatural entities were well beyond the engagement of mortals after all. This thing seemed to fit that description. Flight from such powers was an endeavor not much less mad than confrontation, but we had no other choice.

"Argh, all right! Let's go!"

We raced away. I stifled my thoughts of the Aether Seal, which flashed in my memory as we left the orb in the beast's care. Our mission had changed; all that mattered was survival. The Church would have to wait on its delivery.

Our legs carried us toward daylight, but the enemy was a step ahead. Its suckers clung fast to the roof, and the violet figure clambered over our heads and touched down front and center in our path. Our boots slid in the dirt to a stop. It fixed its singular eye on our delectable frames and unleashed an ear-splitting bellow with hideous raspiness.

"Roooooaaarr!"

The earthen hall rumbled, dust sprinkling down from the ceiling. Our attacker launched its arms at us, reiterating its longing appetite. We cut through the barrage for defense, but of course its limbs stretched into full health again.

"This is bad..." I lamented, afraid of how grim the situation was getting. The exit was blocked off, and there was no other way out of this dark pit of doom. The cave seemed like a steaming pan, and the air felt like seething oil for frying, rippling and splattering around me. I found myself visualizing my meats showered in spices like a juicy steak.

Spices! The word blinked many times in my head and spawned a new idea. It seemed so obvious once I saw it that I wanted to scold myself for being so blind till now. Spices were often pulverized into fine powder, but what other powder was scattered all about the place?

It was dirt.

We were holed up in a cave—a dank, dirty cave. And that slimy monster had one big eye. There was one last-ditch effort I could make, but it was now or never.

"Listen, you big ugly octopus!" I shouted, scooping a handful of earth into my palm. "We're too bland for your tastes! Here's a little cooking lesson: always season your food!"

As soon as I delivered those words, I flung the dirt at the enemy's eye. Immediately the tentacles whipped and thrashed in a tantrum. The beast's face scrunched, and it threw back its head and howled so loudly that I feared the cave's silver roof would collapse. Dust ground under its eyelid, the pain of which slackened its grip on the Aether Seal, and the blue lamp fell and rolled out of its reach.

"You need a better one-liner!" Kiara said in light of what I actually thought was quite clever.

"Whoa!" I yelled, ducking under a stray arm that swept across the tunnel's width. "Now's our chance! Let's go!"

My words preceded a beeline. I leaped into a sprint, my arms pumped like thrusting knives, and Kiara kept up beside me. Any sight of daylight still eluded us; all that lit the path to our escape was the moonlit glow of the Aether Seal. We slipped past the dazed creature's wall-like body. I lunged for the artifact and snatched it up as I strode past the spasmodic tentacles and packed it under my arm like a football. Our legs raced like fluttering wings, and very soon the beast roared like a gale. I bent my gaze round my shoulder and saw a swarm of tentacles blazing toward our fleeing figures. A terribly goatish scream rang out of me, and my adrenaline surged and kicked me into even swifter flight. Hazy streams of sunlight were visible up ahead, but the arms were gaining on us like dark fog, and I feared we wouldn't make it.

"We're almost there!" yelled Kiara.

One tentacle reached her and tried to twine up her arm, but I wouldn't let it. I nimbly swiped my sword through it and batted away the other pursuing arms.

Finally we crossed the threshold of stone gloom to golden light, it became apparent that my eyes had adjusted too much to the black nature of the cave, and they couldn't handle the sudden burst of brightness. My feet lost familiarity with the ground, and I tripped and rolled into the soft grass. There was a *thump* beside me: Kiara had tumbled to the ground in the same way.

Laying there as the adrenaline drained from my veins, my eyes adjusted, and I saw the ends of tentacles emerge from the shady depths.

"Back, you vile beast!" shouted raspy unfamiliar voices.

Two soldiers bounded past my lolled figure brandishing their spearheads and made to engage the enemy. The tentacles clumsily waved about in the air before resigning into the shadows and conceding defeat. It seemed the creature had no fancy for stirring out of its dark den, especially if it meant confronting trouble.

"Wow...you did it," said someone leaning over me from behind. Still laying prostrate, I met the eyes of the Chief Enestir, who stood over me with an astonished look playing on him. My view of him was upside-down. Evidently he had at some point decided he ought to come with the soldiers to offer aid.

"What was that thing?" I asked, my breath still ragged from the intense dash.

"An octoclops," said a soldier. "Horrific monsters known for settling in dark areas and claiming them as their personal territory.
They feed on anything that draws near."

"You don't say," I said with sarcasm as I stood up, the vivid daylight no longer bashing my eyes.

Octoclops—quite the suitable name for its appearance.

"Well, I guess that means the Aether Seal isn't cursed after all,"
said the village chief. "As for the octoclops, it's best left alone. I'll
see to it that not a soul sets foot in Senzaw Cave as long as that slimy
creature lives."

"Good," I said, helping Kiara to her feet. "I still don't see anything special about this artifact. It's supposed power seems totally
ambiguous. But we got our hands on it, and that's all that matters.
I'm glad we didn't have to leave it behind. Now, let's go back to
Cordea and get our payment."

At first, I thought the job was too easy for a hundred Merth Silvers, but after that ordeal, the payment felt unjustifiably low. The
beast had nearly rained its fangs on me, and I would've discarded
the contract had I known what was to come. But it was over now,
and there was no point bathing in regret.

Kiara and I started heading back to the village, but the chief had
something else to say.

"Um..."

"What?" I turned and looked at him.

"Who are you two?"

Ironically this was the last question I'd hoped to hear. It was a
question I was loath to answer truthfully. Having my identity kept
secret since arriving in Maratel was a source of comfort I hadn't
enjoyed in a long time. Being ignored for once was a privilege. The
freedom to exist without all those hateful stabbing looks from others gave me pleasant repose amid my life as an outcast. The risk of
Chief Enestir recognizing my name was a risk I wanted to avoid.

Kiara saw that his question made me queasy and spoke. "As servants of Our Lady Ystaria, we think good deeds are better when performed modestly," she said with a smile you might see on an angel. "I'm afraid giving our names would take away Our Lady's due glory. We're just sinners who want to carry out Her will. For fear of the sin of pride, our names are best kept to ourselves."

"Hah! Have it your way!" He said, laughing at her cajolery. "Well then, may Ystaria lead you to safe travels!

And so in the end the chief joined the rest of Maratel in believing we were an ordinary pair of nonfalia. As soon as he and his soldiers pardoned themselves and traveled down the path to the village, I noticed Kiara staring at me.

"..."

"...?"

Her lips were thinly pursed, her forehead was creased with little ravines, and there was an angry growl in the depths of her throat. Her exacting expression appeared out of nowhere. She seemed to expect a bull's-eye response, but I couldn't identify what I'd done to wreck her mood.

When it became clear what a fool I was, she delivered a playful punch to my arm.

"Ah!" I moaned, rubbing my arm.

"You said we'd get breakfast after this!"

"Oh, right."

Now I remembered. This was the price I had to pay for promising to foster her gluttony. Suddenly our stomachs rolled hungrily in unison, and we quickly looked away, blushing to our ears.

Yeah, breakfast sounded nice.

CHAPTER XI

HOLY RELICS AND STRANGE OMENS

O ur breakfast that morning was more than hearty enough to replenish our weary hearts. The meal consisted of a treat called sweet eggs, which came from birds called hraws, with tsaui cheese melted in the warm scramble, and some white bread with butter. After stuffing ourselves silly with this minuet of flavor, we hailed down a carriage for hire and set off. Since the people around Maratel didn't know my identity, the driver had no qualms about serving us as we were average customers in his view.

Since Anbizia didn't have horses, the most common animal for drawing carriages was the traxid. With their hardbodied legs they had the strength to lug huge heaps of weight for hours on end with minimal exhaustion. The wagon rolled along the road through the dingle of Vethwood, and the brambly shrubs and dense foliage shivered under the soft nibbles of the wind.

"Hahh...this ride is so boring," said Kiara yawning. She let out a small "Unf!" as she flopped down on the wagon bed's seat across from mine, apparently landing too hard.

Rolling my eyes at her klutzy behavior, I quipped, "Too bad you aliens don't have cars."

The driver, who sat on the driver's perch looking on with little interest in our conversation, twisted his head back toward me with a blank stare. I hadn't meant for him to hear my mumbling. I didn't want to reveal my alien background.

You must understand that while I viewed the Anbizians as aliens, my perspective was one of a kind. In their eyes, *I* was the alien. I was the foreigner here, the visitor from a faraway planet. That was why I preferred to keep a low profile. Having enjoyed the pleasure of Maratel's villagers mistaking me for a nonfalius, I drew the obvious conclusion that it was far more desirable for my identity to go unknown. Thus I wanted the driver in the same snare of ignorance. But when I called Kiara an alien, I may have accidentally advertised my alienness.

But before the driver could respond, his attention was stolen by a shout.

"Who goes there?!" The voice tolled some fathoms down the road. The cart had just emerged from the thick tangles of Vethwood and blundered onto a flat heath, and as they passed through the clearing a little cottage came into view with an old man standing hunched over out in front.

"It's just me, you crazy dotard!" shouted the driver. "Getting short sighted in your old age, Old Man Teppy?"

"You try monitoring all the passersby on this road!" bawled Old Man Teppy as the cart strolled past him. "It's a lot of damn work!" Two ulffs, who had been lying bored out of their skulls on the porch, picked up their heads and cocked their ears when they saw us. The pets sprang up from their languor, glided off the porch with the help of their patagia, and landed at the side of the road beside their master. They yipped at us like bratty dogs. *"Heep! Heep!"* was the sound.

"Hah! I'm sure the drudgery would have me quaking!" retorted the driver, flicking his reins.

"You youngsters have no respect for your elders! It'll get you all killed one day!" He shook his fist and cast more jeers our way as his figure fell away behind the cart, but the three of us pretty quickly stopped listening.

As the ulffs' barks slipped away to the ends of our ears and grew fainter, the driver spoke to me and Kiara. "Don't you worry about

Old Man Teppy. He's always got the cranks, but word has it that he's a real softy at heart!" With those words he resumed his attention on the road.

The wide path bent off in the distance across the field dressed in alien heather. A few leagues to the right could be seen the dark eaves of a swamp full of murk and grime, with nasty creatures so slimy and weird that you'd shudder just thinking about them. Gray slopes mottled with small clods of green stood up and frowned upon our carriage. The late morning sun watched the carriage creep across the swath of mixed vegetation, breathing a perfect amount of warmth for comfort.

Kiara tilted her head in light of my previous quip. "What's a car?"

My immediate impulse was to reply with "Never mind," but I figured that would dry up the lubricants for a lively conversation. I thought for a moment and spun up a story that I didn't call a lie but a creative tale. Surely it would be fun to tell an ignorant alien girl about my planet's advanced marvels, but I devised a way to make it even better.

"Look at how slow the traxid pulls the carriage," I said. "A car is sturdier, faster, and more obedient."

"*Squawk...*" whined the traxid as if having its pride insulted. Traxids were known for being competitive creatures.

"Oh, pipe down!" groaned the driver, who probably couldn't hear our conversation as well as the traxid could. "You can eat after we get to Cordea!"

"Wow, really?!" Kiara asked as her eyes sparkled with curiosity. "Are cars cute animals?"

"Uh...no, not really. But they're a million times more reliable and don't require as much care. They feed on a special food that no one else eats called gas. They only sleep when no one's using them, and you can wake them up on demand. Oh, and they can carry mountains more weight, too."

"Whoaaa! That's amazing! These cars sound like the coolest thing ever!"

Now I've got you! I thought. She'd fallen into my allure, and her interest was piqued.

"How fast can they go?" she asked. "Like twice as fast? Three times?"

"So fast that they're notorious for taking people's lives. They can easily be lethal if they crash, so you have to handle them carefully."

"That's so cool." Kiara exhaled a long breath of fascination. She was so captivated that her face was bright with excitement and had a sickle smile. Kiara closed her eyes as if picturing herself riding a car. "I bet they're a lot more comfortable than this wagon's hard wood."

Of course her guess was indisputably correct, but I only shrugged. "Human technology is just inimitable. Too bad I couldn't bring one to Anbizia. A car would suit someone like you."

"Hm? What do you mean?" This question was followed by another sidelong bend of her head. Her excitement was unchanged.

Now it was my turn to take a swing. After all, I deserved to get back at her for eating so much at breakfast (a breakfast bought with *my* money).

"You're so lazy, I'm sure you'd appreciate lounging around in a car during a long trip."

"Oh, you say I'm lazy?" purred Kiara. She stood and sat down beside me. She shifted closer until our shoulders kissed and our thighs pressed against each other. A mischievous smile was creeping up on her face, but what was her scheme? Would our lighthearted banter escalate to brute warfare?

I was too deep in my gibe to turn back now, so I feigned confidence and continued to press. "Uh, yep! Who was it that almost passed up a hundred silver coins because she prioritized sleeping in?"

It had only happened a few hours ago, and it was still clear in my mind. I'd been forced to yank her out of bed because she was devoid of all motivation.

What happened next was like her malice bursting out to attack me. Her smile stretched farther across her face, but before I could strategically back off, she launched her attack. With a swift and hammy motion, she dove toward me and threw her head onto my lap.

"H-hey!" I cried, startled. What was she doing? Why would she make an advance like that?

She laughed at my prudish reaction, and although I tried to push her off, her head was planted in place like a firm boulder. "Ha-ha-ha, maybe you're right," she said, shining rosily with a smile. "Since I'm so lazy, I should reclaim the sleep you stole from me this morning."

We locked eyes as her body lay supine across the wagon seat with her head resting on my thighs. I'd tried to come at her with some light teasing, and yet she accepted it with a smile. Here she was, glorifying my accusation of indolence. She seemed so utterly unbothered by how I thought of her that she was unaffected by criticism. How was I supposed to come back from that? It wasn't fair.

"And as punishment for your theft, I get to use your lap as a pillow," she declared.

"Ah, so you're a judge now? What a pleasure it's been, Your Honor," I said sarcastically.

"Think of it this way: a male ought to attend to a lady's every need and request. *That* is the natural order of things. Right now, I, the lady in question, desire a place to rest my head, so *you* have to observe my wish. Besides, snuggling up in this comfy position in a moving vehicle should give me a taste of what cars are like, wouldn't you agree?"

The princess closed her eyes as if finalizing her demands and signaling that she wouldn't hear any objections. I sighed and lifted my gaze, taking in the scenery. The sweep of pink and orange heather stretched beyond my scope of vision, and the air smelled of the last warm weeks of autumn before cold whisked in. Perhaps the sun's radiance floating in the clean blue sky would act as Kiara's blanket to bask in.

Her laziness was never enough to overthrow her cunning. She'd won our childish banter. It took severe effort not to curse myself for taking her for granted.

When we arrived in Cordea, I shook Kiara awake, and we headed into the hash of busybodies and busy buildings. It was early in the afternoon; the sun had crossed the zenith and was beginning to climb back down. I navigated the streets to our destination. At the end of the long stretch of Abafide Avenue in the market district was the towering pillar of faith on Anbizia. It was the very root of everything holy, stringing together all the moral fibers of society.

With tall spires pointing to the heavens stood Saint Abafide's Cathedral. It wasn't just any church building. This was the center of the Church of Ystaria's authority where the pinnacle of the Church's hierarchy dwelled. It was a burning hearth whose flames diffused out and coursed through the rest of the world. We stood at the foot of the entrance steps and peered up at the magnificent house of worship. The masonry was wrought from expensive trachyte and travertine that joined together in contrasting arrangements of color. All the grandness suggested that the Church's funds were nothing to joke about.

"Wow..." Kiara muttered. Her mouth was wide open in awe. "I've seen it from far away, but seeing it up close is like seeing the glory of heaven itself!"

This sounded like an exaggerated remark, but I wondered if imitating heaven was the intention of the architects. If the Church was supposed to be a shadow of heaven in the mortal world, then its followers might as well use their worship houses to mimic the infinite beauty of that realm. I didn't know much about the Ystarian view of heaven, but what was heaven if not an exquisite painting with immeasurable beauty in every brushstroke? Why wouldn't an artist want to copy such a painting?

The church bells tolled overhead, and out walked a swarm of visitors from inside. They looked like followers leaving some daily liturgy. We ascended the broad stairs leading to the cathedral and passed through the giant double doors.

Kiara's captivation rose to its summit when she saw the church's narthex. She glanced around at the building's every sublime detail with an awestruck smile—glass windows stained with bright colors, stone statues of history's most treasured saints, and walls painted with depictions of ancient stories. While the cathedral looked like a fortress on the outside, it was a palace on the inside.

There were some women dressed every bit like nuns with baggy tunics and veiling wimples, along with men wearing priestly habits. It was a very principled, respectful milieu.

Frankly I wasn't interested in the sacred site. "It says here we have to present the artifact to the supreme hierarch," I said looking at the contract, hoping to get down to business without delay.

"Um...if a liturgy just finished, he might still be in the sanctuary," said Kiara, who knew much more about the Church than I did.

Another set of doors across the narthex revealed a cavernous round sanctuary arrayed with long pews. The chamber was so huge that the nave had extra aisles between pews apart from the center. This all suggested church attendance beyond what you might think possible for any religion. The ceiling was a dome that aspired high enough to touch the sky and was enriched with even more intricate paintings. More stained-glass windows pierced the walls and let in vibrant doses of sunlight. Beyond the myriad rows of seating stood the altar, and behind that stood a giant statue watching over the area where people assembled. The statue was of a beautiful falius woman wearing robes and embroideries too luxurious even for nobility. She was made of lustrous gold and seemed to dominate the whole room. It occurred to me that Saint Abafide's Cathedral was a house not only of worship but of artistry—artistry that could make Earth's greatest painters and sculptors like da Vinci and Michelangelo hang their heads in shame.

"Wow! I've heard tell of the statue, but in all honesty I doubted that it was sculpted from real gold!" said Kiara beside me. "I can't imagine the money shoveled into this single statue, not to mention the rest of the cathedral."

The statue appeared to be playing a roia, an Anbizian lyre-shaped instrument. A halo ringed her head. All things considered—her bewitching beauty, her composition of gold, and her centering smack behind the altar—she must have been a depiction of none other than Ystaria herself.

"…?"

A disturbing feeling suddenly struck me, and I turned my head toward the left shoulder aisle. I was well inured to the energy that had so unexpectedly appeared and torn into me. I'd experienced this feeling plenty of times on this planet. It was the feeling of hard-eyed glares. What I saw across the nave was a small group of nuns, well into old age, watching us as they tossed dirt about us with private murmurs. They averted their gazes when I stared back.

Kiara was too enthralled by all the workmanship to notice any of this and rattled on about her fascination. "Hey, Mr. Nathan, do you know the story behind the roia?"

"No," I said, keeping a watchful eye on the nuns.

"Eh-heh-heh, the story is really famous, and it's one of Her greatest miracles. At the time, ancient Neiklof and Holrich were locked in a war that seemed endless. During the climax of the war's bloodiest battle, both armies had gotten swept up in the fiercest exchange in Anbizia's history. But then Ystaria appeared and walked into the crossfire! Most soldiers thought she was a rogue and tried to shoot her, but every arrow missed. She stood in the center of the fray and started playing her roia. The arrows stopped firing in an instant, and all the soldiers fell to their knees and wept at the beautiful music. Three days later, a peace treaty was signed, and the war ended, saving both nations from destruction!"

"Hm, how very noble of her," I said, mildly disinterested.

"Pardon me, sir," said a voice. We turned and were met with the flaming scowl of one of the wrinkle-faced nuns. "Do you need something?"

Of course, she wasn't really extending a helping hand. She asked the question under the veneer of politeness, but her angry expression said, "You don't belong here."

I looked toward the group of nuns yonder and saw them staring again. Their faces wore the same hatred. My words were stuck, and I wasn't sure how to respond.

"We're not accepting visitors at the moment," she said, raising her voice. "If you don't need anything, please get out. And take that nasty slime with you."

Kiara couldn't help but betray a very offended look.

"Come now, Mother Narlyn." An older man in black and purple robes that draped to the floor approached. "Such malice in the face of newcomers will never give Ystaria a good name. Her grace spreads to all walks of life, even humans and nonfalia. Anyone who follows Her is welcome to enter Repose and be saved from Sedhro."

The reverend mother looked at the man warily and pointed at me. "Saved? Father, let's not pretend there's any salvation for this sinner!"

"The most wicked sinners are the most ripe for a glorious transformation," said the man sternly, unmoved by Mother Narlyn's foulness. "Rebuking is one thing, but slandering is entirely different. Before you shun someone else for his faults...you should evaluate your own sins first."

They traded an intense stare. Then her face turned red with self-chastisement, and she yielded with a humble bow.

"Forgive me, Father. I'm so sorry for offending you."

"It's only Ystaria you offend, not me. I'll handle these guests. Another priest will attend to your penance." His last statement was a command.

Mother Narlyn bowed again and went into one of the penitential chambers, and we three were left alone. Being a reverend mother, the shepherd of her order, she couldn't afford to spend more than a moment in sin. Her state of grace was what kept the rest of her flock pure.

"Most Holy Father!" Kiara practically squealed in delight. She skittered over to the man with a smile bright as day as if she'd crossed paths with her favorite celebrity. "What an honor it is to meet you, Your Holiness!"

"Hello there! How pleased I am to meet you too," he said, smiling warmly. He extended his hand for her, and she kissed his ring. "I'm sorry about the dry welcome you received."

He showered us with polite words, but I couldn't tell if this was true cordiality or mere flattery. Kiara was giddy and relished every breathing moment of the meeting.

"Mr. Nathan, this is Prophet Eternal, the supreme hierarch," she said to me.

I exchanged the usual Anbizian greeting with the leader of the Church and gave my full name. He wore a large crest of the Church around his neck, which was an obsidian disk outlined with a silver ring. An additional arch of silver curved over the middle. The shape reminded me of pictures I'd seen of black holes.

"So, what brings you here, Mr. Tucker?" he asked. "Have you come to inquire about our faith?"

"Actually, I'm here to present this artifact from Maratel," I said, holding out the Aether Seal for him, which I'd been carrying by my waist.

"Really? Why's that?" His voice contained a tinge of suspicion, and he grew thick with confusion.

"The Church filed a contract with the Independent Mercenary Guild," I said as I showed him the contract. "Don't you know about this?"

"Independent Mercenary Guild? That's very abnormal. The Church never hires mercenaries. We have the resources to take care of our own affairs."

While the contract's strangeness had been hanging over me, hearing the supreme hierarch deny any involvement rattled me with frustration. He reigned sovereign over the entire Church, so even if a lower-ranking cleric was responsible for the anomalous contract, shouldn't Prophet Eternal know about it?

"Even if it wasn't you, do you think some other clergyman filed the contract? Could it have been another hierarch or priest?"

The Church's chain of command was structured so that one supreme hierarch sat at the top with several other hierarchs seated below him. I suppose the Church would argue that Ystaria was seated in the true highest chair, but she was canonically in the heavens, and they needed leadership in the land of mortals.

"I just can't imagine it. We just don't have any reason to hire mercenaries."

"Then if it wasn't the Church, then who...?" I trailed off and got lost in my thoughts.

It didn't seem like a fake contract, given that the Independent Mercenary Guild didn't spot any discrepancies in the contract. The bookkeepers were usually persistent about their verification process.

"Well, whether it's true or not, the contract says it's from your Church. Can't you sign it at the bottom, at least?" I asked, figuring it didn't matter as long as I got my cut of the bargain. "*Someone* has to sign it, or I won't get paid."

Anyone who filed a contract was required to send it in with the payment. That prevented the guild from sending people on missions without getting their promised cut. If no guild members accepted a contract, it would be canceled, and the money would get sent back to its original owner. This meant the money was already waiting for me at the guild. All I had to do was get a signature on this sheet of parchment. Of course this meant someone sent the guild a hundred Merth Silvers for this seemingly forged contract, but I was concerned with getting paid and cared little about solving puzzles.

Also, forging a fake signature was not an option, as it was kindred with theft. To receive payment for an uncompleted job was to rob the payer of good money, like a salesman withholding a product his customers bought. If you were discovered lying about completing contracts, you would face the wrath of the law. Avoiding getting caught wasn't possible either—there was a machine that prevented fraud. You could forge the client's signature and get paid, thinking you'd beaten the system, but everything would molder in a matter of weeks. When the client realized that his contract didn't get fulfilled nor did he get his money back, he could send a letter to the guild with his complaints. Then the bookkeepers would launch a thorough investigation, and if it turned out that you hadn't completed your mission...well, you could kiss your life as a mercenary goodbye.

"I don't see why not. I suppose there's no harm done that way," said Prophet Eternal, taking the contract. "...Ah, I'll need a quill. Pardon me a moment." He excused himself to seek out a writing utensil.

Then Kiara stole my attention and indicated the statue.

"I wish all churches had awesome decorations like this! Oh, Mr. Nathan, we should use this moment to pray and give thanks to Our Lady!"

"Uh, wha—?!"

Before I could object, Kiara seized my arm, dragged me to the statue's feet, and knelt in front of the towering figure. She forced me down to the marble floor with her.

Without a moment's delay she joined hands with me and prayed:

> *My dear Lady, I hither pray:*
> *Your faithful slave is come today,*
> *Knelt humbly here in Your presence*
> *Where faith may break to new rev'rence.*
>
> *How fain You are to heed the call*
> *of me, Your servant, weak and small.*
> *How good You are to look on me*
> *with arms of grace to set me free.*
>
> *I pray Ystaria my soul (and Mr. Nathan's) to guide*
> *by holy hands where I'll abide.*
> *This weeping world I pray You mend.*
> *My heartfelt thanks may I extend. Amen, amen.*

Not once did Kiara's tongue falter as she spoke to the heavens. Her mellow words flowed like a ballad, and her eyes were closed as she wore a gentle smile. Oddly enough, the prayer touched me dearly, and it really felt like a message that could reach the ears of a higher being. When she was finished, I took her hand and helped her to her feet. Being a man who was unfamiliar with any kind of faith, I couldn't shake off a strange level of respect for her devotion.

But some disquieting idea came into my head that raised a mystery. What put me at a loss was that the gods of Earth and the gods of Anbizia were unbeknownst to each other. No Earthling knew Ystaria, and no Anbizian knew any of Earth's gods. Why didn't these gods reveal themselves to other planets? What did that mean? And who did the Kadaanites worship, if anyone?

Figuring it was a bad idea to ruin Kiara's sunny mood, I didn't bring this up to her.

"Heh-heh. That's a traditional prayer I memorized when I went to church as a girl," she said. "I just added the part where I mentioned you. I haven't set foot in a church in a while, so I'm grateful I could pray in Ystaria's house again."

At that moment we saw Mother Narlyn emerge from the penitential chamber. She was looking at her hand, which was bleeding.

"Was her hand bleeding before?" I asked.

"Of course not," said Kiara, who was undisturbed by the sight. "We reconcile our sins by performing small blood sacrifices."

"That's incredible! But isn't that a bit much? I mean, that would be unthinkable in any of Earth's major religions!"

"It gives us motivation not to sin," she said bluntly, looking ahead. She spoke as if this was common knowledge among her fellow believers. It was difficult to respond as one who'd never been acquainted with any kind of religion.

Presently the supreme hierarch reappeared in the sanctuary with the signed contract.

"Here," he said, handing over the slip. "I'm sorry I couldn't be more helpful."

"It doesn't really matter," I said. I gave him the Aether Seal. "What matters is the job being done."

"Some mysteries just don't get solved. Too bad, really. We're all called to seek the truth, but it's times like these when we're forced to live in ignorance."

Scanning the contract to make sure it looked right, I said, "Yeah, well, for some people, truth isn't important in the face of money and power. When those things are the end goal, it doesn't matter if the truth crumbles and burns."

That was something I knew from bitter experience. Truth had been on my side since arriving here, yet it never came out and showed itself.

"A shame," he responded, frowning with disapproval. "What a shame."

My explanation, given here in the house of a goddess, was out of touch with the virtues that supported this place by many leagues. But the ways of the world were just as I described. Beyond the ornate walls of this holy place was a land consumed by pride, greed, and desire—it was an undeniable fact.

"Don't worry about this thing," he said about the Aether Seal, moving the conversation along. "I'll have the priests decide what to do with it."

"Uh...okay," I said somewhat dazed by his lax judgment. I had expected more concern from him, but being the Church's shepherd, perhaps he was too busy of a man to trouble himself with such matters.

We exchanged bows for parting's sake, and Kiara kissed his ring one more time.

"May Ystaria bless you two." He flashed a smile—the warmth of the smile pierced me suddenly. Something about his expression was more than just a friendly clergyman's smile. It was the smile of someone who, regardless of your struggles and sins, wanted the best for you. But although his smile granted me a brief sense of comfort, I couldn't bring myself to return the smile strangely.

Kiara, on the other hand, was as happy as could be. She smiled back and said gleefully, "May She bless you too!"

Satisfied, the supreme hierarch nodded and returned to his own business. I headed out of Saint Abafide's Cathedral with Kiara, whose mood was as bright as day. A glowing smile stretched across her face as she hummed along childishly. But although my companion left the building with raised spirits, my mind ached as I stepped into the sunlight. I couldn't shut up the question of how someone could get away with impersonating the Church? The impersonator had wanted the Church to secure the Aether Seal for itself, but why? Where was the gain in that? And who was harvesting those gains?

"Hm? What's wrong?" Kiara asked, noticing the unrest on my

face.

"It's just that...I can't wrap my head around that fake contract."

Could this have been the work of some clergyman who wanted the Aether Seal in the city? Or was it the doing of Maratel's villagers hoping to get rid of it? The latter made sense—they thought it was cursed after all. But that didn't explain how someone slid a fake Church order under the guild's nose.

"You worry too much," said Kiara. "You said it yourself—as long as we get paid, who's to say it's our problem?"

"I guess..."

Kiara's intuition was always reliable. By all odds she was probably right. As long as this disorder didn't come back to haunt me, I was skipping down the path to financial victory. We traversed the city till we reached the Independent Mercenary Guild to retrieve our long-awaited payment. As the cathedral stood at the tail of the marketplace, it didn't take long to reach the guild. The receptionists didn't need to know about the contract's fakeness, so we agreed to keep our mouths shut.

Upon opening the guild hall's front door, I held my breath and glanced around the room.

No sign of the Big Bad Wolf.

With a relieved sigh, I headed inside and made for the reception booth. Kiara was right behind me. Sure enough, when we submitted the signed contract, Miss Chethyr had the money. She disappeared into a room behind the booth. In a moment she came back with a plump burlap sack that jingled metallically. The coins clinked around as if they were caroling, and I could smell the mintage's silver fragrance. I opened the bag of money and stared at the shiny money. They stared back irresistibly. The haul was so satisfying that I forgot all my previous troubles.

"Right," I said after dumping the silver into my much more spacious coin purse. "Let's sit down and eat. I'm starving."

The evening was young, and mercenaries were soon to start pouring in for dinner. The guild's drinking hall was a popular place for members to dine, and it was sequenced only with big round tables that could seat multiple parties, which encouraged people to introduce themselves and mingle together. But I didn't really care to participate in socialization.

At the moment, the room was relatively empty, with only a few people sitting here and there. I sat down at an open table, and Kiara sat beside me.

We ordered some beers, which were quite brown, to kick off the evening. Alcohol eased the pain of being stuck on this hellhole of a planet. That was how I coped with this lonely despair. I wanted to go home. I wanted to return to human life. But the only way to do that was either to figure out how the wormholes worked or pray for NASA to come and rescue me. Maybe I was better off wishing for one of heaven's angels to appear and take me away.

As I took a sip of my beer, my stress forced a sigh out of me. For whatever reason, the Kadaanites wanted to destroy Anbizia, and the Anbizians wanted to destroy Kadaan back. It was a fight to the death in which I was pointlessly in the center.

We ate and drank further into the night. I was still a novice when it came to handling alcohol, so my dosage was more modest than Kiara's, who caroused away in the stuff, pouring tankard after tankard. In the meantime the building gradually filled with diners.

"Hey, can I get another round, please?" Kiara had a buoyant tone as she asked the young lad tending to our table. He looked at me tentatively, knowing full well she'd already taken a great deal more beer than your average fellow could handle. As my confusion matched the lad's, I shared with him a defeated look and shrugged my shoulders.

"R-right away, ma'am."

It had been a while since I lost count of Kiara's drinks. I wondered if I wasn't restricting her intake enough. Her debt of twenty silvers kept her in submission, so my will dominated hers. I could easily say, "No more drinks. You've had enough." She understood my dominance, but it didn't seem to bother her. She'd been so afraid when we first met. I recalled our first meeting as I watched her drink the evening away happily. At first she'd been such a shrinking violet, with not an ounce of hope, and she didn't dare step out of line. But now she shamelessly ordered drinks without a touch of concern for my wallet. The once despondent girl was so galvanic now and showed no fear in her social graces. It was simply amazing how her happiness and confidence saw such a huge boost in such a short time.

As I thought about the way she'd evolved, her tankard suddenly came down with a *clunk*, and she shrank away, her cheeks turning slightly ruddy.

"H-hey, what are you looking at...?"

I'd been staring at her for too long, and I hadn't even noticed. I cleared my throat.

"Nothing," I replied coolly, lowering my gaze to my bowl.

The bowl was filled with some buttery stew with vegetables and beans. There was also a basket of dark bread. This meal couldn't measure up to Maratel's totchin, but it was hearty enough, and its affordability was a convenient perk for guild members, making it a great bargain.

Kiara went back to the beer in her pewter tankard as I slurped some of my stew.

"Mm...this is good alcohol," she said after taking another draft.

"Is that all you ever think about?" I asked.

People often enjoyed using drink to wash down their food, but Kiara seemed to use food to wash down her drink. She was doing it all backward.

She leaned toward me, grinning from ear to ear, and said, "You're always worrying about productivity and profits, but you never kick back and relax. Just look at all these people. What do you see?"

"Everyone's chattering and stuffing themselves with food and beer," I answered after glancing this way and that. "They're indulging...pointlessly. I don't understand your point."

"I see dear people enjoying themselves after a hard day. What's the point in working hard if you never get comfy and eat the fruits of your labor?"

Her metaphor echoed the law of balance, a philosophy I didn't much care for. Her words were admirable. But her logic didn't resonate with me.

"Wouldn't it make sense to replant the fruits so that you can grow even more?"

"Of course, Mr. Nathan! But replanting *all* of them will leave you without food, and you'll starve."

We traded a sidelong stare for many uncomfortable seconds. Those words were a snare I couldn't escape this time. She had backed me into a corner, and I couldn't find any room to extricate myself. I had to think of a defense, but how?

She made a painfully agreeable point, and I squirmed in my seat uncomfortably.

"Look," she continued, slowly leaning back. "I'm not saying you shouldn't buckle down and chase your dreams. I just think you should allow yourself some enjoyment every now and then."

"Okay, okay." I raised my hands in surrender. "I'll ease up a little. But only a little." Feeling a bit more relaxed, I allowed myself to take in some more beer than usual.

The drinking hall continued to fill up with mercenaries. With the sound of men laughing and sharing drinks together, everyone was vivacious and cheery.

Everyone except me.

With everyone acting so merrily, I figured it was best to fan off the black fog around my head and take Kiara's suggestion. I tried to let the lively atmosphere influence me, and my sourness gradually deflated.

Unfortunately, the new leisure was cut short when *that human* threw open the door and sauntered inside. He was surrounded by the same women as before, who were like a pack of loyal dogs swift to follow his every command. Kiara, noticing my grated look, stiffened in alert upon seeing him and knew it was time to leave. I appreciated that she respected my grudges.

I didn't take another bite before standing up. I left a palm-sized sum of coins on the table for payment and hoofed it to the door. Kiara slugged down her remaining beer and trailed behind me. Dimitri's gaze followed me as I stormed past him; his devilish eyes haunted me. An intense strain settled on my head. I glanced back as I passed through the exit and saw him and his companions taking their seats at our exact table. He loved taunting me. With immense self-control I resisted the urge to strut over to him and rip his eyes from their sockets.

"Let's...go find an inn," I muttered drearily.

The sun had fallen below the land by now, and shadows reached over the city, which meant a long day was finally at its end. Some people in Cordea, however, worked well into the night.

We followed the road to our usual inn. Kiara lagged several strides behind me, and her footing was unsteady as she waddled and wobbled. I had to make several stops to wait for her. Something was definitely wrong. I couldn't tell what her deal was, but she wasn't being herself.

Not wanting to linger out here any longer, I swallowed my concern and waited for her patiently. Eventually we reached the inn, and I purchased a room.

We slowly climbed the stairs, until...

"Whoops!" She fell victim to her swoon and toppled over, but I rolled my arms out and caught her.

"Hey, be more careful!"

"Ah-ha-ha...you saved me." Her manner of speaking had shifted away from her earlier festivity; now she sounded like a small child. Her new voice sounded as though every mite of sophistication she'd learned over the years had been suddenly cast out so that she was little more than an animal of raw callowness. She clung to the railing and tried to walk but quickly stumbled.

"Geez! What's the matter with you?!" I asked after breaking her fall again.

My nerves bulged with annoyance. Her ungainly behavior was like some bizarre drama in a theater. If this was one of her pranks, it wasn't funny. I wasn't in the mood.

The next person to speak was the bored innkeeper, who stood behind his counter across the lobby trying to stay awake. "Can't you humans smell? She reeks of so much alcohol, it's practically running in her veins. I can smell it from here!"

"Oh," I said, realizing his implication.

When I looked closely at Kiara, I couldn't believe my prior ignorance. She was totally in a stupor! She had trouble staying upright, her cheeks were burning red, and she looked as though she might nod off at any moment. I pressed my palm against my forehead in irritation. She had always handled alcohol so gracefully, but tonight she must have grown too cocky.

Clutching her firmly by the arm, I dragged her up the stairs. She struggled pathetically like a weak lamb, and it was hard to keep her from losing footing, but I kept my grip squeezed tight. When we reached the top, I let her go, and she grasped enough strength to stagger into our room.

"Ah...we made it," she said, slurring her words. She toppled onto her bed clumsily.

"Yeah, yeah. Whatever." I sat at the end of my mattress as I unlaced my boots.

"Say, what are we doing tomorrow?" she asked in singsong. It surprised me that she had the mental clarity to think about tomorrow.

"We'll start by checking out the contract board at the guild. There should be some good work for us."

"Mmm...can't we sleep in a little?"

She rolled on her side atop her sheets to face me, looking enough the delicate girl for a single rush of wind to push her off the bedside. For an alien, her appearance really was emblematic of a youthful lass. Looking up at me, she awaited my response.

"No. Do you think the Kadaanites wage war against this planet by sleeping in?" I wasn't thinking much about my words, knowing it probably didn't matter since she was drunk.

But her reaction was surprisingly precise for her current state. Her gaze tipped to the floor, giving her a heavy look of grief, and she moaned quietly in displeasure. She may have been putting on a desperate masquerade to play the act of begging, but such tricks wouldn't work here.

"Besides, our work for the guild contributes to the war effort," I added. "The guild donates a lot of money to the military, and our labor grants it the funds to make those donations. We have to do our parts. If we don't, the Kadaanites will slaughter me, you, and all your loved ones."

Kiara's expression seemed to shatter at the end of my words. She closed her eyes as if trying to forget a terrible memory. Her emotion had so suddenly climbed out of what seemed like an inactive mind. Even in the dim candlelight, her new sadness was clear as day.

Where had her dungeon depression come from? I'd grown used to her usual high spirits, but now she mirrored the same desolate Kiara I had seen when we first met.

"What's with that face? Waking up early really isn't that bad if you have discipline. It gets easier when you do it more consistently."

"It's not that," she said, sitting up.

"Then come on," I told her, trying to put her mind somewhere where she wasn't so bothered. "Keep your head up."

Kiara did as I told her, looking up at me, but her sadness hardly abated. She gazed at me like I was the only person who could comfort her.

"What's wrong?" I asked. At this point it dawned on me that neither of us could ignore the problem. Something was ravaging her heart. If it wasn't my schedule's strictness weighing on her, what was it?

Before she spoke, her gaze dropped slightly. She looked as though she wished her next words were the greatest lie she would ever tell. "It's just...that last part you said..."

The room fell dead silent. There in the quivering candlelight, Kiara's eyes glowed in a way that stabbed me. What I saw next made my gut close in on itself. My first instinct was to look away from the sight, but I was too paralyzed to do so.

She was smiling.

It wasn't one of those vibrant, joyous smiles I'd grown familiar with lately. It was a forced smile, full of despair and loneliness. Her gaze was downcast as she balled her fists, clenching the bedsheets tightly. Looking at the pain in that smile was unbearable. I'd never even imagined a smile could contain such torment. Tears stood in her eyes.

Kiara didn't often show this side of her—what had triggered it? Surely it wasn't the alcohol. I quickly sifted through my memories to uncover what had hurt her.

"We have to do our parts. If we don't, the Kadaanites will slaughter me, you, and..."

The realization slammed into me, causing me to suck in a quick breath full of regret—the regret of having taken my own word choice for granted.

"...and all your loved ones."

Her smile grew terrifyingly large upon noticing I'd connected the dots. Recalling such a dark past could only set off your emotions far beyond rationality. Seeing her act like this was agonizing, though I knew she suffered far worse.

And then finally came Kiara's soft, shaky voice.

"That last part...it already happened."

Her smile broke. It flipped over flat, and she gritted her teeth as her grip on the sheets tightened. Her tears sparkled like gems as they squinted out of her eyes, the glassy droplets diving onto the gray sheets one by one.

What had happened to her drunken self? All those drinks had possessed her like a clumsy spirit just moments ago, but now she was fully alert and in control. Had she been faking it all along? Why would she feign drunkenness in the first place? At first, I hadn't put much thought into my words, assuming the conversation with the intoxicated girl would be forgotten by morning. But my duty was different now. I had to select my words very carefully to avoid bungling my response.

Taking a deep breath, I stood and approached her side of the room. Kiara glanced at me once before flinching, and cast her gaze down again. I put her hand in mine and pulled it up from the mattress.

"You've had a lot to drink tonight," I said, speaking gently for comfort. After a deep pause, I asked, "Is it the pain of being so lonely that draws you to all that alcohol?" By now I was positive that she wasn't drunk, but there was no questioning her affinity for drinking. It was just now occurring to me why her fondness of alcohol was so strong.

There was another thing I decided to ask: "Were you forced to take those clothes from that back alley because you were so poor and afraid?" She had done it just before we'd met. The city guards had accused her of stealing someone else's clothes, even though they were merely the clothes I'd abandoned. She would've been executed if I hadn't stepped in and bailed her out. There was a reason she'd taken those crude rags in the first place—she couldn't scrape up anything better.

"It's always..." Her voice was strangled, and her words hesitated to slip out over the river of tears.

Realizing there was no stopping the tempest of sorrow, I sat beside her and drew her in. As I held her she melted into my arms and buried her face in my chest.

"It's always so cold. I've been all alone for...*sniff*...months now. I...I don't want to live like that anymore."

Her crying turned into sobbing. I didn't have any experience when it came to comforting women, so I listened quietly to her woes. I stroked my hands through her hair, which was clammy and smooth like the rest of her slime-body.

"Sometimes I close my eyes...*sniff*...I see them standing before me. I miss them...Mommy...Daddy..."

Taken from her by the Kadaanites.

The pain of losing your parents was something I was all too familiar with. The winds of loneliness had whipped and buffeted me, and I'd had to endure it all alone. There was no one to console me—no one to sop up the pain. I didn't want anyone else to experience such emotional torture. Kiara had said she was cold, but it was me who could offer a little bit of warmth.

"Did you know I lost my parents too? They died a long time ago, and it's been tough to move on."

Kiara was too deep in sorrow to respond. A piece of me wondered whether my words even registered in her ears, but I felt it appropriate to find common ground with her anyway. Our loneliness was a suffering we shared.

"Things have been really hard without them," I continued. "But I just have to press on...because I know that's what they would've wanted."

Many people believed their departed loved ones were watching over them. It was a belief that spurred them to toil away in spite of their loss, knowing their efforts were to honor their bloodline. This was also why so many people were wont to turn to the gods—Ystaria, in Kiara's example.

My jacket soaked up her tears, and she embraced me tighter as if I was the only person she had left.

"But...I just can't bear it anymore. I don't know how to move forward knowing the Kadaanites are out to get me. I'm going to die alone at their hands...and there's nothing I can do."

"You're not alone. You said it yourself, didn't you? We can survive together."

We had agreed to work together to survive. Lifting the pain off of her was just part of that bond.

She was still wrapped in my arms. Her outpouring emotions slowly alleviated. Though still sniffling, she calmly pulled back and turned her gaze up at me. Her face was all sloppy with tears.

"Forgive me," she said, mopping some of the gunk off her face. "I shouldn't be crying to you like this. I'm sorry."

"Not at all. I understand."

Kiara returned my words with a tiny nod and looked down shyly. The crying must have taken a toll on her, and that alcohol was probably influencing her slightly even if her supposed drunkenness had been an act.

"Let's get some sleep," I said, standing, and she stood too. "It's getting late."

Feeling better, she gave a new smile—a *real* smile this time. Seeing her back to her normal self was relieving like a sudden breeze on a hot day. It seemed her rush of emotions had made her forget about waking up early, so that was another victory for me. But when that triumphant feeling reached me, I quickly realized only a scumbag would have such thoughts at a time like this.

Well, everyone thought of me as scum anyway, so what did that matter?

Even so, I could feel my mind changing about our wake-up time.

Maybe we can sleep in just a little, I thought.

"So you weren't really drunk, were you?" I asked, just to be sure. "What was the point of playing pretend?"

"Eh-heh-heh," she gave a timid, girlish laugh. "I'll give you exactly *one* guess." Then she turned away and faced her bed, silently expecting an answer.

"Hmm..." I put my hand to my chin. "I feel like I've passed a great test with flying colors."

I had figured out why she faked it. I had cracked the code.

She turned her head with another smile, bigger and brighter this time. It was a childish smile, a smile that emitted the rays of the sun, a smile that aroused the masculine desire to protect a lady, a smile that glittered with that youthful purity and charm so treasured by every adult. "Your kindness is a real treasure," she said. Then with a sudden burst she shoved me away, and having no time to brace myself I staggered back before toppling onto my bed.

"Whoa—! Hey!"

Kiara was already giggling again and skipping playfully to her bed. I exhaled a sigh at that childish side of her. We got into our beds, beyond ready to get our much-needed rest, and I blew out the candle beside me.

Her comment was the answer to my question. Kiara had feigned drunkenness because she wanted to know if she could truly trust me. Anyone could look out for her in her most clearheaded state, but it was the mark of a true gentleman to care for her when she was so fragile and vulnerable. She wanted to be sure that even when the effects of alcohol invaded her system, I wouldn't abandon her. It was a test, and I passed. Having someone to trust in this world was greater than all the treasures or riches a man could claim. Now she undoubtedly felt more secure in my presence.

Still, I wasn't stupid enough to think she *enjoyed* abiding by me. Her debt forced her into submission, and it was my will alone that kept her in shackles. Even if she was grateful for my petty acts of comforting, she'd be right to fly in a heartbeat should her chains ever be shivered.

I went to sleep that night to the sound of Kiara's soft-trickling breath, which had a soothing rhythm in the night's silence, but at some point she drifted off, and her usual snores took over. Luckily I could sleep through those noises.

Later in the night's final hours, I got a wake-up call.

Clang! Clang! Clang! Clang!

The screaming toll of the bells jolted me awake. It was a far more ear-shattering sound than any terrestrial alarm clock I could recall, and I was quickly roused to fury given I had planned to sleep longer.

"Guh...what the hell? What's happening?" I grumbled groggily, scrubbing my eyes.

Only an idiot would try to sleep through the nonstop clangor. After furiously throwing off my sheets and stamping over to the window, I flung it open and peered into the early morning gloom to see what the rumpus was. In the distance, at the end of Abafide Avenue, the cathedral's bell tower reached for the clouds, and the bell on top swayed back and forth like a swing, carrying its echoes across the entire scope of Cordea. But otherwise the city was silent and rather eerie. The sun was just peeping over the margin of the land, and the ghostly aura whirling through the streets made me shudder.

"Hey...what's going on...?" Kiara asked, anxiety paling her face as she sat up in bed.

Something ugly, it seemed, but what?

Everyone had woken up to the clattering bells. We all craned out of our windows, trying to make sense of the situation, trying to judge what was so horribly wrong for the cathedral to cause such a disturbance. My eyes roved the empty streets to see if anyone was out there. Farther down the cobbly pavement, a lone soldier rushed up and down the streets with a desperate cry:

"Everyone, wake up! Please wake up! The Kadaanites are advancing on the city right now! All civilians must prepare to evacuate!" He flew past each building as he spread the urgent news.

Meanwhile all the people stood rooted with horror behind their sills, fear writ large on their faces, looking at one another as if troubleshooting their hearing, trying to confirm whether their ears were right. I slowly backed away from the window and looked at Kiara, who stared into deep space, turned to stone by the soldier's horrible tidings. Her eyes were pulled wide open, her mouth trembled ajar, and she stood in a cold sweat.

The ghosts of her past.

They had come back to haunt her.

A bloody massacre was on the horizon. The Kadaanites didn't take any prisoners; this city was little more than a graveyard waiting to be filled.

So, what to do?

We'd accepted duties as mercenaries, so the answer was clear. We'd accepted duties as pawns doing our part in the struggle for the good of tomorrow. We'd accepted duties to sacrifice everything to do the right thing. We'd accepted duties to fight until our dying breaths.

I knew what I had to do.

With sweaty hands clutching my sword, I dashed out of the inn and prepared for battle.

CHAPTER XII

THE KADAANITE
ON A PALE HORSE

Howling civilians streamed past me as they fled for safety. I ran the other way, charging through the streets to battle. When I reached the city walls, the alien invaders were already gathered in vast hordes outside the city. The Kadaanites trampled Dirul Field and all its green fairness with their filthy boots.

Their appearances were foreign yet humanoid. They had sea-gray skin, with perfectly contrasting dark gray, navy, or black hair. They stood as bipeds with thick but short tails, and their ears pointed up like spikes. Their colorless frowns made them look as if their innocence had drained long ago.

I saw the massive mob from behind the battlements atop the walls. The Kadaanites used catapults to hurl artillery into the city. Staying untouched by the raining fire was easy enough when sticking near the walls; the enemy was aiming deeper. The Anbizian soldiers traded arrows with the enemy from behind cover. Commanders barked orders trying to get their men in a proper formation, but fear and panic was too thick in the host for any coherent thinking.

"General Prachit!" A trooper came scrambling up to a higher-ranked commander, huffing and puffing, trying to catch his breath, and his face was deathly anxious. "Things are worse than we thought, sir! The Kadaanites have formed a perimeter around the city! We can't evacuate any civilians!"

Cordea's civilian population outnumbered the soldiery by a huge margin. If their escape was sealed off, Anbizian casualties would soar. Worse, the fall of Cordea was no different from the fall of Neiklof itself, and if that happened, Anbizia's chances of winning the war would be crunched nearly to zero. Anbizia hung over a pit of fire by a lone thread—a thread that would be severed if we failed today.

"Damn!" cursed General Prachit. "Then get them to the cathedral! The building won't go down from catapult-fire alone! They'll have protection there! What about His Majesty?!"

"We evacuated King Frieval a while ago, sir!"

Are you kidding?! I screamed in my mind.

Gone already! What kind of leader abandons his people to die in battle? We were in the depths of the trenches where he could show off the height of his leadership, but instead he chose flight like a frightened animal!

"My troops are already working on directing the civilian traffic to the cathedral!" said the soldier. "But it's dangerous with them lobbing catapults and arrows onto our heads!"

"Set up cannons along the walls!" said the general. "Our fire will be more effective from up here! Give those aliens a taste of their own medicine! Use explosive artillery!"

"Yes sir!" The soldier ran off to implore the help of his comrades to set up the cannons.

However, I was positive they wouldn't be ready anytime soon. Priming cannons around the edge of this huge city was like building a house one brick at a time. Such an endeavor would take too long if no one could stall the enemy's advance. At the same time, however, girding cannons with explosives would surely give our foe a keen scare as they were sitting ducks in the field. All we needed was time.

The current effort seemed futile. Arrows lashed down blindly into the alien horde, most of which glanced off their targets' shields, but a few hit their marks. The enemy answered with their own storm of arrows, thick as a cloud. I had taken up a bow and took part in the heated exchange, but my shot was untrained and fired with little luck.

It seemed like the Kadaanites had appeared suddenly from deep mists, which was curious. They didn't control any countries surrounding Neiklof, so they couldn't have marched here from the nearest border without pushing through several other countries first. Strategically their siege seemed so reckless yet so ingenious at the same time.

"Why are we being attacked now of all times?" I growled over the hissing din of the battle.

"I think I can guess what they're here for." The voice was instantly recognizable as the pure, gentle voice of prelacy. It was Prophet Eternal, who had arrived at the scene moments ago. With him he carried the Aether Seal. He shot me a wink and a smile as he walked by nonchalantly.

"Good morning, General!" he declared, upbeat as ever. "Lovely sunrise, eh?"

"I'm glad *you* had time to enjoy it, Your Holiness," replied General Prachit bitterly. While there had been a sunrise, black clouds were gathering over the sun's regions, and thunder rolled in the distance. "What are you doing here? Shouldn't you be at the cathedral, standing by the sanctuary!"

"We can't win this battle without the powers of the heavens! And also, I have a theory," said Prophet Eternal. He approached the edge of the wall and stood in a gap in the battlements. Holding the Aether Seal high above his head, he captured the attention of all the Kadaanites below. Its blue glow grinned like a hot star. The enemy stopped firing as if spellbound by the artifact's allure.

"Demons of Kadaan! Our Lady Ystaria is frowning on you! Tell me, are you after this holy artifact?!"

Moments after he spoke, an arrow came whining over the parapet at his head. That was their answer. He sidestepped the arrow nimbly, and it glided past him, crashing into a building's window and shattering it. Having narrowly avoided death, he stepped away with a wry smile. The two forces resumed volley of arrows as quickly as they'd stopped.

"See how the artifact enthralled those vermin?" he asked the general.

"Ah, I'm sure this discovery will save us all!" the general hissed sarcastically, unthrilled about the holy man's injudicious methods. "And what should we do with your finding? You think their hunt will end if we just hand it over?" Suddenly a stray arrow whistled past General Prachit's ear within a mere inch. He gave a yelp and ducked for cover. "It's not safe up here, Your Holiness! Get yourself to the ground!"

The supreme hierarch nodded and descended from the wall to the surface. Figuring my bowmanship was worthless, I pulled away and hurried to the ground too, where terrified civilians took shelter behind the city's thick walls. The artillery and arrows flinging down into the city couldn't hit them there. Men sat miserably with their heads in their hands, children clung to their mothers crying, and soldiers desperately shouted to try and convert the chaos into order.

An old man blathered about how our fate was already sealed. "There's no hope left for us! We're doomed! Doomed, I tell you!" It certainly felt that way. Cordea was now our tomb, locked shut and unopenable from the inside.

All I could see were disordered streets. The air had a fresh scent of suffering. Civilians cowered for their lives behind cover while the groans of the wounded were audible as medics tended them. Black spires of smoke rose from buildings set aflame by catapult-fire and coiled up into the dark clouds above. Seeing all the chaos and misery made me want to curl up and let my nerves shatter.

Saint Abafide's Cathedral was a stout and sturdy building. No doubt the civilians would find some relief from the artillery. But making a run for the sanctuary was suicide with the relentless hail of projectiles.

It was a gray-faced Kiara who then said to me, "We have to help these people." I knew she'd formed that judgment from the scraps of her past trauma. She didn't want anyone to suffer at the hands of the Kadaanites as she did. For that reason, she hadn't joined me atop the walls and instead worked on steering the civilian crowds to cover.

"They're getting closer!" cried a soldier atop the wall. Time was withering.

I pressed my fingers to my forehead, thinking fast. If there was a way to make the Kadaanites stop firing on the city for a few minutes, it would open a window for the people to flee to the cathedral.

And I knew they had their eyes set on the Aether Seal.

Suddenly an idea clicked. There was one way.

But as I mentally tried to slap together the pieces of a plan, an explosion thundered near the ground just beyond the city walls. The earth itself shook. Then there was another boom of the same species. The roaring blasts repeated and sounded like they occurred in the same place each time. This was new. While previously the enemy's catapults had barraged the Cordea's depths, they hadn't targeted anything near the city's skirts. I looked toward the area of interest, smitten with confusion, but all I saw were ghastly faces brimming with fear.

"Get away from the wall!" a soldier wailed at the civilians taking cover. "They're trying to smash through the—!"

Before he could finish, a huge stone sent by the catapults tore through the wall and took out the distressed soldier. The civilians in its path shrieked but were swiftly silenced, for it ripped through them before crashing into a building. The stone's gray face was fouled with their blood. This was the face of war—the death toll had so casually surged in a heartbeat. It would only get higher from here.

And now there was a perfect opening for the enemy. They had breached the wall, their entry was imminent, and the streets were about to become hot with sword combat.

"Here they come!" shouted General Prachit, who was still atop the wall. "Sergeant Linzer, you're in charge down there! Don't let a single bastard through! Take the fight straight to them!"

"I hear you, General!" replied a soldier on the ground who must have been Sergeant Linzer. He faced his men. "This is your moment, gentlemen! Chaaaaarge!"

All the men met his shout with a fierce cry. "Eyahhh!" they roared, and they rushed into battle, brandishing their swords at the enemy. Brazen horns blared. Linzer's men sped through the hole in the wall and charged. The alien attackers surged forth in response. The two waves met at the foot of the walls, and every sword flashed dimly in the morning light, thirsty for the blood of their targets. Blades swung wildly. Men on both sides dropped in the grass like insects. Inevitably some Kadaanites slipped past the combat and pushed through the wall, taking the battle straight to Cordea's streets.

As the city descended into a mad scrum, the Kadaanites, without hesitation or deliberation, spilled the blood of whatever Anbizian was closest to them, be it soldier or civilian. Men, women, children, all of them—the Kadaanites didn't discriminate. Some tried to run, only to be caught. Others yielded and begged for their lives, only to be denied. Torn limbs and severed heads, spilled organs and extracted bones all plastered the stone roads with crimson stains, and shrill screams rang in the streets. The sounds of innocent people being slaughtered like cattle were haunting.

Nothing could be done about the ensuing carnage. Everyone was caught in a bloodbath that served to feed its own flames, and it all made me shake with rage. Kiara and I stood firm together and cut down any Kadaanite that targeted us.

If I wanted to enact any kind of plan, I had to do it now. If someone could draw enemy fire away from the city, the civilians could break away from the outskirts and hurry for the cathedral, and I could also buy time for the soldiers to set up cannons.

Some soldiers rode their traxids into battle. The beasts could pull carriages with an ocean of strength, but they were also quick on their feet. *Yes!* I thought. Their speed was perfect.

Locating a vacant traxid that hadn't yet entered battle, I mounted it and clutched its reins. Then I trotted it over to the supreme hierarch. Being the great shepherd of the Church, he had a protective ring of soldiers surrounding him.

"Old man!" I barked. "Give me the Aether Seal!"

He shot me a ruffled look as I interrupted his prayers. I snatched the artifact from his hands.

It was time to turn the tide of this battle. So far, the Kadaanites had been pushing forward like a legion of bold lions, and Anbizian strength waned. War was an art that delved much deeper than proud swordsmanship or plentiful forces; victory demanded the ingenuity of a master tactician. Victory demanded the wisdom of a sage. Victory demanded the courage of a true hero. That was what I truly believed, and I was tired of kneeling before this incompetent chain of command. I wanted to do the right thing, even if it meant straying from the conventional ways of the world.

"General!" I called from below. Atop the wall he gave me his attention. "I'm going to draw enemy fire! It'll buy you all some time! Have your soldiers cover me!"

A look of surprise conquered him for a moment, and then he nodded and relayed the plan to his men in a bellowing voice. Here are the orders he gave in full:

"Everyone, listen up! The human down below is going to distract the enemy and buy us some time to prime the cannons! Your new job is to give him covering fire so he can hold out as long as possible! The longer he survives, the more time it'll give us! In other words, don't let the enemy kill him!"

Kiara, astonished by my recklessness, gasped and tugged my pant leg with pleading eyes. "Wait, Mr. Nathan! What are you thinking?! This is suicide! You can't just throw away your life here!"

Looking at her calmly, unmoved by her emotional weight, I saw good light in those eyes, those sweet blue eyes. They were the eyes of someone leagues more deserving of life than a reprobate like me. If someone didn't change the course of this battle, that bright light in her eyes would be smothered by the Kadaanites forever. I couldn't allow that light to stop shimmering.

"Kiara..." I said, trying to tune out all the risks. "...My life has been meaningless ever since the day I arrived on this planet. If my life didn't have meaning, neither will my death. But if I die doing this, I'll be giving *your* life meaning, and then you can live to give meaning to my death. Get these civilians to safety. When the artillery stops, that'll be your cue."

"But...what if you..." She was on the verge of tears.

"At this rate the Kadaanites will obliterate this city! Someone has to step up and lead. If no one else will do it, I will."

Without giving Kiara another chance to protest, I pulled the reins and had my traxid face the breach in the wall. I faced the prairie of alien invaders. Many seemed to be howling and jeering derisively in their unintelligible tongue, seeing the Aether Seal in my hand, certain of their ability to wrest it from my hands. Their savage eyes stared at me, bloodlust swimming in their eyes.

There was a scared voice in my head preaching, *Oh God, Nathan, what are you doing?! You suicidal maniac!* I took a long deep breath, preparing myself for the plunge. If I lost my nerve in this critical moment, I'd surely be slain in the first ten seconds.

"All right, boy," I said to the traxid after gathering my wits. "Your new name is Miles, and I'm taking you for a run. Now go, Miles! Go!"

I flicked the reins. Miles the traxid sprang away like a stone from a slingshot. His legs carried me into the Kadaanite-infested breadths of Dirul. They watched me, frozen stupid by my bold play.

"Over here!" I held the Aether Seal aloft and yelled at the top of my lungs. "You want it?! Come and take it!"

I swerved to the left and sped past the rows of Kadaanites. A shout rang from the horde: "*Hrosnågt ontkúras en vropé!*" I didn't understand the exact meaning, but I quickly gathered that it was an order to concentrate fire, for every enemy bow riveted on me in an instant.

Beyond their knowledge, my plan was working. With the enemy distracted, the Anbizians could mow them down with archery. A shower of arrows knocked down many Kadaanites who had let down their guard focusing on me. Furthermore, my decoy lightened the load of the soldiers engaged in sword combat, for the Kadaanite archers were too distracted to reinforce their blade-wielding allies.

Darts fluttered past my ears. Miles's claws thudded against the grass like a rolling drumbeat, so swift and so adroit. Well-placed shooting on the enemy's part seemed unlikely, but the possibility made my nerves boil with anxiety! I quickly gained a nervous habit of spurring the traxid on with the reins over and over.

The catapults stopped firing; their operators took up bows to fire on me. Prophet Eternal's theory was correct. Their eyes were bent on both Cordea and the Aether Seal alike. But why?

Kiara should have been seeing the civilians to the cathedral by now. I had no way of knowing how many were still breathing, but I hoped my efforts wouldn't go in vain.

Screeching wind streamed my hair back as I barreled along the ocean of aliens like a blur. It seemed impossible for the enemy to land a shot with my wild speed. Even so, I lent myself no liberty to slow my flight.

But suddenly, with a dart an enemy archer sprang into my path.

"Uh-oh!" I screamed unconsciously as he took aim. I was square in his line of sight, speeding toward him too fast to maneuver astray. His bow twanged.

For a moment I saw myself dead. But soon it was apparent that Miles and I were unpierced, still racing through the battlefield at full speed. Astounded by my safety, I reflected on how I survived. The arrow's nose bore down on my head, but the traxid sensed the danger and, as if clearing a hurdle, hopped over the arrow and the archer in a magnificent explosion of height. How brilliant these creatures were for how dumb they looked!

"Watch yourself, human!" shouted General Prachit from the wall. "They have tuskers!"

"Tuskers?" I asked wearily. Then I saw the emerging threat. A furlong ahead, a small company of Kadaanites saddled up unfamiliar animals. They were massive beasts with huge hooves, big round noses, and long tusks like boars. Their chestnut bodies were shaped like pumas with tufty tails. The formidable sight moved me with self-reproach as I started to reconsider the whole plan. Undoubtedly these animals, these tuskers, were native to Kadaan—yet another tool in the enemy's arsenal. Judging by the saddles, I could tell my foes were going to mount them and chase after me. But my trajectory was set, and I had no choice but to rush along. I streaked past them, and with bows in hand the riders brought up my rear in hot pursuit—I was now their fugitive. They seriously wanted this artifact, but why?

My flight became a race: it was Miles the traxid against the tuskers, and it was one against three. While I had a strong start, my lead was tightening. My hopes for survival were wilting. Then an arrow from behind flew over my head, and had I not ducked, it would've struck me clean. The arrow had been shot by my pursuers—they rode as jockeys with bows. This was the closest call yet, and at this rate it was only a matter of time before one of them worked out just the right aim.

When I peered back, they were practically on my tail. At this distance a good shot was very landable. I had to shake them off somehow, and quickly.

There was only one way to win this race. I'd dashed so far around the city's perimeter that I was approaching the fresh blue of Lake Dirul. On one end of the lake was a low bank, but its other side was elevated by a high bluff. The bluff was nearly fifteen fathoms high, so the drop-off down to the water was huge.

And that was the side of the lake I so happened to approach.

The leader of my hunters fitted an arrow to his bowstring, took aim, and drew it back.

"Hey, big guy!" I shouted at my traxid, warning him of the approaching leap. "I hope you know how to swim!"

As I approached the fringe of Lake Dirul, an emphatic voice sounded from the city walls.

"Fire! Fire the cannons now!"

And as my pursuer's bow twanged and the arrow ripped toward my head, the feeling of stable ground beneath me vanished. Miles had taken the leap. I roared in terror, not knowing whether this dive would be the death of me.

Whoosh! By some divine miracle, the arrow narrowly avoided me.

Boom! As I went airborne, a fireball rolled into the sky behind me where my pursuers followed.

Splash! My vision was blurry with motion, so I was only dimly aware of the happenings in the battlefield, but the dark cold immediately wrapped around my body. I only realized I was underwater when I started gurgling.

I tried to swim up, but...

"—!"

A pair of arms flung around my neck and jerked me further under. It tried to strangle me. I already couldn't breathe, but having someone constrict my neck didn't help. Who this assailant was, I didn't know, but there was no time for musings. I struggled against the pair of arms and, using the Aether Seal that I had held onto, struck my foe across the face. His grip came loose, and I wrestled with him under the cold water. But this breathless combat was a race against time; I needed to handle this threat fast for the sake of air. As we fought with bare hands, he drew a dagger and swung at me. By a stroke of sheer luck I blocked his swipe with the Aether Seal. Its frame was stronger than stone, and the knife glanced out of his hand. Without thinking but determined to survive, I snatched the knife in the water before it sank...and before he could reclaim it. Before he could grope for another tool of defense, I immediately punctured his neck. Blood spewed out of the wound, painting the surrounding water red. He stopped moving and sank down to the lake's roots, and my next instinct was to find air. My ears popped, and my muscles drained of energy rapidly, but with all the willpower I could muster I fought not to pass out as I swam up toward the light.

"*Gasp!*" A blast of fresh air filled my lungs as the water opened around my head. "Hah...hah..."

When I examined my attacker's body, I recognized it as the same rider who nearly shot me before I was flung into the lake. He must have taken the leap right behind me. The tusker he'd been riding was already crawling ashore. It shook the water off itself like a dog and ran away grunting in fear.

Boom! Boom! Boom! The battlefield roared with a clamor that tore my ears, and clouds of fire billowed up over Dirul without relenting. The realization dawned on me, and I looked toward the city to see the cannons primed and blasting explosives left and right. Each shot could launch away a whole cluster of Kadaanites at a time, blowing their bodies asunder and tossing their torn chunks into the air. I figured the artillery had taken out my other two pursuers before they could join me in my swim.

With most of the enemy still out in the open, there was nowhere for the sitting ducks to take cover. But the battle still raged, and I was still in shape to fight, so I paddled to the shore. Miles the traxid was already waiting on the wet shingle.

"I'm glad you know how to swim," I panted, mounting him. "Well now, I hope you have enough strength to give me a ride back to the city gates." We were both dripping wet and still huffing for air, but I didn't have time to dry off.

As I steered my traxid toward the city, a blunt but heavy cry came from a Kadaanite commander: "*Îksholé!*" Then all the Kadaanites turned tail and dashed away, and the enemy line receded from the walls. While I knew nothing of the enemy's tongue, I was certain of that sole word's meaning: *Retreat*.

"I can't believe it!" A soldier's faint cry reached my ear. "The Kadaanites are retreating!"

"Kill them all!" replied General Prachit. "Show no mercy to that cancer!"

None of the soldiers stopped shooting despite the retreat. The sky remained thick with arrows and cannon-fire. In a fight to the death, scaring the enemy into retreat wasn't enough—the goal was total extermination.

When Cordea's north gate was in sight, I pulled my reins, and the traxid slowed to a stop. The ground shook as the explosions blasted gigantic waves of dirt and rocks into the air, stirring up spectacular fog-like rags of dust that blanketed the field. I watched the brilliant sight as the alien invaders ran for their lives. While previously Kadaan's legion had laid siege to our city without fear, the raining fire brought out their cowardice.

Eventually all the Kadaanites had flown, and the firing finally ceased. Any enemy that hadn't retreated was sprawled dead in the field. The grassy sweep was like a massacre, at this point more red than green, and I almost couldn't help but feel bad for them—*almost*.

Soon, all was silent. The deafening sounds of explosions had so quickly shifted to the quietness of the cool morning that the world suddenly felt surreal. Why weren't the soldiers in Cordea cheering and celebrating? We won, didn't we? They had fended off the most ruthless, wicked force known to the galaxy, and yet an oppressive hush fell abroad.

"Human!" called a voice. "Human, listen to me!" The voice was from an Anbizian soldier laying among the dead Kadaanites. His body was pierced with many arrows. It was Sergeant Linzer, the man who had led his men into sword-combat.

I approached him on traxidback before alighting and kneeling by him. "Sergeant! We won. Your valor wasn't in vain. You fought well."

"No!" he bawled, grabbing my shirt by the collar and drawing me close. "This battle was doomed from the beginning. I've met my end, but you'll all follow soon enough. *He's* here."

"Who's here?" I asked, startled.

"Get everyone to safety...before it's too late. I don't know what he's planning, but—ACK!" He coughed up a fountain of blood that bubbled in his mouth.

My flesh began to creep. I had been shivering cold from being wet as a fish, but now I was sweating as if I sat in an oven.

"What are you talking about? Who's *he*?" My voice shuddered.

But Sergeant Linzer did not answer. His eyes were sealed shut, and his grip went limp.

Gazing at the lurid scene set before me, I sensed an ominous presence lurking within the dust cloud hanging over the field. The sight was like a giant wisp, too thick and brown to see through. Something seemed to be hiding in there, fixing ill eyes upon me. The few soldiers left on the wall must have sensed the same devilry, for they all stood frozen and watched the field sharply.

Like brown fog the dust cloud lingered over the area. The wind fell dead, and the clouds blotted the sun. There was no chirruping of birds, no singing of the breeze, no shuffling of grass. Time froze.

The air was so quiet, so tense, that my hairs stood stiff on their ends. Miles the traxid felt the same eerie feeling. He screeched and reared like a horse, and bolted for the city where there was safety.

"Hey! Come back!" I cried, but he paid me no mind. He was too spooked to care about anything but his own safety.

A faint noise reached my ears from within the veil. Trembling, I stood my ground. It was a sharp patting sound, like a fleshy surface being slapped. The sound repeated at a sluggish, unnatural tempo like the first slow raindrops of a brewing storm. It didn't take me long to understand.

Someone was clapping.

If any clapping should have occurred, it should have come from the Anbizians. They had battered the Kadaanites till not one was left. They should have been squealing in celebration. And yet the only applause came from within the dust, which only held corpses...or so I thought.

Over and over the claps repeated. *Clap...clap...clap...clap...*

A dreadful feeling rushed over me as the dust settled to the ground, revealing a man. The gloom that seemed to circulate the area devastated me, and seeing the horrible figure standing there made me want to shatter into pieces. What made it so awful was that I'd seen this man before. I'd met him on my first day here.

"You! You're a Kadaanite!" I exclaimed in disbelief. Oh, how naive I was back then! I had never seen a Kadaanite at the time, so of course I couldn't have identified one. If only I had known! If only!

The man stopped clapping as he spoke. "I have to admit, I'm impressed!" His menacing grin was audible in his words. It was the masked man who held me at knifepoint beside Lake Dirul. He still wore the same wooden mask and the same militaristic livery. I knew not how or why he could speak the Falian tongue. A tusker, like the ones that had chased me earlier, appeared from the dust and stood beside him obediently, slavering like a hungry wolf.

"You rushed into the enemy's side to distract them and buy time for your allies!" he said. His eyes were locked onto mine. "I don't think I've ever seen such a tremendously doughty display! Truly, I applaud you!"

Glancing at the city behind me, I saw the soldiers watching from atop the walls, ghastliness abundant throughout their faces. Their cowed expressions suggested that I was beyond saving. Did they recognize this man too? Just who was he? I whipped my head back at him.

"What a wonderful demonstration..." he continued, but I could tell only empty flattery spilled from his mouth. An arrogant predator loved to toy with its prey before sinking in its fangs. That was how our dynamic felt at this moment. "...It's just what I'd expect from the one and only son of Stuart Tucker!"

"Wha—?!"

For about a second, I forgot how to breathe. I immediately clapped my hand over my mouth as I fought not to collapse under the weight of his words. All kinds of instincts were screaming at me now—instincts for survival, for vengeance, for solace, for *answers*, but all I could do was try not to vomit.

He uttered my father's name...and he knew I was his son. How was that possible?!

"Unfortunately, your moment of glory is over," he declared in a voice that was much too cool and collected for a battle. "I'm afraid I'll have to take your artifact."

"Who are you?!" I demanded. "What do you know about my dad?!"

"Oh-ho, rather impatient, are we? Very well! General Tebaldus, at your service!" he shouted pompously as he took a bow. His voice boomed loud enough to reach the soldiers. I could hardly believe my ears. He was a general. Of all things, a general! "I've heard I'm somewhat of a local legend among you folk! What an honor!"

I recalled the name from other talkers. I'd heard it in Maratel while listening in on the bar-goers at *Merrybeard Alehouse*. They had dismissed his character as a fable, too abominable to fit reality. And yet, here he stood...in living flesh, much too real for comfort. Yet looking at him was like staring into the eyes of a nightmare. He knew how feared he was, and he cherished it like it was a part of his soul.

"You sick animal!" I yelled, allowing fury to take the reins. "Do you even know the atrocious things you've done?! Answer me!"

"I've done nothing of the sort! And I can assure you that I'm no animal...but you are. You see, it's only atrocious if the lives I smother are valuable as people. Your lives are *not* valuable because *you're* the animals. In fact, your lives are a nuisance. I'm simply doing my people a favor by exterminating some pests."

"I ought to slice your head off!" I drew my sword.

"Oh? You want to wield a blade against me?" he asked condescendingly. He mounted his tusker. "So be it. Brace yourself."

Although I knew it was futile to stand off against a high-ranking general, I readied my sword. I dropped the Aether Seal and put both hands on the hilt, gripping tightly. Surely, if I could hold off long enough, a band of soldiers would come to my aid.

However, when I took a glance at the city, everyone stood frozen as they watched our exchange. No one even seemed to care about rushing to my aid. What were they dawdling for? Were they afraid of Tebaldus? We had the numbers—we had the manpower—to take him down. Surely, he couldn't be *that* formidable...

"—?!" I had spent too long brooding. When I looked back at Tebaldus, his beast was barreling wildly toward me, brandishing its huge tusks like a sword. I slashed at its face for defense, but its mouth yawned wide open and then clamped my blade between its teeth. Its teeth were so razor-sharp and stout that my blade was caught fast. I tried to pull back, but the beast's maw had ensnared the weapon like a wily hunter. It squeezed its jaw tight until finally my blade shivered into little shards. "What the—?!"

Before I could recover, the beast delivered a mighty headbutt that sent me tumbling to the ground. Then it put its massive hoof onto me, pressing me firmly into the dirt, rendering me immobile. The general had so deftly quelled my fight in one fell swoop. I was just a measly fly that had been swatted away. The humiliation made me want to burst into tears of shame.

"...Pathetic," spat Tebaldus.

With a long tusk the animal picked up the Aether Seal by its handle and gave it to its master. He flaunted it high over his head for the eyes of the Anbizians, mocking the soldiery for their failure.

In those eyes behind his mask, I could see that he was doing all of this for sport. He wasn't fighting out of patriotism. He wasn't following orders from his superiors. He wasn't heroically answering any sort of call of duty. All his atrocities...the towns he plundered, the children he murdered, the women he raped...he committed them because it made him happy. I couldn't accept him as a true warlord. I couldn't accept *this* as a way of fighting wars. No one in their right mind could call this man a soldier—he was a monster! If this was the true nature of the Kadaanites, then the Anbizians were a thousand percent right to seek their extermination.

"Is this what humanity has to offer?" asked the general to Cordea's soldiers. "How sad!"

Struggling was pointless. He found it hilarious to watch me try and win. He was an angel of death who far exceeded the concept of vulnerability.

Why were none of the soldiers coming to help me? Every one of them was rooted atop the walls and seemed unable to breathe or blink. What was stopping them from fighting? What were they waiting for?

Wait...that was exactly it. They were waiting for something, and it didn't take much longer to work out exactly what it was. A wave of rage rushed over me, making my blood boil. I clenched my fists and cursed silently there on the ground as I tried not to lose myself in a rampage. These aliens were disgusting—all of them. They were no better than the general.

They *wanted* Tebaldus to kill me.

Dimitri had condemned the authorities for wanting to execute me, but they could still let the Kadaanites do the dirty work instead.

Why did I have to go through the torment of living among these shameless people? I'd tried to play hero and protect them, yet they still longed to leave me in a ditch to die. As the horrible realization befogged my head with thoughts of wrath, my heart felt poisoned with anguish. But I had to keep hold of my nerve. I wanted to cry, I wanted to scream, I wanted to explode, but if I lit that fuse, Tebaldus would grant the Anbizians their wish. My life balanced on a high glass bridge, and one wrong step would make it shatter.

"Why do you want the Aether Seal so badly?" I asked, my voice husky from all the emotion.

"Do you know how this artifact works?"

"..."

The contract with the Independent Mercenary Guild explained that the Aether Seal would grant divine protection. As a nonreligious man, I'd disregarded the description as blabbering nonsense as I didn't believe in providential happenings.

"How do you think it earned its name? The Aether Seal interferes with Kadaan's destiny of destroying you wretched aliens. It's called the Aether Seal because it emits a field of energy with a massive effective range; the energy disrupts the aether that maintains the wormholes we use to travel to this filthy planet. In a practical sense the artifact sucks the life out of the wormholes, or in other words, it *seals* the required aether. Without the aether, there are no wormholes, and without our wormholes, your existence continues, but I won't allow it."

I didn't know anything about the aether, nor had I known of its relation to the wormholes. No one on Earth or Anbizia had an inkling of how the Kadaanites could create them. It was one of the several mysteries I had originally intended to solve.

On the other hand, I finally had the pleasure of learning the Aether Seal's true function. I didn't understand the science behind it, but at least I knew how it worked and why it bore its name.

"You...how did you know it was in the city?"

"The effect of the Aether Seal works based on proximity. The farther it travels from an area, the lesser its effect on the aether there. I realized it was here because—" Suddenly he bit his tongue. He lasered me with a sharp-eyed stare as if trying to work out an equation in which I was an essential variable. "Hold on...why would you assume I shouldn't know? Did you know it was previously in Maratel? Wait...don't tell me it was *you* who brought it to the Church here!"

"What...?" I managed to croak out as a painfully self-conscious feeling stole over me.

How could he possibly know it was brought to the Church?

"Oh-ho! This is too good to be true," he laughed and pointed at me, and shouted his next words at the Anbizians. "All of you, your annihilation is *his* fault! Remember that in your dying breaths!"

My breath became uneven as he humiliated me. My throat tightened, I choked back sobs, and nausea like I'd never felt before was thick in me. I knew what grievous mistake I'd made.

"You see, my troops needed a place to assemble before attacking this city," he explained. "The village of Maratel was perfect. My country, Hûndark, is ravaged by an awful famine, and Maratel's farms had a huge wealth of food to feed my troops before battle. But we couldn't get there with the Aether Seal suppressing our wormholes. That's why we needed someone to move it away..."

No, no, no! This wasn't real! It couldn't be true—it couldn't! He had to be lying! How could anyone be such an evil master of deception?!

I didn't want to hear another word. I wanted to plug my ears, but my arms were too pinned down.

"...And *that's* why I forged a fake contract for the Independent Mercenary Guild!" he exclaimed excitedly. His words slammed down on me like the wrath of the heavens. Everything had changed. My survival of Senzaw Cave and my retrieval of the Aether Seal wasn't the triumph I thought it was. I'd been set up and used like a puppet, dancing around in Tebaldus's bidding, and I never even noticed the pulling of strings. "But still, I can't believe it was *you* who took up that job! Ha-ha-ha!"

And it was all because I'd been led into greedy temptation by those hundred silvers.

"Once the Aether Seal was gone from Maratel, we were finally able to summon our wormholes and transport enough troops to invade the humble village. Oh, and about the villagers—they hardly put up a fight, so I killed them all! It was almost like they weren't there!"

This Kadaanite kept getting worse and worse. All those kind hearts and smiling people of Maratel...they'd been terminated at Tebaldus's hands. Now the village was infested with the enemy like a disease.

"How many of your people died today? Look at this place! You've sacrificed all these soldiers just to get your hands on that artifact!"

Tebaldus gazed at the corpse-ridden field that was full of his slaughtered subordinates.

"Their deaths won't be in vain," he said calmly. The sight didn't move him at all. "The Aether Seal still has a modest effect on Maratel from here, which prevents my wormholes from reaching optimal power. I didn't anticipate the effect reaching this far. Wormholes are a scientific wonder, but they collapse easily, and this no-good relic only makes it worse, so I can't transport as many men. I'd planned to enter this battle with a greater multitude—ah, I'd *planned* to win this battle in a single assault—but when I only got a fraction of my army through the wormhole before it collapsed, I had to devise a plan B, which is to seize the Aether Seal and destroy it. Now, once I kill this artifact for good, we'll raze your city to the ground, and this time nothing will hold us back!"

It seemed that the Aether Seal's power grew weaker the farther it reached. If Tebaldus managed to destroy it, Neiklof's future would be gone. His army would massacre all of Cordea, and then they'd keep expanding their reign across the planet.

"So you're going kill me, run away, and then come back with more of your pawns?"

"I won't kill you. You delivered the Aether Seal straight into my hands, and I *thank* you for that. I'll spare you for now as a reward."

Standing before all the soldiery with my name engraved on this disaster may have been a fate worse than death. I could see myself getting branded as a traitor, the last remains of my reputation getting decimated. At this point I couldn't tell whether it was the lakewater or my sweat that drenched my clothes.

"Now, I really must be going," he said. The tusker lifted its hoof from my recumbent body. Then, for nobody else's hearing but mine, he said quietly, "Meet me again, and the truth will be yours." He had spoken of the truth during our first meeting. Even now, what he meant I did not know, but I was dying to find out ever since he'd mentioned my father. He looked at the city and yelled, "May your false gods be with you!"

Ironically, he wished blessings on us only because he was convinced the heavens were against us. He believed his mighty hand was more powerful than that of all the gods, from which no amount of undying faith could protect the Anbizian people.

With that he flicked his reins hard before dashing away from the city. None of soldiers moved a muscle.

When I stood and turned around, I saw Kiara standing at the gates having returned from her operation with the civilians. Her expression was wrenched. She and all the soldiery watched as I took the walk of shame back to the city. Dark clouds masked the sky from north to south. Thunder cackled angrily, the wind hummed with a slow crescendo, and little raindrops started diving from the firmament.

There was no future for Neiklof, a fate that was my fault. The penetrating stares of everyone else were all that kept me tied to this terrifying reality.

CHAPTER XIII

NEIKLOF'S DESPERATE MUSTER

By instigating a spirit of terror, Tebaldus was already attacking us from the inside. Cordea had degraded into a madhouse, which was natural with the flames of panic consuming the city. Civilians hurried through the streets in stampedes like loose animals, all so they could gather their things and leave while there was still time.

And yet, all I did was sit on the stoop of a crushed building in empty silence. Kiara was there beside me. The awning was still intact, which protected me from the torrential rain. On the outside, I may have looked unfazed, but deep down a whole stew of emotions tormented me. Fear, anguish, guilt, indignation, disgust—perhaps other things that human understandings of emotion can't identify—all stirred in my heavy heart. We both sat there, listening to the drumming of rain, the crying of civilians, the splish-splashing of carriages in the wet streets.

A group of soldiers came and escorted us away without explanation. We didn't need one, nor did we resist. That was how we wound up on our knees in the throne room of Sidor Nysh, or the Spirit Hall, Cordea's castle.

"Look at what you two have done." King Frieval had shortly returned to Cordea and was quick to summon me after hearing whose fault the attack was. There was nothing I could say in defense, which made his harsh words sting all the more. "You opened the window for the Kadaanites to attack, and now all our lives are in peril. What do you have to say for yourself?"

"..."

Kiara and I hung our heads with our lips sealed silent.

The throne room was packed with guards and nobles. They stood round the fluted pillars along the room's shoulders as they watched our exchange. I felt as though the humiliation from Tebaldus had carried its momentum to this moment.

Dimitri strolled into the room with little trace of worry on his face. "It's obviously because of Nathan's incompetence. I would never have let Tebaldus fool me so easily."

I slowly looked at him and stared through him, pale as ash. Incompetent? *Me*? If I hadn't bought so much time for the soldiers, they would have been overwhelmed. Dimitri hadn't done *anything* during the battle. All he did was fall in with the flock and shoot his bow blindly.

"Certainly," replied King Frieval. "O Dimitri, you're a wise one, aren't you? How should he pay for his failure?"

"Sir!" I spoke up in protest. "We don't have time for this."

"This is all your fault, Nathan," said Dimitri. "All you do is make trouble. We need to take care of you swiftly before you do something even stupider."

What did these people not realize? We were on the cusp of destruction and all they could think about was assigning punishment! They just couldn't work past their own hard feelings!

"If we go after the Kadaanites, we can stop them!" I cried. "We might even retake Maratel!"

"You ignorant child!" barked the king. "We don't have the strength for that now! Our men are all wounded and tired!"

"You think our enemy isn't going through the same thing? They're weakened and low on numbers too!"

"Even if that's true, the clock is ticking too fast! By the time our forces reach the village, General Tebaldus will already have summoned his reinforcements!"

As the room thundered with a fruitless argument, a priest approached the throne.

"Your Majesty. If I may, I'd like to offer a suggestion."

King Frieval bit his bottom lip in surprise. It was unusual that a priest of all people would offer a transgressor's punishment. Or was he here to suggest something else?

"And who the hell are you?" asked the king, foaming with anger.

"I'm called Father Nirië. Last night I found some old writings about the Aether Seal. They taught that the artifact is extremely durable—nearly indestructible. The sheer power it takes even to dent the thing is simply exorbitant. I have no doubt that it would take quite a while for General Tebaldus to find a way to destroy it. Do you know what that means?"

"What?"

"It means there's still time to stop the key from turning."

The king thought to himself deeply at the new intel. While previously it seemed Tebaldus's army would be back for round two within the day, perhaps the Aether Seal would hold them back longer than expected.

"Our troops are still exhausted and run thin," said Dimitri. "We might not be able to muster enough power for a successful raid on Maratel."

"True, but there is another source we can muster from," said King Frieval before addressing General Prachit, who had served as the leading commander in battle. "General, assemble a division of criminals rotting in jail and prepare them for battle. They'll be the first to die for this city."

When the king gave his command, I stared at him in shock with my brows knitted. A memory of Hippocrates's ancient wisdom, which I had read about in school on Earth, came flashing back: "Extreme remedies are very appropriate for extreme diseases." The words seemed to glow in my mind in a horrible, blinding fashion. When the disease of alien invaders threatened life itself, no sacrifice was too great. To King Frieval, if pawns were available—especially pawns of the more disposable type—they ought to be thrown into the bloody struggle for the sole purpose of boosting the army's mass.

"Right away, Your Majesty," said the general before leaving the throne room, and Father Nirië left too.

"As for you, human, to compensate for your failure, you'll be among the first wave in the attack on Maratel. This battle will be suicidal. You will die with your fellow criminals in the name of restoring peace to Neiklof."

This was it. I was going to join them in being expended against the Kadaanites. We would be cannon fodder in hope of overwhelming our foe with sheer numbers. There was something so dehumanizing about being reduced to an expendable pawn that I felt myself swelling with misery. Protesting or resisting these demands was something for which I didn't have the strength—my hopelessness had siphoned off all my energy. As much as I wanted to change my destiny, my will was extinguished. Ordinarily my willfulness would lead me to cast shouts and protests, but today that trait was silent, and this time I only shifted my gaze downward in shame, knowing my final fate was on the horizon.

"Your majesty!" shouted Kiara at my side. "You can't! This isn't just his fault! I was there with him when he accepted that contract with the guild!"

"Ah, yes, that reminds me," said the king. "It's come to my attention, human, that you stopped the execution of this girl."

"Keep her out of this," I growled.

"She carries the blame for Neiklof's jeopardy too. As punishment, I'm going to settle her execution once and for all!"

"What?!" Kiara and I cried in unison.

This couldn't happen. I couldn't lose her. I needed her to work with me so we could survive together. There'd been so many times when I survived thanks only to her. I didn't know how long I'd last without her.

"W-wait! You can't just—!" Before Kiara could utter a complete sentence, a soldier clasped his hand over her mouth and restrained her. She squirmed and kicked and tried to scream, but her resistance came to no avail as he exerted his power over her.

"You keep your hands off her!" I barked fiercely, drawing my sword. "—Ungh!" A spear's shaft thwacked me across the stomach and knocked the wind out of me. I fell over, and three soldiers threw themselves onto me and squashed me into the ground. A hand shielded my mouth like Kiara's. The crowd of nobles gasped and screamed in fear at the surge of brutality. As civilians they could only handle so much violence in one day. Their spirits were ready to melt at this point.

Kiara didn't deserve this. She deserved a shot at life—the shot she'd never gotten the chance to take. The Kiara from all those days ago wasn't the same as today's Kiara. Since then she'd gained hope: hope for her future, hope for life, hope for meaning, hope for the world itself. While before she had bottled up her zest for life, the time we spent together made it plainly clear that she never wanted to die. She wanted to live! That dirty king could put me in a suicide squad all he wanted, but sentencing her to death wasn't execution—it was cold-blooded murder!

"Don't worry about her, Nathan," Dimitri gloated as he crouched over my restrained body. "If the price is low enough, I might buy her out of the execution. She'll be in great hands with me!"

My gaze drifted to Dimitri's lady companions in the crowd. They heard his words, at which jealousy bloomed in their expressions. Those women only followed him because his florid lies won them over. He used his influence to manipulate those who believed in him, and it didn't matter how he treated them—they would always remain by his side as long as he kept that unctuous halo on his head. Those women always quarreled over Dimitri's heart, wore skimpy clothing, and looked askance at everyone they viewed as lesser. I didn't want Kiara to end up like them. I couldn't bear to let her join that stupid harem!

That garbage king must've known how important Kiara was to me. He just wanted to steal her away. Why, why couldn't he just treat me fairly?!

As the soldiers dragged away a struggling and sweating Kiara, I watched with my eyes widened and wrecked with despair. Through the muffling of the soldier's hand over her mouth, I thought I heard her crying my name. The choices were either to have King Frieval butcher her or to let Dimitri take her under his wing. I didn't know which was worse.

"Human!" bellowed King Frieval as he ignored my anguish. "It's time for you to make up for your failure!"

The soldiers lifted me and carried me off. They handed me a spare standard-issue sword to replace my broken one. Destiny called, and battle loomed. I suppose it didn't matter what happened to Kiara in the end. After all, I would be dead soon.

Neiklof's military was quick to prepare a convoy to transport all the combatants. The leading carts were clustered with criminals turned troopers. Behind them were the more dignified soldiers whose value hadn't sunk to mere cannon fodder. I squeezed into a cart up front, which was already cramped beyond comfort, and its occupants stared at me, sneering, perhaps growling, before lapsing back to their own thoughts. I held my head low as I sat down, taking in the smell of the men's unkept hygiene, and eventually the traxids drew the carts forward. The formation was many carts wide and many more carts long.

Though there were more soldiers than could be counted, there was no telling whether it was enough to overwhelm the enemy. We had no way of knowing how many Kadaanites would be waiting to defend Maratel. We could only pray that our mass of firepower was heavy enough. This assault was our final act of desperation and the ultimate gamble. Failure meant death for all of Neiklof, and the rest of the planet would soon follow. Anbizia's fate rested in our hands.

Silence seemed to blast through everyone's ears as the carts rolled along the muddy path. The weeping rain had stopped, but the air was damp and stuffy under the gray sky. While there were usually travelers perched on carriages that could be seen scrolling across the land, today it was all waste. There was only a vast throw of grass and fallen warriors, Anbizians and Kadaanites alike. Guts were strewn about the carcasses, and pools of blood were mixed with the wet earth to produce hideous dark red sludge. A terrible migraine settled over me; it churned round and round unbearably as the festered stench of alien carrion wafted to our noses.

At the moment, the only thing uniting us was the knowledge that our final moments were upon us. The road we followed was paved with the bodies of those who fought before us, and we knew we were next. We were a flock of sheep being led to the slaughter, only to be butchered and replaced by the next wave.

Thinking back on how I ended up here was too painful to bear. The anguish of my failure made me want to tear off my limbs in frustration. I could see them standing before me—all those people who afflicted me. The king, Dimitri, and Tebaldus were all there...and then there was Kiara. Her glistening blue image made me want to cry out at my own worthlessness, but a disgusting taste kept my tongue paralyzed. I couldn't waste energy screaming. I was better off saving it and putting it toward surviving the next battle.

How could I score survival? When I evaluated the question rationally, it seemed like doom was certain. I was expected to rush in and get picked off by enemy arrows—it was what the king wanted. What was I supposed to do about that?

Anxiety flowed through my head like a river's white rapids, and my headache seemed to spread to my body. I wanted to collapse then and there in a breakdown, but the people squishing me from each side kept me sitting upright.

Kiara was in danger. I wanted to turn back and save her, yet I couldn't escape the flowing convoy's current. Besides, Tebaldus was the most immediate threat. He vowed to bring inferno to Anbizia, but the world would survive without Kiara. That was the hard truth I had to swallow.

When I first arrived in Neiklof, I immediately lost my place in society. I wanted somewhere to belong. I wanted some way to rebuild my life, but every time I tried, there was a cannon pointed at me just waiting to demolish it all. Every sword, bow, and spear was poised to strike away all my hope, and all my strides for betterment had been proven vain. I was the victim of a ruse. The general had gone fishing for a puppet, and it was I who excitedly took the bait, little knowing I'd latched onto the fisherman's hook.

The voyage to Maratel wouldn't last long. There wasn't much time. I decided to take some deep breaths and rethink the situation. Since I didn't know how much firepower we were up against, I needed to think of a way to outsmart the enemy—something they wouldn't expect. But this challenge was beyond the usual difficulties of warfare. Tebaldus had proven his aptitude for leading one step ahead of the Anbizians at all times, which was precisely why he was such a successful warrior. It was worth assuming his remaining forces anticipated our raid. Maybe they even *wanted* us to attack.

The real problem was clad in stopping Tebaldus from destroying the Aether Seal and conjuring wormholes with more stability. Given its ability to drain the aether (a substance I knew little about), preserving the artifact's existence seemed like best defense against our enemy. We needed to get it back before it was too late, but how?

I rifled every nook and cranny of the problem in my mind, but the answer was nowhere in sight.

"Um, Kiara—"

As I felt it necessary to ask for her input, my companion's name rolled off my tongue as if it were the most natural thing in the world. I managed to stop a sentence from forming upon remembering she wasn't there. When the other passengers heard me, they stared for a long chain of seconds. This whole time they'd been sitting in silence, but I'd broken it. I atoned with an awkward "Sorry."

The sudden lapse in my train of thought rekindled my awareness of the present. I must have lost sense of time because we'd traveled a healthy distance by now. The city had fallen out of sight, and we were alone on the lonely road to Maratel.

My instinct to consult Kiara reminded me that I really had grown dependent on her. Her absence was what crippled me the most. We had agreed to work together to survive, and without her, it seemed like there was no way out of the enemy's snare. I couldn't help but wonder what she was feeling at the moment.

No...it was time to forget about her. I was nothing but a measly flea without her. I had relied on her so much that I couldn't pull my own weight, but now she was out of the picture. I had to be a man and climb out of this hole myself.

Still, the best option was to approach this challenge logically, and that was Kiara's specialty.

What would Kiara do if she were here? I asked in my mind.

It was a stupid question. I hadn't known the girl very long, and I couldn't possibly mimic her thoughts based on my novice experience. But I knew she always thought what no one else thought. She always had an idea that seemed so simple, yet no one else could see it.

What element was I missing? What was the enemy not thinking?

Closing my eyes, I flipped through the layers of my memory to tap into Kiara's way of thinking. Perspective could easily spawn an unseen vantage point. I just needed the right angle. I thought for a long time and was sure to leave no stone unturned mentally. There were so many factors at play here, so there had to be *some* divine tool waving at me.

"Yuck," said a voice next to me suddenly.

"Damn Kadaanites don't got a shred of mercy," remarked another voice.

"They just murder like it's no one's business."

When I opened my eyes, I found that I was looking at a wooden cottage. An old falius man was sprawled on the porch. It was Old Man Teppy, the man Kiara and I had passed on our way out of Maratel. Blood was puddled around his body, pink intestines were unspooled across the wood, and an eye was suspended from its socket. Lying dead with him were his two pet ulffs. Their fur was slathered red, their ruins were mangled and torn to shambles, and their limbs stuck up at obscene angles.

Looking on at the scene, I was speechless. What kept me from speaking was Tebaldus's wanton cruelty. Just yesterday Old Man Teppy had been screaming full of energy at passersby, and his ulffs could yip their snouts off, but that had all been stamped out with the suddenness of a crack of lightning.

Vethwood was just ahead. A league or two farther, the woods would open up to Maratel's plots of farmland.

"Everyone off your carts!" shouted the raid captain on his driving perch. "The village of Maratel is just beyond these woods!"

This was a bulging problem. The journey had flown by quicker than I expected, and I still hadn't thought of anything. The convoy came to a halt, and everyone poured off their carts. Vethwood's eaves hid us from the enemy's view, but I could see Maratel's thatches in the distance, and the Menuil Hills peeking over the tall pendent crag.

"Listen up, warriors!" boomed the raid captain in front of the vast army. "We'll cut through this wood, reclaim the village, and burn any alien who stands in our way! This may be the most important battle of your lives! Don't let a single Kadaanite escape! Ystaria wills it! Many of you may be charging to your deaths, but remember, Our Lady is on our side, not theirs!" He brandished his sword and roared: "To battle! In the name of—!"

Boom!

The noise came abruptly from across the woods. Many startled flinches and gasps occurred among the soldiers.

"What was that?" asked the raid captain.

It sounded like an explosion. I could see plumes of smoke and dust swirling up near the cliff. But why? Surely combat hadn't been unleashed in the village yet.

A realization suddenly tugged me—a realization no one else reckoned with.

Tebaldus was trying to blow up the Aether Seal.

That was when an idea snapped into place. People feared Tebaldus more than they feared his soldiers, which made *him* the bigger target. After all, the knight was far more powerful than the pawn.

But our plan was to charge headlong against the pawns. Why not change our strategy? Why not take the fight straight to Tebaldus?

"Whatever," said the raid captain, clearing his throat. "As I was saying—"

"Listen up!" I announced, standing over the crowd on a cart. My interruption was immediately greeted by blinking eyes and open mouths. Confounded murmurs shook across the crowd, stunned by my nerve to talk over the raid captain. "I'm going to try and assassinate the general. That's when you should storm the village. The Kadaanites will be vulnerable without a leader commanding them."

"You're an imbecile," said the raid captain with a nasty glare. "That would be suicide. How are you going to reach him without the enemy catching you?"

"Don't worry about me. You just give those parasites everything you've got." I got down from the cart and walked toward the wood, and the raid captain twisted with anger.

"You get back here now, or I'll have you arrested! You fiend!"

And yet in spite of his threat, I kept walking. I went past the front line of carts, past the murdered old man's cottage, and into Veth-wood's matted thicket. The raid captain fumed with rage and cast dangerous shouts my way. But he didn't stop me.

Now was my chance to make up for my failure. I could prove I wasn't a nuisance. With a regal raise of my chin, I set out for Maratel.

CHAPTER XIV

1POTION-HL

If the enemy spotted me, it was over. Knowing this, I stayed in Vethwood's shadows and flanked around the village, sidestepping the Kadaanites by moving along the cliff wall. The battle had run them thin; guards were scarce. While I crept along the far route, three soldiers caught up to me and insisted on joining me in taking down General Tebaldus.

"You want to join me?" I asked, taken aback. A small part of me wondered if their siding with me was a trick, but their eyes looked so bright with innocence that I decided to hear them out. "You know, killing him won't be easy. Are you willing to face that much danger?"

"We're more than up for the challenge!" boasted a soldier.

"Your bravery in standing up to the captain inspired us," said another. "We've always hated his smug superiority."

"We figured that if *you* can rebel against that jerk, so can we!" exclaimed the third. "Besides, you'll need our help. I doubt any of us can hold our own against the general one-on-one, but if we work together, we can beat him."

Since I was well aware that Tebaldus was an awfully tough foe, I ultimately accepted their aid. In truth I'd been making my way through the woods with much agony of mind, but having a group of swords backing me was helpful. Still, I had to nerve myself for the upcoming battle; for it would be a great struggle.

"Well, if we're doing battle together, we might as well share our names," I said as we sneaked through the trees.

My new comrades agreed, and we introduced ourselves. Jourl,

Hálorn, and Morogond were their names.

"We heard about your servant, that slime girl," said Jourl. "I'm sorry about her."

"Yeah, I can't imagine how that feels," added Hálorn in a black tone. "If the king targeted my wife and daughter like that..." He paused for a moment, and the silence weighed heavy on all of us. "...I don't know...I wouldn't be able to bear it. They're the reason why I fight for Neiklof—the reason why I'm fighting at this very moment."

"It's good to have something to fight for, isn't it?" said Morogond. "If we aren't all dead once this war ends, I hope I can get married too. I could live a quiet life, watch the daily sunrise with my family, see my kids grow into some mighty fine ladies and gentlemen. That's the dream, I tell you."

"Not a bad dream," said Jourl. "But after the war ends, I want to be Ystaria's priest. I believe divine love is better than familial love, which is why She's the only woman I want to live for."

"How admirable!" remarked an impressed Morogond. "I hope at least one of my kids chooses the path of priesthood!"

"Mm, so do I," said Hálorn smiling. "But with only one daughter, that's not very likely. I suppose I'll need more kids first. Guess I'll have to get busy with my wife once this is over!"

The three soldiers laughed at Hálorn's implication, but I remained neutral. My stress weighed too heavy for humor.

We marched on and evaded the enemy's sight.

At length Jourl asked, "What about you, Nathan? Anything you're fighting for in particular?"

Had I not been so mentally numb at the time, the question might have moved to tears. For at that moment, I had to ask myself why I fought on this planet's behalf. It wasn't like I owed it anything—Anbizia had handled me like dirt. It was ridiculous to fight for a world that hated you. But this raised a thought I never knew

I'd consider till now. Even when the world dealt you suffering beyond your ability to bear, was that a good reason to turn against it?
Did *that* justify handing over your land to greater evil? Indeed,
Anbizia didn't fight for me, but was I right not to fight for Anbizia? There must have been something about this planet worth protecting, something cherishable, something to fight for. Even if the
ship was sinking, that ship must have had something valuable
enough worth saving. It was then that I realized all this time I'd
been fighting for Kiara.

But she was gone now, and that reason to push forward wasn't
present anymore. That one shred of good for which I'd kept on
was stolen, and now my fight lacked any discernible telos. That was
why I suddenly felt a blow of emotion.

And yet, here I was, still fighting.

"I don't know what I'm fighting for at this point," I answered.
"But if there's anything that keeps me going, I think it's hope.
Hope that at the end of the painful broken road, something good
will be waiting—something that'll make all the tears and bruises
worth it. I think that, without hope, life isn't really worth the trouble."

The three took some time to stomach my words.

"I guess we're all doing this because we have hope," said Hálorn.
"I hope to protect my family, Morogond hopes to get married, and
Jourl hopes to serve Ystaria."

"No arguing with that!" agreed Jourl. He pumped his fist and
said, "Come on, boys! Fulfilling our hopes starts with taking down
the general! Let's go win this fight!"

With fiery passion we all agreed, and quickened our advance to
battle.

We lay prone in a scraggly bush watching the general's procedure.
Tebaldus was alone in his mask holding the Aether Seal near the
crag's base; it was still intact and scratchless.

I sighed slowly. It seemed Father Nirië was right about its dura-
bility. But how was it undented even now? Hadn't he tried to blow
it up? Surely it couldn't have been *that* bulletproof, could it?

"Arghhh!"

He roared like a tiger, and my face went white. His sudden outburst rocked me. More chilling was the certainty that he would
take out his fury on us should we get spotted.

Tebaldus slammed the Aether Seal on the ground and cursed,
"Minshé! Fônú hrosnâgt! Minshé! Minshé!"

It was hard to decide whether I should laugh or be disturbed. I
couldn't understand his speech, but my interest was piqued. No
doubt he was nearing his wits' end. Even after having been hurled
at the ground, the Aether Seal hadn't sustained a dent. I was positive that the artifact was made chiefly of glass, but *this* glass was
markedly enigmatic: it didn't want to shatter.

The cliff was too far from the village for his men to hear his unrest. We stayed quiet and watched what he would do next. Tebaldus kept seething in unintelligible mutterings as he produced
what appeared to be a keg of gunpowder and some earthenware
jars. My face lit up with wonder. He really *did* seek to blow the
Aether Seal to oblivion. But was the glass too durable even for explosives to defeat?

Perhaps there really was some kind of divinity to this bulletproof
artifact. Ystarism was a fairytale, but I couldn't imagine what could
cause such advanced glass in such an unadvanced world except
providence. *Providence.* What other answer was there? Even if the
Church of Ystaria was built on fairytales, I felt there was more to
Ystaria than met the eye. I pondered the idea as the general filled
the jars with gunpowder.

He stacked the explosive jars in a circle around the Aether Seal
and poured a string of gunpowder that rounded a tall boulder near
the cliff wall twenty yards away. He took cover behind the boulder
and lit the fuse.

As the flame reeled toward the explosives, hissing sibilantly down the fuse like a snake, I figured our chance to attack had come. I whispered the plan to the three soldiers, and we collectively agreed on the timing. We all plugged our ears as a gust of fire screeched into the sky, but it was so loud that it rattled my ears anyway. Even so, we had to take advantage of the heat.

The explosion left a dense cloud of smoke and dust. When the shrapnel stopped flying, Tebaldus left his cover, and we sprang into action. Our movements were in sync. We drew our swords, lunged through the brumous veil, and bore down on the general. His focus was occupied with destroying the Aether Seal, so we had a chance to strike a clean blow. It was a perfect ambush—he'd never have time to react for defense!

Clang!

No scream. No swish of blood. No groan of swords sliding through flesh. Only the sound of metal clashing against metal.

"Hah!" He laughed watching our faces go pale.

It just so happened that as we emerged from the smoke, our speed was fruitless. Tebaldus was speedier. He instantly drew his sword and blocked all our attacks at once.

"You thought you could take me by surprise?!" he barked angrily.

When our loss became too pressing to deny, we stepped back and kept our swords up. I prepared for his retaliation, but his blade didn't move. His attention was elsewhere; his gaze wandered beyond us. He was ignoring us and eyeing the site of the explosion. Notwithstanding his rudeness, I turned my head and watched the stirred-up dust clear away.

"No way..." I muttered.

We all stared at the Aether Seal. There it lay in the dirt with its signature blue glow, utterly unscathed. Seeing it so gracefully endure the blast gave it an effect so uncanny that it awoke fear like I'd never felt before. It lay there with such boldness, such cockiness, such absurdity that in this ephemeral instant—this paper-thin glimpse of time—it truly looked like a celestial entity beyond all possibility of disguise.

"Damn it all," said Tebaldus. "Say, Nathan, I don't suppose you know how to erase that thing? I'd hate to ruin that nice jacket of yours."

"Couldn't say," I spat. "Even if I did, I'd die before telling you."

"I suppose it was worth asking," he said, sighing with a pained smile. "And who are these friends of yours? You don't think they'll improve your odds against me, do you?"

"It won't matter who we are once you're dead!" exclaimed Jourl.

"That's right! We'll make you pay!" followed up Hálorn.

"Start thinking about your last words," said Morogond.

Everything they said, I agreed with. We were going to punish this monster for his crimes.

"On my mark, you guys!" I said, and we readied our swords to attack.

"What a shame," said Tebaldus, staring at his sword with a robe of melancholy. "It really is a nice jacket."

Our blades glanced in the Aether Seal's blue shine. While holding a weapon could get one's blood flowing in a matter of seconds, Tebaldus's voice was cold and dry. In his eyes, today was just another day on the job, and we were more grunts in his life as a killing machine.

"..."

"...!"

In a silent flash, Tebaldus moved. He was too fast to register; his figure went unseen as he blitzed forward, but very visibly Morogond's neck was slashed. The soldier, gurgling, grabbed his neck and dropped instantly, blood spewing between his fingers.

Those of us that remained leaped into the offensive. Tebaldus dealt a heavy stroke to Hálorn. The soldier blocked it but tottered back, disoriented. Jourl and I rushed to his aid before our foe could strike him down. As we both swung at our target, the general spun around and batted our swords away. He was so fast, so strong, so terrible! Was the strength of four men not enough to hinder him?

Shouting he swung wildly in a flurry, and my eyes couldn't keep up with the whirlwind of movement. But soon Jourl's body lay in the grass with his front scored up like a carving of doom.

Only two of us remained: me and Hálorn. We charged at Tebaldus from opposite sides, but he twirled swiftly and deflected both blades. Every attack we launched was met with the ringing of metal. The frustration made me grit my teeth.

He delivered Hálorn a powerful kick that sent him tumbling. Clenching my sword I quickly took another swipe, but the general parried, driving me back with such force that I toppled back on my rear.

Before I could recover, Hálorn pounced at Tebaldus from behind, already back on his feet. He leaped and aimed his sword, determined to land a blow from above. "I've got you now!" he shouted with bold vigor. But Tebaldus turned impassively, readied his sword, and clove the airborne Anbizian in half. His legs were swept off in an instant. Before hitting the ground, the soldier's eyes widened, and his mouth gaped in disbelief. His attack, an attack that should have been impossible to ward off, was squelched with ease.

With haste Tebaldus got behind Hálorn, who clung to life after being split in two. My final ally wailed and clawed the dirt, his entrails hanging out of his body in pink strands as he desperately crawled toward me for safety, though I knew not one bit how to help. All I could do was watch the blood pour from his waist. Tebaldus raised his sword to kill. Looking into that soldier's eyes, I saw what true fear looked like. As death loomed over his helpless body, the terror in his expression was a kind of terror that came from a devil. But although his eyes were bursting with fear, the general's eyes were dim and glassy.

"...Run!" wheezed Hálorn as the blade sliced through his neck like butter.

As I sat in the prickly grass, petrified by utter trauma, the severed head rolled toward me and bumped into my foot. His face was covered in gore. His eyes, wide but lifeless, met my gaze with the slow-creeping grimness of the dead. And while the soul that once looked through his eyes was gone, I could feel a penetrating stare coming from them, as if he demanded an answer: "You didn't save me—why didn't you save me?"

Looking at the corpses tossed about me, all I could think about was the irony of their deaths. It seemed like my comrades perished in the blink of an eye, and with them went all their dreams. Morogond's dream of marriage, Jourl's dream of priesthood, Hálorn's dream of family protection, all snuffed out like candles. I had only met them moments ago, and now they were dead before laying a single scratch on the general.

I wanted to scream. I wanted to invest every built-up emotion into that scream. But I couldn't—pure shock stayed my tongue.

Knowing I was next, I slowly looked up to find Tebaldus towering over me. I didn't need to see through his mask to perceive his bloodthirsty expression.

"On your feet, Tucker!" he demanded. "Stand and fight! We'll settle this one-on-one!"

"...?" I stared at him, perplexed. If four of us couldn't fell him, there was no way I could do it alone. He had every chance to finish me off now, so why did he delay it? What was the point in asking me to fight on?

"Don't give me that look!" he steamed as I struggled up. "I saved you for last for a reason! For years I yearned to get revenge on your father, but it got stolen away. But now that you're here, I'll punish you instead. During our previous meetings, the temptation to kill you then and there was unbearable—it planted its claws firmly into my heart from all sides. The voices telling me to stomp your head into mush screamed so loud that I couldn't hear anything else. I only spared you because I figured I'd kill you all soon anyway, so I'd torment you by letting you live your last hours in fear. But since you followed me here, I'll do to you what I wish I'd done to your bastard father."

"Is that why you have a bone to pick with me? Why do you hate my dad so much? What did he ever do to you?"

Tebaldus had told me that if I met him again, the truth would be mine. He must have known my dad pretty personally, and yet *I* hadn't heard from him in years. Although there were all kinds of questions I wanted to ask about him, I hardly had time to ask any of them, for battle was just too urgent. It seemed I would have to go searching for answers another day. But even if I couldn't get all the answers I wanted, it was at least time to extract his truth once and for all.

"You want the truth? Fine. I'll show it to you." As he spoke, his hand floated to his mask and peeled it off. What I saw behind it was a face that seemed to have traveled down to hell and back again. His naked face was ruined with horrible black burns, revealing hideous patches of scorched flesh and red scar tissue. They were the kinds of wounds that would never heal in all his days. He looked like he'd been branded like a farm animal. "Do you understand now?!" he screamed, losing himself in fresh fury. "You see all the shit your father did to me?! That's why I'm getting revenge here and now!"

At that moment I wanted nothing more than to figure out what had happened between the general and my old man, but before I could say a word, Tebaldus was sweeping toward me, his sword glaring. Fire burned in his eyes. If I couldn't prove my worth against Tebaldus now, I had no right to exist on this planet, and so, having no other option, I prepared to strike back. The sound of our swords clattering against each other rang like bells. Several strong clashes we traded, but my speed fell behind, and the edge of his blade slipped past my defense and slit my forearm, tearing my sleeve and leaving a thick incision.

"Agh!" I howled as my arm flared in pain, staggering me and sapping a great draft of strength. Blood dribbled down my arm like a red runny egg, streaming over my hand and staining my clothes from the inside.

"I'll enjoy killing you," said Tebaldus, staring as I clasped my arm. "I wish I could keep you alive. I wish I could take you and give you a fate worse than death. I'd keep you in eternal punishment, not killing but torturing you so that you'd exist an inch away from death at all times. You'd never die, but you'd always yearn for it. But I won't make that mistake again. I won't risk you getting away like your father did." At that moment I knew I was no ordinary kill. For him, killing me was the sweet release of his slow-kindled hatred that had piled up over the years into a mountain. His hatred for me was like a swollen balloon, and it was all about to burst. Then, snarling every word with biting sharpness, he said:

"Nathan, I hate you. No unit of measurement can gauge my hatred. In all the universe's vastness, across all its billions of light-years from corner to corner, there has never been as much hate as the hate I feel for you. Let the word hate echo through every valley of your mind as you bleed to death. I hate you. I HATE YOU!"

He slowly walked forward, his sword dangling at his side. The blazing flames in his eyes seemed hot enough to burn me.

He continued, "I want you to know that it's people like your father who prove that Kadaan is the superior planet, and the rest of you are insects. That's why we'll conquer this world and come for yours next. This galaxy belongs to *us*."

"You couldn't stay in your corner of the galaxy? Where's your respect for other people's peace and quiet?"

"It's not about peace. You're dead wrong if you think there's room for us to coexist."

Coexistence was something I didn't fancy either—not after how

Anbizia had treated me. But why couldn't we just sit in our respective seats? Why did he go out of his way to massacre entire planets?

"What do you hope to gain from all this?"

"Dominion is rightfully ours," he said bluntly. "The galaxy will be better with Kadaan in control. By exterminating you, we'll defend ourselves from the cancer you all conceive. To let you live would be to permit the spread of your disease. Your people only breed weakness. You humans preach nonsense like love and kindness and spirituality and equality and money, and you implement absurd laws and ideologies in the name of a more prosperous world, yet your society only regresses. How much have your leaders helped the poor and sick? And what about happiness? Why does sorrow abound despite all the efforts to help?"

Just how much did he know about Earth? I wondered if he'd learned these things from my father.

Tebaldus launched toward me. Our blades glanced off each other again and again as we fought to strike a blow on the other.

Over the peals of iron, he continued, "Oh, but you and I both know where your weakness really comes from. The very idea of it makes me sick. You people are so weak that you turn to your gods whenever life gets difficult, and you're even willing to coexist with completely contradicting religions! Look around you, Nathan. Your people worship gods unheard of by any Kadaanite or Anbizian. And what about Ystaria? Why hasn't she revealed herself to you or me?"

My assailant leaped back a few paces. My face glistened with sweat, my muscles twitched from stress, and my breath rose and fell in heavy pants. Still, with effort I kept my footing.

Of course I had thought about the religious differences between worlds and found them puzzling. Surely it seemed unfair for a god to favor one planet exclusively. But would a religious person fold at Tebaldus's argument? Was his logic enough to convince all members of creation—if it *was* a creation—to abandon their belief? If I were a man of faith, I knew I wouldn't be convinced so easily. If I believed in spiritual things, I would be more inclined to forge a counterargument.

But ultimately I wasn't interested in religious folly. I was simply indifferent to that stuff. Even Kiara's belief, which was a strong sense of devotion, did not alter my respect for her in any way. "You can hate the gods all you want," I said. "Makes no difference. It's all nonsense anyway. It's like an imaginary friend—you can spit on him, or you can worship him, but in the end it's all fiction."

"I'm not saying there's no god out there. Maybe there is. But what kind of god calls himself universal only to be known by one people? Use some damn reason for once! Look, the height of human morality is being tolerant of people with different beliefs and values...and for what? For people to live blissfully in their delusions? For people to worship their false gods?!"

While these ideas may have been considered extreme by Earthly standards, Tebaldus didn't care. Such standards were what he vowed to destroy. He wanted to breathe death on all seeds of weakness so that they wouldn't sprout in his own society.

The general swung again with a yell, but I betrayed no surprise and dodged his stroke. He must have wanted me to lower my guard while listening to his rant. I had kept at the ready only because I'd been desensitized to such bloodlust over the past weeks.

Once again, the heat of battle consumed us. Our blades locked against each other, and we struggled, our faces separated by mere inches. The air seemed to turn solid from the tension.

This was the closest I had ever seen his eyes. His rage was lava red in his eyes. I returned the hostile gaze. He smiled grimly.

"And where are these gods now?" he asked. "Why aren't they fighting on your side? Have they abandoned you? Ha-ha-ha! You people are frail without their protection! Only the strongest deserve the right to live. Those that can't prove their strength need to be culled."

"Are you crazy?" I uttered throatily under the blade's pressure. "Strength isn't inherited—it's earned. You have to work for it. You think Earth and Anbizia are intrinsically weak, but Kadaan is strong?"

Believing the classic theory that only the strongest could survive was fine. I didn't care if he felt that way. But his vision of strength was totally skewed. Destroying Anbizia and Earth wouldn't extinguish weakness. Surely weak Kadaanites existed, so shouldn't that have held the bulk of Tebaldus's concern?

"If you want to eradicate weakness," I said. "You should start with the weak people in your homeland!"

My last words were bellowed as I poured all my strength into driving him back. He stumbled back a few steps, startled by the sudden gust of force. Seeing the opening was like a flash of hope, hope that I could end this, but I had to act quickly. Wasting no time, I lunged with a fierce shout and thrust my sword at his head.

Clang! Averted again. Trained swordsmen knew speed was an invaluable asset. Even when his guard fell, his mastery of reaction speed allowed him to reset his defense quicker than one could blink.

"Don't you worry," said Tebaldus as our blades gritted in opposition. "The *Flesh* is taking care of that. They've already wiped out the Gryals, the Talithites, and even the Núrivans. They'll kill the Wriftians next. And to answer your question, no, strength isn't inherited. But a weak culture raises weak people. Your pathetic excuse for a society proves that humanity is weak and worthless. Strength isn't important to you people. It's as simple as that. That's why..."

This was not a battle. This was a test of strength between Earthling and Kadaanite.

Suddenly Tebaldus's head fidgeted. A cold wave of force bashed my forehead. For a moment I saw only blurs, and I found myself wobbling, nearly aswoon. When I realized I'd been headbutted, I saw him speeding toward me. I hoisted up my sword to block his blade, but the strain of my gash caught up to me, and I couldn't muster enough strength to fend him off. With a swift stroke Tebaldus launched my sword out of my hands, reversed his sword, and struck my face with a terrible blow with the handle. Red-hot pain blossomed in my conscience, and as lights flashed in my vision like a strobe, my weight seemed to vanish and I went down tumbling. Tebaldus could have killed me then and there, but that was not his intention. Not yet. He had reversed his weapon because he wanted to keep me alive just a little longer.

As I collapsed toward the dirt, however, his thigh opened, and a streak of blood appeared, for I had summoned the minimal strength needed to slide my blade down his leg. I'd finally struck a blow.

But being a warrior, it was natural that he had the grit to muscle through the pain.

My body, prostrate, tensed up with unsteady pressure as Tebaldus hobbled toward me. Bubbly drops of blood rolled over my lips and dribbled to the grass below. My eyes grew blurry with tears as the claws of death dug into my shoulders. I heard the general's boots thud closer from behind. Each slow-passing step was like the ticking of the grandfather clock of doom.

Somewhere out in this vast universe, there was a community of dear hearts, gentle people living amongst each other in solitude. A vision of myself living that future blinked before me. I could see families built on reciprocal love, sharing good times with their neighbors, exchanging smiles and laughter and friendships. They lived slow and simple lives. Much like the lost grace of this humble village, a man's purpose was fulfilled not by strength or wealth or conquest but simply by loving his community. Such peaceful living reflected the dream of all intelligent life.

But in this dark part of the universe, that dream was far out of reach.

As the vision faded out of view, my hope faded with it. But then, my ears made out a new sound: the faint rustle of grass. It wasn't Tebaldus's footsteps—it came from ahead and had that gentle consistency of something sliding along a soft surface. Then I saw it: a small glass vial rolling closer. I blinked rapidly to clear my eyes of the tears, and I could hardly believe what I saw. The bottle was filled with bright red liquid. It was Nefzing's Touch—the healing potion! I'd received it from an apothecary the other day but had hitherto forgotten about it.

What was it doing there? Where had it come from? No, I couldn't waste time brooding. This was my one window for survival: the potion could replenish my strength and provide the fighting spirit I needed. A subtle burst of adrenaline led me to lurch forward and grab the vial.

If I could just open the vial and drink it—!

"Augh!"

Tebaldus's boot came down on my forearm. The cork popped out of the bottle's neck as my hand released it, and the medicine spilled onto the grass. I gasped and shook with horror.

...That was my last chance at turning the tide.

When the bottle was about half-empty, Tebaldus picked it up and examined it. He probably didn't know what the substance was, but seeing me so earnestly trying to drink it was proof enough of how useful it was.

"What's this, some kind of medicine? How convenient! Maybe this will fix what your father did to me!"

"No..." I squeezed out quietly. By now I'd abandoned all hope.

My last saving grace had slipped away and fallen in the hands of the enemy. I couldn't bear the sight of him healing his own wounds knowing he'd walk away from our duel without a scratch.

But as Tebaldus guzzled the potion, I heard the soft sound of leaves rippling. I looked ahead, and to my utter bewilderment I saw the unmistakable color blue among the green and brown earth, and I locked eyes with...

...Kiara!

Her body hid stock-still in the same bush I'd used earlier. She went unnoticed by Tebaldus. Amazement fell on my face, and I briefly forgot about my peril. What was she doing here? How did she escape the king's clutches? She must have thrown me the Nefzing's Touch.

But she'd surely seen Tebaldus steal it away, which meant her attempt to bestow aid had backfired. Shouldn't she try to mend her failure? It was inconceivable enough that she was present, but her behavior seemed ridiculous. If we fought together, we stood a better chance against him. What was she doing in that stupid shrub? What was she trying to accomplish?

I agonized over these thoughts until I noticed her expression. A grin marked her face—a grin full of the same mischief that appeared whenever she played her pranks. Then, crystal clear in my view, she winked at me.

By now I was stupefied. What was going on? Her delighted beam suggested that everything was going to plan. Did she...did she have some kind of trick up her sleeve?

Of course she did. She always did. What was it this time?

"Eugh!" Tebaldus's face contorted after downing the red stuff. "It's spicy! Why is the potion so spicy?!"

When he spoke, I noticed a change in the earth. The grass had caught fire where the potion had spilled.

"W-wha...?" The change taking place before my eyes captured my full attention, and I muttered confused jabber at the sight.

It didn't take long to catch onto Kiara's sleight of hand. I'd solved her trick. Before Tebaldus noticed the emerging flames I quickly blew them out to prevent their spread, and the whiskers of grass were left black as if the sun had charred it.

It was not medicine Kiara had tossed at me. The apothecary had given me two products. The first was Nefzing's Touch, a healing potion that patched wounds and restored strength. But the other was like the broth of the netherworld, scorching everything it touched. That was why Tebaldus whined about it being spicy— he'd poured fire on his tongue! And *that* was why Kiara's smile had since turned into laughing. She *wanted* him to drink it.

But that fire potion was supposed to be black. I couldn't fathom why it was red.

"You damn aliens," moaned the general. "*Cough*...You make your medicine spicy! Why?!"

"What's the matter?" I asked mockingly. "Too weak to handle a bit of heat?"

Tebaldus raised his sword to plunge it down. Just before he let the blade fall, however, the effects of Hell's Liquor kicked in. His face twisted even more, and at that moment, he realized he had ingested no medicine.

An obscene cough possessed him. "*Cough...cough...cough cough!* W-what the—*cough!* What was that stuff?!" He gripped his neck and kept coughing. The pain must have been unbearable, for his insides were burning with the heat of the sun. A literal fire had been kindled inside him, melting his entrails and making a furnace out of his stomach. He squeezed his sword's hilt and readied the blade as if signaling he still had some fight left.

Wielding his blade, he bore down on me, but then Kiara sprang from her hiding spot. She dashed out of the bush with another vial in hand, shouting, "Let's spice up your last moments even more!" and flung it at the enemy. It crashed into his chest and splattered all over him.

"Aaauuggh!" The broken cry escaped him as his body seared under the new coating. The potion hissed as it burned him, and flames erupted on his clothes. He was drenched in so much heat that it even imbued the air around him. It felt like one might melt simply standing near him.

Then a new danger entered the stage. I recalled where we were. Behind him was Senzaw Cave, the lair where the Aether Seal had dwelled for so long. A monster lurked in that murky darkness, and it was natural that Tebaldus's explosives coupled with our raging battle were bound to rouse it from sleep. Now it was hungry to break its fast. The tentacles of the giant one-eyed octopus—the octoclops—crept out of the cave's shadows.

The arms probed the area for food, crawling up behind Tebaldus's vulnerable figure. As for the octoclops's body, it remained concealed in the cave's gloom. The arms loomed up on him with the stealth of a leopard stalking its prey.

"No! *Cough, cough!*" As the Kadaanite coughed, his screams bellowed with brutal hoarseness: his throat was burnt. Blazing sparks and bloody embers sputtered out from his throat. "Killing me won't change a thing! Kadaan will rise above all! You and your false gods will perish!"

"Uh-huh, just shut up and die," I said dispassionately as Kiara helped me to my feet.

An arm curled around his ankle, and his eyes widened before he was jerked back. He flopped to the ground and let his sword fall clattering. The tentacle dragged him toward the cave. Desperately he dug his fingers into the ground but to no avail. The explosives had uncaked the soil, loosening the earth and leaving his hands to slide through it like dry sand. On top of that, the cave beast's incomparable strength hardly wavered against Tebaldus, who was too sapped for resistance.

"This can't be! Only the strongest survive! Kadaan will have its revenge, and when we do—*cough, cough*—we'll remember your name, Nathan Tucker!"

I approached him and stared deep into his eyes. Kiara was right beside me. While the battle left me dripping, the radiating heat drew out even more sweat, but I didn't care. His eyes were colored by so much malice, yet they harbored no fear. Something occurred to me then, as I saw the hateful tone of his eyes. He lamented not because he feared death but because he wanted to be spared from the shame of dying by *my* hand.

"Not so strong after all, eh?" I sneered.

Tebaldus's face glowed red with rage, but there was nothing he could do. No one could swoop in and save him now.

But in one final act of desperation...

"—?!"

Kiara's proud expression suddenly swapped out for a look of horror as she toppled, for Tebaldus had reached out and seized her leg. They slid toward the cave together. With his tightened grip on her, he planned to take her with him.

"Kiara!" I cried as I sprinted after her.

"No! No! Let go!" Kiara's wails rang out. She kicked at Tebaldus with her free leg, but his nails dug through her boots and into her flesh. He wouldn't let go; if he was going to let the octoclops sink its teeth into him, he was determined not to be devoured alone.

When I dove for Kiara, our hands locked, and I was dragged with them. Our formation was like a chain: the octoclops, Tebaldus, Kiara, and I were the links. Within seconds an arched root sticking out of the dirt caught my foot. The sliding chain stopped abruptly. That little root was the final chain-link, the only thing holding us in place.

But the root wouldn't hold on to the ground forever. As the octoclops tugged with its peerless might, the root started breaking out of the ground. The clock was ticking fast, and it wouldn't be long before the chain resumed its flow.

There was only one way I could think of to break this chain.

Holding onto Kiara, who screamed in terror, I reached into my jacket pocket with my free hand. I spent several seconds groping. If I could just find what I was looking for, I could end all of this.

"What's it gonna be, Nathan?" Tebaldus asked, his voice low and guttural. "How many more people...can you save today?"

The root—that one thread holding us in place—was only seconds away from snapping out of the dirt. By what seemed like a miracle, my fingers curled around what I was looking for.

It was now or never.

From my pocket I produced my utility knife. It was the same knife Dimitri had gifted me in the Stiadev Welyn. His gift had proved useful after all. I held it out for Kiara. She stared at me as she processed my movements amid her peril.

"Finish him!" I told her.

When I spoke, the fright and shock that cowed her vanished. Courage strengthened her. Taking the knife, she quickly brought it to her bound leg and thrust it straight into the enemy's wrist. And with one shrill cry from the general, Kiara's leg was free.

General Tebaldus's reign was over.

Her hand released the knife, leaving it in his wrist, and the tentacle dragged him in, but we were left behind, trembling and sweating in the soil.

Inside the cave, however, the octoclops's patience grew thin, and its arm thrashed. A strident shriek rang out with stark gruffness as the beast slammed the Kadaanite into the cliff wall. There was the sound of bones shattering like glass, and I winced at the horror. Tebaldus's body was limp now. He neither screamed nor struggled. Finally, the beast pulled him into the darkness forever.

I stood, staring into the silent shadows of Senzaw. There was no noise except the tweeting of birds. I shuddered as I imagined the fate of Tebaldus's body, but also a pleasant wave of relief washed over me. The souls he had ravaged were free, and a rich plate of justice was served. Moreover, this was surely a crushing blow for the Kadaanites: a valuable general was dead.

Which meant they had one less point of leadership.

As I mused on these things, another tentacle emerged. Why was the beast showing itself again? It had already feasted. Was it still hungry?

Its intentions became clear when I saw the snaky arm's goal.

"—Oh no! The Aether Seal!"

The realization felt like a steel fist. We couldn't let the octoclops have the artifact—not after learning its true function. Anbizia could use it as a tool to suppress Kadaan's wormholes, which seemed likely to be an excellent weapon, but that wouldn't be possible if it fell into the beast's hands.

I fell into a deep sprint. The memory of fighting in the cave for the Aether Seal flashed in my mind, driving me even faster. But the octoclops knew this was a race and didn't want to lose. We dashed against each other to the quiet crater in which it sat. As I desperately dove for the artifact, the tentacle snatched it up just before my arms embraced it.

"No!" I cried as the arm pulled back into the cave with the Aether Seal. Giving myself no time to blink, I leaped to my feet and ran after it, taking up my sword.

But before I could give chase, Kiara's hand fell on my shoulder and held me back. Her expression was like calm waters against my tempestuous spirit, and the mere sight of her could soothe the tides of even the angriest sea. I shot her an addled look, unable to make sense of her relaxation.

"The Hell's Liquor," she said, pointing to the cave. "It's collateral damage."

Shifting my gaze back toward Senzaw, I froze in silence. What in the world did she mean by *collateral*?

"*Roooooaaarr!*" A screech of pain sounded out from the gloom, and the realization hit me. Oh, that Kiara, she had a remarkable flair for thinking things through. One dose of Hell's Liquor was more than enough to incinerate the general's vitals, yet Kiara had hurled another bottle at his chest. I thought the extra dosage had been for good measure, but it was really another limb of her plan. She had actually intended to contaminate him with the stuff, like an assassin spiking a target's drink. "*Roooooaaarr!*"

More cries came. The octoclops must have felt the same sizzling pain as Tebaldus; its innards were blazing. By eating the hellfire-coated Kadaanite, the octoclops absorbed its effects. Then the stuff fatally burned the beast from the inside, leaving not a sliver of hope for survival.

Eventually the octoclops's screams died in the darkness. The Hell's Liquor permeated the beast's system like poison until the carcass lay hushed in the shadows.

With that everything was quiet. I faced Kiara, and she faced me. Her grin was impish, but I was bewildered, and stared like a dummy. My train of thought didn't know which way to turn. My heart seemed to bash my ribs, and my legs shook from weakness, and I could hardly croak a word.

"K...Kiara..." I stammered after some awkward silence. "How...how did you...?" I was too flabbergasted to finish. At length we welcomed each other into a warm embrace.

"Well!" she said, excited to share her story. "I figured that if Tebaldus saw you trying to drink the Hell's Liquor, he'd want to drink it himself. But I knew *you* wouldn't drink the stuff knowing what it really was, so I dyed it red to make it look like Nefzing's Touch." She shrunk slightly, blushing. "I'm sorry for tricking you, Mr. Nathan. But think! The only other option was to let Tebaldus slaughter you! I knew I was playing a huge gamble—I knew you might have drunk it yourself—but it was the only way to win. Either you'd have died to the Hell's Liquor, or you'd have died to Tebaldus. *That's* why the risk was worth—!" Her voice was muffled as I drew her head in.

"Kiara, I'm not mad. We won, and it was all thanks to you. If you hadn't stepped in, I'd be dead."

Such a risky yet genius plan went to show how bright her intuition was. There really was no end to her brilliance.

When I released her head, she was smiling, her expression looking like a flower.

Now I *had* to ask about her mere presence.

"How are you in the flesh? I mean, the king wanted to kill you! How'd you get away?"

"Ah, that! Well, it just so happens that *someone* is still on our side."

When she spoke, a traxid came trotting up the hill leading to Vethwood. The riders were familiar faces. A blast of happy surprise took me as I spotted them.

"Hey there, kid!" said Gad Goldwin the merchant.

Yes, it was him—the one man who showed me kindness by helping me get started on this planet. I should have known—who else would've given me a favor? The two climbed down from the Traxid. "They were *planning* to execute her until they brought up the bailing price of fifty silvers. That other human's hand shot up immediately. What was his name...Dimitri? Something like that. Anyway, I sure as hell wasn't letting him have the prize *that* easily. I gave him a piece of my mind by offering a higher price, and after battling it out for some time, I won with a grand total of ninety silvers."

Dimitri, that rat of a man. He had said he'd take Kiara under his wing, an outcome I feared was worse than her execution. How horrible reality would be if Goldwin hadn't stepped in!

"I'm glad we rode here in time!" said his wife Elowen. "Three people is a lot of weight on a traxid's back!"

Though I was thankful to Goldwin for saving Kiara and giving her a ride to Maratel, the price of ninety Merth Silvers left me flustered. I'd only paid twenty silvers for her. How had it swelled like that? I figured this was an ill time to worry about it, so I decided to compensate him for his troubles. I couldn't let him pay all that money for nothing.

"Here." I produced my coin purse and gave him ninety silvers, which had been most of my payoff for retrieving the Aether Seal.

"Thanks for the help."

But as I handed them over, he held up his palm toward me.

"Ah, don't bother. It's my pleasure."

Although I appreciated his kindness, I couldn't let him pay ninety silvers for something that hardly benefited him. Besides, Kiara was bound to me by a debt of only twenty coins, a price that had just been outweighed. There was no way I'd let her be in more debt to someone else.

That was the only way to keep her by my side.

"Please, I insist. I need you to accept it."

My eyes as I glared at him were severe, relaying that I wouldn't take no for an answer. He stared with a wide mouth and, seeming to feel a bit guilty, looked down and gave a nod as if he knew my reasons. Certainly there was some deeper reason for helping me that he kept secret, and I could tell by his look that it was much more than an attempt to buy customer loyalty. There must have been some other motive that he couldn't reveal, but now wasn't the time to trouble with that. *That* could wait for another day.

"Y-yeah, all right," he said as he accepted my payment in understanding.

With that said and done, I couldn't help but glance at Kiara uneasily. It had suddenly occurred to me that she never *needed* to come all this way. After Goldwin saved her, she could have moved on if she wanted. She could have left me for dead, which would nullify her debt to me. And the merchant had no desire to chain her up, so she gained new freedom. Why did she come back to me? She could have done as she pleased, even pretend I never existed.

And yet, she didn't. It was unsettling.

"Is something wrong?" asked a concerned Kiara, noticing my disquiet.

"Uh...nothing. Hey, what about the village?" I decided to change the subject. "Did the raid go through? Did we win?"

"See for yourself," said Goldwin. He indicated a nearby hill that would offer me a view of the village.

After quickly climbing it, my gaze roved the village streets. The pavement was choked with slain bodies. Stray arrows, notched swords, heavy battle-axes, and broad-headed spears littered the alleys and avenues that wound between the buildings, many of which were torn to ruin. But there was one fantastic sight that lifted the huge burden of stress from my shoulders. Down in the village square, the Anbizian soldiers were busy rounding up surviving Kadaanites as prisoners. Their hands were bound behind their backs, they were stripped of arms, and their faces burned with shame.

"They did it!" I said with a leaping heart. "Well, the general's dead too. I guess we should head down and tell everyone the good news."

After all, the man wanted across all of Anbizia was finally dead. He was a lawless barbarian that plundered the land and laid waste to the innocent. His death was a cause for celebration.

"You'll be on your own for that," said the merchant. "There's still some daylight left, which means there's still time for profit! I'm heading back to Cordea."

"Oh, deary, you think about money more than you actually *think*!" laughed Elowen.

And so, we parted ways till our next meeting. After saying goodbye to the Goldwins, Kiara and I headed for the village. The sound of the traxid's thudding footsteps tickled our ears as the couple rode along the path into Vethwood.

We reached the village square, and everyone fixed their attention on me and awaited the news anxiously. Murmurs circulated among the soldiers in anticipation of what I'd say. In a sonorous announcement I proclaimed the general's death. The crowd took in the triumph for a silent moment, letting my words spin excitement, and cheers erupted.

"Ha-ha! We won!"

"Now those aliens will think twice about who they're screwing with!"

"I'll bet these prisoners'll be crying for their mommas soon!"

They hollered verbal slander across the square, at which the Kadaanite prisoners crimsoned. Though they didn't understand our language, they knew exactly what was happening. Their humiliation was totally transparent!

Kiara was deeply moved by the triumphant scene. Tears hung at the corners of her eyes above a touched smile. The Kadaanites had taken so much from her, but for the first time in her life, she had seen Anbizia fight back. This meant a turning point for her.

"Tebaldus killed a lot of people, and there's no bringing them back," I said to her. "But now their souls—especially the ones of this village—can rest. All that's left is to keep fighting until Kadaan can't steal any more lives."

The scourge of Kadaan had taken Kiara's family. I didn't know how or when her loved ones would see justice, but I wanted her to see that there was hope in making that happen. We had already avenged Maratel's people. One day we would do the same for Kiara's family. I knew we would.

"Yeah," she said, giving a smile and standing taller. "We'll keep fighting."

Suddenly the main doors of Maratel's church swung open, and out bobbed Chief Enestir along with a very weary group of villagers.

"It's about time someone rescued us!" bellowed the chief in a flamboyant outburst.

"You're aliiiiive?!" cried everyone in unison.

"We've all spent the last eighteen hours cooped up in a hidden cellar beneath the church, all praying that we wouldn't be discovered behind a single trapdoor!" said Mr. Merrybeard, who was among the group. "You wouldn't believe how cramped it was!"

His complaints were obviously lighthearted as he sported a broad smile (I daresay he was as merry as his beard itself), but the woeful story did have that sting, and I couldn't help pitying the villagers.

"We thought you were all dead!" remarked a soldier.

"That's what the vermin thought too!" replied Enestir. "But they didn't get all of us! That Tebaldus may be a genius of war, but even *he* can be outsmarted." The soldiery laughed to hear such a jab.

Meanwhile, I noticed Dimitri standing within the crowd of soldiers. Having been present at Kiara's attempted execution, he must have arrived in Maratel just now. As everyone left to their own business, he approached Enestir.

"Hey, mister," he said. "I trust you recognize me, yes?"

"Um..." the chief searched his memory with a polite smile, but nothing seemed to click. "...I'm sorry, but I don't believe we've met."

"I'm Dimitri Volkov, the human."

The chief's smile vanished. His gaze drifted toward me. Undoubtedly he was snapping together all the puzzle pieces in his head. When Dimitri professed his humanity like that, the next obvious conclusion was that *I* was human too. Until today, Maratel's locals were evidently unfamiliar with the defining features of humans; they had fallen for an illusion that I was an Anbizian nonfalius, but now they were being educated. I watched Dimitri and Enestir with a series of restless fidgets. I was annoyed; my true identity was coming out of hiding. Even if Enestir didn't know what humans looked like, he had surely heard of the crimes attached to my name. If the chief found out Dimitri was the widely respected human whom the king loved, he'd know I could only be the traitor whom the public feared. His gaze returned to Dimitri. Surely those common anti-me opinions that took society by storm were emerging in his mind. *That* would only cause more unwanted trouble.

"I see," said the chief a bit solemnly. Sighing, he asked, "How can I help you?"

"I've troubled myself to defeat General Tebaldus and liberate your village. I expect compensation for my efforts by tomorrow morning."

"You can't be serious," I murmured under my breath.

Dimitri's lies were rampant. To casually approach the chief, steal credit for my victory, and demand payment was just like him and yet so irredeemable. This was yet another stain on his imaginary honor. Worse, he was spitting on the graves of those who faced Tebaldus's wrath, but his nonchalant tone suggested not even a dash of shame. I wondered just how low he was willing to stoop.

But Chief Enestir's stare bore into Dimitri like icy shards, and a clear image of disgust hid behind his blank expression. "I'm afraid that's not going to happen."

"What? What do you mean?" Dimitri asked sharply. He looked visibly insulted by the denial. Oh, when would he let go of the delusion that his lies would slip past every radar?

"You didn't do a thing in this battle...and I don't appreciate you exploiting my village."

"What?!" He had a dire expression. "Don't you know who I am? I've saved you today!"

Dimitri was always desperate to bend the truth, but at this point, his efforts were all in vain. Enestir saw the subterfuge, and he didn't like it one bit. He refused to be swayed.

"No, you didn't do a single thing," he said, his expression swelling. "When the raid began, we heard the Kadaanites rush out of the church in a panic, and then I climbed to the top of the bell tower to see what was going on."

Every onlooker of the conversation, myself included, glanced toward the church. The doors were left open; it was a mess in there. Pews were disarrayed and overturned, icons were vandalized, and the head of a priest was skewered on the altar. This was a likely and deliberate attempt on the enemy's part to desecrate the Ystarian faith. But what grabbed our attention at the moment was the bell tower, which stretched tall enough to provide a view of the entire village.

Which could only mean one thing.

"I saw everything from up there. You didn't kill Tebaldus, but I know who did. Leave me be, and don't make any trouble. Good day to you!"

With those words, the village chief had nothing left to say to Dimitri and walked away without feeling. The scalding hot tension between the pair sprinkled across the area, and the villagers stared at the lying scoundrel, contempt burning in their eyes. He lost all comfort at that. Sweat seeped from his forehead, and his breath hitched.

His eyes darted nervously. "The hell are you people looking at?!" he exploded with a sharp bawl, and the stares fell away.

It was the way of the world that being exposed for your lies was a humiliating fate. Still, this was only one of many lies. The rest of his deception survived; his corrupt shell had yet to crack. He was still the hero, and I was the devil.

Someday, I wanted the world to know the truth.

"Now then, I have to admit," said Enestir, approaching me. "*That* was one hell of a show. Your standoff against Tebaldus inspires us all. We may have defeated that general, but..." he paused for a moment as if hoping the wind would sweep the words out of his mouth. "...This victory only follows a loss. Most of my people are dead now. I wish I could have done more for them." He looked down in remorse.

"It's not your fault any more than it is mine," I said. "I was the one who opened the door for the Kadaanites to attack. If I hadn't taken away the Aether Seal, this battle never would've happened." I clasped his shoulder, and he snapped to attention. "You keep leading this village. Help these people rebuild. One day, Anbizia will have its revenge."

An increase in strength seemed to cross him, and he lifted his chin with a ghost of a smile. "You're right. Anyway, I do want to thank you two for saving our village. Please, if there's any way I can repay you, pray tell."

It was my turn to speak, but I was delayed by indecision.

The first idea that flickered into my mind was money. This made perfect sense given the bounty on Tebaldus's head. My gut feeling suggested that King Frieval would invent an excuse to withhold the bounty if I approached him demanding it; but I could at least wring *something* out of Chief Enestir. Obviously he couldn't give enough to make me rich, but I'd still get a much-needed financial boost. However, when I thought more about my decision, a plethora of other choices sprang to life in my head. I could ask for land in the village alternatively. That way, I'd have somewhere to nest myself away from that harsh king. I'd be surrounded by villagers who appreciated me for my deeds, and I wouldn't be spending money on inns either. Another option was to ask for tools or resources. A weapon more suited for combat than our cheap swords would serve us greatly, and I could probably scrape together some medicine—*real* medicine—or perhaps nicer clothes. Maybe I could even score a personal traxid and carriage.

These choices sounded appealing, but they all seemed too temporary. I needed something with an everlasting benefit: revenge. There was one more idea that gripped me. If Dimitri's chagrin hadn't yet been activated, *this* was sure to trigger it. It was a simple request, but I had waited too long for an opportunity like this.

Now was my chance for a taste of sweet revenge, and so, I made up my mind and told the village chief what I wanted.

CHAPTER XV

YOUR PAIN BELONGS TO ME

In the end, Dimitri's face went pale when he got word of my request. Ever since his arrival on this planet, he always got his way, but the times were changing. As he was unadapted to any kind of persecution, it was sure to ruffle his feathers. Never before had he been humbled like this. Finally I'd served him a taste of my pain. And while I couldn't deny that he'd dragged me through darker voids of despair, today's deal of satisfaction was mine. This village belonged to its chief, and there was nothing Dimitri nor King Frieval could do about it.

Pride comes before the fall. I thought about the classic saying as I watched Dimitri depart for Cordea. But *this* was a heavy blow to his pride. My request to Chief Enestir was simple. I had asked him to banish Dimitri from Maratel for life. He would never set foot in this village as long as he lived.

Since that was quite the effortless task for the chief, he let Kiara pick a reward, too. Her expression brightened at the offer, and with little thought she asked him to send supplies to the war effort in the north since that was where her hometown was. Piecing together what little information she'd given me about her past, I could surmise the reasons behind her request. Not wanting to trouble her about it, I refrained from asking questions.

Night fell on the land soon, and the village gathered in the square for a feast. Many soldiers stayed for the night to celebrate the victory. The stars dazzled in the sky with the two plump moons. Round wooden tables were set up neatly, and villagers and soldiers sat alongside each other, making hearty conversation, singing merrily, and laughing as they sipped their ales. Chefs were constantly dishing out food much to their enjoyment.

"To put it simply, it would be a shame to let the remains of the octoclops go to waste," said Enestir when he learned of its demise. Although I warned him that its insides were contaminated with the Hell's Liquor, he expressed little worry, arguing that the stuff could easily be cooked off.

As for the Aether Seal, the chief arranged for it to go back to the Church. If they could study it and learn how it worked, it was a likely tool against Kadaan.

I sat alone at a table nuzzled in the corner of the square, secluded from the throng, sipping my ale dispassionately with some local delicacy on my plate. It had been whipped up as an appetizer as the chefs put their finishing touches on the roasted octoclops. The feast was more than enormous. With a single glance, one could warrant that this village could never finish so much food in one evening—well, everyone was calamitously famished, so perhaps there was a narrow chance.

Oh, and did I mention there was alcohol? Lots and lots of alcohol.

They were the special courtesy of Mr. Merrybeard himself, who probably brewed the brownest beer in all of Neiklof.

Kiara was thrilled when she learned of the free drinks. In her defense, it was indeed a surprise, as free drinks were seldom in Anbizia. But Chief Enestir spared some of the village's funds to pay for the feast, so Mr. Merrybeard gave away his ale with a smile.

Also, Kiara won the drinking contest. She won it with ease. "Ha-ha-ha!" Kiara returned to the table giggling. "That was fun! And the drinks were delicious, too!"

"Uh-huh. Glad you liked it."

As usual, the alcohol had hardly dazed her. "And look at this!" Kiara chirped as she opened her hands for me to see. "I won three silver coins!"

I looked at her cupped hands and saw the tiny haul. Naturally you couldn't win crazy money from a single drinking contest, but her mastery of alcohol was prodigious.

As I was about to give some petty words of congratulation, she put them in her pouch as if they were trivial. Did she forget about them just like that?

"Wow! This looks so yummy!" Her eyes sparkled over the mountains of food on our table. Cheese, bread, crackers, fermented vegetables, tangy fruits, and of course, octoclops meat, were all among the fare. I was pretty sure the chefs had served us the largest of portions, but as our table was somewhat isolated from the celebration, it was hard to tell. Whatever the case, there was plenty to go around, and a long table stood in the middle of the square with heaps of extra food, dedicated to second helpings.

"Enjoy the food. You've earned it," I said before cutting into a crispy tentacle. Kiara smiled and nodded as she dug in.

When I bit into the meat, its tenderness tantalized my tongue, and the blasting flavors were enhanced by a rainbow of spices. Its numbing flavors shot up into my temples and throughout my head, churning a feeling of bliss that I wished would last a lifetime. The food was like an evil army that had infiltrated my mouth to tie up my tastebuds and hold them hostage. Kiara was immediately in love with her plate too.

"*Mph, nom...gulp.* Mmm!"

"Hey, your mouth is all covered in grease."

My comment left her flustered in an instant, and she flushed shyly before scrubbing her face with a napkin. She went back to her food. Contrary to Kiara's eating habits, I took the time to chew and savor my food, whereas she stuffed her cheeks till she had the run of her teeth. She may have been wildly clever, but she was foolhardy when it came to food and drink. Gluttony was the bane of her self-restraint.

The Hell's Liquor seemed to have sizzled off when cooking. A single drop of the stuff could seriously burn your throat, but the fare on my plate was nothing but pleasurable. It didn't even kindle the smallest flame.

"Hah..." My companion swallowed and panted with her tongue lolling out like a dog. "Spicy!" she wheezed, taking a huge swig of her drink.

"Spicy?" I echoed. "It's not *that* bad!"

"It is too!"

At most it had a slight kick, but it didn't sting the senses. She must have been dramatic; her tolerance was poor. She could handle all that alcohol but hardly any spice.

Her reaction left me wondering if the spice was the work of the Hell's Liquor.

"That was great!" said my companion, who had kept gorging in spite of the spice. In the time it took me to finish half of my plate, Kiara had demolished hers. She leaned back in her chair like a bear having feasted on the most heavenly prey.

"You can get more if you want." Many weeks would pass before we received another meal like this, so I wanted Kiara to milk this opportunity while it stood.

"Nah, I'm way too full now...especially after all those drinks."

I almost smiled at that side of her, seeing that her gluttony had already defeated her. She closed her eyes where she sat, as if trying to make the gears in her stomach turn faster to speed up digestion.

Cooking the octoclops must have been an ordeal for the chefs. It was amazing how they turned such a massive beast into little ribbons of meat that burst with flavor, which now rested on my plate, waiting to retire in my mouth.

As I neared my last bits of food, a chef stood atop an empty table and shouted across the village square, "Attention, you big ol' fatties! Dessert is ready! Come and get it while it's hot!"

"Ooh, dessert!" Kiara, who had been lazily lounging in her chair, perked up in delight.

Oh, come on, you just said you were full...

...Was what I wanted to say, but I figured there was no point. Her behavior was ridiculous, of course, but I'd given her the green light to eat what she wanted. Her choice was her choice. Having no interest in the extra course, I wrapped up my meal while Kiara rushed over to the table of sweets. Her comical behavior reminded me of a child bolting out the door after hearing an ice cream truck's music. And of course her childlike etiquette was only highlighted when I saw her nibbling at the sugary dish even before sitting down again.

"Mm...heh-heh...it's been a while since I last had sweets. You want some, Mr. Nathan?"

The treat looked like a crumbled mess of baked dough with sugar and soft fruit, and it was doused in some viscous syrup, which drooled down the sides and glistened in the orange torchlight. The aroma from the spoon filled my nostrils, overwhelming my senses with the murder of the candyish scent. The smell was so rampantly sweet that I wanted to turn it down, but Kiara was already putting the spoon in my face and giving me no room for escape. "Go on! Try it!" said her sparkling look. Realizing I couldn't wriggle out of this one, I drew in a breath of fresh air from the side, and then reluctantly took up her offering of the sweetness. The spoon went in and came out empty. As I chewed and let the flavors dance in my mouth, the sugar was so powerful that it scrubbed my tongue in the most nauseating way possible. I couldn't compare it to any dessert on Earth, but my teeth felt ready to fall out like icicles. What kind of person would eat something so sweet? Well, it did seem like something a child would enjoy.

"It's called an Ashovian Crumble. Gets your sweet tooth going, doesn't it?" said Kiara. She smiled and seemed to assume I *liked* that abomination of a dish.

"*Cough...gag.* Y-yeah...it *really* does," I answered, putting extra emphasis on the "really." The sweetness stuck to the roof of my mouth, and I tactically retreated to my ale. That awful taste wasn't washed down till I slurped down the whole mug.

Maratel was a babel of festive talk and laughter. The loud atmosphere was like a party, which didn't quite fit my style. The noise was getting to my head. This whole celebration felt like a waste of time. I waited for Kiara to finish her dessert, which she *somehow* enjoyed, and after letting our feast digest a little, we slowly got ready to leave. I was positive we would have to get up later than usual tomorrow morning. Our meal was weighing down our bellies and would probably have us in a food coma all night.

Speaking of slumber, tonight's sleep was sure to be an excellent sleep. As thanks for defeating Tebaldus, the innkeeper insisted we stay the night for free. Resting in a fine straw bed without paying was a keen source of delight. We headed over to the inn, walking with slow steps to prevent our digesting meals from sloshing too much in our stomachs.

We really did eat a bit much. Kiara was unbothered by it, and her mood was rather pleased. As I hadn't indulged in much drink, the alcohol was ineffective as it worked its way through my system, and while Kiara was more of a drinker than me, she seemed mostly unfazed as well. At most her walk was slightly rickety, but she was rather steady.

The inn was empty save for the innkeeper, who was nodding toward sleep in his chair until we trudged in. Wary of intruders, he jerked from his sleep but, upon seeing who we were, acknowledged us with a calm nod, and I promptly returned the gesture. We ascended the stairs and entered our room. The door clicked shut, and she slumped down on one of the beds.

"Ah...that was the longest day ever..." she murmured lazily with her eyes closed.

"And grass is green, and the sky is blue," I said in agreement with her remark.

She laughed at my lighthearted sarcasm. "Still, now that I'm with you again, everything's a lot more bearable."

"What do you mean by that?"

"I mean I was worried I wouldn't see you again. When they brought me to the gallows again, I thought it was over. At the time, that all too familiar feeling of loneliness clouded me like a black storm. But...now that I'm here, it's all coming up sunny!"

This was rather difficult. Was she implying that she enjoyed spending time with me? No, that wasn't possible. She must have meant that she was scared of execution and only saw her surrender to me as a slightly better alternative. There was no way she *preferred* following me. No way.

Knock knock!

The sound came from the door. Late-night visitors at this hour? I glanced at Kiara, who bounced back my confusion with a shrug.

I plodded to the door, where I turned the knob and pulled it open. Kiara was frontside-down atop her bed, though her position was backward so that her head was at the bed's foot. Her head was in her hands, and she fluttered her legs. She watched with interest as the door creaked open.

"..."

Standing before me was a lone soldier holding a sheet of parchment paper. His displeased expression matched mine; neither of us were happy to see the other. He cleared his throat, and with a brief "Good evening," read the paper aloud:

"To the human Nathan Tucker: By the order of His Majesty King Frieval, the young female slime by the name Kiara Jaroe in your possession has been relieved of her debt. The nonfalius girl shall be unbound from you to restore her freedom in exchange for her debt, being twenty Merth Silver coins." He held out a small burlap sack of coins, and I took it with a slow, melancholic movement. At some point in his speech, my eyes went wide, and my stomach twisted.

"If you are spotted with the slime again, you are to be arrested imme-diately."

Though it suddenly started feeling very hot, I couldn't keep my-self from shivering. The soldier, who seemed nervous that I might lash out, strode away with quick feet.

As I closed the door and tried to control my trembling hands, the face of that pathetic king appeared in my mind. Why was he doing this? Was his only purpose to target me? Did he not have better matters to attend to? This must have been his final effort to drive me into the ground. I knew his intentions when he deployed me to Maratel—he was sending me to my death. When that didn't work, he must have decided to steal Kiara away just to fuel my suffering. Or was this Dimitri's doing? He must have run crying to the king about how I caused his banishment from the village. Was this his way of getting back at me? Whatever the case, I wanted to punch a hole through the wall in a steaming fury.

They're all animals! Animals, animals, animals! My heart cried the word out but to no one's hearing.

The thought of turning around was too terrifying. I could al-ready picture Kiara frantically trussing up her things to flee. I couldn't possibly bear the sight. But I knew better than to deny reality. The truth was that Kiara was happy to take the leap toward freedom. She was out of my grasp again. The moment she'd fallen back into my hands, she slipped clean through my fingers.

Turning around I fought hard to keep my composure. Sweaty streams rolled down my neck. My expression must have been black with consternation or terror or rage or something else—I didn't know. My thoughts were frozen with Kiara's image burning in my mind. To my surprise, her body was still when I finally looked at her. She sat up now, having heard the soldier's speech. A long stare was drawn between us, and her face was full of concern.

"Um...Mr. Nathan...?" she said in a soft voice.

Hearing her attempt to speak, I froze. I didn't freeze out of shock, misery, or fear...I did so out of anger.

Her senseless behavior was infuriating. She had heard the king's order, yet she sat there like a clueless dope. Her debt was relieved, and her freedom was waiting, so why wasn't she moving? She should have been scrambling to get away from me.

It didn't matter in the end. Kiara would be gone soon, and I would be all alone again. History had shown me my destiny, and history repeated itself. It was my destiny to be alone. It was my destiny to be despised. It was my destiny to live in a snake pit where misery tied me up and gutted me of all hope.

My gaze fell to the wooden planks under my boots. I balled my fists, clenching them so hard that my nails almost dug into my palms, and my teeth grated. The lid to all my pent-up hatred for those who'd hurt me was about to pop off.

This planet made me sick. This planet *was* sick. I hated it. I hated everything about it.

I wanted to go home.

"Mr. Nathan...you're all pale."

Shut up, shut up! I thought. I didn't want to hear it.

She stood up and drew closer, and I spoke in a dry, cold voice.

"Just...leave."

"B-but...I don't..."

She extended her hand by way of comfort. I was hardly conscious when my arm's instincts kicked in.

Smack!

"Get away from me!" I blustered after slapping her hand away.

This world was darker than doom. It was a rathole that pulled me in and tortured me without mercy. I couldn't trust anyone. Everyone wanted to hurt me. Everyone wanted to watch me suffer. As my vision became blurry with all the hatred I could muster, I felt ready to collapse. I just wanted to be left alone. That way, no one could inflict any pain.

But this girl...this stupid girl! Why was she still bothering me?

"Please stop! I don't want to—"

"Just leave me alone!" I refused to listen to whatever she had to say. Why listen to anyone when they all aimed to hurt me? "Didn't you hear that soldier? You're free to go, so just scram! Beat it!"

My hand went up defensively preparing to strike her, but a cool hand squeezed my wrist and held it up. Kiara had seized my arm.

"No! I'm not leaving you to waste away and rot! Please...I don't want to see you suffer anymore..." Her voice throbbed, and her forehead was grooved. She was on the verge of tears.

Still, I knew better than to fall for these traps. Every emotion was an act to reel me in. I was done letting myself be vulnerable.

"Too bad! You're not in my debt anymore! There's nothing left for you here!"

"Forget the debt! I want to stay by your side! Please!"

Our voices were rising. Kiara tugged my arm down to my side and released her grasp.

Stay by my side? Give me a break. Everything she said was a lie. She was just like everyone else; she wanted to manipulate me and deal more harm. I was better off trusting nobody. If I put my faith only in myself, I would never get backstabbed or led astray. It really didn't sound so bad—it was better than *this* torture.

Still, there'd been something bugging me all evening. Even though I knew I couldn't trust her, I couldn't resist asking.

"Why? Why did you come here and save me? You could have gone anywhere after Goldwin freed you, so why did you come here?!"

If Kiara hadn't stepped in at the last moment, Tebaldus surely would have killed me. He could have killed both of us had her plan failed. I didn't understand why, of all the things she could've done, she traveled all this way when she knew she might meet her demise. Why didn't she just abandon me to death?

"Don't you understand?!" said Kiara in desperation. "I did it because I didn't want you to die. I wanted you to live!"

Silence swept over the room for a long moment. Then she spoke again bitterly, looking away with a scowl.

"Well, forget about living. You're always so sullen and angry that it's impossible for you to *live*."

Living—living not as merely staying alive, but as pursuing a life that fulfills. And she was right. How could I possibly *live* on this wretched planet? How could I be fulfilled when everyone and everything knocked me over whenever I stood up?

"Yeah, that's right. I'm a total jerk who can't live his life," I replied. "So just get out of here and live life on your own."

"But I...I also came here because I wanted to stay with you. You saved my life when we first crossed paths; you're the reason I'm alive. Besides, the things you've done for me...they're worth way more than twenty silvers."

"Heh...that's touching, but I'm not that nice of a guy. Do you even know who I am?"

The answer was obvious. I had withheld the shadows of my past so that she'd see me in a more positive light. But I was done hiding.

"Yes! I do!" she cried.

Wrong answer. She was as ignorant as ever.

"No, you don't! You know nothing about me!" Then I lowered my voice, but my fury was still red-hot. "I'm a monster. If you don't believe me, just ask everyone else."

"They're wrong! You're not a monster!" She rounded her fists and squeezed her eyes shut as if finding her next words difficult to get out. "I...I already knew everything!"

"...What?"

I stared at her, open-mouthed in astonishment.

"I'd been putting on an act because I didn't want you to mistrust me, but I already knew all the horrible things about you! I'd already

heard the news that you destroyed your spaceship—that you murdered your fellow humans!"

At her words, my eyes went wider than ever before. This entire
time, I thought she didn't suspect a thing about me...but she knew
everything!

Then I remembered the untruth of my alleged crimes. I'd been
so subjected to scorn that it started to become natural. Kiara knew
everything? No, she knew *nothing* at all. She was among the flock
who'd accepted Dimitri's lies.

"You're wrong!" I said before shouting, "I didn't kill them!" The
words came out like thunder; the roar was like a bear's. Beyond all
doubt it extended past the door, but this was the least of my concern.

Kiara continued, "At...at first, I was terrified. I was so scared you
would do horrible things to me. But now I know you would never
do such things. I even started doubting what everyone else was saying about you. I just *know* you aren't the kind of person to kill your
own companions!"

"—?!"

I couldn't believe my ears. What were these games? What was she
hoping to get? It was an impossible riddle that made me want to
shake the answer out of her.

"So, if you didn't do it..." Kiara began as tears covered her eyes.
"...Then why? Why are your eyes always so full of pain?!"

Her big, diamond, shiny, honeyed, innocent eyes stared at me
and penetrated me like a knife. Within them I saw something...there was nothing evil or deceitful in them. There was only
loyalty and care, and not one bit of trickery. Her question had broken the final seal. Hearing her speak, I collapsed to my knees and
wept.

"Why are you saying these things?" I asked with my head low
while tears cascaded down my face. "What do you want from
me?!"

Suddenly the gentlest sensation enveloped my body. Although I couldn't see much through the blurry tears, I sensed it as a pair of arms wrapping around me. The embrace was more tender than anything I'd felt before. I thought I was imagining things.

Seconds later came the kind words: "Listen, I know the world doesn't believe you, but I do. I'll say it over and over again until you accept it if I have to. You did nothing wrong."

"But the world never believes me. Why you?"

"Because I know you and they don't. They're all wrong. You're not a bad man."

When I mopped my eyes, I saw Kiara crying on her knees with her arms draped around me. She watched me through her teary eyes. Her mouth was curved up in a smile. The way she smiled...it was so full of light. Her face was sticky and dripping wet from crying, and yet she was adorable. While I had never before believed I could see beauty in an alien, her appearance shined clear in my eyes now. Her blue slime-body, her thick willowy tresses, her delicate rosy face. It was all so gorgeous. I couldn't believe her charm had been perched under my nose all along.

It was then that I knew what she was doing. I hadn't received such grace in so long that I'd forgotten it was possible. She was giving me friendship. I'd been blind to what friendship really looked like, but Kiara had opened my eyes. Not knowing how to thank her for such an extraordinary favor, I couldn't manage anything but a gaping stare, dumbfounded and awkward as ever.

"Hey," she said as our eyes locked. "I never thanked you for everything you've done for me. You saved me from being hanged. You gave me food and protected me. You fought for me. You showed me that I have a future when I thought there was no tomorrow. I can't make myself any clearer. You've saved my life. Thank you." Kiara seemed to understand my speechlessness, so she drew me in, and this time she made sure I wouldn't push her away. And I embraced her back. We refused to let go of one another. "You've been

through a lot, haven't you? I'm sorry. I won't let you bear it alone again...because I'll be there. No matter what happens, we'll kill our enemies together."

Although I had no idea before, it was now abundantly clear that Kiara was worth much more than twenty silvers. Much, much more.

As my crying got under control in her heavenly arms, a gentle gust swooped in from the doorway, followed by a shrill sound. *Cre-aaaaak...* The door groaned open. Then came a man's voice.

"I heard shouts. Is everything all right in there?"

Paying him no mind, I inferred that the voice belonged to the innkeeper.

"Yes..." Kiara said softly. "Everything's wonderful." Her voice was so soothing. I wanted to keep hearing it.

The door creaked again before closing, and we were again left to ourselves.

"You promised me we'd survive together," she whispered. "Here's my promise: from now on, when you suffer, I'll suffer with you. And I'll stand firm against anyone who makes you suffer. I swear it."

Kiara's arms were so comforting. It was just the two of us, sharing each other's pain. That was all I needed—someone to believe me. All I needed was someone to understand and support me. And I was willing to do the same for her. In doing so, we could find a way to *live*. We could sprout wings together and soar toward greatness.

If we could continue that mutual feeling—if I could believe what she said today—maybe I could gather the strength to carry on.

EPILOGUE

That night was the best I'd ever slept on this planet. In the night's glory, it became apparent that the bond we'd formed over the past weeks was very real, perhaps more real than reality itself. It must have existed beyond the bounds of time. My wounds weren't healable by time alone, so our friendship must have achieved *some* kind of temporal transcendence. I just knew it— something more powerful than time was at work in our bond, though I didn't know what. Often I awoke with my thoughts swimming, but this morning my mind was quiet like a garden and clear like a blue sky.

I turned to my side in bed. My eyes found Kiara across the room, who was in the slow-operating process of stirring. She faced me on her side, and we took each other in with our eyes.

"Good morning," she said with a warm smile.

Looking at her, I knew she was worth fighting for. Having *something* to fight for was a treasure, and for that, all my gratitude was hers. This was my first time feeling so grateful. As long as I could keep fighting for her, I'd still have hope in my heart. And as long as she handled me with care, I wouldn't break into pieces.

We had made the agreement to survive together not too long ago, but I'd been so mistrusting of others that I didn't truly believe our pact. I'd been so blinded by cynicism that I had assumed everyone's motive was to heap misery onto me. I wanted to heal my blindness. I wanted to start *living* by the agreement we'd made. For real this time.

"Good morning..." I muttered more to myself than to her. Sitting up and looking ahead, I asked, "It's a good morning, but you know what would make it even better?" I looked at Kiara for an answer.

"Uh, no, what?" she responded with a chuckle. Her face was twisted, half-smiling and half-befuddled by my odd language.

"Breakfast!"

In response, my companion beamed in delight. How exactly like her! She was as childish as ever. So childish. I liked her that way.

We got out of bed, headed downstairs, and stepped outside into the morning sunlight. The lukewarm air touched me pleasantly as I looked up at the clear sky. Birds hummed sweet songs, and the air smelled of cedar and rich herbs. The idea crossed me that Anbizian air was cleaner than terrestrial air as there was no emission of smog. I loved the way the air filled my lungs. The sensuous breeze blew back my hair, and I took a deep breath and reflected on everything I'd been through.

How did I get here? I thought as Kiara emerged from the inn behind me.

It seemed like yesterday when I was conforming to the generic student's lifestyle of repeated stress and studies, stress and studies, stress and studies. But quickly I got lost in a foreign land full of nettles and thistles that tore me in every corner. I was so far from home that I felt like I didn't have one. In an act of desperation, I purchased the life of an imperiled flower and used the bonds of debt to shackle her. She became my servant. Eventually her service was cut short, but by then, our chemistry had evolved beyond servant and master. Instead we reestablished our partnership for good, not as crutches or allies, but as friends.

This reflection brought thoughts of friendship into my mind. Many friendships were partial: they favored only one friend and not the other. Other friendships were mutual but still existed only for each friend's personal gain, be it materialism, status, or pleasure. Both species of friendship suffered from the problem of being circumstantial; they dissolved easily when the boons fell away. But there was also a rare kind of friendship that didn't depend on fleeting benefits—it rather stood on the genuine love shared between two friends. In such cases, the friendship didn't serve either friend, but both friends served the friendship. They extended mutual and selfless acts of service. Kiara had been in service to me all this time, but I only saw her as a pair of hands to help me shuffle along. But now our friendship was better than that. Now it was time for the one-sidedness to stop. From here on out, we'd serve *each other*.

Yesterday was gone, and today was the day to start anew.

"Mr. Nathan."

"Hm?" I offered my attention.

"I'll fight alongside you. If we can bring about a better world— no, a better universe—I'll stand with you till I die."

"We'll make it better. I've decided I won't stop fighting until I see it through..."

Kiara extended a hopeful smile. Her smile was perfect, still as bright as ever. And I returned it. It was the first time in a very long time that a smile played upon my face. I'd forgotten how it felt for the corners of my mouth to stand up like that.

However, although I smiled, there were many things that didn't warrant such smiling. There were things I couldn't brush aside. I couldn't dismiss the darkness plaguing my heart. My despair had not faded, and my feelings of utter vengeance toward the people who made me suffer would not stop screaming until satisfied. I wanted to reflect my agony on those who hurt me. I wanted to watch them plunge into the pit of misery into which they'd kicked me, and I wouldn't let them escape.

And although Kiara eased my pain, she did not terminate it. The sharp feeling always slashed at my bruised heart and wouldn't be easily quenched.

This planet was full of injustice. Only I could avenge those who were snuffed and buried under a mound of lies. Hinata, Dutch...I wouldn't let their deaths be in vain. I wanted to ensure that their lives meant something and, most importantly, to bring the *real* gunman to justice.

And then there was my father. Tebaldus had only raised my curiosity even higher. There were so many unanswered questions about him, and I needed answers.

No matter what obstacles this gray world threw at me, I would never give up. I wouldn't yield to satisfaction until I made all these things right.

"...But I won't be able to do it without you, Kiara," I said, looking her dead in the eye. I was challenging her—challenging her to keep up with me as I took after my goals. For a moment she stalled out of surprise, but then she composed herself and accepted.

"I'm with you. Together, we'll do it."

I didn't know how long I'd be on this planet, nor did I know how I'd get home. Surely the wormhole that delivered me here was long gone...collapsed under its own weight. The painful truth was that I was stuck here, and getting home was a nearly impossible equation. There just *had* to be a way to solve it. If Florence could do it, so could I. I wanted to figure it out someday, but until that day came, it looked like I would be stuck in the crossfire of this Great Alien War.

Surely this was only the beginning. There were too many variables—too many people with too many agendas—for this war to get better anytime soon. If the forces on Earth planned to get involved (and I *knew* the United States had such plans), the war would escalate into utter carnage. They would wheel their advanced enginery onto the battlefield. Tanks, bombs, guns, all of it; their sanguine fangs were much more suited for killing than the sticks and stones of Anbizia and Kadaan. There would be blood...more blood than any Anbizian or Kadaanite could imagine, and it would rain down like a storm, flooding every valley and coating every mountain.

"That's right," I said, my heart lifting in spite of the bleak out-look. No doubt there would be more suffering, but I could endure it because of hope. Hope that we would kill our enemies. Hope that I would find a way home. Hope that we would survive to-gether. And for now, all I could do was focus on the present. "You know, it might be hard to find a place to eat given everything that happened yesterday. Most vendors probably aren't selling food on the morning after a battle like *that*."

"Oh yeah?" replied Kiara, who would never let me go back on a promise of food. "Well, you have a knack for doing hard things, so I see no problem!"

"You really think so?" I asked, assuming she was spouting flat-tery. "You're bluffing."

"I mean it!" she exclaimed. "Who was it that dragged me on ad-ventures all the time? Who forced me to get up early every morn-ing? Who made me join the Independent Mercenary Guild? It was *you*! *You* taught me how to work hard even when I don't feel like it. *You* made me do things I never would've dreamed of doing if you hadn't come around. I've already made it clear that I believe in you, Mr. Nathan, but you need to believe in yourself a lot more!"

Kiara had a playfully teasing smile, and I could only laugh at her way with words.

"Then we'd better get started!" I said, to which she also laughed and nodded. Together we set off and receded from the inn. As we strolled through the quiet village in search of a place to eat, we drew ourselves close, leaning into one another ever so slightly.

ABOUT THE AUTHOR

Henry Green Ingram was born on June 17, 2005, in Austin, Texas. He studied philosophy at Baylor University in Waco, Texas and is the creator of the Alien Strike series.

www.henrygingram.com

www.ingramcontent.com/pod-product-compliance
Lightning Source LLC
Chambersburg PA
CBHW031450260626
47154CB00016B/354